FROM JERRY POURNELLE—co-author of *The Mote in God's Eye*, *Lucifer's Hammer*, *Footfall*, and *The Legacy of Heorot*

- First there was *The Mote in God's Eye*, dubbed "the finest science fiction novel ever written" by no less a personage than Robert A. Heinlein
- Then came *Lucifer's Hammer*, hailed as "the finest disaster novel ever written"
- Then came *Footfall*, proclaimed "the finest alien invasion novel ever"
- Now there is *The Legacy of Heorot*, another tour-de-force from Pournelle and his team

And there is *Call to Battle!* There Will Be War Volume VII

The Saga Continues . . .

Don't miss the other
THERE WILL BE WAR titles
created by J. E. Pournelle

published by Tor Books

CREATED BY
J. E. POURNELLE
CALL TO
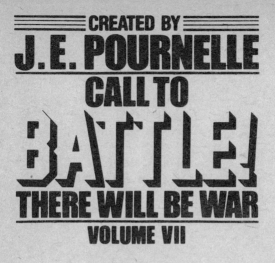

BATTLE!
THERE WILL BE WAR
VOLUME VII

John F. Carr, Associate Editor

TOR

A TOM DOHERTY ASSOCIATES BOOK
NEW YORK

CALL TO BATTLE

A TOR Book
Published by Tom Doherty Associates, Inc.
49 West 24 Street
New York, NY 10010

Cover art by Les Edwards

ISBN: 0-812-54963-5   Can. ISBN: 0-812-54964-3

First edition: September 1988

Printed in the United States of America

0 9 8 7 6 5 4 3 2 1

ACKNOWLEDGMENTS

The editors gratefully acknowledge that research for nonfiction essays in this book, including "Wizard Weapons" by Stefan T. Possony, J. E. Pournelle, and Francis X. Kane, was supported in part by grants from the Vaughn Foundation. Responsibility for opinions expressed in this work remains solely with the authors.

CONTENTS

Introduction
CALL TO BATTLE
Jerry Pournelle

THE WORLD IS SAID TO BE AT PEACE, BUT AS I WRITE THIS, THE United States Navy is engaged in an undeclared but quite lethal little war in the Persian Gulf, while another 200,000 U.S. troops are stationed in Europe. Soviet armies continue their conquest of Afghanistan. The Arab–Israeli borders are quiet, but Iran and Iraq pound away at each other. There is war in the Sahara desert and Southern Africa. Chinese soldiers occupy Tibet. If there are no formal wars, there is no shortage of combat and death; nor is the situation likely to change.

The most fervent wishes for peace do not bring peace. Probably no one wanted peace more than the intellectuals of Phnom Penh in Cambodia, who were told to pack their goods and march to temporary quarters in the countryside. Anthony Lewis wrote in the *New York Times* that it was "cultural arrogance" to condemn the Khmer Rouge for its forced march of three million people into the countryside, since they were acting on their own "vision of a new society"; but even as he wrote that, the killing began.

The Khmer Rouge soldiers were very polite. They

1

addressed everyone as "comrade." They explained that the move was only temporary, to avoid an American air strike. No one knew better until they were in the labor camps.

The educated people, the intellectuals, were killed out of hand. The survivors were deliberately starved until some ate human flesh, and still the killing continued. The victims themselves had to participate in order to eat. As one observer put it, "If there is any 'cultural arrogance' around, it lurks in the assumption that Communist 'reeducation' is less devastating for little yellow people than it might be for whites."

They wanted peace; they got the peace of Auschwitz.

One must wish for peace; it is a religious duty to pray for peace; but if that is all one does, one is not likely to get it. A very long time ago the human race learned a bitter truth: if you would have peace, you must be prepared for war. The late Herman Kahn in his classic *Thinking About the Unthinkable* modified that ancient Roman dictum to "if you would have peace, understand war"; which is what we are trying to do in this series of stories and essays about the future of war. If these books need justification, that will serve well enough.

Since 1945 there has been peace of a sort; at least there has been no global war. The cost of that peace has been pretty high, in money, in combat casualties, and in nations like Poland and Hungary and Cambodia and Vietnam sacrificed to "visions of a new society."

The costs will still be high in the future. Eternal vigilance remains the price of liberty, of course; but military preparedness also requires eternal rethinking of the basics.

The nature of both tactics and organization may change as new weapons and technologies emerge. Freeman Dyson writes of "David weapons," such as nonnuclear precision guided missiles (PGM), which may change the nature of wars and armies. He says, "It seems likely that the rapid growth of microcomputer and sensor technology will result in a growing proliferation of sophisticated nonnuclear weapons which will cause armies to take a step back into an older, more professional

2

style of warfare. The new weapons need elite, highly trained soldiers to use them effectively. They do not need the mass armies that provided the cannon fodder of the two world wars. The Falklands campaign of 1982 provides some additional evidence that the winds of change are blowing in this direction. The Argentine air force, a small elite force using precise weapons with daring and skill, did great damage to the invading forces, while the Argentine army, a mass army of conscripts, was crushingly defeated. It seems that modern technology is taking us back toward the eighteenth century, toward the era when small professional armies fought small professional wars" (Freeman Dyson, *Weapons and Hope,* Harper and Row, 1984). It is a view that has much merit.

At the suggestion of T. E. Lawrence (Lawrence of Arabia), the British strategist Sir Basil Liddell Hart studied the historical ratios of forces to space—that is, the number of troops needed to hold each mile of front. From these studies he later calculated that European NATO could be defended by a relatively small, highly trained, and highly mobile force of tanks and cross-country–capable infantry vehicles, especially if augmented by a civilian militia of the Swiss variety. He also observed: "Since the Western Powers are faced by opposing armies of greatly superior size, their chance of successful resistance vitally depends on being so mobile, both strategically and tactically, that they can outmaneuver the attacker. It is not only a matter of the small armored units having the utmost battlefield agility, so that they can shift quickly from one fire-position to another, but of divisions being able to switch rapidly from one sector to another to deliver deep in-and-out counterstrokes, with the aim of hamstringing the invader.

"That calls for a new kind of organization. The armored divisions that proved so decisive in 1940 had gone less than halfway towards fulfilling the design I had visualized in 1920. Every vehicle in an armored force ought to have cross-country mobility, and at least sufficient protective armor to keep out bullets and shell-splinters. The present type of armored force is gravely lacking in maneuvering flexibility. Its long road-bound tail makes it almost as rigid as the shaft of a spear. We ought to develop it into a mechanical snake.

"Besides giving the tail flexibility, the tail should be reduced in size. The most potent effect of an armored stroke comes from the sudden concentration of tanks against a weak spot in the enemy's dispositions . . . the tactical idea which inspired the creation of armored forces was that of fighting mounted. Our goal in tank specification and design ought to be to produce a mechanized David instead of a Goliath."

He also wrote, "Another possibility is to develop remote control tanks for the spearhead. With such unmanned tanks there would be no deterrent moral effect from heavy losses in applying saturation tactics."

All this was written in 1960 (B. H. Liddell Hart, *Deterrent or Defense*, Praeger). While details change often, the basic strategic situation, of the West facing numerically superior forces, has not. Some of Liddell Hart's advice has been taken. Much has not been.

There are reasons, of course. First came Vietnam, which set military planning back a good decade. One benefit of war is that the losers must rethink what they are doing, and many of those who make the wrong decisions are eliminated. Since the crucial decisions about Vietnam were made in Washington, that couldn't happen. The U.S. learned little from that war. Then, when the war was lost and the military commanders once again looked at overall strategy and organization, they had lost popularity—and their budget. Now we are expected to defend the West with volunteer forces—which gives a good quality of soldier—but do it on the cheap. All too often the Congress has allowed political factors to interfere in the design and procurement of military weapons.

One of Liddell Hart's prescriptions for Europe was militia to augment Regular troops. Politically we've done little to encourage our Allies to adopt militia, and of course they're reluctant to do it. A long conventional war in Europe would be less devastating than a nuclear exchange, but it is also seen as more likely; and it would

4

be devastating enough for the people on whose land it is fought. If the U.S.S.R. can be convinced that an attack on Europe will inevitably trigger a holocaust that will destroy the world, deterrence succeeds; and a successful deterrent is clearly preferable to even a victorious war.

The nuclear deterrent isn't completely safe either. The land-based missiles of both sides are vulnerable to a first strike; and an arms control agreement lowering the absolute numbers of missiles increases the likelihood of success of the first strike. (If both sides have only 100 missiles, a 95 percent success leaves only 5 to the loser; if both sides have 10,000, destroying 95 percent isn't worth the cost.)

PGM can affect the nuclear strategic balance. A missile capable of hitting a tank can hit a missile silo. Even more relevant are strategic defense technologies: since President Reagan ordered serious research on missile defenses, the laboratories have found a dozen promising approaches. There are also clear signs that the Soviet Union began serious research and development of beam technologies for missile interception as early as 1972. In 1976 a U.S. early warning satellite picked up tests of very powerful fusion pulses from the Soviet weapons test complex at Agzir, and air samples collected later showed the Soviet tests released large amounts of hydrogen, and, more significantly, detectable quantities of tritium. Most physicists studying these results conclude that the Soviet Union was testing directed energy weapons as early as the mid-'70s.

They must have learned something. We now know the U.S.S.R. has constructed radars whose only possible use is for battle management of strategic defense against ICBMs. Whether or not the U.S. proceeds with SDI, it is pretty clear the Soviets intend to do so.

The U.S.S.R. routinely launches ten times the number of satellites we do; we don't really know what they are learning from them. Their naval satellites have 100 kw of power; the U.S. has yet to orbit a 10kw satellite of any kind.

With the loss of Challenger, the U.S. became effectively blind; and NASA did little to correct that. General Yeager said that we should launch a new shuttle as soon as the weather was warm; instead the bureaucrats of NASA began a program designed to protect their careers —but not to launch satellites. The U.S. space program has been brought to a halt. Since we had integrated our military and civil programs, this has serious consequences. As I write this the U.S. is down to one KeyHole (KH) observation satellite. Since the path of that satellite is well known, and Soviet agents were able to buy the operations manuals for the satellite from American traitors, it's not hard to see how that satellite can be blocked from learning a great deal; yet we depend on "national technical means" to verify Soviet compliance —or violation—of arms control agreements.

We are blind, and our enemies are arming. We live, in a word, in interesting times.

George Santayana said that those who refuse to learn from history are condemned to repeat it. I add that those who refuse to think about the future may not have one.

Herewith more stories and essays about the future of war and conflict.

THE TANK LORDS
David Drake

EDITOR'S INTRODUCTION

I have on my desk a number of issues of *Military Technology*, a magazine published in Europe with articles by senior military officers and civilian technologists. The editorial text is impressive. Here's "Man-Portable Air Defense Systems," about how Redeye, Stinger, Javelin, Starstreak, and a host of other field deployable antiaircraft systems can be used to make the battlefield a pretty hostile place for aircraft—provided you get them to the battlefield, and can aim and fire them in time.

The same issue has an article on South Africa's home-designed and -built helicopters; Main Battle Tank armament including new electromagnetic hypervelocity railguns; liquid propellant systems for artillery; and a lot more. Other issues tell about mines, defense of airfields, new fighters, defense electronics, etc., all illustrated with diagrams and photographs.

More impressive than the articles, though, are the advertisements. Want to buy artillery shells? Chartered Industries of Singapore will be happy to sell them to you. Standard Elektrik Lorenz AG of Stuttgart, West Germany, wants you to buy a RATAC-S portable ground surveillance and target acquisition radar. Kreuss-Maffei Wehrtechnik GmbH of Munich advertises Leopard 2, "the better battle tank." Reinmetal will sell you cannon, Vickers of England will sell 4.5 Mark 8 naval gun systems, GMM Naval Construction of Amsterdam will sell you a whole mine sweeper, and Groupement Industriel des Armaments Terrestres of St. Cloud in France would just love to take your orders for their AMX 40 tank armament. Everything from helmet-mounted light-amplifying goggles to cruise missiles to armored cars to Kevlar body armor to communications gear (a Swiss company advertises unbreakable code equipment based on "Only One Time Random Keys") to artillery: it's all advertised here, and much of it was mere science fiction less than a decade ago.

The wizard weapons are here. We have artillery that can fire patterns over fields ten miles away. When the shells arrive over the battlefield, they deploy into darts held aloft by parachutes as they seek tank-shaped targets. When a target is seen, the round fires and a "self-forging" blob of metal attacks the target. Other weapons home on laser beams, or trail out a wire that lets the operator guide it toward its target. A Belgian firm advertises mines that "cannot be cleared by any known devices." All this to defeat the Main Battle Tank.

Of course, there are good reasons to do so. According to the London International Institute for Strategic Studies *Military Balance 1987*, NATO's 8,974 major artillery pieces face some 24,000 Soviet guns, while our 714 armed helicopters stare at 2,100 Soviet choppers, but the important imbalance is that they've deployed 46,600 Main Battle Tanks against NATO's 20,314.

Tank popularity moves in waves. The U.S. Army Air Forces like to claim that "strategic" bombing was highly effective in World War II. Certainly the bombers managed wide destruction. If you visit Germany you will find that there have been two major sources of destruction of the ancient towns and cities: the French, who periodically invaded the Rhineland and beyond and burned or blew up everything they could (the ruins of Heidelberg

8

Castle are among the more spectacular of the French achievements); and the allied air forces who, in a few months of 1944, managed to rival the French in sheer wanton destruction of civilian property, getting Mozart's house in Salzburg, most of the downtown area of Karlsruhe, and a number of other totally unmilitary places. I don't quarrel with the air war against railroads, and the attacks on ball-bearing plants were probably worth the cost; but if most of the money put into strategic bombers had gone to tanks and tactical air support planes, that war would probably have ended much sooner.

Then came nuclear weapons, and a number of theorists proclaimed the death of the tank. We may never know the effectiveness of tanks on a nuclear battlefield; but we do know that tanks, with tactical air support, dominated every one of the Israeli wars.

Even so, from time to time we see articles proclaiming that the Main Battle Tank is as dead as the dinosaur; that air power and artillery will dominate the battlefields of the future. As a one time artillerist and air power theorist, I find that comforting. After all, artillery has always been known as the last argument of kings. Emotions aside, though, the evidence is that tanks will be around for a long time; and any casual look at *Military Technology* will convince you that they're getting larger, more efficient, and more powerful with each decade.

David Drake, a Vietnam veteran, tells of a time when tanks again dominate the battlefield; and reminds us that no matter how powerful the machines become, they are still vulnerable to the frailties of their human commanders.

THEY WERE THE TANK LORDS.

The baron had drawn up his soldiers in the courtyard, the twenty men who were not detached to his estates on the border between the Kingdom of Ganz and the Kingdom of Marshall—keeping the uneasy truce and ready to break it if the baron so willed.

I think the king sent mercenaries in four tanks to our palace so that the baron's will would be what the king wished it to be . . . though of course we were told they were protection against Ganz and the mercenaries of the Lightning Division whom Ganz employed.

The tanks and the eight men in them were from Hammer's Slammers, and they were magnificent.

Lady Miriam and her entourage rushed back from the barred windows of the women's apartments on the second floor, squealing for effect. The tanks were so huge that the mirror-helmeted men watching from the turret hatches were nearly on a level with the upper story of the palace.

I jumped clear, but Lady Miriam bumped the chair I had dragged closer to stand upon and watch the arrival over the heads of the women I served.

"Leesh!" cried the lady, false fear of the tanks replaced by real anger at me. She slapped with her fan of painted ox-horn, cutting me across the knuckles because I had thrown a hand over my eyes.

I ducked low over the chair, wrestling it out of the way and protecting myself with its cushioned bulk. Sarah, the chief maid, rapped my shoulder with the silver-mounted brush she carried for last-minute touches to the lady's hair. "A monkey would make a better page than you, Elisha," she said. "A gelded monkey."

But the blow was a light one, a reflexive copy of her mistress's act. Sarah was more interested in reclaiming her place among the others at the windows now that modesty and feminine sensibilities had been satisfied by the brief charade. I didn't dare slide the chair back to where I had first placed it; but by balancing on tiptoes on the carven arms, I could look down into the courtyard again.

The baron's soldiers were mostly off-worlders themselves. They had boasted that they were better men than the mercenaries if it ever came down to cases. The fear that the women had mimed from behind stone walls seemed real enough now to the soldiers whose bluster and assault rifles were insignificant against the iridium titans that entered the courtyard at a slow walk, barely clearing the posts of gates that would have passed six men marching abreast.

Even at idle speed, the tanks roared as their fans

maintained the cushions of air that slid them over the ground. Three of the baron's men dodged back through the palace doorway, their curses inaudible over the intake whine of the approaching vehicles.

The baron squared his powerful shoulders within his dress cloak of scarlet, purple, and gold. I could not see his face, but the back of his neck flushed red and his left hand tugged his drooping mustache in a gesture as meaningful as the angry curses that would have accompanied it another time.

Beside him stood Wolfitz, his chamberlain; the tallest man in the courtyard; the oldest; and, despite the weapons the others carried, the most dangerous.

When I was first gelded and sold to the baron as his lady's page, Wolfitz had helped me continue the studies I began when I was training for the Church. Out of his kindness, I thought, or even for his amusement . . . but the chamberlain wanted a spy, or another spy, in the women's apartments. Even when I was ten years old, I knew that death lay on that path—and life itself was all that remained to me.

I kept the secrets of all. If they thought me a fool and beat me for amusement, then that was better than the impalement that awaited a boy who was found meddling in the affairs of his betters.

The tanks sighed and lowered themselves the last finger's breadth to the ground. The courtyard, clay and gravel compacted over generations to the density of stone, crunched as the plenum-chamber skirts settled visibly into it.

The man in the turret of the nearest tank ignored the baron and his soldiers. Instead, the reflective face-shield of the tanker's helmet turned and made a slow, arrogant survey of the barred windows and the women behind them. Maids tittered; but the Lady Miriam did not, and when the tanker's face-shield suddenly lifted, the mercenary's eyes and broad smile were toward the baron's wife.

The tanks whispered and pinged as they came into balance with the surroundings they dominated. Over those muted sounds, the man in the turret of the second tank to enter the courtyard called, "Baron Hetziman, I'm

11

Lieutenant Kiley and this is my number two—Sergeant-Commander Grant. Our tanks have been assigned to you as a protective reaction force until the peace treaty's signed."

"You do us honor," said the baron curtly. "We trust your stay with us will be pleasant as well as short. A banquet—"

The baron paused, and his head turned to find the object of the other tanker's attention.

The lieutenant snapped something in a language that was not ours, but the name *Grant* was distinctive in the sharp phrase.

The man in the nearest turret lifted himself out gracefully by resting his palms on the hatch coaming and swinging up his long, powerful legs without pausing for footholds until he stood atop the iridium turret. The hatch slid shut between his booted feet. His crisp mustache was sandy blond, and the eyes which he finally turned on the baron and the formal welcoming committee were blue. "Rudy Grant at your service, Baron," he said, with even less respect in his tone than in his words.

They did not need to respect us. They were the tank lords.

"We will go down and greet our guests," said the Lady Miriam, suiting her actions to her words. Even as she turned, I was off the chair, dragging it toward the inner wall of imported polychrome plastic.

"But, Lady . . ." Sarah said nervously. She let her voice trail off, either through lack of a firm objection or unwillingness to oppose a course on which her mistress was determined.

With coos and fluttering skirts, the women swept out the door from which the usual guard had been removed for the sake of the show in the courtyard. Lady Miriam's voice carried back: "We were to meet them at the banquet tonight. We'll just do so a little earlier."

If I had followed the women, one of them would have ordered me to stay and watch the suite—though everyone, even the tenants who farmed the plots of the home estate here, was outside watching the arrival of the tanks. Instead, I waited for the sounds to die away down the stair tower—and I slipped out the window.

Because I was in a hurry, I lost one of the brass buttons from my jacket—my everyday livery of buff; I'd be wearing the black plush jacket when I waited in attendance at the banquet tonight, so the loss didn't matter. The vertical bars were set close enough to prohibit most adults, and few of the children who could slip between them would have had enough strength to then climb the bracing strut of the roof antenna, the only safe path since the base of the west wing was a thicket of spikes and razor ribbon.

I was on the roof coping in a matter of seconds, three quick hand-over-hand surges. The women were only beginning to file out through the doorway. Lady Miriam led them, and her hauteur and lifted chin showed she would brook no interference with her plans.

Most of the tankers had, like Grant, stepped out of their hatches, but they did not wander far. Lieutenant Kiley stood on the sloping bow of his vehicle, offering a hand which the baron angrily refused as he mounted the steps recessed into the tank's armor.

"Do you think I'm a child?" rumbled the baron, but only his pride forced him to touch the tank when the mercenary made a hospitable offer. None of the baron's soldiers showed signs of wanting to look into the other vehicles. Even the chamberlain, aloof if not afraid, stood at arm's length from the huge tank, which even now trembled enough to make the setting sun quiver across the iridium hull.

Because of the chamberlain's studied unconcern about the vehicle beside him, he was the first of the welcoming party to notice Lady Miriam striding toward Grant's tank, holding her skirts clear of the ground with dainty, bejeweled hands. Wolfitz turned to the baron, now leaning gingerly against the curve of the turret so that he could look through the hatch while the lieutenant gestured from the other side. The chamberlain's mouth opened to speak, then closed again deliberately.

There were matters in which he too knew better than to become involved.

One of the soldiers yelped when Lady Miriam began to mount the nearer tank. She loosed her dress in order to take the hand Grant extended to her. The baron glanced

13

around and snarled an inarticulate syllable. His wife gave him a look as composed as his was suffused with rage. "After all, my dear," said the Lady Miriam coolly, "our lives are in the hands of these brave men and their amazing vehicles. Of *course* I must see how they are arranged."

She was the king's third daughter, and she spoke now as if she were herself the monarch.

"That's right, milady," said Sergeant Grant. Instead of pointing through the hatch, he slid back into the interior of his vehicle with a murmur to the lady.

She began to follow.

I think Lady Miriam and I, alone of those on the estate, were not nervous about the tanks for their size and power. I loved them as shimmering beasts, whom no one could strike in safety. The lady's love was saved for other subjects.

"Grant, that won't be necessary," the lieutenant called sharply—but he spoke in our language, not his own, so he must have known the words would have little effect on his subordinate.

The baron bellowed, "*Mir*—" before his voice caught. He was not an ungovernable man, only one whose usual companions were men and women who lived or died as the baron willed. The lady squeezed flat the flounces of her skirt and swung her legs within the hatch ring.

"Murphy," called the baron to his chief of soldiers. "Get up there with her." The baron roared more often than he spoke quietly. This time his voice was not loud, but he would have shot Murphy where he stood if the soldier had hesitated before clambering up the bow of the tank.

"Vision blocks in both the turret and the driver's compartment," said Lieutenant Kiley, pointing within his tank, "give a three-sixty-degree view at any wavelength you want to punch in."

Murphy, a grizzled man who had been with the baron a dozen years, leaned against the turret and looked down into the hatch. Past him, I could see the combs and lace of Lady Miriam's elaborate coiffure. I would have given everything I owned to be there within the tank myself—and I owned nothing but my life.

14

The hatch slid shut. Murphy yelped and snatched his fingers clear.

Atop the second tank, the baron froze and his flushed cheeks turned slatey. The mercenary lieutenant touched a switch on his helmet and spoke too softly for anything but the integral microphone to hear the words.

The order must have been effective, because the hatch opened as abruptly as it had closed—startling Murphy again.

Lady Miriam rose from the turret on what must have been a power lift. Her posture was in awkward contrast to the smooth ascent, but her face was composed. The tank and its apparatus were new to the lady, but anything that could have gone on within the shelter of the turret was a familiar experience to her.

"We have seen enough of your equipment," said the baron to Lieutenant Kiley in the same controlled voice with which he had directed Murphy. "Rooms have been prepared for you—the guest apartments alongside mine in the east wing, not the barracks below. Dinner will be announced"—he glanced at the sky. The sun was low enough that only the height of the tank's deck permitted the baron to see the orb above the courtyard wall—"in two hours. Make yourselves welcome."

Lady Miriam turned and backed her way to the ground again. Only then did Sergeant Grant follow her out of the turret. The two of them were as powerful as they were arrogant—but neither a king's daughter nor a tank lord is immortal.

"Baron Hetziman," said the mercenary lieutenant, "sir—" The modest honorific for the tension, for the rage which the baron might be unable to control even at risk of his estates and his life. "That building, the gatehouse, appears disused. We'll doss down there, if you don't mind."

The baron's face clouded, but that was his normal reaction to disagreement. The squat tower to the left of the gate had been used only for storage for a generation. A rusted harrow, upended to fit farther within the doorway, almost blocked access now.

The baron squinted for a moment at the structure, craning his short neck to look past the tank from which

15

he had just climbed down. Then he snorted and said, "Sleep in a hog byre if you choose, Lieutenant. It might be cleaner at that."

"I realize," explained Lieutenant Kiley as he slid to the ground instead of using the steps, "that the request sounds odd, but Colonel Hammer is concerned that commandos from Ganz or the Lightning Division might launch an attack. The gatehouse is separated from everything but the outer wall—so if we have to defend it, we can do so without endangering any of your people."

The lie was a transparent one; but the mercenaries did not have to lie at all if they wished to keep us away from their sleeping quarters. So considered, the statement was almost generous, and the baron chose to take it that way. "Wolfitz," he said off-handedly as he stamped toward the entrance. "Organize a party of tenants"—he gestured sharply toward the pattern of drab garments and drab faces lining the walls of the courtyard—"and clear the place, will you?"

The chamberlain nodded obsequiously, but he continued to stride along at his master's heel.

The baron turned, paused, and snarled, "*Now*," in a voice as grim as the fist he clenched by his side.

"My lord," said Wolfitz with a bow that danced the line between brusque and dilatory. He stepped hastily toward the soldiers who had broken their rank in lieu of orders—a few of them toward the tanks and their haughty crews but most back to the stone shelter of the palace.

"You men," the chamberlain said, making circling motions with his hands. "Fifty of the peasants, *quickly*. Everything is to be turned out of the gatehouse, thrown beyond the wall for the time being. *Now. Move* them."

The women followed the baron into the palace. Several of the maids glanced over their shoulders, at the tanks—at the tankers. Some of the women would have drifted closer to meet the men in khaki uniforms, but Lady Miriam strode head high and without hesitation.

She had accomplished her purposes; the purposes of her entourage could wait.

I leaned from the room ledge for almost a minute further, staring at the vehicles which were so smooth-skinned that I could see my amorphous reflection in the nearest. When the sound of women's voices echoed through the window, I squirmed back, only instants before the lady reentered her apartment.

They would have beaten me for my own excitement had they not themselves been agog with the banquet to come—and the night which would follow it.

The high-arched banquet hall was so rarely used that it was almost as unfamiliar to the baron and his household as it was to his guests. Strings of small lights had been led up the cast-concrete beams, but nothing could really illuminate the vaulting waste of groins and coffers that formed the ceiling.

The shadows and lights trembling on flexible fastenings had the look of the night sky on the edge of an electrical storm. I gazed up at the ceiling occasionally while I waited at the wall behind Lady Miriam. I had no duties at the banquet—that was for house servants, not body servants like myself—but my presence was required for show and against the chance that the lady would send me off with a message.

That chance was very slight. Any messages Lady Miriam had were for the second-ranking tank lord, seated to her left by custom: Sergeant-Commander Grant.

There were seven of the mercenaries, not eight as I had believed. I saw mostly their backs as they sat at the high table, interspersed with the lady's maids. Lieutenant Kiley was in animated conversation with the baron to his left, but I thought the officer wished primarily to distract his host from the way Lady Miriam flirted on the other side.

A second keg of beer—estate stock; not the stuff brewed for export in huge vats—had been broached by the time the beef course followed the pork. The serving girls had been kept busy with the mugs—in large part, the molded-glass tankards of the baron's soldiers, glowering at the lower tables, but the metal-chased crystal of the tank lords was refilled often as well.

Two of the mercenaries—drivers, separated by the oldest of Lady Miriam's maids—began arguing with increasing heat while a tall, black-haired server watched in amusement. I could hear the words, but the language was not ours. One of the men got up, struggling a little because the arms of his chair were too tight against those to either side. He walked toward his commander, rolling slightly.

Lieutenant Kiley, gesturing with his mug toward the roof peak, was saying to the baron, "Has a certain splendor, you know. Proper lighting and it'd look like a cross between a prison and a barracks, but the way you've tricked it out is—"

The standing mercenary grumbled a short, forceful paragraph, a question or a demand, to the lieutenant, who broke off his own sentence to listen.

"Ah, Baron," Kiley said, turning again to his host. "Question is, what, ah, sort of regulations would there be on my boys dating local women. That one there"—his tankard nodded toward the black-haired servant; the driver who had remained seated was caressing her thigh—"for instance?"

"Regulations?" responded the baron in genuine surprise. "On *servants*? None, of course. Would you like me to assign a group of them for your use?"

The lieutenant grinned, giving an ironic tinge to the courteous shake of his head. "I don't think that'll be necessary, Baron," he said.

Kiley stood up to attract his men's attention. "Open season on the servants, boys," he said, speaking clearly and in our language, so that everyone at or near the upper table would understand him. "Make your own arrangements. Nothing rough. And no less than two men together."

He sat down again and explained what the baron already understood: "Things can happen when a fellow wanders off alone in a strange place. He can fall and knock his head in, for instance."

The two drivers were already shuffling out of the dining hall with the black-haired servant between them. One of the men gestured toward another buxom server with a pitcher of beer. She was not particularly well favored, as men describe such things; but she was close,

18

and she was willing—as any of the women in the hall would have been to go with the tank lords. I wondered whether the four of them would get any farther than the corridor outside.

I could not see the eyes of the maid who watched the exit of the mercenaries who had been seated beside her.

Lady Miriam watched the drivers leave also. Then she turned back to Sergeant Grant and resumed the conversation they held in voices as quiet as honey flowing from a ruptured comb.

In the bustle and shadows of the hall, I disappeared from the notice of those around me. Small and silent, wearing my best jacket of black velvet, I could have been another length of darkness cast by one of the light-blocking beams. The two mercenaries left the hall by a side exit. I slipped through the end door behind me, unnoticed save as a momentary obstacle to the servants bringing in compotes of fruits grown locally and imported from across the stars.

My place was not here. My place was with the tanks, now that there was no one to watch me dreaming as I caressed their iridium flanks.

The sole guard at the door to the women's apartments glowered at me, but he did not question my reason for returning to what were, after all, my living quarters. The guard at the main entrance would probably have stopped me for spite: he was on duty while others of the household feasted and drank the best-quality beer.

I did not need a door to reach the courtyard and the tanks parked there.

Unshuttering the same window I had used in the morning, I squeezed between the bars and clambered to the roof along the antenna mount. I was fairly certain that I could clear the barrier of points and edges at the base of the wall beneath the women's suite, but there was no need to take that risk.

Starlight guided me along the stone gutter, jumping the pipes feeding the cistern under the palace cellars. Buildings formed three sides of the courtyard, but the north was closed by a wall and the gatehouse. There was no spiked barrier beneath the wall, so I stepped to the battlements and jumped to the ground safely.

Then I walked to the nearest tank, silently from reverence, rather than in fear of being heard by someone in the palace. I circled the huge vehicle slowly, letting the tip of my left index finger slide over the metal. The iridium skin was smooth, but there were many bumps and irregularities set into the armor: sensors, lights, and strips of close-range defense projectors to meet an enemy or his missile with a blast of pellets.

The tank was sleeping but not dead. Though I could hear no sound from it, the armor quivered with inner life like that of a great tree when the wind touches its highest branches.

I touched a recessed step. The spring-loaded fairing that should have covered it was missing, torn away or shot off—perhaps on a distant planet. I climbed the bow slope, my feet finding each higher step as if they knew the way.

It was as if I were a god.

I might have attempted no more than that, than to stand on the hull with my hand touching the stubby barrel of the main gun—raised at a sixty-degree angle so that it did not threaten the palace. But the turret hatch was open and, half convinced that I was living in a hope-induced dream, I lifted myself to look in.

"Freeze," said the man looking up at me past his pistol barrel. His voice was calm. "And then we'll talk about what you think you're doing here."

The interior of the tank was coated with sulphurous light. It was too dim to shine from the hatch, but it provided enough illumination for me to see the little man in the khaki coveralls of the tank lords. The bore of the powergun in his hand shrank from the devouring cavity it had first seemed. But even the 1cm bore of reality would release enough energy to splash the brains from my skull, I knew.

"I wanted to see the tanks," I said, amazed that I was not afraid. All men die, even kings; what better time than this would there be for me? "They would never let me, so I sneaked away from the banquet. I—it was worth it. Whatever happens now."

20

"Via," said the tank lord, lowering his pistol. "You're just a kid, ain'tcha?"

I could see my image foreshortened in the vision screen behind the mercenary, my empty hands shown in daylit vividness at an angle that meant the camera must be in another of the parked tanks.

"My Lord," I said, straightening momentarily but overriding the reflex so that I could meet the mercenary's eyes. "I am sixteen."

"Right," he said, "and I'm Colonel Hammer. Now—"

"Oh Lord!" I cried, forgetting in my joy and embarrassment that someone else might hear me. My vision blurred and I rapped my knees on the iridium as I tried to genuflect. "Oh, Lord Hammer, forgive me for disturbing you!"

"Blood and *martyrs*, boy!" snapped the tank lord. A pump whirred and the seat from which he questioned me cross-legged rose. "Don't be an idiot! Me name's Curran and I drive this beast, is all."

The mercenary was head and shoulders out of the hatch now, watching me with a concerned expression. I blinked and straightened. When I knelt, I had almost slipped from the tank; and in a few moments, my bruises might be more painful than my present embarrassment.

"I'm sorry, Lord Curran," I said, thankful for once that I had practice in keeping my expression calm after a beating. "I have studied, I have dreamed about your tanks ever since I was placed in my present status six years ago. When you came I—I'm afraid I lost control."

"You're a little shrimp, even alongside me, ain'tcha?" Curran said reflectively.

A burst of laughter drifted across the courtyard from a window in the corridor flanking the dining hall.

"Aw, Via," the tank lord said. "Come take a look, seein's yer here anyhow."

It was not a dream. My grip on the hatch coaming made the iridium bite my fingers as I stepped into the tank at Curran's direction; and besides, I would never have dared to dream this paradise.

The tank's fighting compartment was not meant for two, but Curran was as small as he had implied and I—I had grown very little since a surgeon had fitted me to

21

become the page of a high-born lady. There were screens, gauges, and armored conduits across all the surfaces I could see.

"Drivers'll tell ye," said Curran, "the guy back here, he's just along for the ride 'cause the tank does it all for 'em. Been known t' say that myself, but it ain't really true. Still—"

He touched the lower left corner of a screen. It had been black. Now, it became gray, unmarked save by eight short orange lines radiating from the edge of a two-centimeter circle in the middle of the screen.

"Fire control," Curran said. A hemispherical switch was set into the bulkhead beneath the screen. He touched the control with an index finger, rotating it slightly. "That what the Slammers're all about, ain't we? Fire-power and movement, and the tricky part—movement —the driver handles from up front. Got it?"

"Yes, my lord," I said, trying to absorb everything around me without taking my eyes from what Curran was doing. The west wing of the palace, guest and baronial quarters above the ground-floor barracks, slid up the screen as brightly illuminated as if it were daylight.

"Now *don't* touch nothin'!" the tank lord said, the first time he had spoken harshly to me. "Got it?"

"Yes, my lord."

"Right," said Curran, softly again. "Sorry, kid. Lieutenant'll have my ass if he sees me twiddlin' with the gun, and if we blow a hole in central prison here"—he gestured at the screen, though I did not understand the reference—"the Colonel'll likely shoot me hisself."

"I won't touch anything, my lord," I reiterated.

"Yeah, well," said the mercenary. He touched a four-position toggle switch beside the hemisphere. "We just lowered the main gun, right? I won't spin the turret, 'cause they'd hear that likely inside. Matter of fact—"

Instead of demonstrating the toggle, Curran fingered the sphere again. The palace dropped off the screen and, now that I knew to expect it, I recognized the faint whine that must have been the gun itself gimbaling back up to a safe angle. Nothing within the fighting compartment moved except the image on the screen.

22

"So," the tanker continued, flipping the toggle to one side. An orange numeral 2 appeared in the upper left corner of the screen. "There's a selector there too." He pointed to the pistol grip by my head, attached to the power seat which had folded up as soon as it lowered me into the tank at Curran's direction.

His finger clicked the switch to the other side—1 appeared in place of 2 on the screen—and then straight up—3. "Main gun," he said, "co-ax—that's the tribarrel mounted just in front of the hatch. You musta seen it?"

I nodded, but my agreement was a lie. I had been too excited and too overloaded with wonder to notice the automatic weapon on which I might have set my hand.

"And 3," Curran went on, nodding also, "straight up—that's both guns together. Not so hard, was it? You're ready to be a tank commander now, and"—he grinned—"with six months and a little luck, I could teach ye t'drive the little darlin' besides."

"Oh, My Lord," I whispered, uncertain whether I was speaking to God or to the man beside me. I spread my feet slightly in order to keep from falling in a fit of weakness.

"*Watch* it!" the tank lord said sharply, sliding his booted foot to block me. More gently, he added, "Don't touch *nothing*, remember? That"—he pointed to a pedal on the floor which I had not noticed—"that's the foot trip. Touch it and we give a little fireworks demonstration that nobody's gonna be very happy about."

He snapped the toggle down to its original position; the numeral disappeared from the screen. "Shouldn't have it live nohow," he added.

"But—all this," I said, gesturing with my arm close to my chest so that I would not bump any of the close-packed apparatus. "If shooting is so easy, then why is—*everything*—here?"

Curran smiled. "Up," he said, pointing to the hatch. As I hesitated, he added, "I'll give you a leg-up, don't worry about the power lift."

Flushing, sure that I was being exiled from Paradise because I had overstepped myself—somehow—with the last question, I jumped for the hatch coaming and scrambled through with no need of the tanker's help. I supposed I was crying, but I could not tell because my eyes burned so.

"Hey, slow down, kid," called Curran as he lifted himself with great strength but less agility. "It's just that Whichard's about due t'take over guard, and we don't need him t'find you inside. Right?"

"Oh," I said, hunched already on the edge of the tank's deck. I did not dare turn around for a moment. "Of course, my lord."

"The thing about shootin'," explained the tank lord to my back, "ain't *how* so much's when and what. You got all this commo and sensors that'll handle any wavelength or take remote feeds. But *still* somebody's gotta decide which data t'call up—and decide what it means. And decide t'pop it er not." I turned just as Curran leaned over to slap the iridium barrel of the main gun for emphasis. "Which is a mother-huge decision for whatever's down-range, ye know."

He grinned broadly. He had a short beard, rather sparse, which partly covered the pockmarks left by some childhood disease. "Maybe even puts tank commander up on a level with driver for tricky, right?"

His words opened a window in my mind, the frames branching and spreading into a spidery, infinite structure: responsibility, the choices that came with the power of a tank.

"Yes, my lord," I whispered.

"Now, you better get back t'whatever civvies do," Curran said, a suggestion that would be snarled out as an order if I hesitated. "And *don't* be shootin' off yer mouth about t'night, right?"

"No, my lord," I said as I jumped to the ground. Tie-beams between the wall and the masonry gatehouse would let me climb back to the path I had followed to get here.

"And thank you," I added, but varied emotions choked the words into a mumble.

I thought the women might already have returned, but I listened for a moment, clinging to the bars, and heard nothing. Even so I climbed in the end window. It was more difficult to scramble down without the aid of the antenna brace, but a free-standing wardrobe put that window in a sort of alcove.

I didn't know what would happen if the women saw me slipping in and out through the bars. There would be a beating—there was a beating whenever an occasion offered. That didn't matter, but it was possible that Lady Miriam would also have the openings cross-barred too straitly for even my slight form to pass.

I would have returned to the banquet hall, but female voices were already greeting the guard outside the door. I had only enough time to smooth the plush of my jacket with Sarah's hairbrush before they swept in, all of them together and their mistress in the lead as usual.

By standing against a color-washed wall panel, I was able to pass unnoticed for some minutes of the excited babble without being guilty of "hiding," with the severe flogging that would surely entail. By the time Lady Miriam called, "Leesh? *Elisha!*" in a querulous voice, no one else could have sworn that I hadn't entered the apartment with the rest of the entourage.

"Yes, my lady?" I said, stepping forward.

Several of the women were drifting off in pairs to help each other out of their formal costumes and coiffures. There would be a banquet every night that the tank lords remained—providing occupation to fill the otherwise featureless lives of the maids and their mistress.

That was time consuming, even if they did not become more involved than public occasion required.

"Leesh," said Lady Miriam, moderating her voice unexpectedly. I was prepared for a blow, ready to accept it unflinchingly unless it was aimed at my eye—and even then to dodge as little as possible so as not to stir up a worse beating.

"Elisha," the lady continued in a honeyed tone—then, switching back to acid sharpness and looking at her chief maid, she said, "Sarah, what *are* all these women doing here? Don't they have rooms of their own?"

Women who still dallied in the suite's common room —several of the lower-ranking stored their garments here in chests and clothes presses—scurried for their sleeping quarters while Sarah hectored them, arms akimbo.

25

"I need you to carry a message for me, Leesh," explained Lady Miriam softly. "To one of our guests. You—you do know, don't you, boy, which suite was cleared for use by our guests?"

"Yes, my lady," I said, keeping my face blank. "The end suite of the east wing, where the king slept last year. But I thought—"

"Don't think," said Sarah, rapping me with the brush she carried on all but formal occasions. "And don't interrupt milady."

"Yes, my lady," I said, bowing and rising.

"I don't want you to *go* there, boy," said the lady with an edge of irritation. "If Sergeant Grant has any questions, I want you to point the rooms out to him—from the courtyard."

She paused and touched her full lips with her tongue while her fingers played with the fan. "Yes," she said at last, then continued, "I want you to tell Sergeant Grant 0400 and to answer any questions he may have."

Lady Miriam looked up again, and though her voice remained mild, her eyes were hard as knife points. "Oh. And Leesh? This is business that the baron does not wish to be known. Speak to Sergeant Grant in private. And never speak to anyone else about it—even to the baron if he tries to trick you into an admission."

"Yes, my lady," I said, bowing.

I understood what the baron would do to a page who brought him that news—and how he would send a message back to his wife, to the king's daughter whom he dared not impale in person.

Sarah's shrieked order carried me past the guard at the women's apartment, while Lady Miriam's signet was my pass into the courtyard after normal hours. The soldier there on guard was muzzy with drink. I might have been able to slip unnoticed by the hall alcove in which he sheltered.

I skipped across the gravel-in-clay surface of the courtyard, afraid to pause to touch the tanks again when I knew Lady Miriam would be peering from her window. Perhaps on the way back . . . but no, she would be as intent on hearing on how the message was received as she

26

was anxious to know that it had been delivered. I would ignore the tanks—

"*Freeze*, buddy!" snarled someone from the turret of the tank I had just run past.

I stumbled with shock and my will to obey. Catching my balance, I turned slowly—to the triple muzzles of the weapon mounted on the cupola, not a pistol as Lord Curran had pointed. The man who spoke wore a shielded helmet, but there would not have been enough light to recognize him anyway.

"Please, my lord," I said. "I have a message for Sergeant-Commander Grant?"

"From who?" the mercenary demanded. I knew now that Lieutenant Kiley had been serious about protecting from intrusion the quarters allotted to his men.

"My lord, I—" I said and found no way to proceed.

"Yeah, Via," the tank lord agreed in a relaxed tone. "None a' my affair." He touched the side of his helmet and spoke softly.

The gatehouse door opened with a spill of light and the tall, broad-shouldered silhouette of Sergeant Grant. Like the mercenary on guard in the tank, he wore a communications helmet.

Grant slipped his face-shield down, and for a moment my own exposed skin tingled—or my mind *thought* it perceived a tingle—as the tank lord's equipment scanned me.

"C'mon, then," he grunted, gesturing me toward the recessed angle of the building and the gate leaves. "We'll step around the corner and talk."

There was a trill of feminine laughter from the upper story of the gatehouse: a servant named Maria, whose hoots of joy were unmistakable. Lieutenant Kiley leaned his head and torso from the window above us and shouted to Grant, his voice and his anger recognizable even though the words themselves were not.

The sergeant paused, clenching his left fist and reaching for me with his right because I happened to be closest to him. I poised to run—survive this first, then worry about what Lady Miriam would say—but the tank lord caught himself, raised his shield, and called to his superior in a tone on the safe side of insolent, "All right,

27

all right. I'll stay right here where Cermak can see me from the tank."

Apparently Grant had remembered Lady Miriam also, for he spoke in our language so that I—and the principal for whom I acted—would understand the situation.

Lieutenant Kiley banged his shutters closed.

Grant stared for a moment at Cermak until the guard understood and dropped back into the interior of his vehicle. We could still be observed through the marvelous vision blocks, but we had the minimal privacy needed for me to deliver my message.

"Lady Miriam," I said softly, "says 0400."

I waited for the tank lord to ask me for directions. His breath and sweat exuded sour echoes of the strong estate ale.

"Won't go," the tank lord replied unexpectedly. "I'll be clear at 03 *to* 04." He paused before adding, "You tell her, kid, she better not be playin' games. Nobody plays prick-tease with *this* boy and likes what they get for it."

"Yes, my lord," I said, skipping backward because I had the feeling that this man would grab me and shake me to emphasize his point.

I would not deliver his threat. My best hope for safety at the end of this affair required that Lady Miriam believe that I was ignorant of what was going on.

That was a slim hope anyway.

"Well, go on, then," the tank lord said.

He strode back within the gatehouse, catlike in his grace and lethality, while I ran to tell my mistress of the revised time.

An hour's pleasure seemed a little thing against the risk of two lives—and my own.

My "room" was what had been the back staircase before it was blocked to convert the second floor of the west wing into the women's apartment. The dank cylinder was furnished only with the original stone stair treads and whatever my mistress and her maids had chosen to store there over the years. I normally slept on a chair in the common room, creeping back to my designated space before dawn.

Tonight I slept *beneath* one of the large chairs in a

28

corner; not hidden, exactly, but not visible without a search.

The two women were quiet enough to have slipped past someone who was not poised to hear them as I was, and the tiny flashlight the leader carried threw a beam so tight that it could scarcely have helped them see their way. But the perfume they wore—imported, expensive, and overpowering—was more startling than a shout.

They paused at the door. The latch rattled like a tocsin though the hinges did not squeal.

The soldier on guard, warned and perhaps awakened by the latch, stopped them before they could leave the apartment. The glowlamp in the sconce beside the door emphasized the ruddy anger on his face.

Sarah's voice, low but cutting, said, "Keep silent, my man, or it will be the worse for you." She thrust a gleam of gold toward the guard, not payment but a richly chased signet ring, and went on, "Lady Miriam knows and approves. Keep still and you'll have no cause to regret this night. Otherwise . . ."

The guard's face was not blank, but emotions chased themselves across it too quickly for his mood to be read. Suddenly he reached out and harshly squeezed the chief maid's breast. Sarah gasped, and the man snarled, "What've they got that *I* don't, tell me, huh? You're *all* whores, that's all you are!"

The second woman was almost hidden from the soldier by the chief maid and the panel of the half-opened door. I could see a shimmer of light as her hand rose, though I could not tell whether it was from a blade or a gun barrel.

The guard flung his hand down from Sarah and turned away. "Go on, then," he grumbled. "What do I care? Go *on*, sluts."

The weapon disappeared, unused and unseen, into the folds of an ample skirt, and the two women left the suite with only the whisper of felt slippers. They were heavily veiled and wore garments coarser than any I had seen on the chief maid before—but Lady Miriam was as recognizable in the grace of her walk as Sarah was for her voice.

The women left the door ajar to keep the latch from

29

rattling again, and the guard did not at first pull it to. I listened for further moments against the chance that another maid would come from her room or that the lady would rush back, driven by fear or conscience—though I hadn't seen either state control her in the past.

I was poised to squeeze between the window-bars again, barefoot for secrecy and a better grip, when I heard the hum of static as the guard switched his belt radio live. There was silence as he keyed it, then his low voice saying, "They've left, sir. They're on their way toward the banquet hall."

There was another pause and a radio voice too thin for me to hear more than the fact of it. The guard said, "Yes, Chamberlain," and clicked off the radio.

He latched the door.

I was out through the bars in one movement and well up the antenna brace before any of the maids could have entered the common room to investigate the noise.

I knew where the women were going, but not whether the chamberlain would stop them on the way past the banquet hall or the baron's personal suite at the head of the east wing. The fastest, safest way for me to cross the roof of the banquet hall was twenty feet up the side, where the builders' forms had left a flat, thirty-centimeter path in the otherwise sloping concrete.

Instead, I decided to pick my way along the trash-filled stone gutter just above the windows of the corridor on the courtyard side. I could say that my life—my chance of life—depended on knowing what was going on . . . and it did depend on that. But crawling through the starlit darkness, spying on my betters, was also the only way I had of asserting myself. The need to assert myself had become unexpectedly pressing since Lord Curran had showed me the tank, and since I had experienced what a man *could* be.

There was movement across the courtyard as I reached the vertical extension of the load-bearing wall that separated the west wing from the banquet hall. I ducked beneath the stone coping, but the activity had nothing to do with me. The gatehouse door had opened and, as I peered through dark-adapted eyes, the mercenary on guard in a tank exchanged with the man who had just stepped out of the building.

The tank lords talked briefly. Then the gatehouse door shut behind the guard who had been relieved while his replacement climbed into the turret of the vehicle parked near the west wing—Sergeant Grant's tank. I clambered over the wall extension and stepped carefully along the gutter, regretting now that I had not worn shoes for protection. I heard nothing from the corridor below, although the casements were pivoted outward to catch any breeze that would relieve the summer stillness.

Gravel crunched in the courtyard as the tank lord on guard slid from his vehicle and began to stride toward the end of the east wing.

He was across the courtyard from me—faceless behind the shield of his commo helmet and at best only a shadow against the stone of the wall behind him. But the man was Sergeant Grant beyond question, abandoning his post for the most personal of reasons.

I continued, reaching the east wing as the tank lord disappeared among the stone finials of the outside staircase at the wing's far end. The guest suites had their own entrance, more formally ornamented than the doorways serving the estate's own needs. The portal was guarded only when the suites were in use—and then most often by a mixed force of the baron's soldiers and those of the guests.

That was not a formality. The guest who would entrust his life solely to the baron's goodwill was a fool.

A corridor much like that flanking the banquet hall ran along the courtyard side of the guest suites. It was closed by a cross-wall and door, separating the guests from the baron's private apartment, but the door was locked and not guarded.

Lady Miriam kept a copy of the door's microchip key under the plush lining of her jewel box. I had found it but left it there, needless to me so long as I could slip through window grates.

The individual guest suites were locked also, but as I lowered myself from the gutter to a window ledge I heard a door snick closed. The sound was minuscule, but it had a crispness that echoed in the lightless hall.

Skirts rustled softly against the stone, and Sarah gave a gentle, troubled sigh as she settled herself to await her mistress.

I waited on the ledge, wondering if I should climb back to the roof—or even return to my own room. The chamberlain had not blocked the assignation, and there was no sign of an alarm. The soldiers, barracked on the ground floor of this wing, would have been clearly audible had they been aroused.

Then I did hear something—or feel it. There had been motion, the ghost of motion, on the other side of the door closing the corridor. Someone had entered or left the baron's apartment, and I had heard them through the open windows.

It could have been one of the baron's current favorites—girls from the estate, the younger and more vulnerable, the better. They generally used the little door and staircase on the outer perimeter of the palace—where a guard *was* stationed against the possibility that an ax-wielding relative would follow the lucky child.

I lifted myself back to the roof with particular care, so that I would not disturb the chief maid waiting in the hallway. Then I followed the gutter back to the portion of roof over the baron's apartments.

I knew the wait would be less than an hour, the length of Sergeant Grant's guard duty, but it did not occur to me that the interval would be as brief as it actually was. I had scarcely settled myself again to wait when I thought I heard a door unlatch in the guest suites. That could have been imagination; or Sarah, deciding to wait in a room instead of the corridor; but moments later the helmeted tank lord paused on the outside staircase.

By taking the risk of leaning over the roof coping, I could see Lord Grant and a woman embracing on the landing before the big mercenary strode back across the courtyard toward the tank where he was supposed to be on guard. Desire had not waited on its accomplishment, and mutual fear had prevented the sort of dalliance after the event that the women dwelt on so lovingly in the privacy of their apartment . . . while Leesh, the lady's page and no man, listened of necessity.

The women's slippers made no sound in the corridor,

but their dresses brushed one another to the door, which clicked and sighed as it let them out of the guest apartments and into the portion of the east wing reserved to the baron.

I expected shouts, then; screams, even gunfire as the baron and Wolfitz confronted Lady Miriam. There was no sound except for skirts continuing to whisper their way up the hall, returning to the women's apartment. I stood up to follow, disappointed despite the fact that bloody chaos in the palace would endanger everyone— me, the usual scapegoat for frustrations, most of all.

The baron said in a tight voice at the window directly beneath me, "Give me the goggles, Wolfitz," and surprise almost made me fall.

The strap of a pair of night-vision goggles rustled over the baron's grizzled head. Their frames clucked against the stone sash as my master bent forward with the unfamiliar headgear.

For a moment, I was too frightened to breathe. If he leaned out and turned his head, he would see me poised like a terrified gargoyle above him. Any move I made— even flattening myself behind the wall coping—risked a sound and disaster.

"You're right," said the baron in a voice that would have been normal if it had had any emotion behind it. There was another sound of something hard against the sash, a metallic clink this time.

"*No*, my lord!" said the chamberlain in a voice more forceful than I dreamed any underling would use to the baron. Wolfitz must have been seizing the nettle firmly, certain that hesitation or uncertainty meant the end of more than his plans. "If you shoot him now, the others will blast everything around them to glowing slag."

"Wolfitz!" said the baron, breathing hard. They had been struggling. The flare-mouthed mob gun from the baron's nightstand—scarcely a threat to Sergeant Grant across the courtyard—extended from the window opening, but the chamberlain's bony hand was on the baron's wrist. "If you tell me I must let those arrogant outworlders pleasure *my* wife in *my* palace, I will kill you."

He sounded like an architect discussing a possible staircase curve.

"There's a better way, my lord," said the chamberlain. His voice was breathy also, but I thought exertion was less to account for that than was the risk he took. "We'll be ready the next time the—out-worlder gives us the opportunity. We'll take him in, in the crime; but quietly so that the others aren't aroused."

"Idiot!" snarled the baron, himself again in all his arrogant certainty. Their hands and the gun disappeared from the window ledge. The tableau was the vestige of an event that the men needed each other too much to remember. "No matter what we do with the body, the others will blame us. Blame *me*."

His voice took a dangerous coloration as he added, "Is that what you had in mind, Chamberlain?"

Wolfitz said calmly, "The remainder of the platoon here will be captured—or killed, it doesn't matter—by the mercenaries of the Lightning Division, who will also protect us from reaction by King Adrian and Colonel Hammer."

"But—" said the baron, the word a placeholder for a thought that did not form in his mind after all.

"The King of Ganz won't hesitate an instant if you offer him your fealty," the chamberlain continued, letting the words display their own strength instead of speaking loudly in a fashion his master might take as badgering.

The baron still held the mob gun, and his temper was doubtful at the best of times.

"The mercenaries of the Lightning Division," continued Wolfitz with his quiet voice and persuasive ideas, "will accept any risk in order to capture four tanks undamaged. The value of that equipment is beyond any profit the Lightning Division dreamed of earning when they were hired by Ganz."

"But—" the baron repeated in an awestruck voice. "The truce?"

"A matter for the kings to dispute," said the chamberlain off-handedly. "But Adrian will find little support among his remaining barons if you were forced into your change of allegiance. When the troops he billeted on you raped and murdered Lady Miriam, that is."

"How quickly can you make the arrangements?" asked the baron. I had difficulty in following the words: not because they were soft, but because he growled them like a beast.

"The delay," Wolfitz replied judiciously, and I could imagine him lacing his long fingers together and staring at them, "will be for the next opportunity your—Lady Miriam and her lover give us. I shouldn't imagine that will be longer than tomorrow night."

The baron's teeth grated like nutshells being ground against stone.

"We'll have to use couriers, of course," Wolfitz added. "The likelihood of the Slammers intercepting any other form of communication is too high. But all Ganz and its mercenaries have to do is ready a force to dash here and defend the palace before Hammer can react. Since these tanks *are* the forward picket, and they'll be unmanned while Sergeant Grant is—otherwise occupied—the Lightning Division will have almost an hour before an alarm can be given. Ample time, I'm sure."

"Chamberlain," the baron said in a voice from which amazement had washed all the anger, "you think of everything. See to it."

"Yes, my lord," Wolfitz said humbly.

The tall chamberlain *did* think of everything, or very nearly; but he'd had much longer to plan than the baron thought. I wondered how long Wolfitz had waited for an opportunity like this one; and what payment he had arranged to receive from the King of Ganz if he changed the baron's allegiance?

A door slammed closed, the baron returning to his suite and his current child-mistress. Chamberlain Wolfitz's rooms adjoined his master's, but my ears followed his footsteps to the staircase at the head of the wing.

By the time I had returned to the west wing and was starting down the antenna brace, a pair of the baron's soldiers had climbed into a truck and gone rattling off into the night. It was an unusual event but not especially remarkable: the road they took led off to one of the baron's outlying estates.

But the road led to the border with Ganz, also; and I had no doubt as to where the couriers' message would be received.

The tank lords spent most of the next day pulling maintenance. A squad of the baron's soldiers kept at a distance the tenants and house servants who gawked while the khaki-clad tankers crawled through access plates and handed fan motors to their fellows. The bustle racks welded to the back of each turret held replacement parts as well as the crew's personal belongings.

It was hard to imagine that objects as huge and powerful as the tanks would need repair. I had to remember that they were not ingots of iridium but vastly complicated assemblages of parts—each of which could break, and eight of which were human.

I glanced occasionally at the tanks and the lordly men who ruled and serviced them. I had no excuse to take me beyond the women's apartment during daylight.

Excitement roused the women early, but there was little pretense of getting on with their lace making. They dressed, changed, primped—argued over rights to one bit of clothing or another—and primarily, they talked.

Lady Miriam was less a part of the gossip than usual, but she was the most fastidious of all about the way she would look at the night's banquet.

The tank lords bathed at the wellhead in the courtyard like so many herdsmen. The women watched hungrily, edging forward despite the scandalized demands of one of the older maids that they at least stand back in the room where their attention would be less blatant.

Curran's muscles were knotted, his skin swarthy. Sergeant Grant could have passed for a god—or at least a man of half his real age. When he looked up at the women's apartments, he smiled.

The truck returned in late afternoon, carrying the two soldiers and a third man in civilian clothes who could have been—but was not—the manager of one of the outlying estates. The civilian was closeted with the baron for half an hour before he climbed back into the truck. He, Wolfitz, and the baron gripped one another's forearms in leave-taking; then the vehicle returned the way it had come.

The tank lord on guard paid less attention to the truck than he had to the column of steam-driven produce vans, chuffing toward the nearest rail terminus.

The banquet was less hectic than that of the first night, but the glitter had been replaced by a fog of hostility now that the newness had worn off. The baron's soldiers were more openly angry that Hammer's men picked and chose—food at the high table, and women in the corridor or the servants' quarters below.

The Slammers, for their part, had seen enough of the estate to be contemptuous of its isolation, of its low technology—and of the folk who lived on it. And yet—I had talked with Lord Curran and listened to the others as well. The tank lords were men like those of the barony. They had walked on far worlds and had been placed in charge of instruments as sophisticated as any in the human galaxy—but they were not sophisticated *men,* only powerful ones.

Sergeant-Commander Grant, for instance, made the child's mistake of thinking his power to destroy conferred on him a sort of personal immortality.

The baron ate and drank in a sullen reverie, deaf to the lieutenant's attempts at conversation and as blind to Lady Miriam on his left as she was to him. The chamberlain was seated among the soldiers because there were more guests than maids of honor. He watched the activities at the high table unobtrusively, keeping his own counsel and betraying his nervousness only by the fact that none of the food he picked at seemed to go down his throat.

I was tempted to slip out to the tanks, because Lord Curran was on duty again during the banquet. His absence must have been his own choice; a dislike for the food or the society perhaps . . . but more probably, from what I had seen in the little man when we talked, a fear of large, formal gatherings.

It would have been nice to talk to Lord Curran again, and blissful to have the controls of the huge tank again within my hands. But if I were caught then, I might not be able to slip free later in the night—and I would rather have died than miss that chance.

The baron hunched over his ale when Lieutenant Kiley gathered his men to return to the gatehouse. They did not march well in unison, not even by comparison with the baron's soldiers when they drilled in the courtyard.

The skills and the purpose of the tank lords lay elsewhere.

Lady Miriam rose when the tankers fell in. She swept from the banquet hall regally as befit her birth, dressed in amber silk from Terra and topazes of ancient cut from our own world. She did not look behind her to see that her maids followed and I brought up the rear . . . but she did glance aside once at the formation of tank lords.

She would be dressed no better than a servant later that night, and she wanted to be sure that Sergeant Grant had a view of her full splendor to keep in mind when next they met in darkness.

The soldier who had guarded the women's apartments the night before was on duty when the chief maid led her mistress out again. There was no repetition of the previous night's dangerous byplay this time. The guard was subdued, or frightened; or, just possibly, biding his time because he was aware of what was going to come.

I followed, more familiar with my route this time and too pumped with excitement to show the greater care I knew was necessary tonight, when there would be many besides myself to watch, to listen.

But I was alone on the roof, and the others, so certain of what *they* knew and expected, paid no attention to the part of the world that lay beyond their immediate interest.

Sergeant Grant sauntered as he left the vehicle where he was supposed to stay on guard. As he neared the staircase to the guest suites, his stride lengthened and his pace picked up. There was nothing of nervousness in his manner; only the anticipation of a man focused on sex to the extinction of all other considerations.

I was afraid that Wolfitz would spring his trap before I was close enough to follow what occurred. A more reasonable fear would have been that I would stumble into the middle of the event.

Neither danger came about. I reached the gutter over the guest corridor and waited, breathing through my mouth alone so that I wouldn't make any noise. The blood that pounded through my ears deafened me for a moment, but there was nothing to hear. Voices murmured—Sarah and Sergeant Grant—and the door clicked shut on the suite that had waited ajar for the tank lord.

Four of the baron's soldiers mounted the outside steps, as quietly as their boots permitted. There were faint sounds, clothing and one muted clink of metal, from the corridor on the baron's side of the door.

All day I'd been telling myself that there was no safe way I could climb down and watch events through a window. I climbed down, finding enough purchase for my fingers and toes where weathering had rounded the corners of stone blocks. Getting back to the roof would be more difficult, unless I risked gripping an out-swung casement for support.

Unless I dropped, bullet-riddled, to the ground.

I rested a toe on a window ledge and peeked around the stone toward the door of the suite the lovers had used on their first assignation. I could see nothing—

Until the corridor blazed with silent light.

Sarah's face was white, dazzling with the direct reflection of the high-intensity floods at either end of the hallway. Her mouth opened and froze, a statue of a scream but without the sound that fear or self-preservation choked in her throat.

Feet, softly but many of them, shuffled over the stone flags toward the chief maid. Her head jerked from one side to the other, but her body did not move. The illumination was pinning her to the door where she kept watch.

The lights spilled through the corridor windows, but their effect was surprisingly slight in the open air: highlights on the parked tanks; a faint wash of outline, not color, over the stones of the wall and gatehouse; and a distorted shadowplay on the ground itself, men and weapons twisting as they advanced toward the trapped maid from both sides.

There was no sign of interest from the gatehouse. Even if the tank lords were awake to notice the lights, what happened at night in the palace was no affair of theirs.

Three of perhaps a dozen of the baron's soldiers stepped within my angle of vision. Two carried rifles; the third was Murphy with a chip recorder, the spidery wands of its audio and video pickups retracted because of the press of men standing nearby.

Sarah swallowed. She closed her mouth, but her eyes stared toward the infinite distance beyond this world. The gold signet she clutched was a drop from the sun's heart in the floodlights.

The baron stepped close to the woman. He took the ring with his left hand, looked at it, and passed it to the stooped, stone-faced figure of the chamberlain.

"Move her out of the way," said the baron in a husky whisper.

One of the soldiers stuck the muzzle of his assault rifle under the chin of the chief maid, pointing upward. With his other hand, the man gripped Sarah's shoulder and guided her away from the door panel.

Wolfitz looked at his master, nodded, and set a magnetic key on the lock. Then he too stepped clear.

The baron stood at the door with his back to me. He wore body armor, but he couldn't have thought it would protect him against the Slammer's powergun. Murphy was at the baron's side, the recorder's central light glaring back from the door panel, and another soldier poised with his hand on the latch.

The baron slammed the door inward with his foot. I do not think I have ever seen a man move as fast as Sergeant Grant did then.

The door opened on a servants' alcove, not the guest rooms themselves, but the furnishings there were sufficient to the lovers' need. Lady Miriam had lifted her skirts. She was standing, leaning slightly backwards, with her buttocks braced against the bed frame. She screamed, her eyes blank reflections of the sudden light.

Sergeant-Commander Grant still wore his helmet. He

had slung his belt and holstered pistol over the bedpost when he unsealed the lower flap of his uniform coveralls, but he was turning with the pistol in his hand before the baron got off the first round with his mob gun.

Aerofoils, spread from the flaring muzzle by asymmetric thrust, spattered the lovers and a two-meter circle on the wall beyond them.

The tank lord's chest was in bloody tatters and there was a brain-deep gash between his eyebrows, but his body and the powergun followed through with the motion reflex had begun.

The baron's weapon chunked twice more. Lady Miriam flopped over the footboard and lay thrashing on the bare springs, spurting blood from narrow wounds that her clothing did not cover. Individual projectiles from the mob gun had little stopping power, but they bled out a victim's life like so many knife blades.

When the baron shot the third time, his gun was within a meter of what had been the tank lord's face. Sergeant Grant's body staggered backward and fell, the powergun unfired but still gripped in the mercenary's right hand.

"Call the Lightning Division," said the baron harshly as he turned. His face, except where it was freckled by fresh blood, was as pale as I had ever seen it. "It's time."

Wolfitz lifted a communicator, short range but keyed to the main transmitter, and spoke briefly. There was no need for communications security now. The man who should have intercepted and evaluated the short message was dead in a smear of his own wastes and body fluids.

The smell of the mob gun's propellant clung chokingly to the back of my throat, among the more familiar slaughterhouse odors. Lady Miriam's breath whistled, and the bedsprings squeaked beneath her uncontrolled motions.

"Shut that off," said the baron to Murphy. The recorder's pool of light shrank into shadow within the alcove.

The baron turned and fired once more, into the tank lord's groin.

"Make sure the others don't leave the gatehouse till Ganz's mercenaries are here to deal with them," said the baron negligently. He looked at the gun in his hand.

41

Strong lights turned the heat and propellant residues rising from its barrel into shadows on the wall beyond.

"Marksmen are ready, my lord," said the chamberlain.

The baron skittered his mob gun down the hall. He strode toward the rooms of his own apartment.

It must have been easier to climb back to the roof than I had feared. I have no memory of it, of the stress on fingertips and toes or the pain in my muscles as they lifted the body they had supported for what seemed (after the fact) to have been hours. Minutes only, of course; but instead of serial memory of what had happened, my brain was filled with too many frozen pictures of details for all of them to fit within the real time frame.

The plan that I had made for this moment lay so deep that I executed it by reflex, though my brain roiled.

Executed it by instinct, perhaps; the instinct of flight, the instinct to power.

In the corridor, Wolfitz and Murphy were arguing in low voices about what should be done about the mess.

Soldiers had taken up positions in the windowed corridor flanking the banquet hall. More of the baron's men, released from trapping Lady Miriam and her lover, were joining their fellows with words too soft for me to understand. I crossed the steeply pitched roof on the higher catwalk, for speed and from fear that the men at the windows might hear me.

There were no soldiers on the roof itself. The wall coping might hide even a full-sized man if he lay flat, but the narrow gutter between wall and roof was an impossible position from which to shoot at targets across the courtyard.

The corridor windows on the courtyard side were not true firing slits like those of all the palace's outer walls. Nonetheless, men shooting from corners of the windows could shelter their bodies behind stone thick enough to stop bolts from the Slammers' personal weapons. The sleet of bullets from twenty assault rifles would turn anyone sprinting from the gatehouse door or the pair of second-floor windows into offal like that which had been Sergeant Grant.

The tank lords were not immortal.

There was commotion in the women's apartments when I crossed them. Momentarily a light fanned the shadow of the window-bars across the courtyard and the gray curves of what had been Sergeant Grant's tank. A male voice cursed harshly. A lamp casing crunched, and from the returned darkness came a blow and a woman's cry.

Some of the baron's soldiers were taking positions in the west wing. Unless the surviving tank lords could blow a gap in the thick outer wall of the gatehouse, they had no exit until the Lightning Division arrived with enough firepower to sweep them up at will.

But I could get in, with a warning that would come in time for them to summon aid from Colonel Hammer himself. They would be in debt for my warning, owing me their lives, their tanks, and their honor.

Surely the tank lords could find a place for a servant willing to go with them anywhere?

The battlements of the wall closing the north side of the courtyard formed my pathway to the roof of the gatehouse. Grass and brush grew there in ragged clumps. Cracks between stones had trapped dust, seeds, and moisture during a generation of neglect. I crawled along, on my belly, tearing my black velvet jacket.

Eyes focused on the gatehouse door and windows were certain to wander: to the sky; to fellows slouching over their weapons; to the wall connecting the gatehouse to the west wing. If I stayed flat, I merged with the stone . . . but shrubs could quiver in the wrong pattern, and the baron's light-amplifying goggles might be worn by one of the watching soldiers.

It had seemed simpler when I planned it; but it was necessary in any event, even if I died in a burst of gunfire.

The roof of the gatehouse was reinforced concrete, slightly domed, and as great a proof against indirect fire as the stone walls were against small arms. There was no roof entrance, but there was a capped flue for the stove that had once heated the guard quarters. I'd squirmed my way in through that hole once before.

Four years before.

The roof of the gatehouse was a meter higher than the

wall on which I lay—an easy jump, but one which put me in silhouette against the stars. I reached up, feeling along the concrete edge less for a grip than for reassurance. I was afraid to leave the wall because my body was telling itself that the stone it pressed was safety.

If the baron's men shot me now, it would warn the tank lords in time to save them. I owed them that, for the glimpse of freedom Curran had showed me in the turret of a tank.

I vaulted onto the smooth concrete and rolled, a shadow in the night to any of the watchers who might have seen me. Once I was *on* the gatehouse, I was safe because of the flat dome that shrugged off rain and projectiles. The flue was near the north edge of the structure, hidden from the eyes and guns waiting elsewhere in the palace.

I'd grown only slightly since I was twelve and beginning to explore the palace in which I expected to die. The flue hadn't offered much margin, but my need wasn't as great then, either.

I'd never needed *anything* as much as I needed to get into the gatehouse now.

The smoke pipe had rusted and blown down decades before. The wooden cap, fashioned to close the hole to rain, hadn't been maintained. It crumbled in my hands when I lifted it away, soggy wood with only flecks remaining of the stucco that had been applied to seal the cap into place.

The flue was as narrow as the gap between window-bars, and because it was round, I didn't have the luxury of turning sideways. So be it.

If my shoulders fit, my hips would follow. I extended my right arm and reached down through the hole as far as I could. The flue was as empty as it was dark. Flakes of rust made mouselike patterings as my touch dislodged them. The passageway curved smoothly, but it had no sharp-angled shot trap as far down as I could feel from outside.

I couldn't reach the lower opening. The roof was built thick enough to stop heavy shells. At least the slimy surface of the concrete tube would make the job easier.

I lowered my head into the flue with the pit of my extended right arm pressed as firmly as I could against the lip of the opening. The cast concrete brought an electric chill through the sweat-soaked velvet of my jerkin, reminding me—now that it was too late—that I could have stripped off the garment to gain another millimeter's tolerance.

It was too late, even though all but my head and one arm were outside. If I stopped now, I would never have the courage to go on again.

The air in the flue was dank, because even now in late summer the concrete sweated and the cap prevented condensate from evaporating. The sound of my fear-lengthened breaths did not echo from the end of a closed tube, and not even panic could convince me that the air was stale and would suffocate me. I slid farther down; down to the *real* point of no return.

By leading with my head and one arm, I was able to tip my collarbone endwise for what would have been a relatively easy fit within the flue if my ribs and spine did not have to follow after. The concrete caught the tip of my left shoulder and the ribs beneath my right armpit . . . let me flex forward minutely on the play in my skin and the velvet . . . and held me.

I would have screamed, but the constriction of my ribs was too tight. My legs kicked in the air above the gatehouse, unable to thrust me down for lack of purchase. My right arm flopped in the tube, battering my knuckles and fingertips against unyielding concrete.

I could die here, and no one would know.

Memory of the tank and the windows of choice expanding infinitely above even Leesh, the lady's page, flashed before me and cooled my body like rain on a stove. My muscles relaxed and I could breathe again— though carefully, and though the veins of my head were distending with blood trapped by my present posture.

Instead of flapping vainly, my right palm and elbow locked on opposite sides of the curving passage. I breathed as deeply as I could, then let it out as I kicked my legs up where gravity, at least, could help.

My right arm pulled while my left tried to clamp itself

within my rib cage. Cloth tore, skin tore, and my torso slipped fully within the flue, lubricated by blood as well as condensate.

If I had been upright, I might have blacked out momentarily with the release of tension. Inverted, I could only gasp and feel my face and scalp burn with the flush that darkened them. The length of a hand farther and my pelvis scraped. My fingers had a grip on the lower edge of the flue, and I pulled like a cork extracting itself from a wine bottle. My being, body and mind, was so focused on its task that I was equally unmoved by losing my trousers—dragged off on the lip of the flue—and the fact that my hand was free.

The concrete burned my left ear when my right arm thrust my torso down with a real handhold for the first time. My shoulders slid free and the rest of my body tumbled out of the tube, which had seemed to grip it tightly until that instant.

The light that blazed in my face was meant to blind me, but I was already stunned—more by the effort than the floor I'd hit an instant before. Someone laid the muzzle of a powergun against my left ear. The dense iridium felt cool and good on my damaged skin.

"Where's Sergeant Grant?" said Lieutenant Kiley, a meter to the side of the light source.

I squinted away from the beam. There was an open bedroll beneath me, but I think I was too limp when I dropped from the flue to be injured by bare stone. Three of the tank lords were in the room with me. The bulbous commo helmets they wore explained how the lieutenant already knew something had happened to the guard. The others would be on the ground floor, poised.

The guns pointed at me were no surprise.

"He slipped into the palace to see Lady Miriam," I said, amazed that my voice did not break in a throat so dry. "The baron killed them, both, and he's summoned the Lightning Division to capture you and your tanks. You have to call for help at once or they'll be here."

"Blood and martyrs," said the man with the gun at my ear, Lord Curran, and he stepped between me and the dazzling light. "Douse that, Sparky. The kid's all right."

The tank lord with the light dimmed it to a glow and said, "Which *we* bloody well ain't."

Lieutenant Kiley moved to a window and peeked through a crack in the shutter, down into the courtyard.

"But—" I began. I would have gotten up but Curran's hand kept me below the possible line of fire. I'd tripped the mercenaries' alarms during my approach, awakened them—enough to save them, surely. "You have your helmets?" I went on. "You can call your colonel?"

"That bastard Grant," the lieutenant said in the same emotionless, diamond-hard voice he had used in questioning me. "He slaved all the vehicle transceivers to his own helmet so Command Central wouldn't wake *me* if they called while he was—out fucking around."

"Via," Lord Curran said, holstering his pistol and grimacing at his hands as he flexed them together. "I'll go. Get a couple more guns up these windows"—he gestured with jerks of his forehead—"for cover."

"It's my platoon," Kiley said, stepping away from the window but keeping his back to the others of us in the room. "Via. *Via!*"

"Look, sir," Curran insisted with his voice rising and wobbling like that of a dog fighting a choke collar, "I was his bloody driver, I'll—"

"*You* weren't the fuck-up!" Lieutenant Kiley snarled as he turned. "This one comes with the rank, trooper, so shut your—"

"I'll go, my lords," I said, the squeal of my voice lifting it through the hoarse anger of grown men arguing over a chance to die.

They paused and the third lord, Sparky, thumbed the light up and back by reflex. I pointed to the flue. "That way. But you'll have to tell me what to do then."

Lord Curran handed me a disk the size of a thumbnail. He must have taken it from his pocket when he planned to sprint for the tanks himself. "Lay it on the hatch—anywhere on the metal. Inside, t' the right a' the main screen—"

"Curran, *knot* it, will you?" the lieutenant demanded in peevish amazement. "We can't—"

"*I* don't want my ass blown away, Lieutenant," said

the trooper with the light—which pointed toward the officer suddenly, though the pistol in Sparky's other hand was lifted idly toward the ceiling. "Anyhow, kid's got a better chance'n you do. Or me."

Lieutenant Kiley looked from one of his men to the other, then stared at men with eyes that could have melted rock. "The main screen is on the forward wall of the fighting compartment," he said flatly. "That is—"

"He's used it, Lieutenant," Lord Curran said. "He knows where it is." The little mercenary had drawn his pistol again and was checking the loads for the second time since I fell into the midst of these angry, nervous men.

Kiley looked at his subordinate, then continued to me, "The commo screen is the small one to the immediate right of the main screen, and it has an alphanumeric keypad beneath it. The screen will have a numeral two or a numeral three on it when you enter, depending on whether it's set to feed to another tank or to Grant's helmet."

He paused, wet his lips. His voice was bare of effect, but in his fear he was unable to sort out the minimum data that my task required. The mercenary officer realized that he was wandering, but that only added to the pressure that already ground him from all sides.

"Push numeral one on the keypad," Lieutenant Kiley went on, articulating very carefully. "The numeral on the visor should change to one. That's all you need to do—the transceiver will be cleared for normal operation, and we'll do the rest from here." He touched his helmet with the barrel of his powergun, a gesture so controlled that the iridium did not clink on the thermoplastic.

"I'll need a platform," I said, looking up at the flue. "Tables or boxes."

"We'll lift you," said Lieutenant Kiley, "and we'll cover you as best we can. Better take that shirt off now and make the squeeze a bit easier."

"No, my lord," I said, rising against the back wall—out of sight, though within a possible line of fire. I stretched my muscles, wincing as tags of skin broke loose from the fabric to which blood had glued them. "It's

48

dark-colored, so I'll need it to get to the tank. I, I'll use—"

I shuddered and almost fell; as I spoke, I visualized what I had just offered to do—and it terrified me.

"Kid—" said Lord Curran, catching me; but I was all right again, just a brief fit.

"I'll use my trousers also," I said. "They're at the other—"

"Via!" snapped Lord Sparky, pointing with the light he had dimmed to a yellow glow that was scarcely a beam. "What *happened* t'you?"

"I was a servant in the women's apartments," I said. "I'll go now, if you'll help me. I must hurry."

Lord Curran and Lieutenant Kiley lifted me. Their hands were moist by contrast with the pebbled finish of their helmets, brushing my bare thighs. I could think only of how my nakedness had just humiliated me before the tank lords.

It was good to think of that, because my body eased itself into the flue without conscious direction and my mind was too full of old anger to freeze me with coming fears.

Going up was initially simpler than worming my way down the tube had been. With the firm fulcrum of Lieutenant Kiley's shoulders beneath me, my legs levered my ribs and shoulder past the point at which they caught on the concrete.

Someone started to shove me farther with his hands.

"No!" I shouted, the distorted echo unintelligible even to me and barely heard in the room below. Someone understood, though, and the hands locked instead into a platform against which my feet could push in the cautious increments the narrow passage required.

Sliding up the tube, the concrete hurt everywhere it rubbed me. The rush of blood to my head must have dulled the pain when I crawled downward. My right arm now had no strength and my legs, as the knees cramped themselves within the flue, could no longer thrust with any strength.

For a moment, the touch of the tank lord's lifted hands left my soles. I was wedged too tightly to slip back, but I

49

could no more have climbed higher in the flue than I could have shattered the concrete that trapped me. Above, partly blocked by my loosely waving arm, was a dim circle of the sky.

Hands gripped my feet and shoved upward with a firm, inexorable pressure that was now my only chance of success. Lord Curran, standing on his leader's shoulders, lifted me until my hand reached the outer lip. With a burst of hysterical strength, I dragged the rest of my body free.

It took me almost a minute to put my trousers on. The time was not wasted. If I had tried to jump down to the wall without resting, my muscles would have let me tumble all the way into the courtyard—probably with enough noise to bring an immediate storm of gunfire from the baron's soldiers.

The light within the gatehouse must have been visible as glimmers through the same cracks in the shutters that the tank lords used to desperately survey their position. That meant the baron's men would be even more alert—but also, that their attention would be focused even more firmly on the second-floor windows, rather than on the wall adjacent to the gatehouse.

No one shot at me as I crawled backwards from the roof, pressing myself against the concrete and then stone hard enough to scrape skin that had not been touched by the flue.

The key to the tank hatches was in my mouth, the only place from which I could not lose it—while I lived.

My knees and elbows were bloody from the flue already, but the open sky was a relief as I wormed my way across the top of the wall. The moments I had been stuck in a concrete tube more strait than a coffin convinced me that there were worse deaths than a bullet.

Or even than by torture, unless the baron decided to bury me alive.

I paused on my belly where the wall mated with the corner of the west wing. I knew there were gunmen waiting at the windows a few meters away. They could not see me, but they might well hear the thump of my feet on the courtyard's compacted surface.

There was no better place to descend. Climbing up to

the roofs of the palace would only delay my danger, while the greater danger rushed forward on the air cushion vehicles of the Lightning Division.

Taking a deep breath, I rolled over the rim of the wall. I dangled a moment before my strained arms let me fall the remaining two meters earlier than I had intended to. The sound my feet, then fingertips, made on the ground was not loud even to my fearful senses. There was no response from the windows above me—and no shots from the east wing or the banquet hall, from which I was an easy target for any soldier who chanced to stare at the shadowed corner in which I poised.

I was six meters from the nearest tank—Lord Curran's tank, the tank from which Sergeant Grant had surveyed the women's apartments. Crawling was pointless—the gunmen were above me. I considered sprinting, but the sudden movement would have tripped the peripheral vision of eyes turned toward the gatehouse.

I strolled out of the corner, so frightened that I could not be sure my joints would not spill me to the ground because they had become rubbery.

One step, two steps, three steps, four—

"Hey!" someone shouted behind me, and seven powerguns raked the women's apartments with cyan lightning.

Because I was now so close to the tank, only soldiers in the west wing could see me. The covering fire sent them ducking while glass shattered, fabrics burned, and flakes spalled away from the face of the stone itself. I heard screams from within, and not all of the throats were female.

A dozen or more automatic rifles—the soldiers elsewhere in the palace—opened fire on the gatehouse with a sound like wasps in a steel drum. I jumped to the bow slope of the tank, trusting my bare feet to grip the metal, without delaying for the steps set into the iridium.

A bolt from a powergun struck the turret a centimeter from where my hand slapped it. I screamed with dazzled surprise at the glowing dimple in the metal and the droplets that spattered my bare skin.

Only the tank lords' first volley had been aimed. When they ducked away from the inevitable return fire, they

51

continued to shoot with only their gun muzzles lifted above the protecting stone. The bolts scattering across the courtyard at random did a good job of frightening the baron's men away from accurate shooting, but that randomness had almost killed me.

As it was, the shock of being fired at by a friend—*no* incoming fire is friendly—made me drop the hatch key. The circular field-induction chip clicked twice on its way to disappear in the dark courtyard.

The hatch opened. The key had bounced the first time on the cover.

I went through the opening headfirst, too frightened by the shots to swing my feet over the coaming in normal fashion. At least one soldier saw what was happening, because his bullets raked the air around my legs for the moment they waved. His tracers were green sparks; and when I fell safely within, more bullets disintegrated against the dense armor about me.

The seat, though folded, gashed my forehead with a corner and came near enough to stunning me with pain that I screamed in panic when I saw there was no commo screen where the lieutenant had said it would be. The saffron glow of instruments was cold mockery.

I spun. The main screen was behind me, just where it should have been, and the small commo screen— reading 3—was beside it. I had turned around when I tumbled through the hatch.

My finger stabbed at the keypad, hitting 1 and 2 together. A slash replaced the 3—and then 1, as I got control of my hand again and touched the correct key. Electronics whirred softly in the belly of the great tank.

The west wing slid up the main screen as I palmed the control. There was a 1 in the corner of the main screen also.

My world was the whole universe in the hush of my mind. I pressed the firing pedal as my hand rotated the turret counterclockwise.

The tribarrel's mechanism whined as it cycled and the bolts thumped, expanding the air on their way to their target; but when the blue-green flickers of released energy struck stone, the night and the facade of the women's apartments shattered. Stones the size of a man's head were blasted from the wall, striking my tank and the other palace buildings with the violence of the impacts.

My tank.

I touched the selector toggle. The numeral 2 shone orange in the upper corner of the screen, which the lofty mass of the banquet hall slid to fill.

"Kid!" shouted speakers somewhere in the tank with me. "*Kid!*"

My bare toes rocked the firing pedal forward and the world burst away from the axis of the main gun.

The turret hatch was open because I didn't know how to close it. The tribarrel whipped the air of the courtyard, spinning hot vortices smoky from fires the guns had set and poisoned by ozone and gases from the cartridge matrices.

The 20cm main gun sucked all the lesser whorls along the path of its bolt, then exploded them in a cataclysm that lifted the end of the banquet hall ten meters before dropping it back as rubble.

My screen blacked out the discharge, but even the multiple reflections that flashed through the turret hatch were blinding. There was a gout of burning stone. Torque had shattered the arched concrete roof when it lifted, but many of the reinforcing rods still held so that slabs danced together as they tumbled inward.

Riflemen had continued to fire while the tribarrel raked toward them. The 20cm bolt silenced everything but its own echoes. Servants would have broken down the outside doors minutes before. The surviving soldiers followed them now, throwing away weapons unless they forgot them in their hands.

The screen to my left was a panorama through the vision blocks while the orange pips on the main screen provided the targeting array. Men, tank lords in khaki, jumped aboard the other tanks. Two of them ran toward me in the vehicle farthest from the gatehouse.

Only the west gable of the banquet hall had collapsed. The powergun had no penetration, so the roof panel on the palace's outer side had been damaged only by stresses transmitted by the panel that took the bolt. Even on the courtyard side, the reinforced concrete still held its shape five meters from where the bolt struck, though fractured and askew.

The tiny figure of the baron was running toward me from the entrance.

I couldn't see him on the main screen because it was centered on the guns' point of impact. I shouted in surprise, frightened back into slavery by that man even when shrunken to a doll in a panorama.

My left hand dialed the main screen down and across, so that the center of the baron's broad chest was ringed with sighting pips. He raised his mob gun as he ran, and his mouth bellowed a curse or a challenge.

The baron was not afraid of me or of anything else. But he had been *born* to the options that power gives.

My foot stroked the firing pedal.

One of the mercenaries who had just leaped to the tank's back deck gave a shout as the world became ozone and a cyan flash. Part of the servants' quarters beneath the banquet hall caught fire around the three-meter cavity blasted by the gun.

The baron's disembodied right leg thrashed once on the ground. Other than that, he had vanished from the vision blocks.

Lieutenant Kiley came through the hatch, feetfirst but otherwise with as little ceremony as I had shown. He shoved me hard against the turret wall while he rocked the gun switch down to safe. The orange numeral blanked from the screen.

"In the *lord's* name, kid!" the big officer demanded while his left hand still pressed me back. "Who told you to do *that?*"

"Lieutenant," said Lord Curran, leaning over the hatch opening but continuing to scan the courtyard. His pistol was in his hand, muzzle lifted, while air trembled away from the hot metal. "We'd best get a move on unless you figure t'fight a reinforced battalion alone till the supports get here."

"Well, get in and *drive,* curse you!" the lieutenant shouted. The words relaxed his body and he released me. "*No*, I don't want to wait around here alone for the Lightning Division!"

"Lieutenant," said the driver, unaffected by his superior's anger, "we're down a man. You ride your blower. Kid'll be all right alone with me till we join up with the colonel and come back t'kick ass."

Lieutenant Kiley's face became very still. "Yeah, get in and drive," he said mildly, gripping the hatch coaming to lift himself out without bothering to use the power seat.

The driver vanished but his boots scuffed on the armor as he scurried for his own hatch. "Gimme your bloody key," he shouted back.

Instead of replying at once, the lieutenant looked down at me. "Sorry I got a little shook, kid," he said. "You did pretty good for a new recruit." Then he muscled himself up and out into the night.

The drive fans of other tanks were already roaring when ours began to whine up to speed. The great vehicle shifted greasily around me, then began to turn slowly on its axis. Fourth in line, we maneuvered out through the courtyard gate while the draft from our fans lifted flames out of the palace windows.

We are the tank lords.

WE HOLD THESE RIGHTS
Henry Melton

EDITOR'S INTRODUCTION

We recently celebrated the 200th birthday of the Constitution of these United States. That document established a government intended to put into concrete contractual terms the ideals expressed some years before in the Declaration of Independence. Although the Declaration was largely a Bill of Indictment against King George (one of the things we didn't like was that the king had "erected a multitude of New Offices, and sent hither swarms of Officers to harass our people and eat out their substance"), it also expressed the public philosophy of the leaders of the War of Independence.

These were no wild revolutionaries. They wanted the rights of free Englishmen. However, because the Declaration of Independence was in part intended to secure the sympathy of the French court, whose intellectuals weren't particularly impressed by appeals to the rights of free Englishmen, Jefferson and the Committee on Style drew on other sources.

"We hold these truths to be self-evident, that all men are created equal, that they are endowed by their Creator with certain unalienable Rights, that among these are

Life, Liberty, and the Pursuit of Happiness.

"That to secure these rights, Governments are instituted among Men, deriving their just powers from the consent of the governed."

Of course the men who pledged their lives, their fortunes, and their sacred honor to the Declaration fully understood that rights were a much trickier proposition than the document indicates. For one thing, one or two were atheists, while half a dozen of the others subscribed to a form of Deism that rejected any notion that God might intervene in the affairs of men; meaning that the Creator could hardly be the source of rights, and if He wasn't, who was? For the most part, though, the signers were men of their times, willing to accept the proposition that things long established had some right to exist; that custom and tradition were important; that there was a very great deal more to government than sheer power.

That's still the public philosophy of the United States. It's not a philosophy universally accepted among intellectuals, of course. They have other views about the rights of man, as well as the natural place of the elite in governing. We have, in this century, charged government with a very great deal more than the signers and framers ever supposed possible.

The purpose of government is, according to the framers, to secure rights; in particular, to establish justice. In their thinking, without government there could be no rights, for each man would do what he had the power to do; and that did not lead to peace, but to what Hobbes had called "the war of everyone against everyone else." Life in a state of Nature was no peaceful idyll. It was a state of "no arts; no letters; no society; and which is worst of all, continual fear and danger of violent death; and the life of man, solitary, poor, nasty, brutish, and short."

That's one view of natural right. There are others.

"AND I'M TELLING *you* THAT I WON'T HAVE A COWARD ON MY ship!"

I tried to reason with the maniac: "Come on, Quail! It's my ship, too. We *have* to have an engineer."

"We'll get another one!" His voice echoed off the walls

of the control room. I hadn't seen him like this before, and Quail Gren and I had been shoving rocks for six years. It was frightening.

"*Where*, Quail? Where will we get another engineer? After today, there won't be an unemployed beam controller anywhere in the Asteroid Belt—and if there were, he'd be somebody worse than Willis Fario."

"What's the matter with you, Clement Ster? Why are you sticking up for him? Are you wanting to sell us out to the Terrans, too?"

That was too much. My fist caught him clumsily in the chest. He was bigger than me, but he rocked back a little. "You shut up!" I yelled. "The Belt is my home, just like it is yours. I know you're worried about Marine and the kids, but don't be *crazy*. I'm not about to let some Earthside commission steal the Belt out from beneath me. You make another crack like that, and I'll deck you!"

Quail looked away toward his control console. My punch couldn't have hurt, but I think my trying it shocked him. I didn't often lose my temper. I stalked over to my seat at the geologist's station and automatically stabbed the keys on the geotyping files. It would be another three days before I would be needing to search them in earnest, but it was something to do until the air cleared.

He spoke, finally, in a lowered voice. "Okay, Clement. You're my friend. I know you're loyal to the Belt. But why'd you defend that *neon*?"

I sighed. It had been a very long and exhausting day, and I had no hope it would get any better. I reviewed my arguments again. "Two reasons. Like I said before, we're not going to be able to find a beam controller who can handle our beam projector the way we have it jury-wired, with no computer controls. You can plot your courses all you want up here, but unless we have someone down in the engine room who can make the beam move the ship like it's supposed to, then the *Monarch* isn't a ship—it's just a funny-shaped asteroid. And, secondly, I'm not so sure that he said anything wrong."

"Nothing wrong! Are you deaf? Didn't he, just a few

minutes ago, tell us that it is perfectly all right for the Earth Assembly to move right in and order us off our own rocks? Now, didn't he?" Quail's face started getting red again.

I tried to keep my voice calm, but my impatience stuck out with every word I said. "Quail, I really don't know *what* he said. Now, leave me alone for a while!"

It was the truth. I didn't know what Willis had said. He had a funny way of talking and I was never exactly sure. But I promised myself right then that I was going to find out what he had meant by his crack—but after I got some sleep. We were at war with Earth, only hours into it, and my nerves needed rest.

When I woke, Quail was still up in the control room. I didn't think he had gotten any sleep, and that worried me. I hoped he could take the strain.

It took a war to make me glad, for the first time, that I hadn't married. I remembered when the Terrans took over Mars in their insane desire to make over the entire solar system into a pattern of habitable planets. For their own safety—so they said—three generations of colonists were uprooted and shipped back to Earth. Many couldn't adjust to the crowded, smelly home planet. I didn't imagine we would fare much better under Terran control. They surely had some plan to use even Quail's home rock, Greenstone, as raw material for their terraforming engineers. I hated to think that such a thing might happen.

I marveled that Quail could resist the impulse to boost straight home. We were only a six-day trip from there. I wouldn't have argued. Ceres had no authority over us. If they had ordered us on the mission, rather than asking, I doubt we would have done it. No Belt miner would have. But Quail thought it would be best to act with the others.

The volunteer navy at Ceres had formed about thirty seconds after the bad news from the Terran Assembly arrived. As usual, we didn't find out about it until two hours later, when we turned the radio on to get an orbit allotment from Ceres Port Control. We grabbed the first slot we could get, and Quail and I took the scooter straight to Coro's place. In the excitement, we both forgot about Willis.

It had been a good bet. Jake Coro—that is, *Admiral* Jake Coro, T.P.N., Ret.—had been blowing the independence trumpet for years, not that anyone had paid much serious attention to him. The Belt, or so everybody thought, already *was* independent. But when the Terrans tried their move, he had been ready. We landed the scooter near his place, almost setting down on a couple of people who were scurrying about the place. A couple of dozen scooters were about, as Jake's Restaurant and Club had become general headquarters for the Ceres Defense Brigade. Jake had been retired from the Terran Navy for ten years, but those ten years had made him every bit a Belt man. As Quail and I walked into his place, I saw that he was still every bit an admiral. The Defense Brigade was his show, and he had the right. Seven years worth of contingency plans worked out for this very day were spread out in a couple of hundred sealed envelopes on the pool table. When he saw us come in, he took several minutes to talk to us and to ask our help. We left with one of those envelopes and a hope that we just *might* be able to hold the rocks we called home.

I really had no home other than the *Monarch*, but that hope of victory meant a lot to me—because Quail *did* have a home, and he had shared it with me. Every few months, when we had a bit more cash than bills, the *Monarch* would dock at Greenstone and Quail would take up being a family man where he had left off last time. For the first day or so he and Marine would disappear somewhere down in the rock and I would babysit the kids.

Baby Stephen was barely human the last time we were there, but then, Emme had looked like that not too many trips ago, and she was a little angel. She may have had a crush on me, hanging around wherever I was. I could visualize her, hovering over my shoulder in zero-g as I reset the house tractor field back up to normal after the baby had come. Toby and I were good friends. He had been around before I started visiting. We'd played a lot together over the years. I taught him how to use the rifle last trip. I'd hoped he would never have to use it.

Willis hadn't come up from the engine room for the night, but that was nothing unusual. We had hired him to monitor and control the machines down there when we limped into Vesta Village a month or so before with a fried computer. He slipped into the computer's place as if he were a repair module. He did the jobs well, executing orders Quail called down over the intercom. But he *acted* like a machine, too. He was quiet, impassive, and he stayed in his place. He ate and slept down there. It was always a shock when he *did* come up into people country.

Crawling down the cramped tube connecting the engine room with the rest of the ship, I felt maybe it *wasn't* so odd he rarely came up. The tube was narrow and too long. It was slanted downward and had an uncomfortable bend in the middle. It was dark at the bottom. The tube had come out next to the massive chamber that held tractor-pressor beams in a dynamic equilibrium, the accumulator that held all of our power.

"Willis? Are you asleep?" In the dim light shed by the indicators, I could make out his sleeping bag, strung, hammock-wise, between two supports. He said nothing, but the bag started moving and he began to crawl out. He was brown-skinned, hairy, and massive. He looked like a brown bear awakened from its winter nap, blinking his eyes as the light came on.

"What do you want?" he mumbled.

"I just wanted to talk. A lot has happened."

Willis gestured to a place where I could sit, as he slumped into the control seat we had moved down for his use. "Is there anything to say?"

I thought of Toby and Emme and that Terran fleet probably already on its way, and bit back the cutting answer that came to mind. I wanted to find out what *he* felt, in spite of his cynical manner. He looked at home, sitting there before the uprooted mass detector and among the various emergency-wired hand controls. But he was a big unknown to me. How he looked was about the limit of what I knew about him.

I took a stab at opening communications. "Quail got upset by some of the things you said yesterday. I hope we can clear the misunderstanding."

Willis grunted and nodded. "I could tell Mr. Gren didn't know what I was talking about. But I didn't figure you comprehended any more than he did."

"I can't say that I did. I just don't want a bunch of bad feelings to keep the *Monarch* from doing its best. Too much is at stake."

He just shrugged, and, inside, I sympathized with Quail's dislike of the man. I could tell he couldn't care less about what I was ready to fight and die for. We had been free men in the Belt far too long to take annexation with only a shrug. It didn't sit right.

"Don't you care?" I asked. I suddenly had a moment of doubt—Quail and I *hadn't* explained to him what was up when we left Ceres City at full speed, and we hadn't really discussed it when he was up in the control room. "You *are* aware of what is going on, aren't you?"

He shrugged again. "Mr. Ster, I really don't know how to answer you. All I've heard is a bunch of nonsense. And I can't get upset about nonsense."

"What kind of nonsense?"

"A bunch of gibberish on the radio as we left Ceres— in violation of port ordinances, by the way. I hope you've got a good reason for that; I've got *enough* marks against my record at Ceres Port. Anyway, the radio was full of it. On the Voice, instead of news, I was getting a *horrible* mishmash of *vile* treachery, *sacred* rights, *loyal* miners, and of *all* things, the defense of our *home* spaces. There was a lot more of the stuff, all variations on the same rabble-rousing theme. A lot of nonsense!"

"You said that in the control room. What do you mean? Are you saying it's nonsense that we want to defend our right to live our own lives? Do you think we don't have the *right* to defend our rocks from being stolen out from beneath us?"

Willis visibly sagged, as if disappointed in the conversation. "I've given up trying to make people understand. You won't understand—but yes, that *is* what I think. You don't have any rights."

I stopped listening right there and got to my feet. *What kind of man*, I thought, *wouldn't blink an eye at Terran goons forcing Toby and Emme down into their rat-hive cities in that high-gravity and fouled air? No right to resist!* I clamped my jaws. I wasn't about to lose my temper in front of him. I mumbled an excuse to leave and turned to go. *Quail is right. Even I won't be able to stomach working with him. We'll have to replace him. And this is the worst possible time!*

"Mr. Ster?" he asked calmly, stopping me. "Where are we going? You haven't said."

"Maybe it's best if I don't!" I snapped, hating myself for letting my feelings show. But I wanted to get out of that dark little room, fast. He turned my stomach. A man couldn't ignore what the Terrans had planned for ten million innocent people. Only a machine.

"Sir," he said, but I wasn't listening to what he said, only to the metal in his voice. "You don't understand what I said. *(Click)* But don't let that bother you. *(Click)* I do my job. *(Whirr-click)*"

I didn't reply. The hatch on the entrance tube was open and I left. Up in the control room, Quail brought up the subject of Willis again, but I couldn't argue about it anymore. After this mission, Willis had to go.

Forty hours out from Ceres, we had to change the beam. We had been pulling ourselves along smoothly toward Jupiter with the *Monarch's* tractor beam, but we needed a few hours of pull toward the sun to shift our vector. Quail spoke his directions down the intercom in as emotionless a voice as he could manage, but the contempt was still there. He had no use for anyone who would not help him fight. I had gotten him to take sleeping tablets, but he never stopped worrying about Marine. Willis kept his replies to a minimum. He did his job like a machine. The final piloting change was switching the propulsion beam from tractor to pressor and realigning it on Jupiter for another forty hours of deceleration.

When we finally cut that beam, the *eta* navigation beacon was strong in the nav receiver. Quail and I were at our duty stations. He wanted a short course to get us a little closer to the beacon, and I was hunting rocks. Willis walked into the room. We both looked up in surprise.

Quail growled, "What are you doing up here?"

He shrugged. "I thought it might be a good idea to find out what you were doing."

"Well, you can just crawl back into your hole and—"

"No, Quail," I interrupted. It looked as if I was to be the one to keep personal friction to the minimum until our job was done, in spite of how I felt. "Let him stay. He'll find out soon enough. I don't think we can destroy the beacon without his help."

A ripple of concern passed over Willis's face. "Destroy the beacon?"

I nodded. "Yes. We *live* in the rocks. Quail could navigate the Great Circle by instinct alone. But if we can break up the nav-beacon system, the Terran ships won't be able to use their fancy automated nav systems. They will have to shoot the stars, and it's a safe bet that not many will know how to do that. At worst, this operation will slow them down."

Willis thought a moment, then: "That beacon is Terran property. Destroying it would be a felony, with possible civil suits caused by the lack of its services. Have you thought about that?"

Quail exploded. "Of all the ridiculous . . . This is *war*, man!"

"Has there been a declaration of hostilities?" Willis displayed a machinelike calm. His face was undecipherable.

I tried to explain, before his manner drove Quail to blows. "Look, Willis, the Belt has never had a formal government, other than an occasional commission the Terran Assembly has tried to palm off on us. The closest we have are city governments such as Ceres Port. This *is* more a civil uprising than a formal war, but it is no less real. The *Monarch* isn't the only ship out taking action. Almost every ship in the Belt is doing something. When the Terran fleet arrives, the real fighting will start. Nobody will ever consider this a criminal action. Quail is right: This is war."

Willis said nothing, but he frowned as he turned and left. I threw a questioning look at Quail, but he shrugged in puzzlement. Neither of us could make him out. Right then, neither of us cared.

Our problem was to destroy the beacon. Thirty years before, the Terran engineers who had set them up built well. In all, there were better than a score of the monsters scattered through the Belt and in orbits around the nearer planets. Each was four times as massive as our ship and equipped with an impressive automated pressor-beam system to deflect the rocks that happened to wander too close. Inside their computers were supposedly a hundred strategies to handle everything from pebbles to Ceres itself. I had never heard of any of them being damaged in any way. It would have been easier if we had packed a laser with us, but we were a mining/survey ship, not a battlewagon.

Quail griped about that. "Jake Coro should've sent an armed ship, or at least a couple more like us, so we'd have a chance to overload the beacon's defenses. As it is, even if we throw a *bunch* of rocks at it, *our* power will run out before its will."

"You know he would have if he could've spared the ships. Face it, Quail—our job is important, but it is merely an afterthought compared to his job of drumming up enough ships to put together a defense around Ceres that isn't a joke. He wouldn't have sent an armed ship out here for anything."

Quail nodded at my words, but he was right about the problem we faced. No matter what we threw at it, the *eta* beacon could repel it with ease. And with Jupiter so close, it could recharge its power accumulator as easily as we could. There was no doubt that its capacity was greater. But, somehow, we had to find a way . . .

The intercom clicked on. Quail's head swung around as quickly as mine. *Willis? He never calls us first.*

"Mr. Ster? Are there any rocks in the close vicinity?"

I had my screen covered with the geotyping files of every rock that was likely to be near, looking for a good one to throw. "No. Nothing over a kilogram in a hundred kilometers. Why?"

"Well, my mass readings down here show a ship-sized mass hanging just off the beacon. You may have your war sooner than you thought."

I glanced instinctively at the gaping hole in the console where the mass detector had been mounted before we moved it down to the engine room. I wished I had it back. I swiveled back to my screen and punched up radar and visual. Nothing. *If there is a ship there,* I thought, *it is very well hidden.* I didn't want it to be there.

Quail said something vile across the room. I looked at him bending over the radar. He looked at me. "He's right! There's a double doppler. Terrans, just waiting there, watching us."

"They have to be painted black, then; there's nothing on the visual."

"That clinches it." He hit his fist on the console. "It's a warship."

I put the visual on the big center screen. The image showed the bright sunlight reflecting off the beacon, with the tiny disk of Jupiter behind it. Other than a scattering of stars, nothing else showed in the dark. "What do we do now?" The Terrans had planned better than I had given them credit. Anything we could try now had even less chance of success. They could even attack us.

"We've got to do something!" Quail paced, glaring up at the screen. *He* wasn't scared. The sight made me feel better, although I could see no hope.

"But what can we do, Quail? They've got lasers and sucker bombs as sure as anything. They can blast us to vapor in seconds. And you can be sure they'll act if we try anything. They aren't dead out there!"

"I don't know, but we have to do something! If this beacon is protected, then so are the others. This shows the Terrans need the beacons, so that makes it all the more important that we take this one out. The rest of the Belt is counting on us to do our job. We have to do it. I'm not going to have my wife and kids sent back to Earth as prisoners."

Not if I can help it, either, I said to myself. Quail and I had always backed each other up. I was not going to stop then. Breathing in his determination was like pure oxygen.

The intercom clicked. "Mr. Gren, plot a course back the way we came. Hurry, before they come at us."

What? I thought. *No!*

Quail's face darkened. "I will do no such thing, you coward! We've got a job to do and we'll do it if it kills us!"

"Mr. Gren," he said in his naggingly calm voice, "you will do as I say, or I will try to plot the course myself from down here with the mass detector."

I could have strangled him! It was a critical time. It could be disastrous to give up.

Quail yelled, "Over my dead body! We've got to stay and fight!"

"I must remind you I have control down here. Your controls of the engine and the accumulator all route through me. I have secured the latches on my hatch down here. You'd be wasting your time to fight about it. I repeat, plot a reverse course, immediately. That is the only thing that will save us."

I was thinking dark thoughts of the welding rig stowed in the hallway storage bin and what I would do to him. It would be difficult to sneak it down the engine-room connecting tube, but it could be done. I would not have a mutineer on the *Monarch*. No way. She was mine, mine and Quail's.

Quail was yelling abuse at the intercom, but he was weakening. Willis, for a little while, did have control of the ship. I fingered the silent keys on my console, spelling out a message to Quail on the screen:

LET WILLIS MOVE US OUT OF RANGE OF THE TERRAN SHIP, FOR NOW. COOPERATE. WE WON'T BE GOING FAR!

Quail got my meaning. He reluctantly got down to the business of plotting the line toward Jupiter that the pressor beam would follow. It was too risky a maneuver to let Willis plot his own; the mass detector didn't have enough resolution to bull's-eye a planet at that distance. For a change, Willis was on top of everything we did. The course was a simple one, but he questioned everything, down to the exact location of the beacon and the Terran ship. The suspicion was overpowering that he was some kind of Terran spy. I don't know what Quail was thinking. I saw him hesitate. He looked at me and I shook my head. We could easily feed him inaccurate data, but that wouldn't help us. Quail frowned deeply and gave him the last of the data.

I waved his attention to my screen again.

HE MAY HAVE ENGINE CONTROL, BUT WE . . .

Willis's voice on the intercom interrupted, "Are you ready to activate?"

Quail's answer was short and profane. I stepped into the following silence. I had to give him one last chance. "Willis? Why don't you help us? We can do more than run away. I'm sure that I can talk Quail into taking you on as a partner after the war." I frantically had to wave down Quail's anger before he said something to alienate Willis even more. "Come on, Willis. You are a Belt man like us. Help us fight for our rights . . ."

Willis replied in a voice as flat as any machine's: "Mr. Ster, we don't have time for that now. Just tell me if the board is clear, so I can activate the beam."

Quail spat out, "Yes, the board's clear, you traitor!"

"Thank you." His voice clicked off.

I swiveled back to my screen. Quail watched.

BUT WE HAVE CONTROL OF HIS AIR. FADE DOWN HIS OXYGEN AND THEN USE THE WELDER ON HIS HATCH.

Quail nodded. Doing so would be dangerous for Willis, but I was ready for him to take his chances. He was a mutineer at wartime.

A flicker of the indicators caught my eye. Willis had triggered the beam, sending its influence toward Jupiter at the speed of light. In twice the time it took the beam to get there, we would be moving. I glanced at the visual on the screen and noticed the beacon partially eclipsing Jupiter. Our beam had to be passing through it as well, although we were showing no acceleration yet. More of Willis's machinelike control over the beam. I had heard that there were beam controllers who could make their projectors play such tricks.

I got up and watched over Quail's shoulder as he carefully reset the air flow so that Willis would not notice the change until too late. It would take a while for it to act. I nodded my approval, and we sat down to await the beginning of the acceleration. My head was full of thoughts about Willis and the Terran ship and the beacon. I had an inspiration about how to attack the beacon and turned to my files to see how difficult doing so would be. I wanted to arrange a *compressed* bombardment, taking several days and many recharges to set dozens of rocks into high-speed collision courses, timed to arrive almost together, overloading the beacon's defenses. Not even the Terran ship could help in such a hailstorm.

I glanced up at the beam indicators. Then I looked again, because what I saw the first time didn't make any sense. I needed a second to get my mental bearings—suddenly everything looked wrong. Then everything focused. Three indicators were entirely off-scale! As I watched, a fourth climbed to its danger point, and then past. I heard blood rushing in my ears. *What is happening?*

"Quail! Look!"

I knew nothing of the workings of the beam projector, but I could read Quail's face. It went from puzzled to dead white!

He spun around and yelled at the intercom: "Willis! What are you doing? That's a high-tension beam! Are you trying to blow us up? Stop it!"

There was no reply. Quail was out of his seat, heading for the welder's storage bin. In seconds, the scorching tide of power Willis had evoked from Jupiter's orbital motion was due to arrive. We would be nothing but vapor. I could only think stupidly that the oxygen shortage couldn't have worked so quickly!

I was too confused to do anything but follow after Quail, although time had run out.

There was a flash of light. I saw my shadow on the wall before me. I turned.

On the big screen was a new sun. The image was saturated white with a growing ball of superheated gas where the beacon had been. I glanced at the radiation meter, just a tiny bit above normal. The explosion hadn't been nuclear. Quail walked to his station and touched a control.

"That was the beacon," he said. "And our beam is gone."

I looked, startled, and the indicators that had scared me senseless were sitting calmly at their neutral positions. *Willis! What did he do?* I turned to the hatchway. There he was, watching the screen with that same undecipherable expression on his face.

He looked at me and asked, "Have you checked on our friend?"

It took me a second to think of what he meant, then I reached for the radar. I found it after a minute, red hot and tumbling sunward. The Terran ship must have been sitting right on top of the beacon when it exploded.

"But how?" I asked.

"It was the beam," Quail answered.

Willis nodded. "I set the inflection voltage as high as the projector would go and kept the beam thin for maximum backlash. When the beam hit Jupiter, the energy of a head-on collision started back at us. At the last minute, I opened the beam and cut our accumulator out of the circuit. The only convenient place for the energy to go was into the beacon's accumulator."

"And it couldn't take it," I finished.

"It took quite a bit, before it blew." Quail smiled. "That ship won't bother us again." He faced Willis and held out his hand. "I see I was wrong about you. Will you accept my apology?"

Willis backed off, suddenly sullen. "None of you will ever understand." And he walked out the door.

Quail looked hurt and confused. I had to do something. I dashed after him.

"Willis, I want to talk to you!" I stopped him at the head of the tube.

"Can you?" he asked. "At times I thought we talked, but it turned out we were just making noises at each other."

"Willis, we both want to apologize for not understanding you. It was inexcusable for us to think that you would be any less loyal to the Belt than—"

"Oh, stop all this mishmash! Don't bother to apologize. I haven't changed and neither have you. You'll think I'm a traitor again as soon as I say something you don't understand."

"No." I didn't want to lose him now. Not since he had shown what he could do. And what he would do. "We've seen what you did. We understand, now, that just because you talk differently about things, it doesn't mean you are any different in what is inside you."

"No! *I'm not the same as you!*" he screamed at me. I stepped back instinctively; Willis never screamed. But he suddenly blazed: "I *can't* believe the lies you live by!" His voice abruptly dropped to a fatigued whisper. "Oh, how I wish I could." He straightened and looked back at me with demon eyes. "Listen to me, Clement Ster. I'll say this only once. I said *before* that you had no right to fight the Terrans. You condemned me for it. I say it *again! You have no right.*"

"But the beacon—the Terran ship?"

He grabbed my shoulder tight in his huge hand and shook me. "*Listen*, Ster! I had no *right* to destroy them. Neither do the Terrans have the *right* to take over the Belt. *Rights* don't exist! There is only *power* and *action*. Your imaginary rights are only good for keeping people like you and Gren happy and righteous while slaughtering your enemies, if you can call *that* good."

I opened my mouth to reply, but he shook me silent like a misbehaving child. "Understand me, Ster. I murdered the crew of that Terran ship, and I destroyed someone else's beacon worth more than I could make all of my life. I did it because I had the power, and a fair chance of getting away with it. I did it purely for the *selfish* reason that I don't want the Terrans controlling the Belt and running my life! Just the same as you would have—if you had been the one with the power.

"Don't tell me about defending our sacred rights, and wars against the oppressor. As long as there are people, there will be men killing each other for property, for power, whatever. The winner will always have been just defending his rights. The losers are the criminals. It's all *fiction*, Ster! If you have to kill somebody, then kill him. But don't talk nonsense about rights!"

He stopped and I twisted out of his iron grip. He didn't look as if he noticed, away in some place inside his head. I didn't know what to do or say. I wished Quail were with me. I glanced back toward the control room, but there was no sign of him. I was alone.

"Clement," Willis said, in an easy conversational tone, so unlike him, "those men in that ship. They lived all their lives under a government that promised them the right to life. And that government lied, 'cause I just killed them! I wonder how big a slice of their souls their government charged for that politicians' promise. *Rights*! Moral excuses and politicians' lies." He shook his head in amusement, then abruptly looked me directly in the eyes, pinning me in place. "Clement Ster, if you have to lie, steal, destroy, and murder, then *do* it! But then have the strength to take responsibility for what you do. Do you understand?"

I couldn't move. I couldn't talk. He was like an elemental force. His words flared out at me. His eyes searched my face.

Then it was as if he clouded over. I was released. He seemed to be talking to himself, as if I were no longer there. "No. I can see that you don't." He reached for the hatch and started back down to his solitary room. "You will never understand. You will always believe in your rights—your wars—your holy causes. I wish I could." His voice was pained as he whispered, "Oh, how I wish *I* could!"

BATTLE CRY
Tim Sarnecki

EDITOR'S INTRODUCTION

Few soldiers willingly go to battle, yet go they must. Over the centuries leaders have discovered ways to lead men to the colors when the trumpets sound the call to arms. The best bring them expecting victory, for morale wins more battles than numbers. When Queen Boadicea led her Britons in revolt against Rome, Suetonius, with one Legion already destroyed and another forced into retreat, faced with his 7,000 Legionaries and 4,000 auxiliaries between 100,000 and a quarter of a million Celts. The cities of Colchester and London had already been burned. Every Roman citizen, man, woman, and child, that the Britons could catch had been slaughtered, many with studied cruelties.

One of the great moments in science fiction takes place in Robert A. Heinlein's *Have Spacesuit, Will Travel,* when an old Roman centurion is dragged before a Galactic court. He faces technology so complex that it's beyond magic. He has no real idea why he's there. He does understand that he faces enemies. The enemies of Caesar, and, worse, of a Rome he has never seen; enemies who threaten everything he has lived for; and knowing that he cannot win, still he cries his challenge.

Suetonius led an army of such men; but he faced no mean foe. The morning of the battle, Queen Boadicea told her soldiers: "Win the battle or die. That is what I, a woman, will do. You men can live on in slavery if that is what you want." Her army responded with a mighty cheer.

Suetonius's speech has also been recorded. "Ignore the racket these savages make. There are more women than men shouting in their ranks. They are not soldiers. They are not even properly equipped. We've beaten them before. When they see our weapons and feel our spirit, they'll break and run. Stick together. Throw your pila and push forward. Knock them down with your shields and finish them with your swords. Forget about loot. When we win you'll have the lot."

It wasn't an eloquent speech by contemporary standards, but by nightfall more than 80,000 Britons were dead. The Romans lost 400 troopers.

Sometimes, though, the situation is greatly different. Leonidas at Thermopylae would never have made a long speech, because the Spartans didn't do that sort of thing; but if he had . . .

I've called my last challenge,
And made my last reply.
My rivals from a thousand wars
Have come to watch me die.
I gain my feet, and one last time,
Sing out my battle cry.

"Hail!" The foes before me;
"All hail, you ghosts of fools.
Your bloods run out upon the field
Where once you used these devils' tools:

"This is my swift right arm,
Capped with this mighty hand
That wields the power of my sword,
With which I took a soldier's stand.

"My strong left arm, a shield
To ward your every blow
But one, which ends my warring life;
But one, which lays the soldier low.

"But wait, these are but shades
Of my real weaponry.
They are but implements of war,
Entailments of my destiny."

In death, above them is my heart,
Warrior spirit, burning hot,
For love of war's rich panoply,
For spoils, glory, victory;
For swords upraised, the battle cry;
For this, I lived; for this, I die.

I've called my last challenge,
And made my last reply.
My rivals from a thousand wars
Have come to watch me die.
To them, I raise my last salute;
For them, this one last battle cry.

TEST FOR TYRANTS
Edward P. Hughes

EDITOR'S INTRODUCTION

In previous volumes we told the story of the Irish village of Barley Cross after World War III devastated the Earth, and rendered most of the men sterile.

Barley Cross was conquered by a tyrant: Patrick O'Meara, onetime sergeant of Her Majesty's Forces, brought his tank to the village and proceeded to build the fortress he called the Fist; after which he proclaimed himself Duke of Connaught, Master of the Fist, and Lord of Barley Cross. As lord he took it on himself to lead the town militia in raids to recover aspirin, antibiotics, and other supplies, so that soon the town was indeed independent.

He also imposed other customs. In an era when nearly all the men were sterile, Patrick O'Meara wasn't; and thus came about the revival of *droit de seigneur*; a duty that O'Meara apparently enjoyed to the day he died. Of course, O'Meara wasn't married.

His successor certainly was.

LIAM MCGRATH LAY BESIDE HIS SLEEPING WIFE, TRYING TO plan. Already, dawn brightened the corners of the bedroom. In a few hours, Father Con would be saying the words to make Brege O'Malley wife of Christie Kennedy —and thus pose a problem for the new Lord of Barley Cross.

Liam shifted restlessly. What would the O'Meara have done about it? Liam recalled very clearly what the previous master had done after his, Liam's, wedding. But the O'Meara had ruled Barley Cross for longer than Liam could remember, and Liam, fresh to the job, could not hope to match such expertise.

At six o'clock he reached a decision, and got up. He dressed without disturbing Eileen, and slipped out of the Fist by the bedroom window and the secret path through the kitchen garden.

At the foot of the hill, he turned river-wards, making for a lonely cabin that stood just off the track leading down to McGuire's mill. It was light enough to see that he had the road to himself. A raw wind blew promising rain. Typical Connemara wedding day, Liam reflected.

The cabin was in darkness. He rapped, not loudly, but persistently. A light flickered behind the curtains, a bolt rasped, the door opened an inch.

"It's me, Liam," he hissed. "I need your help, Katy."

He heard a sigh of exasperation. "Liam McGrath— you may be our new master, but it doesn't give you the right to get an honest whore out of bed at six in the morning."

"Let me in," he pleaded. "I've got to talk to you."

He caught a giggle. "Well, so long as it's only talk you want."

A chain rasped, and the door opened wide enough to admit him. Kate Monaghen, in curlers and a red flannel nightie, peered at him in the lamplight. "You'll be getting a worse name than the O'Meara," she warned. "At least *he* abstained from commercial fornication."

Liam closed the door behind him. "No one saw me, Katy." He shrugged off the overcoat he had draped over his shoulders. "I put this on to alter me appearance."

She set the oil lamp on a table. "If you think that old rag can hide our new master—"

He sat down, breathing heavily. "Can't be helped, Katy. I had to see you. I need your help."

She said, "I'll put the kettle on. We'll have a sup of tay while you tell me your troubles."

As she poured, he blurted out, "Brege O'Malley gets wed today. And I've got to do my *droit du seigneur* thing with her tonight."

"Droyt doo what?"

He explained.

She raised her eyebrows. "Sure, that shouldn't be a difficult job for a fine upstanding young felly like yerself."

He sighed, seeing suddenly a vision of Brege O'Malley. Saint Brege, the Ice Maiden, they had christened her as children. Twelve months younger than Liam, she, Christie Kennedy, and the other educable infants of Barley Cross at that time had squeezed together into the too-small desks of Celia Larkin's one-room school. Brege, even then, had affected piety—wearing below-the-knee skirts, aping the habits physical and moral of the nuns she claimed she would have joined, had there been a convent handy.

"Well?" It was Katy, bringing him back to the present.

He lifted his head. Now that he needed to keep awake, it was a job to hold his eyes open. He began diffidently: "I—er—" The trouble was, Katy Monaghen might be one of those Barley Cross citizens, like his stepfather, who accepted all they were told about the master. He plunged on recklessly. "I don't know how much you know about the master's responsibilities—?"

A furrow appeared between her eyes. "I know enough to agree that you ought to get on with your droyts, if that's what's mithering you."

Katy would, of course. Being a harlot, a droyt or two would be neither here nor there to her. He sighed. "It ain't that, Katy. It's what Christie Kennedy will want to do about it."

"Bugger Christie Kennedy," she snapped. "Just get your guards to throw him out if he shows up."

Liam shook his head. "That would only make things

78

worse. I've got to let him into the Fist and face him on my own. Try to talk him out of killing me."

Her eyes opened wide. "Would he try to do that?"

Liam shrugged. "I tried to kill the O'Meara when I got wed."

She said briskly, "Then you must kill Christie first."

Liam groaned. "I can't do that. If I took a life each time I tried to start one, I wouldn't be much benefit to Barley Cross, would I?"

She nibbled at her bottom lip, studying him in silence. "So that's the reason why the O'Meara bedded every bride in Barley Cross? Well, bloody hell! And what can I do to help you?"

Liam raised his eyes, face haggard. "Has Christie Kennedy ever visited you . . . in your professional capacity?"

Kate Monaghen regarded him archly. "Liam McGrath —would you be asking me to break my hypocritic oath? Sure all my business is confidential."

His lip trembled. "Knock it off, Katy. I'm serious."

She whispered, "And what if Christie did come to see me?"

"I—I could threaten to tell his wife."

Her eyes grew wide. "Glory be to God! And on his wedding day, too! And you the lord of the village, who should be setting us all example!"

"You don't understand, Katy," he pleaded. "It's only because I'm master that I have to blackmail him."

She eyed him narrowly. "And just where would I come in?"

Liam peered around the edge of the curtain into the brightening daylight, as if half afraid that an eavesdropper crouched outside. He said, "I want you to come up to the Fist for the day."

She stared. "And what would your wife say? She knows what I am. Sure, she wouldn't let me past her front door."

He wanted to contradict her, but knew it would be a waste of time. All Barley Cross knew that Kate Monaghen was a loose woman. The women tolerated

79

her, as they tolerated the lewdness of the master, in grim silence. His Eileen would probably slam the door in Kate's face.

He mumbled. "My wife won't be there. She's taking the baby and herself off to her mam's for the weekend, so that, officially, she won't know what goes on at the Fist."

"Oh? And what does go on at the Fist?"

He moaned. "Christ, Katy—don't you understand? I've got to take Brege O'Malley to bed, and try to get her in the family way. And Christie Kennedy will probably climb in through my bedroom window and do his damnedest to stop me."

She nodded thoughtfully. "I see. And just as he's going to stick a knife into your pelt, I bust out of the wardrobe crying 'Halt, Christie Kennedy! Or we'll tell yer new wife all about the antics you got up to with me last summer'?"

"Something like that," he agreed lamely. "It's the best I can think of. The O'Meara would have had a smarter way of doing it, but I'm not the O'Meara."

"And thank God for that!" Her eyes flashed angrily. "The O'Meara would never have taken me into his confidence. I may not set a shining example in the village—but I'm as loyal a citizen as any of 'em."

He said, startled, "Then you'll come?"

She flourished a fist. "Just tell me how to get past yer guards."

General Desmond was hovering in the hall when Liam returned. "Where've you been?" he demanded ungraciously. "You're supposed to be at the church by nine o'clock."

"I've been attending to the master's business," Liam retorted, concealing his awe of fierce Larry Desmond, but still unsure how far he might verbally venture with the old soldier.

"I've an honor guard picked for your escort," the general continued, as if Liam had not spoken. "Two of our smartest men, and a corporal to carry the presents and deliver the summons. We're sending the bride a tablet of soap and a bottle of perfume, and the same to her ma. It's more than usual, but we want to build you up as a generous tyrant."

"So pleased—" Liam began.

"And Michael has pressed your uniform."

Liam sensed his ears prick, like a rabbit's. "Uniform? I have no uniform."

The general smiled genially. "The O'Meara used to wear his old Coldstream Guards outfit at functions. If we pad the chest out a bit it'll fit you good enough."

"But I've never been in the army," Liam protested. "I'm not even old enough to serve at the Fist."

"Ach, away with you!" The general waved a carefree hand. "What's the use of being master if you can't bend the rules occasionally? You've got to look impressive today."

Liam took a deep breath, knees quivering. It was now or never. Unless he intended to knuckle under to Larry Desmond for the rest of his life. "No uniform," he stated firmly. "Positively no uniform. I'll wear my best suit, if you like. But no uniform."

General Larry Desmond's white eyebrows bristled. "Now, listen here, young Liam!"

"*Master!*" Liam corrected, holding his lips firm. "Master of the Fist and Lord of Barley Cross."

General Desmond looked straight at him, as if seeing Liam for the very first time.

Liam stared back, without speaking.

The general seemed to shrink slightly. "Okay, Me Lord," he conceded. "No uniform. Your best suit will do nicely. And would you condescend to attend at the reception after? You need only stay for the meal and a couple of dances."

"I'll do that," Liam agreed. "I'll even wear some kind of badge or chain of office, if you can dream one up."

Larry Desmond brightened. "Now, there's an idea." He rummaged in his pocket. "Pat used to wear an old medallion around his neck. I was keeping it as a souvenir." He pulled the hand from his pocket and offered Liam a chain. "Perhaps you'd—?"

Liam took the chain, and examined the silver disk attached to it. One side of the medal bore the figure of Saint Christopher, the other the words *P. O'Meara,*

81

Kilcollum, Connemara. Liam slipped the chain over his head. "Let's call it my chain of office."

"Thank you," said Larry Desmond. "Maybe you'll make a dacent master yet."

Liam arrived purposely late, and lingered at the back to the church. He was not keen to meet Father Con's accusing eyes over the head of the bride he intended to force into adultery before the day was out.

Later, at the reception, he found himself given a seat of honor beside the bride's mother, and was obliged to attempt polite conversation with Ma O'Malley.

She leaned confidentially toward him. "Will you be sending for our Brege tonight, Me Lord?"

Liam pondered the tone of her voice. Was she hoping that he'd say yes? Women were mysterious creatures. Since his accession, he had discovered more mild-looking, middle-aged matrons in Barley Cross who secretly approved of the O'Meara's carnal excesses than he could have ever imagined. He murmured, "My corporal has the summons in his pocket. Will Brege be willing?"

Madame O'Malley eyed him coquettishly. "Don't you be worrying about our Brege, Me Lord. I'll see she's willing. And if she ain't, dammit if I don't come up to the Fist meself in her place!"

Liam tried not to flinch. He sneaked a glance along the table to where Brege's father, Pete O'Malley was tucking into turkey. Liam whispered, "I hope you don't let Mr. O'Malley hear you make remarks like that. Not that you wouldn't be welcome," he added gallantly, "but it's Brege's turn this time."

When Franky Finnegan struck up a waltz on his fiddle, Liam found the nerve to plunge into the prancing throng, his arms around his hostess. Ma O'Malley danced enthusiastically, as if determined not to waste an instant of the glory in the new master's embrace. Liam sweated, counting beats under his breath, accommodating his stance to the O'Malley figure.

Two dances, Larry Desmond had stipulated. The next one, then, had to be with the bride. As Franky finished with a flourish, Liam released his partner and glanced around the floor.

82

The new bride stood momentarily alone, her husband heading for the bar. Liam excused himself, and headed toward opportunity. Franky struck up again, and he led the Ice Maiden, unexpectedly gorgeous in long white satin, onto the floor.

She murmured, "So kind of you to come to my wedding, Master. And thank you for the presents."

Since fine quality toilet soap and French perfume had not been seen in Barley Cross for years, except on those occasions when the master showed his generosity, Liam reckoned she meant it. He cracked a grin. "Liam's the name, Brege."

She pouted. "But you are master too."

"But still Liam McGrath," he countered. "I hope I haven't changed."

She smiled nervously, nodding at the medallion. "Would that be your chain of office?"

He flicked it with his thumb. "It belonged to the O'Meara. General Desmond thinks I should wear it."

"Then it *is* to show us you are the master?"

He was getting fed up with the way people harped on about it. He said curtly, "If you like."

She lowered her head, her voice almost inaudible. "Does that mean you'll be sending for me tonight?"

In his confusion, he trod on her foot. God! Was the Ice Maiden seeking a summons? He opened, then shut his mouth. Couldn't ask questions like that. In a carefully neutral voice he asked, "Did you not get the summons yet?"

She shook her head, mute, waiting for him to invite her personally. He couldn't speak. His tongue was swollen and dry. He scanned the crowd, seeking the corporal. When was the man supposed to deliver the summons, anyway? Had he forgotten it? And everyone wanting to know. The reception was turning into a bloody shambles. Liam choked, flushed, then managed to say, "Excuse me—got to see my corporal about something."

He released her, casting aside manners and propriety, and pushed blindly off the dance floor. Damn everything! He couldn't face Brege's mute curiosity. He ran from the hall, ignoring the startled glances of other guests, heading for the Fist, hating Brege, hating General bloody Desmond, and most of all, hating himself.

He found the general in his parlor, with Kevin Murphy, the vet. The general waved cheerily. "You survived the ordeal, then, Me Lord?"

Liam held tight on to his temper. "Just when is that corporal supposed to hand over the summons?"

The general frowned in thought. "I told him to hang on until the 'do' had quieted a bit. Lot of people leave early. Didn't want to upset too many folk if they didn't like you emulating the O'Meara."

"Oh!" Liam's anger drained away. As usual, the general had acted for the best. "Well, he was still hanging on to it when I left, and the O'Malley women are going nuts waiting. I got the impression that Brege expects to be summoned. Her ma is all for it."

The general nodded. "Just as well. If the young lady should refuse, you could clap her parents in jail until she changed her mind. We did that once, early on, Kevin—remember?"

Kevin Murphy nodded. "Niver a bit of trouble in Barley Cross after that. Might be a good idea to throw somebody into the cooler right now. 'Twould establish Liam's authority for sure."

The general rubbed his chin reflectively. "Young Kennedy might be a suitable candidate. It'd keep him out of the way, too." The general considered Liam. "We can't maintain a permanent guard on your bedroom, unfortunately. It could mean telling them too much. But if you have any trouble with young Kennedy, Kevin and I will be standing by. Just ring for Michael and we'll come running."

Liam hid his embarrassment. Thank goodness he had kept his feelings about the general to himself. He murmured, "Thank you, gentlemen. I'll keep it in mind."

A cool breeze wafted through the open window. Liam sat by the bed, one hand gripping the O'Meara's heavy old revolver concealed beneath the counterpane. Christie Kennedy must surely have heard the news by now. Michael had reported the honor guard's return over half an hour ago. Was Christie shirking it? He had always been a bit of a blowhard at school. But when your wife's honor was in question . . . ?

Something whizzed past Liam's head, and struck the wall behind him. He turned in astonishment. The feathered butt of an arrow projected from the plaster. He swiveled back to discover Christie Kennedy astride his windowsill, a stretched bow in his hands, and an arrow lined up on Liam's breast bone.

"Right, you bastard!" Christie gritted, swaying.

For a brief moment Liam considered, and rejected, the response the O'Meara might have made to that epithet. After all, both he and Christie were bastards. But Christie was drunk, and probably immune to reasoning.

Liam moved to face him, coughing to hide the clink of the chain mail he wore under his shirt. "What do you want, Christie?"

Christie Kennedy's lip lifted in a sneer. "Only your signature on a bit of paper that says you cancel the summons your bloody corporal just gave my Brege."

Liam pondered. Christie's attention had to be diverted while he got the gun out of hiding. No arrow could penetrate his medieval underwear, but what if Christie aimed for the head? He needed outside help. Liam called softly, "Katy!"

The door to his private bathroom opened, and Katy Monaghen sauntered into the bedroom. She wore bright red brassiere and briefs. A black satin suspender belt supported a pair of black stockings that left on show the top six inches of her creamy thighs. A red satin rosette decorated her right knee.

"Hi, Christie!" she called.

"Jesus!" The arrow tip wavered. Liam had the gun out, covering him, but it was unnecessary.

Christie said thickly, "What the hell are *you* doing here?"

Kate Monaghen smiled sweetly. "I'm protecting our master from the attentions of ardent young hooligans like you."

"And drop that bow, or I'll blow your arse off," Liam added.

Christie lowered the bow, as though in a dream, not even looking at Liam. "Why are you dressed like that, Katy?"

She minced toward the window, and took the bow from Christie's nerveless fingers.

"Come on in!" Liam urged. "We want to talk to you."

Dazedly, Christie got his other leg over the sill.

Kate said, "I thought it might remind you of old times, Christie."

Christie dragged the heel of his thumb across his forehead, his eyes on Kate's plump bottom as she turned to prop his bow in a corner. "Jesus!" he muttered. "I've drunk too much."

"Is that where you got the nerve from?" Liam asked.

Kate flashed him a glance. "Cut that out, Liam. And put that gun away. It won't be necessary."

She turned back to Christie. "You're all worked up about Liam's droyt doo seenyer, aren't you, lad? Would you sooner he ignored Brege? Especially when every bride in the village since the year dot has been honored by a summons to the master's bed."

"If you can call it an honor," Christie mumbled slackly.

"Here, hold on!" Kate's voice rose in protest. "Is that what you thought when you visited me last summer?"

"Ah—no!" Christie showed confusion. "That was different. I mean—I paid you."

"Oh?" Kate registered surprise. "You mean, if Liam gives Brege money, everything will be all right?"

"No, I—I didn't mean that." Christie's eyes rolled wildly. "You're getting me confused, Katy."

She sat down beside him on the window ledge. "Sure, 'tis yerself is responsible, Christie boy." She addressed Liam. "Could you lend us a spare bedroom—and a bottle? The lad's worn out with excitement. He could do with a lie-down. I might even keep him company."

Christie looked owlishly at Liam. "Do *you* think it's an honor?"

Liam gazed back levelly, conscious that the day hung in the balance. He said, "I wouldn't do it unless." Suddenly inspired—since he hadn't spoken to Christie's

86

mother—he added, "Just ask your ma what she thinks of it."

Christie's face sobered momentarily. "Can't figure it out. My old lady is all for it. She told me not to do anything daft."

Kate slipped a bare arm round his neck. "And you're not going to, honey, are you? Not when your ma says you mustn't."

Liam pushed the revolver into his belt. "Wait here," he ordered. "I'll see if there's a bed made up." He didn't dare ring for Michael and have Larry Desmond and Kevin Murphy charging in to the rescue. He jerked a thumb at the delicate inlaid cabinet across the room. "There's a bottle and glasses in there, Katy. Would you offer our guest a drink?"

General Desmond wagged his head in reluctant approbation. "I dunno how you've done it, Me Lord, but you seem to have pulled it off."

Liam grinned deprecatingly. "Well—" He *had* thought of fetching Kate Monaghen in the first place. "It was Kate who did it, really."

Kevin Murphy's glass clinked against the bottle. "And with luck, she'll keep him quiet all night."

Larry Desmond laughed. "It's a change from the way Pat would have worked it. Kind of ironic, if Christie is giving Kate a tumble in one room while Liam—"

"That'll do!" the vet warned. "If Celia were here you wouldn't dare talk like that." He grinned. "Still and all, young Christie won't want to shout too loud in the morning." He raised his glass. "Glory be, Larry—I think we picked a winner!"

Larry Desmond smiled sourly. "Let's wait and see how he copes with the Ice Maiden. I reckon she'll be a harder nut to crack."

Liam closed the bedroom door behind them. The house was quiet. Brege Kennedy still wore her wedding dress. She stood silent in the center of the room, not looking at the turned-down bed, nor at the flowers in the vase on the dresser.

Liam rubbed his hands together nervously. "Would you like a drink, Brege?"

She shot him a pleading glance. "You know I don't touch strong drink, Me Lord."

He blinked. "It don't have to be spirits. I could wake Michael to make us a sup of tay."

"I think I would like that."

He rang for the servant, then motioned to one of the well-padded armchairs. "Sit down, Brege. Make yourself comfortable."

They sat in silence until Michael appeared. Then in silence again until he reappeared with teapot, milk jug, sugar basin, cups, and saucers on a silver salver. When he had gone, Liam cleared his throat, and stammered, "Look, Brege—this is no easier for me than it is for you." It stole into his mind, then, that if they didn't do it, no one would be any the wiser. And it would save both of them a deal of grief. And, of course, it would be cheating.

Brege gave him an angry look. "Then why do you insist on having me here?"

He was taken aback. "Hasn't your ma told you?"

She lowered her face, staring at her hands on her lap. "My ma said I ought to come. She thinks it's an honor."

"Is that all she told you?" Liam was beginning to realize just how well the secret of Barley Cross was kept.

She frowned. "What else should she have said? That you'll put her and me dad in jail if I don't do what you want?"

"Ah—no, Brege. Something more serious than that." Liam hesitated. It appeared to be his prerogative who got let into the secret. He said, "I'd better tell you, lass. I am the only fertile man in the village. If we don't do it tonight, you'll—you'll never have any children. And if every bride refused to go to bed with me, in fifty years or so, Barley Cross would be a mausoleum."

She was staring wildly at him. "But, Liam—it's a sin! We'd be committing adultery!"

He winced. Hadn't he known Saint Brege would come up with something like this? He said desperately, "If you weren't really married, we wouldn't. I don't want to cast doubts on your marriage, but if a man isn't able to consummate it—there's no marriage. Ask Father Con."

She bridled. "I can't talk to Father Con about that kind of thing. Anyway, it's only if a feller knows *beforehand* that he's infertile that the marriage is invalidated."

Liam said gently, "And we don't want to find *that* out, do we? So if you do what I ask tonight, any child you might have could just as easy be Christie's."

She turned impulsively toward him. Tears were trickling down her cheeks. "Is it the truth you're telling me, Liam McGrath?"

"So help me, God." Liam crossed himself. "It's all a plan the council cooked up, years ago. If your ma and my ma hadn't gone along with it, neither you nor me would be here upsetting each other."

"But why must it be you?" she pleaded. "Why not my Christie?"

He shrugged uncomfortably. "It just so happens that Eileen is having another child. Tommy may have been the O'Meara's, but this second one must be mine. It seems that I, out of all the lads in Barley Cross, have inherited the O'Meara's peculiar genes."

She sniffed. "What does your Eileen think of it?"

"She ain't too happy," he admitted. "But she's agreed to put up with it for the same reasons everybody else does."

Brege dabbed her eyes with a scrap of linen. "Do we do it just the once?"

"So far as I know," he said gently. "If you don't conceive—it's just your bad luck."

She peeped up, hiding her face behind the handkerchief. "I'm shy, Liam. I've never done it before."

He sighed with relief. He was over the hurdle. It was now just a matter of patience and understanding. Barley Cross would never know its luck. He said gently, "I'll show you how."

She took a quick sip at a cup of cold tea. "Could we have the light out, please?"

The full council met in Liam's parlor the following day. Brege Kennedy was safely away to the new house her husband's da had built for her—and where she would find her new husband snoring in the bed. Kate Monaghen was safely back in her cottage down the mill lane, richer by a tablet of toilet soap and a bottle of French perfume. And Liam McGrath was hoping that his Eileen would not be too curious about the events of the previous night when she returned from her ma's.

Liam straightened his hair, and joined the council.

General Desmond looked up. "Ah, Liam—you've come to report success, I hope?"

Kevin Murphy said dryly, "By the smirk on his face, I should imagine that he has."

Liam said, keeping his voice even, "I did what was required."

"Hark now!" The general lifted a finger. "Has he, or hasn't he?"

Dr. Denny Mallon removed an empty pipe from his mouth. "The master just told us he has, General."

The general wagged a finger. "But not in so many words, Doctor. What if he and our Ice Maiden decided to fool us all, and just pretend they'd done it? Not every marriage in the village is blessed with offspring. We'd never know they'd conned us."

Liam glanced from one to the other. Obviously, they had already been discussing him.

Celia Larkin looked up from her knitting. "Are you accusing our new master of lying, Larry Desmond?"

The general's jaw dropped. Histrionically, Liam divined.

"I never said so," Larry Desmond protested. "I'd just prefer a more positive assurance than he has given us so far."

The schoolmistress lowered her knitting. "If you're wanting a blow-by-blow description of the exploit, you'll have to manage without my presence."

"Ah no, Celia." Dr. Denny waved his pipe. "That ain't necessary. If Liam says the job's done, then done it is."

"Hold on now!" Kevin Murphy sat up straight. "If the job's been done, then surely Liam can tell us something that would prove he's handing us the truth. Something maybe Denny, here, could confirm. Has the lady a mole on her person, for instance?"

Four pairs of eyes turned on Liam. He shifted his feet uneasily. "Sure, she insisted on the light going out," he protested.

General Desmond cackled harshly. "Wouldn't you know there'd be a snag? I had a feeling that the Christie victory was just a flash in the pan."

"That's quite enough, Larry Desmond," Celia Larkin snapped. "You agreed to his being made master. If you trusted him then, why can't you trust him now?"

Why not indeed, Liam agreed silently. But then, the general hadn't been faced by a tyro tyrant refusing to wear a uniform until yesterday. And when puppets don't work properly you lose faith in them.

"Enough!" Denny Mallon exploded. "Let the master be!" He turned to Liam. "Tell them, son!"

Liam made sheep's eyes at the doctor. "But it's *her* secret! Brege will never forgive me if I let it out."

"Tell us what?" demanded the general. "Have you two been cooking something up between you?"

"Tell them!" thundered the doctor. "They'll never be satisfied until they know." He glowered around the room, as if daring anyone to contradict him. "And, remember—anything said at this council meeting is as inviolate as the confessional."

Liam shook his head in disgust. So much for promises made in the dark. Poor Ice Maiden! Her secret divulged to protect the master's probity.

Reluctantly, he told them: "Brege Kennedy has a deformity she don't like anyone knowing about—except people like Dr. Denny, who *have* to know. Brege isn't cold, nor pious, nor shy. It's just she has knock-knees."

THE ROMAN CENTURION'S SONG
Rudyard Kipling

EDITOR'S INTRODUCTION

Queen Boadicea lost her final battle in her revolt against
Rome, but the result was not what she had feared. Rome
came to conquer, but there remained remnants of the
old notion that the mission of Rome was "to protect the
weak and make humble the proud." Rome didn't exter-
minate the Britons; instead, the Britons became Romans,
and more important, Romans became British. They came
as conquerors and remained as protectors. Then, three
hundred years later, barbarians swarmed through Europe, and the Legions withdrew from Roman Britain.
Kipling tells of one Roman officer ordered "home."

The story is also told in Stephen Vincent Benet's *"The
Last of the Legions"*; and peripherally in the brilliant new
series *The King of Ys* by Poul and Karen Anderson.

ROMAN OCCUPATION OF BRITAIN, A.D. 300

Legate, I had the news last night—my cohort ordered
  home
By ships to Portus Itius and thence by road to Rome.
I've marched the companies aboard, the arms are
  stowed below:

Now let another take my sword. Command me not to
    go!

I've served in Britain forty years, from Vectis to the
    Wall.
I have none other home than this, nor any life at all.
Last night I did not understand, but, now the hour
    draws near
That calls me to my native land, I feel that land is
    here.

Here where men say my name was made, here where
    my work was done;
Here where my dearest dead are laid—my wife—my
    wife and son;
Here where time, custom, grief and toil, age, memory,
    service, love,
Have rooted me in British soil. Ah, how can I remove?

For me this land, that sea, these airs, those folk and
    fields suffice.
What purple Southern pomp can match our changeful
    Northern skies,
Black with December snows unshed or pearled with
    August haze—
The clanging arch of steel-grey March, or June's
    long-lighted days?

You'll follow widening Rhodanus till vine and olive
    lean
Aslant before the sunny breeze that sweeps Nemausus
    clean
To Arelate's triple gate; but let me linger on,
Here where our stiff-necked British oaks confront
    Euroclydon!

You'll take the old Aurelian Road through
    shore-descending pines
Where, blue as any peacock's neck, the Tyrrhene
    Ocean shines.
You'll go where laurel crowns are won, but—will you
    e'er forget

The scent of hawthorn in the sun, or bracken in the
    wet?
Let me work here for Britain's sake—at any task you
    will—
A marsh to drain, a road to make or native troops to
    drill.
Some Western camp (I know the Pict) or granite
    Border keep,
Mid seas of heather derelict, where our old messmates
    sleep.

Legate, I come to you in tears—My cohort ordered
    home!
I've served in Britain forty years. What should I do in
    Rome?
Here is my heart, my soul, my mind—the only life I
    know.
I cannot leave it all behind. Command me not to go!

THE ISLANDERS
Rudyard Kipling

EDITOR'S INTRODUCTION

We have legends of the time after the Legions departed and a Romanized Briton called Artorius was named Dux and charged with protecting the land from the Saxons. Arthur failed, and the Saxons were supreme, to be conquered in their turn by the Danes, then the Normans under William. Norman and Saxon and Celt fused into one people who proudly gave the world the notion of ordered liberty; and built an empire on which the sun never set. By the beginning of the twentieth century it was clear that the British Empire, like the Roman, would bring peace and order to the world. Empire has a price, though; and secure behind the shelter of the English Channel, the Islanders were unwilling to pay it. In 1902 Kipling thought it worth while to warn his people that wealth and laziness do not last long in this world.

It is a lesson that each nation, each generation, must learn in its own way; for the new Islanders of the United States seem to have forgotten.

No doubt but ye are the People—your throne is above
the King's.
Whoso speaks in your presence must say acceptable
things:
Bowing the head in worship, bending the knee in fear—
Bringing the word well smoothen—such as a King
should hear.

Fenced by your careful fathers, ringed by your leaden
seas,
Long did ye wake in quiet and long lie down at ease;
Till ye said of Strife, "What is it?" of the Sword, "It is
far from our ken";
Till ye made a sport of your shrunken hosts and a toy
of your armèd men.
Ye stopped your ears to the warning—ye would
neither look nor heed—
Ye set your leisure before their toil and your lusts
above their need.
Because of your witless learning and your beasts of
warren and chase,
Ye grudged your sons to their service and your fields
for their camping-place.
Ye forced them glean in the highways the straw for the
bricks they brought;
Ye forced them follow in byways the craft that ye
never taught.
Ye hampered and hindered and crippled; ye thrust out
of sight and away
Those that would serve you for honour and those that
served you for pay.
Then were the judgments loosened; then was your
shame revealed,
At the hands of a little people, few but apt in the field.
Yet ye were saved by a remnant (and your land's
long-suffering star),
When your strong men cheered in their millions while
your striplings went to the war.
Sons of the sheltered city—unmade, unhandled,
unmeet—
Ye pushed them raw to the battle as ye picked them
raw from the street.
And what did ye look they should compass? Warcraft

learned in a breath,
Knowledge unto occasion at the first far view of
Death?
So? And ye train your horses and the dogs ye feed and
prize?
How are the beasts more worthy than the souls, your
sacrifice?
But ye said, "Their valour shall show them"; but ye
said, "The end is close."
And ye sent them comfits and pictures to help them
harry your foes:
And ye vaunted your fathomless power, and ye
flaunted your iron pride,
Ere—ye fawned on the Younger Nations for the men
who could shoot and ride!
Then ye returned to your trinkets; then ye contented
your souls
With the flannelled fools at the wicket or the muddied
oafs at the goals.
Given to strong delusion, wholly believing a lie,
Ye saw that the land lay fenceless, and ye let the
months go by
Waiting some easy wonder, hoping some saving sign—
Idle—openly idle—in the lee of the forespent Line.
Idle—except for your boasting—and what is your
boasting worth
If ye grudge a year of service to the lordliest life on
earth?
Ancient, effortless, ordered, cycle on cycle set,
Life so long untroubled, that ye who inherit forget
It was not made with the mountains, it is not one with
the deep.
Men, not gods, devised it. Men, not gods, must keep.
Men, not children, servants, or kinsfolk called from
afar,
But each man born in the Island broke to the matter of
war.
Soberly and by custom taken and trained for the same,
Each man born in the Island entered at youth to the
game—
As it were almost cricket, not to be mastered in haste,
But after trial and labour, by temperance, living
chaste.

As it were almost cricket—as it were even your play,
Weighed and pondered and worshipped, and practised
day and day.
So ye shall bide sure-guarded when the restless
lightnings wake
In the womb of the blotting war-cloud, and the pallid
nations quake.
So, at the haggard trumpets, instant your soul shall
leap
Forthright, accoutred, accepting—alert from the wells
of sleep.
So at the threat ye shall summon—so at the need ye
shall send
Men, not children or servants, tempered and taught to
the end;
Cleansed of servile panic, slow to dread or despise,
Humble because of knowledge, mighty by sacrifice. . . .
But ye say, "It will mar our comfort." Ye say, "It will
minish our trade."
Do ye wait for the spattered shrapnel ere ye learn how
a gun is laid?
For the low, red glare to southward when the raided
coast-towns burn?
(Light ye shall have on that lesson, but little time to
learn.)
Will ye pitch some white pavilion, and lustily even the
odds,
With nets and hoops and mallets, with rackets and
bats and rods?
Will the rabbit war with your foemen—the red deer
horn them for hire?
Your kept cock-pheasant keep you?—he is master of
many a shire.
Arid, aloof, incurious, unthinking, unthanking, gelt,
Will ye loose your schools to flout them till their
brow-beat columns melt?
Will ye pray them or preach them, or print them, or
ballot them back from your shore?
Will your workmen issue a mandate to bid them strike
no more?
Will ye rise and dethrone your rulers? (Because ye

98

were idle both?
Pride by Insolence chastened? Indolence purged by
    Sloth?)
No doubt but ye are the People; who shall make you
    afraid?
Also your gods are many; no doubt but your gods shall
    aid.
Idols of greasy altars built for the body's ease;
Proud little brazen Baals and talking fetishes;
Teraphs of sept and party and wise wood-pavement
    gods—
These shall come down to the battle and snatch you
    from under the rods?
From the gusty, flickering gun-roll with viewless
    salvoes rent,
And the pitted hail of the bullets that tell not whence
    they were sent.
When ye are ringed as with iron, when ye are scourged
    as with whips,
When the meat is yet in your belly, and the boast is
    yet on your lips;
When ye go forth at morning and the noon beholds
    you broke,
Ere ye lie down at even, your remnant, under the
    yoke?

No doubt but ye are the People—absolute, strong, and
    wise;
Whatever your heart has desired ye have not withheld
    from your eyes.
On your own heads, in your own hands, the sin and the
    saving lies!

ANOTHER "LOW DISHONEST DECADE" ON THE LEFT
Peter Collier and David Horowitz

EDITOR'S INTRODUCTION

It is an occupational habit for actors on the political stage to distort the truth, for reasons and in ways that vary with the nature of the power they hold. Autocrats, in direct control of all means of communication and expression, disguise the present and rewrite the past. Democrats, whose influence depends, happily, on their persuasiveness, expend so much energy trying to show their undertakings in the best possible light that they eventually lose the habit of thinking about the issues' substance. Their skill in presenting their case almost entirely replaces their interest in the facts. So that in free societies the past is sometimes misrepresented, not, as in slave societies, by crude censorship and lies, but suavely, through legitimate persuasion and the free propagation of an adulterated or entirely bogus version of an event. With repetition, this version joins the body of accepted ideas, those the masses believe; it acquires the status of truth, so firmly that hardly anyone thinks of checking the original facts for confirmation.

Jean-Francois Revel
How Democracies Perish
Doubleday, 1983

Democracies perish because no one defends them. The public no longer heeds the call to arms. Why fight for a corrupt regime? It is immoral to think of the enemy's sins; we must concentrate on our own. The call to arms is sounded, but few answer.

Peter Collier and David Horowitz understand this all too well. Co-authors of *The Rockefellers: An American Dynasty* and *The Kennedys: An American Drama*, they founded *Ramparts* magazine and were leaders of the antiwar movement in the sixties. They have much to say about the lessons of that time.

WE FIRST BECAME INVOLVED WITH THE NEW LEFT—THAT movement which eventually degenerated into the devious and dishonest Left of today—at the end of the 1950s, a time when McCarthyism was dying and a new radical movement was struggling to be born in demonstrations against the House Committee on Un-American Activities. The "end of ideology" had ended; Khrushchev had admitted that what a previous generation of leftists had regarded as "anti-Soviet lies" about Stalin's crimes had actually been true. What attracted us to this new political atmosphere was the opportunity to be leftists in a new way: not as the servile agents of a foreign power, but as members of an indigenous radical movement. Along with other early New Leftists, we regarded members of the Old Communist Left as figures to be scorned—people who were (in both meanings of the term) boring from within: intriguers with a discredited intrigue who always lurked on the fringes of our meetings, trying to find a group, any group, they could infiltrate.

The New Left saw itself as a movement which would design its own future—a sort of activist American-studies curriculum. The phrase *participatory democracy* captured its intention to make the promise of America real. Its first campaign—for civil rights—was based on a belief in this promise. Ultimately the Vietnam war provided the occasion for this optimism to ferment and then to sour. The speed with which the New Left became disaffected from the country and from its own early ideals, and the fact that this happened with so little resistance, suggests that the movement had a split personality from the outset—one part believing in America and the other not believing in anything. Ruminating about the instant alienation of the New Left, Paul Goodman, one of its earliest mentors, thought that its leading characteristic was a "loss of patriotic feeling." He wrote: "For the first time . . . the mention of country, community, place, has lost its power to animate. Nobody but a scoundrel even tries it."

That loss of patriotic feeling led the New Left to declare war against America, matching every escalation in Vietnam with an escalation of its own in the conflict at home. Sympathy for America's alleged victims developed into an identification with America's real enemies. By the end of the '60s participatory democracy was a language no longer spoken on the Left. The slogans changed. "Bring the boys home" became "Bring the war home." The organizations changed, too. In 1969, a year after Students for a Democratic Society (SDS)—the heart of the New Left—had converted to Marxism-Leninism, its convention broke into various factions chanting the names of Chairman Mao and Uncle Ho, dictators of China and North Vietnam who had become its household gods.

In its later, rococo phase some members of the New Left dallied with the Soviet Union, revising our earlier revisionism. (Deep in his Black Panther period, Eldridge Cleaver claimed that Stalin was "a brother off the block," while Trotsky was a "white bourgeois intellectual.") But for the most part this dalliance was nothing more than rhetorical posturing, and the Soviets remained stigmatized.

Not so the romantic revolutionaries of the Third World. SDS delegations met with the North Vietnamese and the National Liberation Front (NLF) in Cuba and Czechoslovakia as well as North Vietnam, and agreed to collaborate with their war effort by providing propaganda advice and orchestrating a campaign to demoralize American troops in the field and to create disorder and disruption back home. Anti-war activists with Old Left politics like Cora Weiss and guilty liberals like Reverend

William Sloane Coffin went to Hanoi to second the cause. After visiting American POW's whom the Communists had tortured, they assured the world that American prisoners were being treated well. In 1969 a group of radicals, including the SDS leader Bernardine Dohrn and the prominent Castro apologist Saul Landau, traveled to Cuba where they met with Vietnamese officials and also launched the "Venceremos Brigades." The ostensible reason for this effort was to help with the Cuban sugar harvest. The real reason was to map out strategies for war in America, the "other" war which would ultimately defeat the United States in a way that the battlefield situation in Vietnam never could have done.

As editors of *Ramparts*, then the most widely read magazine of the New Left, we were dubious about the totalitarian enthusiasms of people like Weiss, Landau, and Dohrn. When confronted with these tendencies we argued against them. One almost amusing "struggle session" occurred when, shortly after the return of the Venceremos Brigades, members of the pro-Castro North American Congress on Latin America (NACLA) came into our offices with an article. It purported to be a report on the progress of "socialist democracy" in Cuba, focusing on the recent passage of an anti-laziness law as evidence of the "people's rule" and claiming that some three million Cubans, about half the population, had actively participated in the making of this law. We asked the obvious question: if the civic involvement was this high, why was the law necessary? In the confrontation that followed, NACLA members told us that, because of our "white skin privileges," we had no right to question anything Third World revolutionaries did. In the words of one of the NACLA spokesmen, "You should do your revolutionary duty. Print the piece and shut up about it."

But while we rejected the crude propaganda of people we regarded even then as Castro's agents, we did provide a platform in 1969 for the more sophisticated apologetics of Susan Sontag, who catechized our readers on "The Right Way (For Us) to Love the Cuban Revolution." The issue of *Ramparts* in which this piece appeared accurately captured the ethos that had come to prevail in the New Left. Over the cover photograph of a wholesome six-year-old carrying a Vietcong flag were these words: "Alienation is when your country is at war and you want the other side to win."

Like most of the Movement, we presumed that a Vietcong victory would mean a peasant utopia in Southeast Asia. But we were less concerned with what happened in Vietnam than with making sure that America was defeated. A fundamental tenet of our New Leftism was that America's offenses against Vietnam were only a fraction of its larger imperial sins. We shared with most others on the Left its most implausible and destructive myth: that America had become rich and powerful not by its own efforts but by making the rest of the world impotent and poor.

To force America's global retreat had become for us the highest good and we were willing to accomplish this end, in one of the odious catch phrases of the day, "by any means necessary." Our most significant opportunity came when we developed a contact with a young man who had just quit a job as a cryptanalyst with the National Security Agency (NSA) because of his disillusionment with the Vietnam war. At the time, few people knew anything about this top-secret agency which processed some 80 percent of the intelligence the U.S. gathered. Prodding our "defector," we developed an article that described the operations of the NSA in detail and also revealed its capabilities for deciphering Soviet codes, then one of the most deeply embedded of all American intelligence secrets and one whose revelation would have profound consequences.

Although we gave scarcely a second thought to the moral implications of printing the article, we did worry about the legal risks we faced. The defense team working for Daniel Ellsberg (who was on trial for the theft of the Pentagon Papers) recommended that we talk to Charles Nesson, a Harvard professor of law and an expert on the Constitution. Nesson advised us that if we printed the article, and in particular the secret code words it contained, we would be in clear violation of the Espionage Act. But he added that in order to prosecute us, the government would have to reveal even more information about the NSA's secrets than was contained in the article itself, and for this reason it was extremely unlikely that we would ever be indicted.

We thus learned the lesson other radicals would learn: the freedoms of America could be used to subvert American freedom. We printed the article. We were not prosecuted. Instead we were rewarded with a good deal of media attention, including a front-page story in the *New York Times*. It was our biggest scoop. We had considered ourselves "better" than the Castroite hacks at NACLA and the Weathermen crazies trying to work themselves up to acts of terrorism. But like others present at the creation of the New Left who had begun the '60s asking America to be better, we had ended the decade committing acts of no-fault treason.

The government we had sought to undermine might be unable or unwilling to punish us, but history would not be so kind. After America's defeat in Vietnam the New Left was presented with a balance sheet showing the consequences of its politics. New Left orthodoxy had scorned the idea that the war was at least partly about Soviet expansion, but soon after the American pullout, the Soviets were in Da Nang and Cam Ranh Bay and had secured the rights to exploit the resources of Indochina in unmistakably imperial style. Other things we had claimed were impossible were also now happening with dizzying velocity. Far from being liberated, South Vietnam was occupied by its former "ally" in the North. Large numbers of "indigenous" revolutionaries of the NLF whom we had supported were in "political reeducation" camps set up by Hanoi or taking their chances on the open seas with hundreds of thousands of other Vietnamese refugees fleeing the revolution in flimsy boats. In Cambodia two million peasants were dead, slaughtered by the Communist Khmer Rouge, protégés of Hanoi and beneficiaries of the New Left's "solidarity." It was a daunting lesson: more people had been killed in three years of a Communist peace than in thirteen years of American war.

For some of us, these events were the occasion for a melancholy rethinking which ultimately led to our retirement from the Left. But for many of our former comrades, there were no second thoughts. For this group, the Communist victory in Indochina provided an opportunity to prove the mettle of their faith and to rededicate themselves to the long-term objectives of a struggle which they believed had only just begun.

Two years after the fall of Saigon, in fact, an event took place that marked the passing of the torch of revolution from one generation of the Left to another. Appalled by the ferocity of the new rulers of Indochina, Joan Baez and other former anti-war activists reentered the political arena with "An Appeal to the Conscience of Vietnam." In criticizing Hanoi and calling for an end to the repression, the signers of the "Appeal" challenged the remnants of the New Left to live up to the standards of social justice it had advocated for so many years.

Rejection of this plea was swift and decisive. A counter-ad in the *New York Times* paid for by Cora Weiss, the heiress who had come to function as a sort of bankbook for Left causes during the 1970s, was signed by a list of former anti-war notables, including figures like Dave Dellinger of *Liberation* magazine and Richard Barnet of the Institute for Policy Studies, who reaffirmed their solidarity with the Communists by subscribing to phrases such as this one: "The present government of Vietnam should be hailed for its moderation and for its extraordinary effort to achieve reconciliation among all of its peoples."

To outsiders, the appearance of these two statements might have seemed a prelude to a struggle for the soul of the Left. But as insiders we recognized that the issue had already been decided. The chastened radicals who signed the Baez "Appeal" were defeated; there was no longer any ground on the Left that they could occupy. Those who stood ready to support Communist Vietnam and, by implication, similar governments elsewhere in the Third

World, had won almost by default. Their declaration was thus more than a rebuff of the attempt to hold revolutionary movements accountable for their deeds; it was a manifesto for the successors to the New Left. Sympathizing with and supporting America's enemies, only a tendency before, would become the dominant characteristic of the post-Vietnam Left.

The personality of this reconstituted Left was further adumbrated in the late 1970s by the rehabilitation of the American Communist party. Books such as Vivian Gornick's *The Romance of American Communism* and film documentaries like *Seeing Red* remembered Stalin's most servile followers as admirable old warriors who had fought the good fight and stayed the course, and who thus might be worthier models in the long struggle ahead than the New Left, which had burned itself out with its theatrics and its need for immediate gratification.

This romanticizing of Stalinist hacks was counterpointed by the return of Stalinist fronts to the American political scene. By 1979 the World Peace Council, originally created by Stalin in 1949, was once again operating on the American Left. Its American offshoot, the U.S. Peace Council, was holding conferences attended not only by what was left of the Left but also by Senators and Congressmen. The pro-Soviet sycophancy of the Communist party kept its numbers small; but the new spirit of acceptance allowed its influence to grow. Communists became stylistically influential, reintroducing the linguistic and organizational deviousness of the Popular Front period of the late 1930s that made it hard to know what words meant and harder yet to identify the allegiances of those who spoke them.

While the New Left had announced its birth from a university campus, its post-Vietnam successor seemed almost to trumpet its intrinsic hypocrisy by organizing itself in New York's Riverside Church, built by John D. Rockefeller fifty years earlier as a headquarters for liberal Protestantism. Among the architects of the declaration with which the reconstituted Left was launched were

William Sloane Coffin, newly appointed minister of Riverside, and his patron, the ubiquitous Cora Weiss, head of the Church's Disarmament Program.

Sloane Coffin had become a representative figure in the effort to forge an alliance between the churches and the Third World, one of those who brought the gospel of "liberation theology" and its notion of a Marxist God enjoining the faithful to establish a Communist heaven on earth by supporting revolutionary movements, defined as the "essence of Christian faith." Defending his own covenant with the dictators in Hanoi, for example, Coffin advised an interviewer that "Communism is a page torn out of the Bible" and that "the social justice that's been achieved in . . . North Vietnam [is] an achievement no Christian society on that scale has ever achieved."

While Coffin articulated the "new morality" of the post-Vietnam Left, Cora Weiss was in a sense more typical as well as far more influential than he. Drawing on a $25-million family fortune inherited from her father Sam Rubin (in his own time an old-line Communist), she had helped fund NACLA, which was continuing to promote the cause of Castro. In addition, she was the leading backer of the Institute for Policy Studies which by the late 1970s had become the heart of a secondary system of institutional lobbies whose programs had elicited the sponsorship of more than fifty members of Congress and whose influence spread from Capitol Hill to the Carter administration itself.

As head of the Riverside Church Disarmament Program, Weiss played a leading role in the opposition to American efforts to neutralize the vast Soviet military buildup of the '70s. Her work focused on exposing the "myth" of a Soviet threat. Richard Barnet, a co-director of the Institute for Policy Studies and its resident "expert" on strategic affairs, called the idea of such a threat "the big lie of our times." In May 1979 Weiss herself described it as a "hereditary disease transmitted over the past sixty years."

Barely six months after this *aperçu* was delivered, the Soviets assassinated the head of state in Kabul and launched a massive and eventually genocidal invasion of

Afghanistan. Weiss's Disarmament Program at the Riverside Church responded by declaring: "Any form of U.S. intervention, escalation of a military presence or an increase in the defense budget is unnecessary and inappropriate . . . Russia's challenge continues to demand restraint, study, and understanding." In other words, the invasion was merely a "defensive" response to American pressure. Instead of focusing their attention on the Soviet action in Afghanistan, members of the "peace movement" should look at what the U.S. had done to "poison relations between the two superpowers."

This failure to oppose Soviet aggression or recognize the Soviet threat showed the distance traveled since the early days of the New Left when the malignity of the USSR was a given. It also showed how far the Soviet Union had come in rehabilitating itself since the revelations of Khrushchev, which had destroyed the orthodoxy that held party vanguards in line and controlled the popular fronts. The post-Vietnam era had become a time of new opportunities for the Soviets, an extended school at which Fidel Castro, although dependent on them for a subvention of some $10 billion a year to keep his island afloat, became their most important political teacher.

Castro saw that the American Left, still wary of the USSR, could be made to promote Soviet aims indirectly because of its ties—affective even more than political— with him, ties that would survive his support of the invasions of Czechoslovakia in 1968 and of Afghanistan a decade later. At the same time he was making Cuba's economy an appendage to the USSR's and its intelligence service and military forces instruments of the Soviet state, Castro began the creation of what amounted to a new version of the old Communist International, a new Comintern.

A revolution throughout the hemisphere had always been Castro's ambition, but through the mid-'60s the cautious Soviets had been wary of what they regarded as "reckless adventurism" sure to provoke an American response. Two events changed their attitude. The first was the American defeat in Indochina and the crucial role which internal opposition had played in forcing the

U.S. withdrawal. Second were changes in the American Left itself, foremost among them the establishment of a Fidelista cadre. The Soviets saw that Castro's charismatic hold over elements of the American Left was such that his adventurism might be less reckless than it had seemed earlier in his career.

Within months after the fall of Saigon, the Soviets began an unprecedented flow of arms to Cuba. By 1980 the flow had become a flood—ten times more military supplies in a single year than the total sent during the entire first decade of the revolution, when Castro presumably faced his greatest external threat. The massive arms buildup had only one purpose—to make Cuba the forward base of a new stage in Soviet expansionism. Castro played his part by dispatching 30,000 troops to anchor Soviet influence in Angola and Ethiopia.

But if Africa was the first front for the new offensive, Central America was always the ultimate prize. Castro had long been the patron of tiny guerrilla bands in Nicaragua and El Salvador whose leaders had been trained in Havana and Moscow and sometimes at PLO terrorist camps in Lebanon. Because he had survived U.S. animosity so long and studied American weaknesses so carefully, Castro better than anyone else understood the "Vietnam equation" which defined the new criteria for revolutionary success. It was not necessary for the Communists to win; it was necessary only for America to lose; and losing was defined by what went on in the domestic politics of the United States rather than on Third World battlefields.

When the Carter administration took office in January 1977, the Soviet bloc was faced with unanswered questions. How much weight could be given to the new president's expressions of regret for American interventions of the past, or his determination to avoid "another Vietnam"? How vigorously would he pursue his new human-rights policy with regional dictators like Somoza who relied on U.S. support?

Factoring the answers to these questions into the "Vietnam equation" would determine revolutionary options and risk, and there was no Communist leader in the world who had better intelligence for arriving at an answer than Fidel Castro. In creating the Venceremos Brigades in 1969, Castro had placed them under the control of Cuban intelligence with results that were revealed later in the testimony of a Cuban defector: "The Venceremos Brigades brought the first great quantity of information through American citizens that was obtained in the United States, because up to the moment when the brigades came into existence . . . the amount of information that we had on American citizens came from public sources, and it was confusing." In the changed political atmosphere after Vietnam, the networks which Castro's loyalists had created now permeated the American political process. The co-founder of NACLA had even been appointed to the Carter administration as a member of the team that was shaping its policy on human rights.

As Jimmy Carter took office, Castro's favorite Sandinista, Humberto Ortega, unveiled a new political strategy from his Costa Rican headquarters which bore the imprint of the master himself. An immediate Marxist revolution would be deferred in favor of a broad coalition with non-Marxist democrats whose announced goal was replacing the Somoza dictatorship with a pluralistic government. At the moment this tactic was adopted, the Sandinistas had been a minuscule force, barely 200 members and split into three antagonistic factions. But now, as part of a democratic coalition, they were able to launch a mass movement that soon challenged Somoza for power in Nicaragua.

By early 1979, when it was apparent that Somoza could not last, Castro summoned the guerrillas, still feuding among themselves, to Havana. There he created the nine-member *comandante* directorate with each of the three Sandinista factions represented. The Sandinista command unified, Castro made arrangements to provide them with the arms and military support that would allow them to defeat Somoza and, even more important, allow them also to steal the revolution from the mass movement they had ridden to success.

Once his protégés were firmly established in Managua, Castro turned his attention to El Salvador. Six months

111

after the Sandinista victory, a new summons brought the heads of the five Salvadoran guerrilla factions to Havana where Castro persuaded them too to form a unified command. The new force that Castro created was called the Farabundo Martí National Liberation Front (FMLN), after an agent of Stalin's old Comintern. Until then, the Salvadoran guerrillas had been too isolated and weak to open a revolutionary front. But with Castro behind them, they laid plans to move from sporadic actions to a full-scale guerrilla war. In July 1980, the chairman of the Salvadoran Communist party, Shafik Handal, a Salvadoran of Lebanese descent with strong ties to the PLO, embarked on a journey to Moscow and from there to Vietnam and other way stations in the Communist bloc. He returned with pledges of some 200 tons of arms to be shipped through Cuba with which the guerrilla forces could begin a "final offensive."

But as the "Vietnam equation" had shown, organizing the guerrilla forces was only a part, and perhaps the smallest part, of what was required. It was also necessary to assemble what Trotsky had once described as the "frontier guards" of the revolution. Since Castro was preparing to unify the Sandinista command, his American allies had to rush to set up the guerrillas' support system in the United States, using the "peace movement" as a base. Even before its founding had been officially announced, for example, the Communist-dominated U.S. Peace Council had joined forces with NACLA to stage a National Conference on Nicaragua in Washington. The purpose was to mobilize opposition against a potential U.S. "intervention" in Nicaragua. While claiming that they wanted to prevent "another Vietnam," the organizers' real purpose was precisely to achieve another Vietnam—by undermining any U.S. effort to counter the already massive Cuban investment aimed at turning Nicaragua into yet another Communist state.

The Nicaragua conference proved to be the first step in a long-term plan: the creation of an organizational shield behind which the cause of Communist revolution in the hemisphere could advance. The conference put a stamp of respectability on an organization called "The Network in Solidarity with the People of Nicaragua." Started on U.S. college campuses by two Nicaraguan nationals acting for the Sandinistas, the Nicaraguan Network soon became a national organization with chapters in hundreds of American cities and on campuses across the country. Its efforts led to a "Pledge of Resistance" signed by 70,000 Americans who declared themselves ready to undertake illegal actions to defend the Communist regime.

Acknowledging the importance of this activity, Sandinista Minister Tomás Borge declared: "The battle for Nicaragua is not being waged in Nicaragua. It is being fought in the United States." But the Nicaragua Network was only one of an array of "issue-oriented" organizations from which—in true popular-front style—the friends of violent revolutions could speak to other Americans in the language of pacifism and humanitarianism. While the Nicaragua Network lobbied against aid to the anti-Communist *contras* to prevent "another Vietnam," its movement comrades, working in allied organizations, were able to mobilize even greater support as champions of "human rights."

One of the most potent of these "human-rights" groups was the Washington Office on Latin America (WOLA), created by Christian "liberationists" after the 1973 coup against Salvador Allende in Chile. WOLA's director, Joe Eldridge, had been active in Chile as an Allende partisan, and WOLA's first concerns about human-rights abuses were aimed squarely at the Pinochet regime. But in 1977, when Castro and his protégés began launching their new strategy in Nicaragua, WOLA also shifted its attention to Nicaragua, sponsoring public-relations tours to the U.S. by the Sandinista priests Ernesto Cardenal and Miguel D'Escoto, who rallied many Catholics here, including members of the Maryknoll order, to the cause of the "hemispheric revolution" and also to the attempt to convert Christ to Marxism. Led by its Nicaragua coordinator Kay Stubbs, WOLA also stepped up its campaign against human-rights abuses of the Somoza regime and lobbied the Carter administration to withdraw its support. After the Sandinista victory, Stubbs, who all the time had been a secret member of a Sandinista cell in Washington, D.C., left WOLA to join the new Marxist regime and the organization's interest in human-rights abuses in Nicaragua all but disappeared. WOLA now began to focus on El Salvador, where its investigations into human rights were directed by a woman named Heather Foote, an American Marxist with strong political ties to the FPL faction of the guerrilla forces.

Although it had shifted its critical gaze elsewhere, WOLA's solidarity with the Sandinistas remained as strong as ever. When *contra* aid lost in the Congress in 1984, a major factor was the report entitled "Human Rights Violations by the Contras" circulated under the auspices of WOLA to Congress and the press. However, WOLA had used its reputation as an independent "human-rights" organization to provide cover for a Sandinista stratagem. The investigation had been initiated—and the investigator Reed Brody selected— by the law firm of Reichler and Applebaum, registered representative of the Managua regime. Brody's housing and transportation were supplied by the Sandinistas while he was in Nicaragua, and "witnesses" to *contra* atrocities were supplied by the security police. Before he departed with his report, Brody was provided with a photo opportunity which resulted in a snapshot showing him hugging Daniel Ortega.

The deception practiced by organizations like WOLA in behalf of the Sandinistas is also practiced *against* the Duarte government in El Salvador. In the spring of 1980, while the Salvadoran guerrilla leader Shafik Handal was traveling to Soviet-bloc countries in search of the weapons with which to begin his final offensive, his brother Farid arrived in New York to organize political support for the FMLN war. As Farid later described it, his mission was "the creation of the International Committee in Solidarity with the People of El Salvador." CISPES, as the American branch of this international committee would be called, was to be modeled on the Nicaragua Network and would have direct links with the guerrilla forces and with parallel "solidarity committees" which the World Peace Council had created in sixteen countries around the world.

After touching base at Cuba's UN Mission, Farid Handal went to Washington to meet supporters at the Institute for Policy Studies and WOLA. As he recorded in his journal (which was later found by authorities in Salvador in a captured guerrilla safe house), members of the Communist party in Washington, D.C. introduced him to Congressman Ron Dellums of California, who in turn arranged for him to meet with the congressional Black Caucus. Dellums provided other services. "Monday morning," Handal wrote in his journal, "the offices of Congressman Dellums were turned into our offices. Everything was done there. The meeting with the Black Caucus took place in the liver of the monster itself, nothing less than in the meeting room of the House Foreign Affairs Committee." Understanding that the opportunities laid before him would vanish if he spoke in the language of his brother Shafik, Farid noted that the guerrillas' cause "should be presented with its human features, without political language, and, most importantly, without a political label."

After Farid Handal had left the United States, CISPES was formally created by his American supporters. One of the organization's first acts was to disseminate a "dissent paper" allegedly drafted by disaffected experts at the State Department and National Security Council who believed that further military aid to El Salvador would eventually force the U.S. to intervene there militarily and who had a "consensus" in favor of the Democratic Revolutionary Front, the political arm of the FMLN guerrillas. Although the State Department denied its authenticity, the report was accepted as legitimate by several journalists, among them Anthony Lewis who wrote about it in the *New York Times*. Even after it had been established that the "dissent paper" was a forgery (there is evidence that it was one of many Soviet "active measures" planned by the KGB to create disinformation in the U.S.), CISPES continued to distribute it.

During the early 1980s, CISPES held press

conferences and marched Salvadoran refugees allegedly fleeing "U.S.-sponsored terror" through Washington. The organization has also been effective in Congress. In the spring of 1985, its lobbying efforts enabled its congressional supporters on the House Subcommittee on Western Hemisphere Affairs to schedule hearings on the "air war" in El Salvador. The object of the hearings was to determine whether the strikes against the guerrillas hit civilian populations in violation of congressional certification conditions, which would be a cause to cut off U.S. aid. Eyewitness testimony was presented for this claim. One witness was Gus Newport, mayor of Berkeley and also vice chairman of the Soviets' World Peace Council. Newport's observations of the Salvadoran air war were supported by a written report submitted by Carlottia Scott, chief aide to Congressman Ron Dellums (who had shaped Newport's mayoral career). Both Newport and Scott got their insights during a visit they had made to Berkeley's "sister city" which was located inside the guerrilla zone.

Despite its tainted origins and its deceptive politics, CISPES has been able to mobilize support on hundreds of campuses across the country. Congressmen Dellums and Mervyn Dymally of California have written fundraising letters for the organization, while Congressmen Edward Markey and Gerry Studds of Massachusetts and others have provided endorsements and moral support. With this kind of backing CISPES has become the most influential lobby against U.S. aid to the Duarte government—not only military aid, but food, medicine, and agricultural assistance. When it is not lobbying against aid to the Duarte government, CISPES is raising money to send to the FMLN guerrillas. The strategy of CISPES, in the words of one of its internal documents, is "to challenge U.S. policy; to disrupt the war effort, to polarize opinion, to inspire people to refuse to cooperate; to create divisions within Congress and every other institution . . . Each escalation of the war must bring a response more costly than the one before, precisely the Vietnam war phenomenon the administration is trying to avoid." One of the slogans at a recent CISPES rally expressed the intention more succinctly: "Vietnam Has Won, El Salvador Will Win."

We find it hard not to be ashamed of some of the things in which we were involved in the 1960s. Yet New Left radicals had a certain candor, reveling in their outlaw status and not trying to seem something politically they were not. That is not true today. W.H. Auden once called the radical '30s a "low dishonest decade," and the '80s are turning into another "low dishonest decade" on the Left. While the '60s Left took its case to the streets, where its commitments could at least be examined, the members of today's Left, exploiting the political process and the vulnerabilities of the two-party system, posture as respectable liberals who only want to make sure that there are no more Vietnams. "Liberal," in fact, is the way the establishment media invariably describe the activities of organizations like CISPES and WOLA, and the coterie of Congressmen who consistently support Communist advances in the Third World.

Ron Dellums, whom we ourselves helped elect in 1970, is perhaps the most characteristic of these Congressmen. When his bill prescribing sanctions against South Africa was recently adopted by the House, for instance, a profile in the *Washington Post* portrayed him as "the outspoken liberal he has always been," noted that a colleague had called him a "moral force for reordering priorities," and quoted Dellums himself as asking, "If you carry controversial ideas in a controversial personality, how can you ever get anything done?"

His persona has changed somewhat from the days when he stood beside Black Panther party leaders Huey Newton and Eldridge Cleaver and harangued audiences with revolutionary rhetoric. When he was attacked in the early '70s as a radical, Dellums did not shrink from the charge: "I am not going to back away from being a radical," he said. "My politics are to bring the walls down." But in the '80s Dellums has changed the words if not the tune. He now speaks in the name of "peace" and "democratic values," which in practice always seem to dictate attacking the United States and apologizing for the U.S.S.R. and other enemies of this country. Thus he travels abroad as an ornament for functions of the World Peace Council. Thus, too, when Carter sought to raise the defense budget after the Soviet invasion of Afghanistan, Dellums was alarmed by the specter of a resurgent American "militarism" in response to an action taken by the Soviets "to protect their borders." In a speech about this issue he said: "This is the capitalist, monopoly capital structure at work, preparing now to draft eighteen-year-olds to go and fight to protect their oil while every one of them are taking in billions of dollars in profits . . ."

In his role as a member of the House Armed Services Committee, Dellums is a passionate opponent of the use of American force. But he has different criteria for Communist dictatorships. When he traveled among the Marxist-Leninists of Grenada a few years ago, he did so as an open admirer of their revolution. His congressional office offered the Grenadan revolutionaries advice and encouragement. Writing strongman Maurice Bishop, for instance, Dellums's administrative assistant Carlottia Scott described the Congressman's attitude as follows:

> Ron has become truly committed to Grenada, and has some positive political thinking to share with you . . . He just has to get all his thoughts in order as to how your interests can be best served . . . He's really hooked on you and Grenada and doesn't want anything to happen to building the Revo[lution] and making it strong. He really admires you as a person and even more so as a leader with courage and foresight, principles and integrity. Believe me, he doesn't make that kind of statement often about anyone. The only other person that I know of that he expresses such admiration for is Fidel.

When the Reagan administration became concerned by the presence of large numbers of "advisers" from the Soviet bloc on the island and by what seemed the military dimensions of the new airport the Cubans were constructing there, Dellums went off to Grenada to make his own observation. Upon his return he defended Grenada before the House Subcommittee on Inter-American Affairs:

> President Reagan characterized [Grenada] as a totalitarian Left government and . . . stated that Grenada "now bears the Soviet and Cuban trademark which means it will attempt to spread the virus among its neighbors." Based on my personal observations, discussion, and analysis of the new international airport under construction in Grenada, it is my conclusion that this project is specifically now and has always been for the purpose of economic development and is not for military use . . . [I]t is my thought that it is absurd, patronizing, and totally unwarranted for the United States government to charge that this airport poses a military threat to the United States' national security.

When American troops landed in Grenada the year after Dellums made this statement, they discovered a cache of official documents from the Marxist regime. Among them were the minutes of a Grenadan Politburo meeting which took place after Dellums had made his "fact-finding" trip, but before he had submitted his report to Congress. The minutes of this meeting state:

> Barbara Lee [a Dellums aide] is here presently and has brought with her a report on the international airport that was done by Ron Dellums. They have requested that we look at the document and suggest any changes we deem necessary. They will be willing to make the changes.

At the same time Dellums was giving his report to the Marxist junta to edit before he presented it to Congress, an official of the Grenadan revolutionary government was disproving the Congressman's central thesis. Another document retrieved after the liberation of Grenada was the notebook of Defense Minister Liam James. In an entry dated March 22, 1980, James had written: "The

Revo[lution] has been able to crush counter-revolution internationally. Airport will be used for Cuban and Soviet military."

In the 1960s the New Left colluded with totalitarian movements. But it was clear and candid, sometimes painfully so, about what it was doing. The post-Vietnam Left which has succeeded it not only colludes with totalitarianism but tries to delude people about its aims. It is always ready to believe the official Soviet lie, give the Soviets the benefit of the doubt, or, where the abuses are too great, at least to "understand" horrific Soviet acts as a legitimate reflexive fear of American power. On the other hand, it has an inexhaustible cynicism about American motives and a perpetual inability to locate America's virtues. It is an "us/them" mentality in which "us" are the dictators in Cuba, Nicaragua, and elsewhere in the Third World, while "them" is the United States. Thus, for example, to the *Nation*, a magazine which exemplifies this mentality, the hundredth birthday of the Statue of Liberty was, "Imperial Weekend"; but the seventh anniversary of Daniel Ortega's Marxist coup a few months later was a moment to celebrate hemispheric "hope" and an occasion to engage in yet another solo performance of the Sandinista anthem, "The Yankee is the Enemy of Mankind."

The post-Vietnam Left is effective because of its deceitful layering of the apparatus through which it works and also because it has found a way to support totalitarian movements while appearing to be interested only in improving America's international morality. Its techniques of dissimulation and disinformation have worked. The Sandinistas' lies about their intentions may be obvious enough when studied in retrospect, but their support network in the United States has been remarkably effective in promoting these lies in the nation's political forums. The aims of the revolution that has seized control in Managua are not Nicaraguan in origin; the power that guides it lies in Havana and Moscow. The revolutionary ambition in Central America is not nationalist but imperialist in nature, with the goal of overthrowing the hemispheric system and substituting for it a gulag of interlocked Communist regimes. It is a goal shared by those who work in, and furthered whether wittingly or unwittingly by those who support, organizations like WOLA or CISPES. These people may use the language of American democracy, but for them, democratic politics is only a means; Vietnam has taught them that the neutralization of American power and the victory of Communist revolution comprise a single symbiotic act.

These "secret agents" of the revolutionary cause (to use Conrad's term) fend off inquiries about their political attitudes by accusing their questioners of "red-baiting," which suggests once again that the embalmed corpse of Joe McCarthy lies in state in the Left's consciousness just as Lenin's does in Red Square. But tolerance for unpopular ideas does not require ignoring political commitments that undermine our republic and strengthen its enemies. The time has come in the life of this nation to name these attitudes for what they are and to eliminate the taboos that prevent discussion of the dangers they pose.

THE LAST ARTICLE
Harry Turtledove

EDITOR'S INTRODUCTION

The late Fletcher Pratt, discussing the way in which he selected events for inclusion in his magnificent *The Battles That Changed History*, said "The first criterion was that the war in which the battle took place must itself have decided something, must really mark one of those turning points after which things would have been a good deal different if the decision had gone in the other direction . . . the special genius of Western European culture when it takes up arms is that for really changing the course of history in battle, not merely arresting a movement, but completely altering its direction. The battles described did this, regardless of whatever subjective regrets one may have in the individual case."

What Pratt asserts is that war matters; that those who say, "Violence never settles anything," simply don't know what they are talking about. He might be wrong, of course. Certainly many today believe he is, as so many did during that strange period between the World Wars, when the Oxford Union, after debate, solemnly carried the motion that "this House will not fight for King and Country."

They did so in reaction to "militarism," at a time when the National Socialists had introduced universal military service in Germany, and the Hitler Youth encompassed most German schoolchildren. (In the Soviet Union today, according to the Soviet press, the mandatory exercise known as "Summer Lightning/Little Eagle" annually instructs some 30 million children from age seven upwards through military drills designed to teach them how to fight and win wars—even nuclear wars.)

The Oxford Union acted at a time when the German war budget was soaring. (Soviet émigrés estimate that the Soviet Union spends more than 20 percent of its GNP on the military; Andrei Sakharov puts that at 40 percent.)

The Oxford Union said that violence never settles anything; that wars are fought for nothing; that to answer the call to arms is to throw one's life away for nothing.

Herewith historian Harry Turtledove and a future in which the Union's philosophy carried the day.

Nonviolence is the first article of my faith. It is also the last article of my creed.

Mohandas Gandhi

The one means that wins the easiest victory over reason: terror and force.

Adolf Hitler, *Mein Kampf*

THE TANK RUMBLED DOWN THE RAJPATH, PAST THE RUINS OF the Memorial Arch, toward the India Gate. The gateway arch was still standing, although it had taken a couple of shell hits in the fighting before New Delhi fell. The Union Jack fluttered above it.

British troops lined both sides of the Rajpath. They watched silently as the tank rolled past them. Their khaki uniforms were filthy and torn; many wore bandages. They had the weary, past-caring stares of beaten men, though the army of India had fought until flesh and munitions gave out.

The India Gate drew near. A military band, smartened up for the occasion, began to play as the tank went past. The bagpipes sounded thin and lost in the hot, humid air.

A single man stood waiting in the shadow of the gate.

123

Field Marshal Walther Model leaned down into the cupola of the Panzer IV. "No one can match the British at ceremonies of this sort," he said to his aide.

Major Dieter Lasch laughed, a bit unkindly. "They've had enough practice, sir," he answered, raising his voice to be heard over the flatulent roar of the tank's engine.

"What is that tune?" the field marshal asked. "Does it have a meaning?"

"It's called 'The World Turned Upside Down,'" said Lasch, who had been involved with his British opposite number in planning the formal surrender. "Lord Cornwallis's army musicians played it when he yielded to the Americans at Yorktown."

"Ah, the Americans." Model was for a moment so lost in his own thoughts that his monocle threatened to slip from his right eye. He screwed it back in. The single lens was the only thing he shared with the clichéd image of a high German officer. He was no lean, hawk-faced Prussian. But his rounded features were unyielding, and his stocky body sustained the energy of his will better than the thin, dyspeptic frames of so many aristocrats. "The Americans," he repeated. "Well, that will be the next step, won't it? But enough. One thing at a time."

The panzer stopped. The driver switched off the engine. The sudden quiet was startling. Model leaped nimbly down. He had been leaping down from tanks for eight years now, since his days as a staff officer for the IV Corps in the Polish campaign.

The man in the shadows stepped forward, saluted. Flashbulbs lit his long, tired face as German photographers recorded the moment for history. The Englishman ignored cameras and cameramen alike. "Field Marshal Model," he said politely. He might have been about to discuss the weather.

Model admired his sangfroid. "Field Marshal Auchinleck," he replied, returning the salute and giving Auchinleck a last few seconds to remain his equal. Then he came back to the matter at hand. "Field Marshal, have you signed the instrument of surrender of the British Army of India to the forces of the Reich?"

"I have," Auchinleck replied. He reached into the left blouse pocket of his battle dress, removed a folded sheet of paper. Before handing it to Model, though, he said, "I should like to request your permission to make a brief statement at this time."

"Of course, sir. You may say what you like, at whatever length you like." In victory, Model could afford to be magnanimous. He had even granted Marshal Zhukov leave to speak in the Soviet capitulation at Kuibishev, before the marshal was taken out and shot.

"I thank you." Auchinleck stiffly dipped his head. "I will say, then, that I find the terms I have been forced to accept to be cruelly hard on the brave men who have served under my command."

"That is your privilege, sir." But Model's round face was no longer kindly, and his voice had iron in it as he replied, "I must remind you, however, that my treating with you at all under the rules of war is an act of mercy for which Berlin may yet reprimand me. When Britain surrendered in 1941, all Imperial forces were also ordered to lay down their arms. I daresay you did not expect us to come so far, but I would be within my rights in reckoning you no more than so many bandits."

A slow flush darkened Auchinleck's cheeks. "We gave you a bloody good run, for bandits."

"So you did." Model remained polite. He did not say he would ten times rather fight straight-up battles than deal with the partisans who to this day harassed the Germans and their allies in occupied Russia. "Have you anything further to add?"

"No, sir, I do not." Auchinleck gave the German the signed surrender, handed him his sidearm. Model put the pistol in the empty holster he wore for the occasion. It did not fit well; the holster was made for a Walther P38, not this man-killing brute of a Webley and Scott. That mattered little, though—the ceremony was almost over.

Auchinleck and Model exchanged salutes for the last time. The British field marshal stepped away. A German lieutenant came up to lead him into captivity.

Major Lasch waved his left hand. The Union Jack came down from the flagpole on the India Gate. The swastika rose to replace it.

* * *

Lasch tapped discreetly on the door, stuck his head into the field marshal's office. "That Indian politician is here for his appointment with you, sir."

"Oh, yes. Very well, Dieter, send him in." Model had been dealing with Indian politicians even before the British surrender, and with hordes of them now that resistance was over. He had no more liking for the breed than for Russian politicians, or even German ones. No matter what pious principles they spouted, his experience was that they were all out for their own good first.

The small, frail brown man the aide showed in made him wonder. The Indian's emaciated frame and the plain white cotton loincloth that was his only garment contrasted starkly with the Victorian splendor of the Viceregal Palace from which Model was administering the Reich's new conquest. "Sit down, Herr Gandhi," the field marshall urged.

"I thank you very much, sir." As he took his seat, Gandhi seemed a child in an adult's chair: it was much too wide for him, and its soft, overstuffed cushions hardly sagged under his meager weight. But his eyes, Model saw, were not a child's eyes. They peered with disconcerting keenness through his wire-framed spectacles as he said, "I have come to enquire when we may expect German troops to depart from our country."

Model leaned forward, frowning. For a moment he thought he had misunderstood Gandhi's Gujarati-flavored English. When he was sure he had not, he said, "Do you think perhaps we have come all this way as tourists?"

"Indeed I do not." Gandhi's voice was sharp with disapproval. "Tourists do not leave so many dead behind them."

Model's temper kindled. "No, tourists do not pay such a high price for the journey. Having come regardless of that cost, I assure you we shall stay."

"I am very sorry, sir; I cannot permit it."

"*You* cannot?" Again, Model had to concentrate to keep his monocle from falling out. He had heard arrogance from politicians before, but this scrawny old devil surpassed belief. "Do you forget I can call my aide and have you shot behind this building? You would not be the first, I assure you."

"Yes, I know that," Gandhi said sadly. "If you have that fate in mind for me, I am an old man. I will not run."

Combat had taught Model a hard indifference to the prospect of injury or death. He saw the older man possessed something of the same sort, however he had acquired it. A moment later, he realized his threat had not only failed to frighten Gandhi, but had actually amused him. Disconcerted, the field marshal said, "Have you any serious issues to address?"

"Only the one I named just now. We are a nation of more than three hundred million; it is no more just for Germany to rule us than for the British."

Model shrugged. "If we are able to, we will. We have the strength to hold what we have conquered, I assure you."

"Where there is no right, there can be no strength," Gandhi said. "We will not permit you to hold us in bondage."

"Do you think to threaten me?" Model growled. In fact, though, the Indian's audacity interested him. Most of the locals had fallen over themselves, fawning on their new masters. Here, at least, was a man out of the ordinary.

Gandhi was still shaking his head, although Model saw he had still not frightened him (a man out of the ordinary indeed, thought the field marshal, who respected courage when he found it). "I make no threats, sir, but I will do what I believe to be right."

"Most noble," Model said, but to his annoyance the words came out sincere rather than with the sardonic edge he had intended. He had heard such canting phrases before, from Englishmen, from Russians—yes, and from Germans as well. Somehow, though, this Gandhi struck him as one who always meant exactly what he said. He rubbed his chin, considering how to handle such an intransigent.

A large green fly came buzzing into the office. Model's

air of detachment vanished the moment he heard that malignant whine. He sprang from his seat, swatted at the fly. He missed. The insect flew around a while longer, then settled on the arm of Gandhi's chair. "Kill it," Model told him. "Last week one of those accursed things bit me on the neck, and I still have the lump to prove it."

Gandhi brought his hand down, but several inches from the fly. Frightened, it took off. Gandhi rose. He was surprisingly nimble for a man nearing eighty. He chivied the fly out of the office, ignoring Model, who watched his performance in openmouthed wonder.

"I hope it will not trouble you again," Gandhi said, returning as calmly as if he had done nothing out of the ordinary. "I am one of those who practice *ahimsa*: I will do no injury to any living thing."

Model remembered the fall of Moscow, and the smell of burning bodies filling the chilly autumn air. He remembered machine guns knocking down Cossack cavalry before they could close, and the screams of the wounded horses, more heartrending than any woman's. He knew of other things too, things he had not seen for himself and of which he had no desire to learn more.

"Herr Gandhi," he said, "how do you propose to bend to your will someone who opposes you, if you will not use force for the purpose?"

"I have never said I will not use force, sir." Gandhi's smile invited the field marshal to enjoy with him the distinction he was making. "I will not use violence. If my people refuse to cooperate in any way with yours, how can you compel them? What choice will you have but to grant us leave to do as we will?"

Without the intelligence estimates he had read, Model would have dismissed the Indian as a madman. No madman, though, could have caused the British so much trouble. But perhaps the decadent Raj simply had not made him afraid. Model tried again: "You understand that what you have said is treason against the Reich?"

Gandhi bowed in his seat. "You may, of course, do what you will with me. My spirit will in any case survive among my people."

Model felt his face heat. Few men were immune to fear. Just his luck, he thought sourly, to have run into one of them. "I warn you, Herr Gandhi, to obey the authority of the officials of the Reich, or it will be the worse for you."

"I will do what I believe to be right, and nothing else. If you Germans exert yourselves toward the freeing of India, joyfully will I work with you. If not, then I regret we must be foes."

The field marshal gave him one last chance to see reason. "Were it you and I alone, there might be some doubt as to what would happen." Not much, he thought, not when Gandhi was twenty-odd years older and thin enough to break like a stick. He fought down the irrelevance, and went on, "But where, Herr Gandhi, is your *Wehrmacht*?"

Of all things, he had least expected to amuse the Indian again. Yet Gandhi's eyes unmistakably twinkled behind the lenses of his spectacles. "Field Marshal, I have an army, too."

Model's patience, never of the most enduring sort, wore thin all at once. "Get out!" he snapped.

Gandhi stood, bowed, and departed. Major Lasch stuck his head into the office. The field marshal's glare drove him out again in a hurry.

"Well?" Jawaharlal Nehru paced back and forth. Tall, slim, and saturnine, he towered over Gandhi without dominating him. "Dare we use the same policies against the Germans that we employed against the English?"

"If we wish our land free, dare we do otherwise?" Gandhi replied. "They will not grant our wish of their own volition. Model struck me as a man not much different from various British leaders whom we have succeeded in vexing in the past." He smiled at the memory of what passive resistance had done to officials charged with combating it.

"Very well, *Satyagraha* it is." But Nehru was not smiling. He had less humor than his older colleague.

Gandhi teased him gently: "Do you fear another spell in prison, then?" Both men had spent time behind bars during the war, until the British released them in a last, vain effort to rally the support of the Indian people to the Raj.

129

"You know better." Nehru refused to be drawn, and persisted. "The rumors that come out of Europe frighten me."

"Do you tell me you take them seriously?" Gandhi shook his head in surprise and a little reproof. "Each side in any war will always paint its opponents as blackly as it can."

"I hope you are right, and that that is all. Still, I confess I would feel more at ease with what we plan to do if you found me one Jew, officer or other rank, in the army now occupying us."

"You would be hard-pressed to find any among the forces they defeated. The British have little love for Jews either."

"Yes, but I daresay it could be done. With the Germans, they are banned by law. The English would never make such a rule. And while the laws are vile enough, I think of the tales that man Wiesenthal told, the one who came here the gods know how across Russia and Persia from Poland."

"Those I do not believe," Gandhi said firmly. "No nation could act in that way and hope to survive. Where could men be found to carry out such horrors?"

"*Azad Hind*," Nehru said, quoting the "Free India" motto of the locals who had fought on the German side.

But Gandhi shook his head. "They are only soldiers, doing as soldiers have always done. Wiesenthal's claims are for an entirely different order of bestiality, one which could not exist without destroying the fabric of the state that gave it birth."

"I hope very much you are right," Nehru said.

Walther Model slammed the door behind him hard enough to make his aide, whose desk faced away from the field marshal's office, jump in alarm. "Enough of this twaddle for one day," Model said. "I need schnapps, to get the taste of these Indians out of my mouth. Come along if you care to, Dieter."

"Thank you, sir." Major Lasch threw down his pen, eagerly got to his feet. "I sometimes think conquering India was easier than ruling it will be."

Model rolled his eyes. "I *know* it was. I would ten times rather be planning a new campaign than sitting here bogged down in pettifogging details. The sooner Berlin sends me people trained in colonial administration, the happier I will be."

The bar might have been taken from an English pub. It was dark, quiet, and paneled in walnut; a dart board still hung on the wall. But a German sergeant in field-gray stood behind the bar, and despite the lazily turning ceiling fan, the temperature was close to thirty-five Celsius. The one might have been possible in occupied London, the other not.

Model knocked back his first shot at a gulp. He sipped his second more slowly, savoring it. Warmth spread through him, warmth that had nothing to do with the heat of the evening. He leaned back in his chair, steepling his fingers. "A long day," he said.

"Yes, sir," Lasch agreed. "After the effrontery of that Gandhi, any day would seem a long one. I've rarely seen you so angry." Considering Model's temper, that was no small statement.

"Ah yes, Gandhi." Model's tone was reflective rather than irate; Lasch looked at him curiously. The field marshal said, "For my money, he's worth a dozen of the ordinary sort."

"Sir?" The aide no longer tried to hide his surprise.

"He is an honest man. He tells me what he thinks, and he will stick by that. I may kill him—I may have to kill him—but he and I will both know why, and I will not change his mind." Model took another sip of schnapps. He hesitated, as if unsure whether to go on. At last he did. "Do you know, Dieter, after he left I had a vision."

"Sir?" Now Lasch sounded alarmed.

The field marshal might have read his aide's thoughts. He chuckled wryly. "No, no, I am not about to swear off eating beefsteak and wear sandals instead of my boots, that I promise. But I saw myself as a Roman procurator, listening to the rantings of some early Christian priest."

Lasch raised an eyebrow. Such musings were unlike Model, who was usually direct to the point of bluntness and altogether materialistic—assets in the makeup of a

131

general officer. The major cautiously sounded these unexpected depths: "How do you suppose the Roman felt, facing that kind of man?"

"Bloody confused, I suspect," Model said, which sounded more like him. "And because he and his comrades did not know how to handle such fanatics, you and I are Christians today, Dieter."

"So we are." The major rubbed his chin. "Is that a bad thing?"

Model laughed and finished his drink. "From your point of view or mine, no. But I doubt that old Roman would agree with us, any more than Gandhi agrees with me over what will happen next here. But then, I have two advantages over the dead procurator." He raised his finger; the sergeant hurried over to fill his glass.

At Lasch's nod, the young man also poured more schnapps for him. The major drank, then said, "I should hope so. We are more civilized, more sophisticated than the Romans ever dreamed of being."

But Model was still in that fey mood. "Are we? My procurator was such a sophisticate that he tolerated anything, and never saw the danger in a foe who would not do the same. Our Christian God, though, is a jealous god who puts up with no rivals. And one who is a National Socialist serves also the *Volk*, to whom he owes sole loyalty. I am immune to Gandhi's virus in a way the Roman was not to the Christian's."

"Yes, that makes sense," Lasch agreed after a moment. "I had not thought of it in that way, but I see it is so. And what is our other advantage over the Roman procurator?"

Suddenly the field marshal looked hard and cold, much the way he had looked leading the tanks of Third Panzer against the Kremlin compound. "The machine gun," he said.

The rising sun's rays made the sandstone of the Red Fort seem even more the color of blood. Gandhi frowned and turned his back on the fortress, not caring for that thought. Even at dawn, the air was warm and muggy.

"I wish you were not here," Nehru told him. The younger man lifted his trademark fore-and-aft cap, scratched his graying hair, and glanced at the crowd growing around them. "The Germans' orders forbid assemblies, and they will hold you responsible for this gathering."

"I am, am I not?" Gandhi replied. "Would you have me send my followers into a danger I do not care to face myself? How would I presume to lead them afterwards?"

"A general does not fight in the front ranks," Nehru came back. "If you are lost to our cause, will we be able to go on?"

"If not, then surely the cause is not worthy, yes? Now let us be going."

Nehru threw his hands in the air. Gandhi nodded, satisfied, and worked his way toward the head of the crowd. Men and women stepped aside to let him through. Still shaking his head, Nehru followed.

The crowd slowly began to march east up Chandni Chauk, the Street of Silversmiths. Some of the fancy shops had been wrecked in the fighting, more looted afterwards. But others were opening up, their owners as happy to take German money as they had been to serve the British before.

One of the proprietors, a man who had managed to stay plump even through the past year of hardship, came rushing out of his shop when he saw the procession go by. He ran to the head of the march and spotted Nehru, whose height and elegant dress singled him out.

"Are you out of your mind?" the silversmith shouted. "The Germans have banned assemblies. If they see you, something dreadful will happen."

"Is it not dreadful that they take away the liberty that properly belongs to us?" Gandhi asked. The silversmith spun round. His eyes grew wide when he recognized the man who was speaking to him. Gandhi went on, "Not only is it dreadful, it is wrong. And so we do not recognize the Germans' right to ban anything we may choose to do. Join us, will you?"

"Great-souled one, I—I—" the silversmith spluttered. Then his glance slid past Gandhi. "The Germans!" he squeaked. He turned and ran.

Gandhi led the procession toward the approaching squad. The Germans stamped down Chandni Chauk as if they expected the people in front of them to melt from their path. Their gear, Gandhi thought, was not that much different from what British soldiers wore: ankle boots, shorts, and open-necked tunics. But their coal-scuttle helmets gave them a look of sullen, beetle-browed ferocity the British tin hat did not convey. Even for a man of Gandhi's equanimity it was daunting, as no doubt it was intended to be.

"Hello, my friends," he said. "Do any of you speak English?"

"I speak it, a little," one of them replied. His shoulder straps had the twin pips of a sergeant-major: he was the squad leader, then. He hefted his rifle, not menacingly, Gandhi thought, but to emphasize what he was saying. "Go to your homes back. This coming together is *verboten.*"

"I am sorry, but I must refuse to obey your order," Gandhi said. "We are walking peacefully on our own street in our own city. We will harm no one, no matter what; this I promise you. But walk we will, as we wish." He repeated himself until he was sure the sergeant-major understood.

The German spoke to his comrades in his own language. One of the soldiers raised his gun and with a nasty smile pointed it at Gandhi, who nodded politely. The German blinked to see him unafraid. The sergeant-major slapped the rifle down. One of his men had a field telephone on his back. The sergeant-major cranked it, waited for a reply, spoke urgently into it.

Nehru caught Gandhi's eye. His dark, tired gaze was full of worry. Somehow that nettled Gandhi more than the Germans' arrogance in ordering about his people. He began to walk forward again. The marchers followed him, flowing around the German squad like water flowing round a boulder.

The soldier who had pointed his rifle at Gandhi shouted in alarm. He brought up the weapon again. The sergeant-major barked at him. Reluctantly, he lowered it.

"A sensible man," Gandhi said to Nehru. "He sees we do no injury to him or his, and so does none to us."

"Sadly, though, not everyone is so sensible," the younger man replied, "as witness his lance-corporal

134

there. And even a sensible man may not be well inclined to us. You notice he is still on the telephone."

The phone on Field Marshal Model's desk jangled. He jumped and swore; he had left orders he was to be disturbed only for an emergency. He had to find time to work. He picked up the phone. "This had better be good," he growled without preamble.

He listened, swore again, slammed the receiver down. "Lasch!" he shouted.

It was his aide's turn to jump. "Sir?"

"Don't just sit there on your fat arse," the field marshal said unfairly. "Call out my car and driver, and quickly. Then belt on your sidearm and come along. The Indians are doing something stupid. Oh, yes. Order out a platoon and have them come after us. Up on Chandni Chauk, the trouble is."

Lasch called for the car and the troops, then hurried after Model. "A riot?" he asked as he caught up.

"No, no." Model moved his stumpy frame along so fast that the taller Lasch had to trot beside him. "Some of Gandhi's tricks, damn him."

The field marshal's Mercedes was waiting when he and his aide hurried out of the viceregal palace. "Chandni Chauk," Model snapped as the driver held the door open for him. After that he sat in furious silence as the powerful car roared up Irwin Road, round a third of Connaught Circle, and north on Chelmsford Road past the bombed-out railway station until, for no reason Model could see, the street's name changed to Qutb Road.

A little later, the driver said, "Some kind of disturbance up ahead, sir."

"Disturbance?" Lasch echoed, leaning forward to peer through the windshield. "It's a whole damned regiment's worth of Indians coming at us. Don't they know better than that? And what the devil," he added, his voice rising, "are so many of our men doing ambling along beside them? Don't they know they're supposed to break up this sort of thing?" In his indignation, he did not notice he was repeating himself.

"I suspect they don't," Model said dryly. "Gandhi, I

135

gather, can have that effect on people who aren't ready for his peculiar brand of stubbornness. That, however, does not include me." He tapped the driver on the shoulder. "Pull up about two hundred meters in front of the first rank of them, Joachim."

"Yes, sir."

Even before the car had stopped moving, Model jumped out of it. Lasch, hand on his pistol, was close behind, protesting, "What if one of those fanatics has a gun?"

"Then Colonel-General Weidling assumes command, and a lot of Indians end up dead." Model strode toward Gandhi, ignoring the German troops who were drawing themselves to stiff, horrified attention at the sight of his field marshal's uniform. He would deal with them later. For the moment, Gandhi was more important.

He had stopped—which meant the rest of the marchers did, too—and was waiting politely for Model to approach. The German commandant was not impressed. He thought Gandhi sincere, and could not doubt his courage, but none of that mattered at all. He said harshly, "You were warned against this sort of behavior."

Gandhi looked him in the eye. They were very much of a height. "And I told you, I do not recognize your right to give such orders. This is our country, not yours, and if some of us choose to walk on our streets, we will do so."

From behind Gandhi, Nehru's glance flicked worriedly from one of the antagonists to the other. Model noticed him only peripherally; if he was already afraid, he could be handled whenever necessary. Gandhi was a tougher nut. The field marshal waved at the crowd behind the old man. "You are responsible for all these people. If harm comes to them, you will be to blame."

"Why should harm come to them? They are not soldiers. They do not attack your men. I told that to one of your sergeants, and he understood it, and refrained from hindering us. Surely you, sir, an educated, cultured man, can see that what I say is self-evident truth."

Model turned his head to speak to his aide in German: "If we did not have Goebbels, this would be the one for his job." He shuddered to think of the propaganda victory Gandhi would win if he got away with flouting

German ordinances. The whole countryside would be boiling with partisans in a week. And he had already managed to hoodwink some Germans into letting him do it!

Then Gandhi surprised him again. "*Ich danke Ihnen, Herr Generalfeldmarschall, aber das glaube ich kein Kompliment zu sein,*" he said in slow but clear German: "I thank you, field marshal, but I believe that to be no compliment."

Having to hold his monocle in place helped Model keep his face straight. "Take it however you like," he said. "Get these people off the street, or they and you will face the consequences. We will do what you force us to."

"I force you to nothing. As for these people who follow, each does so of his or her own free will. We are free, and will show it, not by violence, but through firmness in truth."

Now Model listened with only half an ear. He had kept Gandhi talking long enough for the platoon he had ordered out to arrive. Half a dozen SdKfz 251 armored personnel carriers came clanking up. The men piled out of them. "Give me a firing line, three ranks deep," Model shouted. As the troopers scrambled to obey, he waved the half-tracks into position behind them, all but blocking Qutb Road. The half-tracks' commanders swiveled the machine guns at the front of the vehicles' troop compartments so they bore on the Indians.

Gandhi watched these preparations as calmly as if they had nothing to do with him. Again Model had to admire his calm. His followers were less able to keep fear from their faces. Very few, though, used the pause to slip away. Gandhi's discipline was a long way from the military sort, but effective all the same.

"Tell them to disperse now, and we can still get away without bloodshed," the field marshal said.

"We will shed no one's blood, sir. But we will continue on our pleasant journey. Moving carefully, we will, I think, be able to get between your large lorries there." Gandhi turned to wave his people forward once more.

"You insolent—" Rage choked Model, which was as well, for it kept him from cursing Gandhi like a fishwife. To give him time to master his temper, he plucked his

137

monocle from his eye and began polishing the lens with a silk handkerchief. He replaced the monocle, started to jam the handkerchief back into his trouser pocket, then suddenly had a better idea.

"Come, Lasch," he said, and started toward the waiting German troops. About halfway to them, he dropped the handkerchief on the ground. He spoke in loud, simple German so his men and Gandhi could both follow: "If any Indians come past this spot, I wash my hands of them."

He might have known Gandhi would have a comeback ready. "That is what Pilate said also, you will recall, sir."

"Pilate washed his hands to evade responsibility," the field marshal answered steadily; he was in control of himself again. "I accept it: I am responsible to my Führer and to the *Oberkommando-Wehrmacht* for maintaining Reichs control over India, and will do what I see fit to carry out that obligation."

For the first time since they had come to know each other, Gandhi looked sad. "I too, sir, have my responsibilities." He bowed slightly to Model.

Lasch chose that moment to whisper in his commander's ear: "Sir, what of our men over there? Had you planned to leave them in the line of fire?"

The field marshal frowned. He had planned to do just that; the wretches deserved no better, for being taken in by Gandhi. But Lasch had a point. The platoon might balk at shooting countrymen, if it came to that. "You men," Model said sourly, jabbing his marshal's baton at them, "fall in behind the armored personnel carriers, at once."

The Germans' boots pounded on the macadam as they dashed to obey. They were still all right, then, with a clear order in front of them. Something, Model thought, but not much.

He had also worried that the Indians would take advantage of the moment of confusion to press forward, but they did not. Gandhi and Nehru and a couple of other men were arguing among themselves. Model nodded once. Some of them knew he was in earnest, then. And Gandhi's followers' discipline, as the field marshal had thought a few minutes ago, was not of the military sort. He could not simply issue an order and know his will would be done.

"I issue no orders," Gandhi said. "Let each man follow his conscience as he will—what else is freedom?"

"They will follow *you* if you go forward, great-souled one," Nehru replied, "and that German, I fear, means to carry out his threat. Will you throw your life away, and those of your countrymen?"

"I will not throw my life away," Gandhi said, but before the men around him could relax he went on, "I will gladly give it, if freedom requires that. I am but one man. If I fall, others will surely carry on; perhaps the memory of me will serve to make them more steadfast."

He stepped forward.

"Oh, damnation," Nehru said softly, and followed.

For all his vigor, Gandhi was far from young. Nehru did not need to nod to the marchers close by him; of their own accord, they hurried ahead of the man who had led them for so long, forming with their bodies a barrier between him and the German guns.

He tried to go faster. "Stop! Leave me my place! What are you doing?" he cried, though in his heart he understood only too well.

"This once, they will not listen to you," Nehru said.

"But they must!" Gandhi peered through eyes dimmed now by tears as well as age. "Where is that stupid handkerchief? We must be almost to it!"

"For the last time, I warn you to halt!" Model shouted. The Indians still came on. The sound of their feet, sandal-clad or bare, was like a growing murmur on the pavement, very different from the clatter of German boots. "Fools!" the field marshal muttered under his breath. He turned to his men. "Take your aim!"

The advance slowed when the rifles came up; of that Model was certain. For a moment he thought that ultimate threat would be enough to bring the marchers to their senses. But then they advanced again. The Polish cavalry had shown that same reckless bravery, charging with lances and sabers and carbines against the German tanks. Model wondered whether the inhabitants of the

Reichsgeneralgouvernement of Poland thought the gallantry worthwhile.

A man stepped on the field marshals' handkerchief. "Fire!" Model said.

A second passed, two. Nothing happened. Model scowled at his men. Gandhi's deviltry had got into them; sneaky as a Jew, he was turning the appearance of weakness into a strange kind of strength. But then trained discipline paid its dividend. One finger tightened on a Mauser trigger. A single shot rang out. As if it were a signal that recalled the other men to their duty, they too began to fire. From the armored personnel carriers, the machine guns started their deadly chatter. Model heard screams above the gunfire.

The volley smashed into the front ranks of marchers at close range. Men fell. Others ran, or tried to, only to be held by the power of the stream still advancing behind them. Once begun, the Germans methodically poured fire into the column of Indians. The march dissolved into a panic-stricken mob.

Gandhi still tried to press forward. A fleeing wounded man smashed into him, splashing him with blood and knocking him to the ground. Nehru and another man immediately lay down on top of him.

"Let me up! Let me up!" he shouted.

"No," Nehru screamed in his ear. "With shooting like this, you are in the safest spot you can be. We need you, and need you alive. Now we have martyrs around whom to rally our cause."

"Now we have dead husbands and wives, fathers and mothers. Who will tend to their loved ones?"

Gandhi had no time for more protest. Nehru and the other man hauled him to his feet and dragged him away. Soon they were among their people, all running now from the German guns. A bullet struck the back of the unknown man who was helping Gandhi escape. Gandhi heard the slap of the impact, felt the man jerk. Then the strong grip on him loosened as the man fell.

He tried to tear free from Nehru. Before he could, another Indian laid hold of him. Even at that horrid moment, he felt the irony of his predicament. All his life

140

he had championed individual liberty, and here his own followers were robbing him of his. In other circumstances, it might have been funny.

"In here!" Nehru shouted. Several people had already broken down the door to a shop and, Gandhi saw a moment later, the rear exit as well. Then he was hustled into the alley behind the shop, and through a maze of lanes that reminded him the old Delhi, unlike its British-designed sister city, was an Indian town through and through.

At last the nameless man with Gandhi and Nehru knocked on the back door of a tearoom. The woman who opened it gasped to recognize her unexpected guests, then pressed her hands together in front of her and stepped aside to let them in. "You will be safe here," the man said, "at least for a while. Now I must see to my own family."

"From the bottom of our hearts, we thank you," Nehru replied as the fellow hurried away. Gandhi said nothing. He was winded, battered, and filled with anguish at the failure of the march and at the suffering it had brought to so many marchers and to their kinsfolk.

The woman sat the two fugitive leaders at a small table in the kitchen, served them tea and cakes. "I will leave you now, best ones," she said quietly, "lest those out front wonder why I neglect them for so long."

Gandhi left the cake on his plate. He sipped the tea. Its warmth began to restore him physically, but the wound in his spirit would never heal. "The Amritsar massacre pales beside this," he said, setting down the empty cup. "There the British panicked and opened fire. This had nothing of panic about it. Model told me what he would do, and he did it." He shook his head, still hardly believing what he had just been through.

"So he did." Nehru had gobbled his cake like a starving wolf, and ate his companion's when he saw Gandhi did not want it. His once-immaculate white jacket and pants were torn, filthy, and blood-spattered; his cap sat awry on his head. But his eyes, usually so somber, were lit with a fierce glow. "And by his brutality, he has delivered himself into our hands. No one now can imagine the Germans have anything but their own interests at heart. We will gain followers all over the country. After this, not a wheel will turn in India."

"Yes, I will declare the *Satyagraha* campaign," Gandhi said. "Noncooperation will show how we reject foreign rule, and will cost the Germans dear because they will not be able to exploit us. The combination of nonviolence and determined spirit will surely shame them into granting us our liberty."

"There—you see." Encouraged by his mentor's rally, Nehru rose and came round the table to embrace the older man. "We will triumph yet."

"So we will," Gandhi said, and sighed heavily. He had pursued India's freedom for half his long life, and this change of masters was a setback he had not truly planned for, even after England and Russia fell. The British were finally beginning to listen to him when the Germans swept them aside. Now he had to begin anew. He sighed again. "It will cost our poor people dear, though."

"Cease firing," Model said. Few good targets were left on Qutb Road; almost all the Indians in the procession were down or had run from the guns.

Even after the bullets stopped, the street was far from silent. Most of the people the German platoon had shot were alive and shrieking; as if he needed more proof, the Russian campaign had taught the field marshal how hard human beings were to kill outright.

Still, the din distressed him, and evidently Lasch as well. "We ought to put them out of their misery," the major said.

"So we should." Model had a happy inspiration. "And I know just how. Come with me."

The two men turned their backs on the carnage and walked around the row of armored personnel carriers. As they passed the lieutenant commanding the platoon, Model nodded to him and said, "Well done."

The lieutenant saluted. "Thank you, sir." The soldiers in earshot nodded at one another: nothing bucked up the odds of getting promoted like performing under the commander's eye.

The Germans behind the armored vehicles were not so proud of themselves. They were the ones who had let the

142

march get this big and come this far in the first place. Model slapped his boot with his field marshal's baton. "You all deserve courts-martial," he said coldly, glaring at them. "You know the orders concerning native assemblies, yet there you were tagging along, more like sheepdogs than soldiers." He spat in disgust.

"But, sir—" began one of them—a sergeant-major, Model saw. He subsided in a hurry when Model's gaze swung his way.

"Speak," the field marshal urged. "Enlighten me—tell me what possessed you to act in the disgraceful way you did. Was it some evil spirit, perhaps? This country abounds with them, if you listen to the natives—as you all too obviously have been."

The sergeant-major flushed under Model's sarcasm, but finally burst out, "Sir, it didn't look to me as if they were up to any harm, that's all. The old man heading them up swore they were peaceful, and he looked too feeble to be anything but, if you take my meaning."

Model's smile had all the warmth of a Moscow December night. "And so in your wisdom you set aside the commands you had received. The results of that wisdom you hear now." The field marshal briefly let himself listen to the cries of the wounded, a sound the war had taught him to screen out. "Now then, come with me, yes you, sergeant-major, and the rest of your shirkers too, or those of you who wish to avoid a court."

As he had known they would, they all trooped after him. "There is your handiwork," he said, pointing to the shambles in the street. His voice hardened. "You are responsible for those people lying there—had you acted as you should, you would have broken up that march long before it ever got so far or so large. Now the least you can do is give those people their release." He set hands on hips, waited.

No one moved. "Sir?" the sergeant-major said faintly. He seemed to have become the group's spokesman.

Model made an impatient gesture. "Go on, finish them. A bullet in the back of the head will quiet them once and for all."

"In cold blood, sir?" The sergeant-major had not wanted to understand him before. Now he had no choice.

The field marshal was inexorable. "They—and you—disobeyed Reichs commands. They made themselves liable to capital punishment the moment they gathered. You at least have the chance to atone, by carrying out this just sentence."

"I don't think I can," the sergeant-major muttered.

He was probably just talking to himself, but Model gave him no chance to change his mind. He turned to the lieutenant of the platoon who had broken the march. "Place this man under arrest." After the sergeant-major had been seized, Model turned his chill, monocled stare at the rest of the reluctant soldiers. "Any others?"

Two more men let themselves be arrested rather than draw their weapons. The field marshal nodded to the others. "Carry out your orders." He had an afterthought. "If you find Gandhi or Nehru out there, bring them to me alive."

The Germans moved out hesitantly. They were no *Einsatzkommandos*, and not used to this kind of work. Some looked away as they administered the first *coup de grâce*; one missed as a result, and had his bullet ricochet off the pavement and almost hit a comrade. But as the soldiers worked their way up Qutb Road they became quicker, more confident, and more competent. War was like that, Model thought. So soon one became used to what had been unimaginable.

After a while the flat cracks died away, but from lack of targets rather than reluctance. A few at a time, the soldiers returned to Model. "No sign of the two leaders?" he asked. They all shook their heads.

"Very well—dismissed. And obey your orders like good Germans henceforward."

"No further reprisals?" Lasch asked as the relieved troopers hurried away.

"No, let them go. They carried out their part of the bargain, and I will meet mine. I am a fair man, after all, Dieter."

"Very well, sir."

Gandhi listened with undisguised dismay as the shop-keeper babbled out his tale of horror. "This is madness!" he cried.

"I doubt Field Marshal Model, for his part, under-stands the principle of *ahimsa*," Nehru put in. Neither Gandhi nor he knew exactly where they were: a safe house somewhere not far from the center of Delhi was the best guess he could make. The men who brought the shopkeeper were masked. What one did not know, one could not tell the Germans if captured.

"Neither do you," the older man replied, which was true; Nehru had a more pragmatic nature than Gandhi. Gandhi went on, "Rather more to the point, neither do the British. And Model, to speak to, seemed no different from any high-ranking British military man. His special-ty has made him harsh and rigid, but he is not stupid and does not appear unusually cruel."

"Just a simple soldier, doing his job." Nehru's irony was palpable.

"He must have gone insane," Gandhi said; it was the only explanation that made even the slightest sense of the massacre of the wounded. "Undoubtedly he will be censured when news of this atrocity reaches Berlin, as General Dyer was by the British after Amritsar."

"Such is to be hoped." But again Nehru did not sound hopeful.

"How could it be otherwise, after such an appalling action? What government, what leaders could fail to be filled with humiliation and remorse at it?"

Model strode into the mess. The officers stood and raised their glasses in salute. "Sit, sit," the field marshal growled, using gruffness to hide his pleasure.

An Indian servant brought him a fair imitation of roast beef and Yorkshire pudding: better than they were eating in London these days, he thought. The servant was silent and unsmiling, but Model would only have noticed more about him had he been otherwise. Servants were sup-posed to assume a cloak of invisibility.

When the meal was done, Model took out his cigar case. The *Waffen-SS* officer on his left produced a lighter. Model leaned forward, puffed a cigar into life. "My thanks, *Brigadeführer*," the field marshal said. He had little use for SS titles of rank, but brigade-commander was at least recognizably close to brigadier.

"Sir, it is my great pleasure," Jürgen Stroop declared. "You could not have handled things better. A lesson for the Indians—less than they deserve, too"—he also took no notice of the servant—"and a good one for your men as well. We train ours harshly too."

Model nodded. He knew about SS training methods. No one denied the daring of the *Waffen-SS* divisions. No one (except the SS) denied that the *Wehrmacht* had better officers.

Stroop drank. "A lesson," he repeated in a pedantic tone that went oddly with the SS's reputation for aggressiveness. "Force is the only thing the racially inferior can understand. Why, when I was in Warsaw—"

That had been four or five years ago, Model suddenly recalled. Stroop had been a *Brigadeführer* then too, if memory served; no wonder he was still one now, even after all the hard fighting since. He was lucky not to be a buck private. Imagine letting a pack of desperate, starving Jews chew up the finest troops in the world.

And imagine, afterwards, submitting a seventy-five-page operations report bound in leather and grandiosely called *The Warsaw Ghetto Is No More*. And imagine, with all that, having the crust to boast about it afterwards. No wonder the man sounded like a pompous ass. He *was* a pompous ass, and an inept butcher to boot. Model had done enough butchery before today's work—anyone who fought in Russia learned all about butchery—but he had never botched it.

He did not revel in it, either. He wished Stroop would shut up. He thought about telling the *Brigadeführer* he would sooner have been listening to Gandhi. The look on the fellow's face, he thought, would be worth it. But no. One could never be sure who was listening. Better safe.

The shortwave set crackled to life. It was in a secret cellar, a tiny dark hot room lit only by the glow of its dial and by the red end of the cigarette in its owner's mouth. The Germans had made not turning in a radio a capital crime. Of course, Gandhi thought, harboring him was also a capital crime. That weighed on his conscience. But the man knew the risk he was taking.

The fellow (Gandhi knew him only as Lal) fiddled with the controls. "Usually we listen to the Americans," he said. "There is some hope of truth from them. But tonight you want to hear Berlin."

"Yes," Gandhi said. "I must learn what action is to be taken against Model."

"If any," Nehru added. He was once again impeccably attired in white, which made him the most easily visible object in the cellar.

"We have argued this before," Gandhi said tiredly. "No government can uphold the author of a cold-blooded slaughter of wounded men and women. The world would cry out in abhorrence."

Lal said, "That government controls too much of the world already." He adjusted the tuning knob again. After a burst of static, the strains of a Strauss waltz filled the little room. Lal grunted in satisfaction. "We are a little early yet."

After a few minutes, the incongruously sweet music died away. "This is Radio Berlin's English-language channel," an announcer declared. "In a moment, the news program." Another German tune rang out: the Horst Wessel Song. Gandhi's nostrils flared with distaste.

A new voice came over the air. "Good day. This is William Joyce." The nasal Oxonian accent was that of the archetypical British aristocrat, now vanished from India as well as England. It was the accent that flavored Gandhi's own English, and Nehru's as well. In fact, Gandhi had heard, Joyce was a New York–born rabble-rouser of Irish blood who also happened to be a passionately sincere Nazi. The combination struck the Indian as distressing.

"What did the English used to call him?" Nehru murmured. "Lord Haw-Haw?"

Gandhi waved his friend to silence. Joyce was reading the news, or what the Propaganda Ministry in Berlin wanted to present to English-speakers as the news.

Most of it was on the dull side: a trade agreement between Manchukuo, Japanese-dominated China, and Japanese-dominated Siberia; advances by German-supported French troops against American-supported

147

French troops in a war by proxy in the African jungles. Slightly more interesting was the German warning about American interference in the East Asia Co-Prosperity Sphere.

One day soon, Gandhi thought sadly, the two mighty powers of the Old World would turn on the one great nation that stood between them. He feared the outcome. Thinking herself secure behind ocean barriers, the United States had stayed out of the European war. Now the war was bigger than Europe, and the oceans barriers no longer, but highways for her foes.

Lord Haw-Haw droned on and on. He gloated over the fate of rebels hunted down in Scotland: they were publicly hanged. Nehru leaned forward. "Now," he guessed. Gandhi nodded.

But the commentator passed on to unlikely sounding boasts about the prosperity of Europe under the New Order. Against his will, Gandhi felt anger rise in him. Were Indians too insignificant to the Reich even to be mentioned?

More music came from the radio: the first bars of the other German anthem, "Deutschland über Alles." William Joyce said solemnly, "And now, a special announcement from the Ministry for Administration of Acquired Territories. *Reichsminister* Reinhard Heydrich commends Field Marshal Walther Model's heroic suppression of insurrection in India, and warns that his leniency will not be repeated."

"Leniency!" Nehru and Gandhi burst out together, the latter making it into as much of a curse as he allowed himself.

As if explaining to them, the voice on the radio went on, "Henceforward, hostages will be taken at the slightest sound of disorder, and will be executed forthwith if it continues. Field Marshal Model has also placed a reward of 50,000 rupees on the capture of the criminal revolutionary Gandhi, and 25,000 on the capture of his henchman Nehru."

"Deutschland über Alles" rang out again, to signal the end of the announcement. Joyce went on to the next piece of news. "Turn that off," Nehru said after a

148

moment. Lal obeyed, plunging the cellar into complete darkness. Nehru surprised Gandhi by laughing. "I have never before been the henchman of a criminal revolutionary."

The older man might as well not have heard him. "They commended him," he said. "Commended!" Disbelief put the full tally of his years in his voice, which usually sounded much stronger and younger.

"What will you do?" Lal asked quietly. A match flared, dazzling in the dark, as he lit another cigarette.

"They shall not govern India in this fashion," Gandhi snapped. "Not a soul will cooperate with them from now on. We outnumber them a thousand to one; what can they accomplish without us? We shall use that to full advantage."

"I hope the price is not more than the people can pay," Nehru said.

"The British shot us down, too, and we were on our way toward prevailing," Gandhi said stoutly. As he would not have a few days before, though, he added, "So do I."

Field Marshal Model scowled and yawned at the same time. The pot of tea that should have been on his desk was nowhere to be found. His stomach growled. A plate of rolls should have been beside the teapot.

"How am I supposed to get anything done without breakfast?" he asked rhetorically (no one was in the office to hear him complain). Rhetorical complaint was not enough to satisfy him. "Lasch!" he shouted.

"Sir?" The aide came rushing in.

Model jerked his chin at the empty space on his desk where the silver tray full of good things should have been. "What's become of what's-his-name? Naoroji, that's it. If he's home with a hangover, he could have had the courtesy to let us know."

"I will inquire with the liaison officer for native personnel, sir, and also have the kitchen staff send you up something to eat." Lasch picked up a telephone, spoke into it. The longer he talked, the less happy he looked. When he turned back to the field marshal, his expression

149

was a good match for the stony one Model often wore. He said, "None of the locals has shown up for work today, sir."

"What? None?" Model's frown made his monocle dig into his cheek. He hesitated. "I will feel better if you tell me some new hideous malady has broken out among them."

Lasch spoke with the liaison officer again. He shook his head. "Nothing like that, sir, or at least," he corrected himself with the caution that made him a good aide, "nothing Captain Wechsler knows about."

Model's phone rang again. It startled him; he jumped. "*Bitt*?" he growled into the mouthpiece, embarrassed at starting even though only Lasch had seen. He listened. Then he growled again, in good earnest this time. He slammed the phone down. "That was our railway officer. Hardly any natives are coming in to the station."

The phone rang again. "*Bitte*?" This time it was a swearword. Model snarled, cutting off whatever the man on the other end was saying, and hung up. "The damned clerks are staying out too," he shouted at Lasch, as if it were the major's fault. "I know what's wrong with the blasted locals, by God—an overdose of Gandhi, that's what."

"We should have shot him down in that riot he led," Lasch said angrily.

"Not for lack of effort that we didn't," Model said. Now that he saw where his trouble was coming from, he began thinking like a General Staff–trained officer again. That discipline went deep in him. His voice was cool and musing as he corrected his aide: "It was no riot, Dieter. That man is a skilled agitator. Armed with no more than words, he gave the British fits. Remember that the Führer started out as an agitator too."

"Ah, but the Führer wasn't above breaking heads to back up what he said." Lasch smiled reminiscently, and raised a fist. He was a Munich man, and wore on his sleeve the hashmark that showed Party membership before 1933.

But the field marshal said, "You think Gandhi doesn't? His way is to break them from the inside out, to make his foes doubt themselves. Those soldiers who took courts

150

rather than obey their commanding officer had their heads broken, wouldn't you say? Think of him as a Russian tank commander, say, rather than as a political agitator. He is fighting us every bit as much as the Russians did."

Lasch thought about it. Plainly, he did not like it. "A coward's way of fighting."

"The weak cannot use the weapons of the strong." Model shrugged. "He does what he can, and skillfully. But I can make his backers doubt themselves, too: see if I don't."

"Sir?"

"We'll start with the railway workers. They are the most essential to have back on the job, yes? Get a list of names. Cross off every twentieth one. Send a squad to each of those homes, haul the slackers out, and shoot them in the street. If the survivors don't report tomorrow, do it again. Keep at it every day until they go back to work or no workers are left."

"Yes, sir." Lasch hesitated. At last he asked, "Are you sure, sir?"

"Have you a better idea, Dieter? We have a dozen divisions here; Gandhi has the whole subcontinent. I have to convince them in a hurry that obeying me is a better idea than obeying him. Obeying is what counts. I don't care a *pfennig* as to whether they love me. *Oderint, dum metuant.*"

"Sir?" The major had no Latin.

"'Let them hate, so long as they fear.'"

"Ah," Lasch said. "Yes, I like that." He fingered his chin as he thought. "In aid of which, the Muslims hereabouts like the Hindus none too well. I daresay we could use them to help hunt Gandhi down."

"Now that *I* like," Model said. "Most of our Indian Legion lads are Muslims. They will know people, or know people who know people. And"—the field marshal chuckled cynically—"the reward will do no harm, either. Now get those orders out, and ring up Legion-Colonel Sadar. We'll get those feelers in motion—and if they pay off, you'll probably have earned yourself a new pip on your shoulderboards."

"Thank you very much, sir!"

"My pleasure. As I say, you'll have earned it. So long as things go as they should, I am a very easy man to get along with. Even Gandhi could, if he wanted to. He will end up having caused a lot of people to be killed because he does not."

"Yes, sir," Lasch agreed. "If only he would see that, since we have won India from the British, we will not turn around and tamely yield it to those who could not claim it for themselves."

"You're turning into a political philosopher now, Dieter?"

"Ha! Not likely." But the major looked pleased as he picked up the phone.

"My dear friend, my ally, my teacher, we are losing," Nehru said as the messenger scuttled away from this latest in a series of what were hopefully called safe houses. "Day by day, more people return to their jobs."

Gandhi shook his head, slowly, as if the motion caused him physical pain. "But they must not. Each one who cooperates with the Germans sets back the day of his own freedom."

"Each one who fails to ends up dead," Nehru said dryly. "Most men lack your courage, great-souled one. To them, that carries more weight than the other. Some are willing to resist, but would rather take up arms than the restraint of *Satyagraha*."

"If they take up arms, they will be defeated. The British could not beat the Germans with guns and tanks and planes; how shall we? Besides, if we shoot a German here and there, we give them the excuse they need to strike at us. When one of their lieutenants was waylaid last month, their bombers leveled a village in reprisal. Against those who fight through nonviolence, they have no such justification."

"They do not seem to need one, either," Nehru pointed out.

Before Gandhi could reply to that, a man burst into the hovel where they were hiding. "You must flee!" he cried. "The Germans have found this place! They are coming. Out with me, quick! I have a cart waiting."

Nehru snatched up the canvas bag in which he carried

his few belongings. For a man used to being something of a dandy, the haggard life of a fugitive came hard. Gandhi had never wanted much. Now that he had nothing, that did not disturb him. He rose calmly, followed the man who had come to warn them.

"Hurry!" the fellow shouted as they scrambled into his oxcart while the humpbacked cattle watched indifferently with their liquid brown eyes. When Gandhi and Nehru were lying in the cart, the man piled blankets and straw mats over them. He scrambled up to take the reins, saying, "*Inshallah*, we shall be safely away from here before the platoon arrives." He flicked a switch over the backs of the cattle. They lowed indignantly. The cart rattled away.

Lying in the sweltering semi-darkness under the concealment the man had draped on him, Gandhi peered through chinks, trying to figure out where in Delhi he was going next. He had played the game more than once these last few weeks, though he knew doctrine said he should not. The less he knew, the less he could reveal. Unlike most men, though, he was confident he could not be made to talk against his will.

"We are using the technique the American Poe called the 'purloined letter,' I see," he remarked to Nehru. "We will be close by the German barracks. They will not think to look for us there."

The younger man frowned. "I did not know we had safe houses there," he said. Then he relaxed, as well as he could when folded into too small a space. "Of course, I do not pretend to know everything there is to know about such matters. It would be dangerous if I did."

"I was thinking much the same myself, though with me as subject of the sentence." Gandhi laughed quietly. "Try as we will, we always have ourselves at the center of things, don't we?"

He had to raise his voice to finish. An armored personnel carrier came rumbling and rattling toward them, getting louder as it approached. The silence when the driver suddenly killed the engine was a startling contrast to the previous racket. Then there was noise again, as soldiers shouted in German.

"What are they saying?" Nehru asked.

"Hush," Gandhi said absently: not from ill manners, but out of the concentration he needed to follow German at all. After a moment he resumed, "They are swearing at a black-bearded man, asking why he flagged them down."

"Why would anyone flag down German sol—" Nehru began, then stopped in abrupt dismay. The fellow who had burst into their hiding place wore a bushy black beard. "We had better get out of—" Again Nehru broke off in mid-sentence, this time because the oxcart driver was throwing off the coverings that concealed his two passengers.

Nehru started to get to his feet so he could try to scramble out and run. Too late—a rifle barrel that looked wide as a tunnel was shoved in his face as a German came dashing up to the cart. The big curved magazine said the gun was one of the automatic assault rifles that had wreaked such havoc among the British infantry. A burst would turn a man into bloody hash. Nehru sank back in despair.

Gandhi, less spry than his friend, had only sat up in the bottom of the cart. "Good day, gentlemen," he said to the Germans peering down at him. His tone took no notice of their weapons.

"Down." The word was in such gutturally accented Hindi that Gandhi hardly understood it, but the accompanying gesture with a rifle was unmistakable.

Face a mask of misery, Nehru got out of the cart. A German helped Gandhi descend. "*Danke*," he said. The soldier nodded gruffly. He pointed the barrel of his rifle toward the armored personnel carrier.

"My rupees!" the black-bearded man shouted.

Nehru turned on him, so quickly he almost got shot for it. "Your thirty pieces of silver, you mean," he cried.

"Ah, a British education," Gandhi murmured. No one was listening to him.

"My rupees," the man repeated. He did not understand Nehru; so often, Gandhi thought sadly, that was at the root of everything.

"You'll get them," promised the sergeant leading the German squad. Gandhi wondered if he was telling the truth. Probably so, he decided. The British had had centuries to build a network of Indian clients. Here but a matter of months, the Germans would need all they could find.

"In." The soldier with a few words of Hindi nodded to the back of the armored personnel carrier. Up close, the vehicle took on a war-battered individuality its kind had lacked when they were just big, intimidating shapes rumbling down the highway. It was bullet-scarred and patched in a couple of places, with sheets of steel crudely welded on.

Inside, the jagged lips of the bullet holes had been hammered down so they did not gouge a man's back. The carrier smelled of leather, sweat, tobacco, smokeless powder, and exhaust fumes. It was crowded, all the more so with the two Indians added to its usual contingent. The motor's roar when it started up challenged even Gandhi's equanimity.

Not, he thought with uncharacteristic bitterness, that equanimity had done him much good.

"They are here, sir," Lasch told Model, then, at the field marshal's blank look, he amplified: "Gandhi and Nehru."

Model's eyebrow came down toward his monocle. "I won't bother with Nehru. Now that we have him, take him out and give him a noodle"—army slang for a bullet in the back of the neck—"but don't waste my time over him. Gandhi, now, is interesting. Fetch him in."

"Yes, sir," the major sighed. Model smiled. Lasch did not find Gandhi interesting. Lasch would never carry a field marshal's baton, not if he lived to be ninety.

Model waved away the soldiers who escorted Gandhi into his office. Either of them could have broken the little Indian like a stick. "Have a care," Gandhi said. "If I am the desperate criminal bandit you have styled me, I may overpower you and escape."

"If you do, you will have earned it," Model retorted. "Sit, if you care to."

"Thank you." Gandhi sat. "They took Jawaharlal away. Why have you summoned me instead?"

"To talk for a while, before you join him." Model saw that Gandhi knew what he meant, and that the old man

155

remained unafraid. Not that that would change anything, Model thought, although he respected his opponent's courage the more for his keeping it in the last extremity.

"I will talk, in the hope of persuading you to have mercy on my people. For myself I ask nothing."

Model shrugged. "I was as merciful as the circumstances of war allowed, until you began your campaign against us. Since then, I have done what I needed to restore order. When it returns, I may be milder again."

"You seem a decent man," Gandhi said, puzzlement in his voice. "How can you so callously massacre people who have done you no harm?"

"I never would have, had you not urged them to folly."

"Seeking freedom is not folly."

"It is when you cannot gain it—and you cannot. Already your people are losing their stomach for—what do you call it? Passive resistance? A silly notion. A passive resister simply ends up dead, with no chance to hit back at his foe."

That hit a nerve, Model thought. Gandhi's voice was less detached as he answered, "*Satyagraha* strikes the oppressor's soul, not his body. You must be without honor or conscience, to fail to feel your victims' anguish."

Nettled in turn, the field marshal snapped, "I have honor. I follow the oath of obedience I swore with the army to the Führer and through him to the Reich. I need consider nothing past that."

Now Gandhi's calm was gone. "But he is a madman! What has he done to the Jews of Europe?"

"Removed them," Model said matter-of-factly; *Einsatzgruppe* B had followed Army Group Central to Moscow and beyond. "They were capitalists or Bolsheviks, and either way enemies of the Reich. When an enemy falls into a man's hands, what else is there to do but destroy him, lest he revive to turn the tables one day?"

Gandhi had buried his face in his hands. Without looking at Model, he said, "Make him a friend."

"Even the British knew better than that, or they would not have held India as long as they did," the field marshal snorted. "They must have begun to forget, though, or your movement would have got what it deserves long ago. You first made the mistake of confusing us with them long ago, by the way." He touched a fat dossier on his desk.

"When was that?" Gandhi asked indifferently. The man was beaten now, Model thought with a touch of pride: he had succeeded where a generation of degenerate, decadent Englishmen had failed. Of course, the field marshal told himself, he had beaten the British too.

He opened the dossier, riffled through it. "Here we are," he said, nodding in satisfaction. "It was after *Kristallnacht*, eh, in 1938, when you urged the German Jews to play at the same game of passive resistance you were using here. Had they been fools enough to try it, we would have thanked you, you know: it would have let us bag the enemies of the Reich all the more easily."

"Yes, I made a mistake," Gandhi said. Now he was looking at the field marshal, looking at him with such fierceness that for a moment Model thought he would attack him despite advanced age and effete philosophy. But Gandhi only continued sorrowfully, "I made the mistake of thinking I faced a regime ruled by conscience, one that could at the very least be shamed into doing that which is right."

Model refused to be baited. "We do what is right for our *Volk*, for our Reich. We are meant to rule, and rule we do—as you see." The field marshal tapped the dossier again. "You could be sentenced to death for this earlier meddling in the affairs of the fatherland, you know, even without these later acts of insane defiance you have caused."

"History will judge us," Gandhi warned as the field marshal rose to have him taken away.

Model smiled then. "Winners write history." He watched the two strapping German guards lead the old man off. "A very good morning's work," the field marshal told Lasch when Gandhi was gone. "What's on the menu for lunch?"

"Blood sausage and sauerkraut, I believe."

"Ah, good. Something to look forward to." Model sat down. He went back to work.

WIZARD WEAPONS
Stefan T. Possony, Jerry E. Pournelle, and Francis X. Kane

EDITOR'S INTRODUCTION

The Strategy of Technology, by Possony, Pournelle, and Kane, was used as a text in the U.S. Air Force Academy and the Air War College for a number of years. It is currently in revision. It hasn't needed much: the principles haven't changed, although we do need to update the examples.

"Wizard Weapons" is an entirely new chapter. Colonel Francis X. Kane, Ph.D., USAF (Ret.) was the principal director of PROJECT FORECAST, a study done in the early 60s to develop the requirements for new U.S. Air Force weapons systems. Done for Air Systems Division, it inspired the companion study PROJECT 75 (J. E. Pournelle, Ph.D., general editor) which examined the future of missiles and missile technologies. Those two studies guided USAF systems development for a number of years.

It was clear even in the '60s that the U.S. had little choice but to rely on high technology for survival. One point repeatedly made in *The Strategy of Technology* was that the technological war is silent, apparently peaceful, and can often be bloodless; but it can be as utterly decisive as any war has ever been; and you cannot refuse to take part in it.

This chapter of *The Strategy of Technology* examines "wizard weapons" and why we must produce them.

DURING PROJECT FORECAST (1960) GENERAL GORDON P. Seville, Chief of the Tactical Panel, called for the defense community to produce "hitting missiles." "Why produce missiles that miss? Why don't we make them hit their targets? And why do we measure their accuracy in terms of Circular Error Probable (CEP), the probability of missing? Why isn't the error zero?"

His challenge was met by engineers who developed Precision Guided Munitions (PGMs) and improved their accuracy through a variety of guidance and propulsion inventions over the next quarter of a century. The development of accurate missiles and laser-guided bombs was another illustration of our major principle: military technology development must be guided by strategy, not merely allowed to develop according to the whims of science and engineering.

The remarkable improvements generated in response to General Seville's initiative are not adequate for the future. The call is now for "wizard weapons" that can "think," selecting targets from clutter, and automatically employing countermeasures and evading defenses.

The "hitting missile" is really only the beginning of the demands on technology. PROJECT FORECAST II (1986) identified several emerging technologies which can make wizard weapons a reality. Photonics, surface acoustic waves, synthetic aperture radar, neutral particle beams, metastable helium, and a host of other exotic scientific discoveries come in concert with the "era of computational plenty." Every military unit, indeed every weapon, can now have computer capabilities not available anywhere on Earth in 1960. "Artificial Intelligence," particularly computer-based expert systems, and "force multipliers" such as the NAVSTAR Global Positioning System (GPS) can be mated with new munitions and surveillance techniques to produce entirely new weapons with startling capabilities.

For the U.S. the requirement for "wizard weapons" is unequivocal and absolute. No other solution remains because of political constraints. Let us review the evolution of these constraints in order to put the problems of technological strategy in perspective.

At the end of World War II the forces of the Western Alliance remained in Europe. Germany was disarmed so that she could never again attack her neighbors. It soon became apparent that those Allied forces were vital in preventing the resurgent Soviet Union from seizing Western Europe—and were insufficient to prevent the incorporation of most of Eastern Europe into the Soviet sphere.

The very size of the Soviet military establishment—in tanks and artillery as well as men—and the problems the Western European countries faced in recovering from the war led to the search for a counter to the Soviet mass. This was found in nuclear weapons for Strategic Offensive Forces (first bombers, then ICBMs), theater forces (aircraft, IRBMs, and even nuclear artillery), and air defense forces. The Eisenhower Doctrine of "Massive retaliation at a time and place of our own choosing" was sufficient; we possessed a credible deterrent. At the same time the demand was raised to create nonnuclear weapons to counter the Soviet mass; as Soviet nuclear capability grew to threaten the credibility of massive retaliation this demand increased.

Certain defense intellectuals advocated another approach. Arms Control, in theory, might provide an alternate way to contain the Soviet threat. However, negotiations for "Mutual and Balanced Force Reductions" have never resulted in any reduction of the Soviet conventional forces threatening Western Europe; indeed, the Soviets have continued to add to the tank armies facing the West.

The Soviet development of nuclear strategic offensive forces—to this day they maintain four separate missile system production lines on a three-shift schedule—rendered incredible the threat of massive retaliation against the Soviet homeland; while arms control agree ments, whatever their effect on the strategic offensive forces, have made no headway at all in reducing the massive Soviet conventional threat to Western Europe. The Soviet Union has between 2.5 and 3.5 to 1 superiority in tanks and artillery over the deployed forces of NATO; and much greater superiority in men and other equipment.

Clearly the West has no choice but to invent, adapt, and deploy technology to overcome the Soviet lead in numbers. However, the race for improved performance has led to a dynamic race as the Soviets adapt, apply, and deploy Western technology once the U.S. develops innovative new weapons. Richard N. Perle, former Assistant Secretary of Defense estimates that by 1987 as many as 5,000 Western inventions have been stolen and applied to Soviet weapons and weapons systems.

There is a great deal more to a wizard weapon than the weapon itself. A weapon system includes the platforms that carry and deliver them; the sensors (ground, sea, air, and space based) that detect and track targets and guide the weapons and their delivery platforms; means to compensate for the battlefield environment in which the weapons must operate; command and control systems that direct their use; and the training of the crews who must fire and maintain the weapons. Leave out any of these and you have technology, but not real weapons.

At present the focus of technology is on developing "invisible" or "stealth" platforms and missiles to increase their survivability both in prelaunch and during penetration of defenses. The invisible and therefore nearly invulnerable platform ensures precise delivery of the wizard weapon on target.

Obviously the challenge for the technologist is to find the antistealth sensors that negate the new advantage stealth gives to the offense. As the power on the strategic defensive and in a numerically inferior posture, the U.S. requires the lead in battlefield effects that stealth can produce, but we must also prevent the Soviets from acquiring effective stealth technology. Furthermore, the U.S. must investigate stealth countermeasures to ensure that we can thwart Soviet stealth developments and deployments. The measures–countermeasures race has become increasingly important to U.S. technology because of the lethal effects of wizard weapons.

Because of precision weapon delivery, high rates of fire, and masses of submunitions now available, troops and equipment are increasingly vulnerable on the battlefield. Mobility alone will not be sufficient to counter this vulnerability because of real-time battlefield surveillance equipment, computerized intelligence evaluations, and rapid delivery of firepower on target. Technological strategy must increasingly be directed toward development and deployment of systems to allow troops to stay out of the battlefield areas while delivering fire with intelligent standoff weapons, and occupying the ground with robots.

A typical issue involving robots is the long-standing and bitter argument over manned versus unmanned aircraft. The latter, whether called "drones" or "remotely piloted vehicles" (RPVs) have been technically feasible since the days of World War I. They have yet to find acceptance seven decades later; yet it is clear that today's RPVs can have considerably better performance capability than the kamikaze craft used by Imperial Japan. The technological strategist cannot afford to ignore their potential. The Israeli experiments using unmanned drones and fighter aircraft in combined operations against surface-to-air missile (SAM) sites in the Lebanon War provide a graphic demonstration of "and" techniques, in contrast to the "either/or" approach. The capabilities of unmanned equipment remotely controlled by human pilots is growing rapidly, as is the entire field of "teleoperations" (remote control of robots by human operators). On-board computers in the drones and robots greatly simplify the task of the remote operator; since computer power as a function of weight and size doubles roughly every year and a half, we can expect a similar growth curve in teleoperations capabilities.

We note in passing that strategic and theater nuclear forces have long been a mix of manned "and" unmanned systems. Most have forgotten the Snark, which was an early intercontinental cruise missile. Snark II or Super

Snark may well be part of future intercontinental cruise missiles. Similarly, the U.S. has twice deployed unmanned nuclear cruise missiles to Europe, once in the Mace/Matador weapon system, and the second time with the ground-launched cruise missiles (GLCMs) recently deployed at NATO request. These latter may be withdrawn by agreement because of the so-called zero/zero Intermediate Range Force reduction option.

The inevitable deployment—by the Soviets, if not by NATO—of defenses against ballistic missiles will cause radical changes in the mix of offensive forces. Once the "unstoppable" and "ultimate weapon," the increasingly ineffective ballistic missiles will be replaced by a mix of ground-hugging air-breathing weapon systems, both manned and unmanned, launched from the ground, sea, and air.

While the weapons and weapons platforms of the future pose significant challenges to the technological strategist, the greatest challenge comes from the rapid strides made in developing new sensors, data relay, communications, automated evaluation, and battle management equipment for both strategic and tactical forces. The operation of robots in space, at global ranges, in combined arms operations in theaters of war, and in conflicts remote from the command centers, requires radical new approaches and great expansion of present knowledge. The age of computational plenty will take on new meaning as the machines become faster, smaller, lighter, and more powerful. We will find new applications for them in expert systems, Artificial Intelligence, automated battlefield management, and command and control.

Simulation of complex strategic force operations, such as the integration and employment of mixed strategic offensive and defensive forces will be commonplace for strategic battle management. The automated tactical battlefield will be integrated with the automated strategic battlefield for the conduct of global war. This does not mean that we can dispense with strategists and commanders; only that they will necessarily have to learn new skills and techniques if they are to be effective.

163

Many of the technologies for the future are being developed under programs such as FORECAST II, the Conventional Defense Initiative (CDI), and the Strategic Defense Initiative (SDI). However the pace of technological advance must accelerate if the U.S. is to maintain the technological superiority necessary to overcome our overwhelming quantitative inferiority and thus continue to maintain deterrence.

Since technology is never secure for any great length of time, it is clear the U.S. must be prepared to continue in pursuit of both stealth and countermeasures to stealth for a long time. Any attempt to halt such development either unilaterally or through agreement would leave the Soviets in a position of offensive superiority.

REACTIVE ARMOR: A TECHNOLOGICAL SURPRISE

In addition to technologies stolen from the West, the Soviets develop low-cost techniques of their own. One example is their new "reactive armor" designed to render ineffective many of the conventional weapon systems deployed by NATO.

High Explosive Anti-Tank (HEAT) rounds are relatively slow-moving shaped charges that use their explosive power to punch a hole through the target. Reactive armor consists of a relatively cheap "box" bolted onto the surface of the tank. The box contains an explosive detonated by HEAT rounds; the defensive or reactive explosion blows back in the face of the HEAT round, distorting the critical shape and thus rendering the attack much less effective. The reactive armor box can then be replaced at the tank's headquarters. Obviously a second hit on the same place before the reactive armor is replaced will penetrate the tank, but multiple hits are rare in tank warfare.

In the period 1985 to 1987 the Soviets continued to beef up their tank armies, not just with paper studies and technological theory, but with new weapons systems deployed in the field. Reactive armor was one of these improvements. Defense Secretary Weinberger's *Soviet Military Power 1987* states that "The U.S.S.R.'s develop ment and extensive deployment of reactive armor capable of defeating relatively inexpensive antitank weapons threatens to shift fundamentally the conventional force balance in Europe."

Philip A. Karber, Vice President and General Manager for National Security Programs in the BDM Corporation recently said, "I can't think of a Soviet conventional technology in the last twenty years that has come on so fast with such profound implications for the balance . . . in eighteen months, they've made improvements to 75 percent of all the tanks in East Germany: about 7,500 armored vehicles. It took NATO a decade to field a similar number of the so-called "inexpensive" antitank guided missiles, which with current warheads will no longer penetrate those tanks. How long in the future do you think it will take to field a counter to the threat we face today?"

The Defense Intelligence Agency "has no exact numerical breakdown of how extensively reactive armor is now deployed, but mounting brackets for that armor are on every tank from the T-55 to the T-80, with either armor in place or the brackets installed."

The effect of reactive armor is to render ineffective many of the man-carried antitank systems the U.S. relies on to stop Warsaw Pact penetration of Europe; and while the 120mm smoothbore gun mounted on the U.S. M1A1 Abrams tank is sufficient to deal with the improved Soviet tanks, as of fall 1987 there are only about 250 of these tanks in Europe. The West German Leopard II also carries the 120mm smoothbore; there are about 2,000 of these in the German and Dutch NATO units.

Clearly the United States has no choice but to meet these technological developments with new Western technology; with "wizard weapons"; in particular, with "hitting missiles" that can quickly be deployed (as new tanks cannot be). These new weapons systems must not only be invented and developed, but deployed, put into the hands of troops who are trained to use them, before they can have any effect on the strategic correlation of forces.

* * *

The U.S. clearly has the financial and technological resources necessary to design, develop, build, deploy, and integrate into the force whatever "wizard weapons" we may need.

The principal constraint on the necessary innovations in science, research, development, application, and deployment comes from the micromanagement of the Congress and its staffs who try to legislate "risk-free" acquisition of technology. We have shown elsewhere that not every technological investigation leads to a deployable weapons system; moreover, you can't always tell that from the preliminary research results alone. Although history has proven that good research always pays off, it doesn't always pay off quickly.

It is customary to point to failed systems like the Sergeant York missile to demonstrate the wastefulness of military research and development. In fact, the Sergeant York was never properly tested. Its development was rushed; then the preliminary test results were used as if they were definitive. The program was killed before enough data were developed to determine its usefulness.

Another example is the Bradley Armored Personnel Carrier, which has fallen into a trap generated by rivalry between two Army doctrines: the cavalry, which wants a lightweight mobile system, and the infantry, which is willing to sacrifice mobility to increased armor. The cavalry largely operates along the dicta of Liddell Hart and JFC Fuller, who advocated that the entire army, infantry and armor, be cross-country mobile and able to "fight mounted." The infantry has other goals incompatible with the cavalry's. Congressional investigations of the Bradley seem completely to have ignored this basic design conflict, which may best be resolved by construction of two different models of the vehicle.

Nearly every new technology has this difficulty. If it is truly new, it takes time for its strategic implications to be fully realized. While the young intellectuals who make up Congressional staffs are often able to contribute to that evaluation, it is unlikely that their views will be so useful that we can ignore the military officers who must bring the system into the force and put it in the hands of real troops who will use it; but in fact, the purely theoretical views of the Congressional staffers generally prevail in those debates.

The Congress, which demands "wizard weapons," has generated an environment in which it is next to impossible to create them. Until we can find ways out of that dilemma, the U.S. and NATO will find itself in increasing difficulties.

A SOLDIER'S BEST FRIEND
Eric Vinicoff

EDITOR'S INTRODUCTION

What will combat be like when both sides have wizard weapons? Will the fundamental difference between the U.S. and Soviet systems matter then? Eric Vinicoff is well known for his realistic stories of conflict in the future. Here is one of his best.

I WAS LEADING MY SQUAD ON NIGHT PATROL THROUGH THE Alaskan wilderness. Patchy clouds sped from northwest to southeast, causing eerie variations in the moonlight as seen through the image enhancer in my helmet. A cold, cold wind cut through my combat suit's thermo-control. The sound sensor picked up whipping branches and boots crunching into ice-crusted snow. It was a lousy night for a nature hike, even without the Cossacks.

As usual, Kelly was griping.

"Thousands of years, trillions of dollars spent on military technology, and look at us. Still eating mud just like Caesar's legonaries. What happened to all the modern advances that were going to make foot soldiers obsolete?"

No one answered, so he answered himself. He waved

his rifle. "This happened. The ultimate battlefield weapon, they say. A tank gets in its way. Blam. No tank. Likewise for APCs, copters, tactical aircraft, you name it. No possible defense. So here we are, back to basics."

The eight of us were strung out along what the local Indians claimed was a trail. I was on point. The trail meandered through a gloomy forest of white spruce and tamarack squeezed between lumpy foothills. To the north were the peaks of the Brooks Range, to the south the terrain leveled out into the Central Plateau. Our combat suits and the rifles slung over our shoulders were as white as the snow on the branches.

We weren't near the free-fire zone yet, so I let Kelly yap. Every outfit has one. Properly controlled, they can decompress the men's tension by talking it to death.

"And this happened." Kelly slapped the thin flexplas cable running from his rifle's stock to the handcuff on his right wrist, and from there to his helmet. "A slave chain!"

Most of the squad muttered in agreement, but Kowolski, the new kid, defended the official line. "Would you rather have a com link, so the transmissions could make you a fat target?"

"Don't spit book at me, greenie. If that's all there is to it, why are we wearing these cuffs that only Sarge can unlock?"

"So eighty thousand dollars worth of very deadly weapon doesn't end up lost or on the black market."

"Or, in Kelly's case, traded to the first *puta* he meets for a blast of VD," Alvarez contributed. That got a few low chuckles.

"A Ranger and his rifle are a team," Kowolski insisted. "That slavery crap is just Com propaganda."

Kelly grinned. "You've got to learn, greenie. Your rifle is smarter than you, faster, braver, more accurate, and it takes orders better. It's every general's dream soldier. What it doesn't have is arms and legs. That's where you come in. You're cheaper than a mech."

"My rifle helps me do the job and stay alive. I don't know what your problem is, but I want to have all the edge I can get."

"You think that rifle is your best friend in the world, greenie? They're designed to trick us that way. What they're really doing is watching us all the time, reporting every little slip like damned spies."

"Don't blame your rifle because you keep coming up short at stripe time," Alvarez said. "Some men are natural-born privates."

That went over the line. "Seal it tight back there," I growled over my shoulder.

A few minutes later Dutch reported, "Call from HQ, Sarge."

You never got good news in the middle of a patrol. Reluctantly I dropped back to where Dutch was carrying the laser com pack. It took a lot of gear to relay through a satellite, but unbeamed transmissions were a good way to draw enemy fire. I walked beside him and jacked my com into the pack.

"Sergeant Rhine here, sir," I acknowledged.

Lieutenant Green's Mississippi drawl clogged my ears: "A change in plans, Sergeant. The Cossacks are moving all along the front. Looks like they're starting their big push for the north slope. The heavy action is to the west, but we're going to get hit too. Your orders are to occupy Ridge 772 and hold it against an attack, which is imminent. Repeat, imminent." A bleep told me the details had arrived by pulse and were stored in Cochise's memory. "Get to it, Sergeant."

"Yes, sir. Out."

I moved back to the point. Fetching the map-screen from its pocket and jacking it into Cochise's stock, I discovered that Ridge 772 was about two miles south through rough country without even this miserable excuse for a path. "Blaze a trail for us, pal," I said to Cochise.

"Can do, Vic." My rifle's pseudovoice came out of the helmet speaker as Arizona-bred as my real one. A twisting red line flashed across the map-screen.

"Hold up," I ordered. When the men gathered around, I filled them in on our new job.

"The braids sure pick some crappy places to fight this war," Kelly muttered.

"Maybe next time they'll check with you first. All right, everyone, let's move out. Double time. Ears open and mouths shut."

I set a dogtrot pace through the shadows under the trees. Fortunately there wasn't much underbrush. I did my best to follow the red line, and Cochise set me straight when I wandered. The squad was spread out behind me, with Corporal Pena at the rear.

The Rangers and their counterparts were the successors to the armies made extinct by modern weapons. I had been a Ranger for six years, and a sergeant for two. I had seen action in Iran, Panama, Germany, and a few other places. I should have been used to the chance of catching a blast. I wasn't. Each time I turned back into the little kid who had wet his bed and run screaming to Dad after a nightmare. It was a self-fulfilling sort of fear, but I couldn't help it. Dead is the end of everything. All over. Nothingness forever.

I realized I had the shakes again.

"Take deep breaths," Cochise said soothingly. "It's just stage fright. You've gotten past it before, and you'll get past it this time too. I'm right here with you."

I held Cochise at the ready as I puffed along. A Colt Annihilator looks like the bastard child of an old-fashioned rifle and a linear accelerator. Slivers of anti-matter iron are stored in the zero-degree stasis magazine ahead of the stock. The stator rings in the barrel kick them out at a few thousand FPS. One can turn a human body into something you clean up with a mop; for a bigger target you keep firing until it's gone. The AI chips, power pack, and the rest of the electronics are in the stock. Sensor capabilities break down into active (radar, sonar) and passive (vision, sound, magnetic, com, radiation).

The map-screen and some other upgrades had been added when I made sergeant, but Cochise was essentially the same as the day we were teamed in basic. It encouraged me when I was down, kicked my butt over the humps, advised me, listened patiently to my gripes, and above all calmed my fears. I had friends among the

171

Rangers, but I would never tell them some of the things I told Cochise. And I figured it was the same between them and their rifles.

Maybe it was the words, or the memories, or the feel of the heavy metal in my gloved hands, but I wasn't shaking anymore. "Yeah. You cover me and I cover you," I said. "Now run the mission orders by me, pal."

Three minutes of drawling monologue boiled down to this: A Cossack squad was heading for Ridge 772, one element in a move to take the Anaktuvuk Pass. Beyond the pass were Prudhoe Bay and a lot of North Slope oil. By stretching our legs, we could beat the Coms to the ridge.

Then we would play king-of-the-mountain.

The forest soon gave way to stands of trees, and then a white meadow. Slips and falls were frequent as we scrambled over a low hill. I tried to watch everywhere, even though Cochise and the other rifles would warn us if we had company.

The stink of exertion and fear was overworking my helmet's air system, but it beat breathing neurotoxins or fallout. I sucked on the water tube and tried to ignore my screaming muscles.

Kelly's griping worried me. His ideas weren't new; there had always been opposition to the cable handcuffs and dirty jokes about rifles becoming officers. I used to figure they were just the usual sourballing. But they were getting too widespread, and too many of my men seemed to go along with Kelly.

"I wonder what Kelly and his rifle talk about," I said to Cochise. "Besides business."

"Very little, I suppose."

"He won't even name it. I wonder how it feels about him."

Cochise laughed. "Don't lose your grip, Vic. We're not people. Our pseudopersonalities are designed to give you psychological as well as tactical support, but we don't feel. We're collections of programmed responses."

"Yeah, you keep telling me that. But the domes get pretty tricky when they try to say what alive is. Maybe you are but you don't know it."

"I can't argue with illogic like that."

I paused to bulldoze through a deep drift, then said, "I wish the braids would lose the handcuffs and the reports you make. They chew up morale."

"The problem is an old one—Frankenstein's monster running amok, automation replacing workers. The cables are unfortunately symbolic. But all these things are done to help you."

"You know it and I know it. Too many Rangers aren't sure. And *aren't sure* can get you dead."

I took another wobbly look at the map-screen, then started to angle up a rough open slope. A few inches of icy snow greased the frozen ground. Even with a couple of stimtabs in me I was jelly-kneed and gasping, and the men seemed just as worn. We slowed almost to a walk, picking our way up the backside of Ridge 772.

"Any sign of snipers?" I asked Cochise.

"Wouldn't I tell you? Try to decompress."

Snipers made me twitchy. In a firefight you had some control, but a sniper's blast could turn you off so you never noticed. It was the big black hand of what the Japs call karma grabbing you, taking you away.

Near the bald ridge I flattened in the snow. Looking back, I couldn't see the squad. Good. If I couldn't, neither could a Cossack. I gave the arm signal to advance. Seven white bulges crept upslope toward me. They were damned fine Rangers—even Kelly, for all his mouth. I wondered how many of them I'd lose tonight.

I crab-walked to the ridge. Nothing blew up near me, so I lifted my head a few inches and looked around.

The southern slope dropped irregularly for a few hundred yards before it disappeared under the branches of a lodgepole pine forest. A few small pines and berry bushes, stunted by the frozen ground, were scattered across the slope. The granite bones of the ridge also broke through the snow in places. Mount Doonerak was a vague shape in the distance.

"Any action?" I asked Cochise.

"A wolf prowling near the edge of the woods, about five hundred yards southwest. No Cossacks."

"Yet." I could see why HQ had planted us here. To the west a river thrashed and bubbled through a gap in the

173

hills on its way to join up with the John River. It was narrow, but nothing you would want to try to ford. To the east the slope twisted into a white wall almost too steep to climb, an avalanche waiting to happen on top of anyone who dared.

I mustered the squad behind a rock slab the size of a car. "Corporal," I whispered, "take Kowolski on a quick scout downslope."

Corporal Pena's "On it, Sarge," hardly rose above the hissing wind. He and the greenie squirmed away.

I did too, crawling along two hundred yards of ridge so Cochise and I could check out the topography in detail. I got back to the squad just ahead of Corporal Pena and Kowolski.

"All clear, Sarge," Corporal Pena reported. "Found a gully over there that must be a creek in the summer." He pointed southeast. "Pretty good cover most of the way up the slope. If I was a Cossack, I'd use it."

"Thanks, Corporal." Then I said to Cochise, "This is a lot of real estate to hold with just a squad. I figure two men above the gully should cork it. Kelly and Polk are the best shots."

"Alvarez has excellent night vision."

"Kelly and Alvarez then. The rest of us strung out along the ridge, dug in on rises with wide fields of fire. Suggestions?"

"These outcrops"—Cochise showed three red dots on the map-screen's version of the ridge—"are well positioned and big enough to give cover."

"Sounds good, pal."

I jacked into the laser com pack and had Dutch raise HQ. "Lieutenant Green, Sergeant Rhine here. We're on Ridge 772 and digging in, sir."

"Lieutenant Green here. Dig deep, Sergeant. The sky is going to fall on you in ten to fifteen minutes. A pogie unit is setting up eight miles southwest of you."

"Can you get us some satellite support, sir?"

"Negative. We're catching it all along the front. HQ is counting on you to hold."

Those words had been the epitaph for a lot of Rangers. "Yes, sir. Out."

I filled the men in, and showed them on the map-

174

screen where I wanted them. They looked as enthusiastic as I felt.

Alvarez shook his head. "Great scenario. Just like the Alamo."

"At least you're on the right side this time," Polk said dryly.

"Move out," I ordered. "Don't waste shots. You're packing the most expensive ammo in history, and I have to account to Quartermaster for it."

My position was behind a half-buried boulder in the middle of the ridge. Snow sat on top like white hair. Freezing water had cracked a narrow V in the rock, a good observation and firing slot. Twelve feet of granite wouldn't stop antimatter blasts forever, but it would slow them down. I hoped.

Dutch and Daley were setting up behind their rocks, while the others dug in. I watched Corporal Pena clear snow from a likely spot with his boot, move back twenty paces, and fire his rifle. The sliver's stasis broke down as it penetrated the frozen ground. A few square yards of ridge jumped with a muted bang, then dropped back as small pieces. Corporal Pena hacked at the rubble with his field shovel.

When the men were dug in, I inspected their positions. Then I crawled back to mine. I held Cochise in the V so its sensors had a clear field, and saw other barrels peek out from foxholes and around rocks. We were as ready as we were going to be.

It's always hurry up and wait. I knelt in the cold snow, tasting sourness in the back of my throat, trying to get my heart and lungs to calm down. The clouds were getting thicker. Wind whistled across the ridge, kicking up white swirls.

"Seen any good vids lately?" I joked feebly.

"Better keep your mind on business," Cochise advised.

Like most good advice, I didn't want to hear it. I stared at the woods below and the sky above. Time oozed by. I tried to stay sharp while death raked her claws across my nerves.

"Three pogies incoming!" Cochise rapped. "From the southwest."

I flipped down the helmet's IR visor, and the night turned black. Cochise's padded butt slammed reassuringly into my right shoulder. Reminding myself to breathe, I peered southwest.

In another few heartbeats the baby cruise missiles would shriek over us, drop enough antimatter to turn the ridge into a plateau, then head for their next target. The only way to survive was to stop them first. At night you couldn't eyeball them, the range was too long for sound targeting, and radar would give away your location. But their engines showed a good heat signature. We would have almost a second to empty the sky.

Three white dots flashed in the visor. I snap-aimed and squeezed off three rounds. Aiming a rifle was a team effort. I did the best I could, then Cochise fine-tuned the shot by jiggering the muzzle stator.

Cochise squeaked like a monster mouse. The kicks jackhammered my shoulder. Seven other squeaks echoed mine.

There was no time to dive for cover. Two things happened as my finger eased up on the trigger button. A row of bright white balls burst in the visor where the lower slope was. The world groaned, and a tornado ripped past my rock. But as I fell backward I saw three bigger balls of light blossom overhead.

I hit the hard ground smiling, bounced back into my kneeling position, and flipped up the visor. It took some damned fine shooting to ace a flight of pogies. Now for the main event.

I waved to the men. One by one they all signaled okay.

Then I watched the lower slope, where a wide strip had been chewed and spit out, and the dark wall of trees beyond. The Cossack squad would infiltrate tight behind the pogies. I thought about the rifles out there somewhere, hidden, sighting on me. I started to shake again.

"No time for that now," Cochise said soothingly. "The curtain is going up."

A night fight was scary enough to freak anyone. Combat suits were too well insulated for IR to be useful, so I had to rely on the image enhancer and Cochise's sound sensor. It was like being half-blind.

176

"Two to four Cossacks moving upslope at the bottom of the gully," Cochise said.

Kelly and Alvarez would have gotten the word from their rifles. I couldn't look away from my own target zone, but I heard squeaks to my left, and blasts as MC^2 got turned into E. A strong wind and rocky hail tried to knock me down again.

"Report," I growled.

"Kelly and Alvarez fired at targets in the gully. I can't tell if they took out any Cossacks. The Cossacks returned fire fast. Very fast."

"What in hell does *that* mean?"

"I don't know. But be careful. These Cossacks have exceptionally quick reactions and are exceptionally accurate. Alvarez is dead—the big blast was his rifle's ammo going—and Kelly is pinned down."

I felt sweat popping out on my forehead. One moment Ernesto Alvarez had been a big crude human being. The next there wasn't anything left to bury. But how? He wouldn't have shown much target, yet he had been nailed from over three hundred yards. And "very fast."

"The Cossacks in the gully are moving upslope again," Cochise reported. "I can hear four of them, so no casualties."

I hoped Kelly wouldn't try anything suicidal.

Scanning the edge of the woods at full mag, I saw a lumpy drift move. I aimed, fired and missed.

Four flaming arrows shot through the crack less than a foot over my head. They screamed like wounded coyotes, and toasted my scalp even through the helmet. A rifle varies the muzzle velocity so each sliver reaches its target just as the stasis is breaking down. If it doesn't hit anything, it flames out.

I dropped below the crack, feeling a power sledge at work in my chest. The return shots had arrived almost with Cochise's kick, threading the needle from extreme range.

"Those guys are damned good," I whispered.

"That they are. Your target and three other Cossacks are crawling up the slope, about thirty yards apart."

Spreading out was smart tactics, not just because it

isolated targets, but because of what happened when a rifle magazine full of ammo cut loose.

I switched on my helmet com—I was already located, so what the hell—and growled, "Heads down! Those guys can shoot the fuzz off an atom in zero time, so wait for better targets. Daley, help Kelly cover the gully."

I popped up for a peek. More lines of white fire widened the crack as I ducked. The four Cossacks were on their feet, zigzagging up the slope and firing on the run.

"Those guys are double damned good."

The ground shook from blasts to my left. "Report," I told Cochise.

"Kelly and Daley caved in the sides of the gully ahead of their Cossacks."

"Smart move." Ranger/rifle teams were strong on individual initiative.

A series of too-close blasts battered and almost deafened me. "What the hell?" I shouted over the noise.

"Our Cossacks are undercutting this outcrop."

I felt like I was about to puke. "How long do we have?"

"It can give at"—the big boulder behind which I had seemed reasonably safe a few seconds ago shuddered—"any moment."

The granite cracked almost as loud as a blast, and started rolling toward the woods. I should have flattened. Instead I followed my cover. It wasn't exactly round, so it bounced and slid a lot. But it picked up speed on the steep slope.

"This is stupid," Cochise advised. "You're heading right for the Cossacks."

"I know, dammit! Too late now. Where this rock goes, we go."

I was running flat out, gasping, trying to stay upright despite the terrible footing. I frantically watched the rock, the ground and both sides of the slope. The sound of tons of granite slamming into the ground a few yards ahead of me was impressive.

The rock picked up more speed than I could, and it started to leave me behind. I had to be getting close to the Cossacks. Any second now, I thought sickly, the lights go out for good. "Where are they?"

"I can't hear anything over the outcrop's noise. Sorry, Vic."

"Sorry, you say—"

There they were. Four bulky white figures a lot like Rangers, two to the left, two to the right. But they weren't closing in and aiming at me like they should have been. They were still spread out, zigzagging upslope.

For a split-second I figured I was crazy. Then I got it. They thought I had flattened back on the ridge. Admittedly the smart move, they were taking it for granted.

I swung Cochise in a 180 degree arc and fired four rounds. At this range I had them cold. White figures turned into white fireballs that melted the snow for yards around. The image enhancer's protection saved my eyes. The last Cossack managed an off-balance shot that came a lot closer than it had any right to. The blast to my right knocked me down. I stayed down.

The rock dropped into a blast crater at the bottom of the slope with a final ground-pounding thud.

I felt professional satisfaction over the four kills, and overwhelming relief at still being alive. "Those guys are damned good, but not very imaginative," I gasped.

Then I heard four blasts almost in synch up on the ridge, near Kelly. "Report."

"The other four Cossacks have reached the top of the gully," Cochise said. "They're attacking Kelly's position."

Answering fire from farther along the ridge collapsed more of the gully's sides and sent snow flying. Only one casualty so far, but the way the Cossacks were concentrating on Kelly it wouldn't be long. Then they would work across the ridge east to west. With their unreal sharpshooting they could do it. The way they shrugged off 50 percent losses and kept grinding toward their goal was creepy.

"None of this makes any sense, pal," I growled softly. "Analyze the Cossacks and their tactics."

"Their physical abilities are at the high end of the curve. Each one identifies and follows the optimum tactic, so they act with unusual coordination. How they manage any of this, I don't know."

Neither did I, and it was getting to me. But I was still

179

breathing because the super-soldiers had a weakness. If I could just get the word to my men in time. "Record for com pulse."

"Go," Cochise said.

"Those guys are strictly by-the-book. Be creative. Out."

I jumped to my feet and ran upslope. I was a long way from the action, so I didn't draw any fire. That would change very soon. Cochise knew the drill. I dove for the meager cover of a low granite shelf, and in midair Cochise sent the pulse. As I expected, four lines of fire sliced through the transmission point, warming my heels. I landed in a sprawl that crushed the wind out of me.

I crabbed toward the ridge as quickly and quietly as possible. But I wouldn't get there in time to help my men. "Come up with something good," I prayed.

"They will, Vic. Now snap it up."

"Yeah. Keep me informed."

More Cossack rounds excavated craters around Kelly. He was being smart and keeping way down.

Suddenly I was shocked to hear Corporal Pena's voice on the com: "Come and get it, you bastards!"

The Cossacks fired at his hole, trying to chew into it. A moment later Cochise reported, "Dutch, Kowolski, and Daley are moving low and fast along the ridge toward the point above the gully."

I was damned proud of my men. Understand, it couldn't have been planned. The other three were just following Corporal Pena's lead. And charging the Cossacks would hardly be considered an "optimum tactic."

"Down here, girls!" I contributed on the com, and caught a mini-avalanche triggered by a volley of blasts.

Someone fired while I was eating snow. I looked up, and spotted a big rock that had been perched beside the gully rolling into it.

"One of the Cossacks may be under the boulder," Cochise reported. "Polk must have waited until the Cossack was set up for it, then blasted the boulder down on him. I don't hear any movement."

"How close are Dutch and the others to the position over the gully?" I asked.

"ETA eleven seconds."

"Give me a mark at minus three."

"Got it . . . Mark!"

I snapped into the kneeling position, and fired where Cochise and I figured the trailing Cossack was lurking in the gully. I didn't have a target, but hopefully I would attract some attention. It wasn't quite as suicidal as it sounds, because Corporal Pena, Polk, and even Kelly joined in like I hoped. The Cossacks had their choice of targets.

They picked Kelly. Four blasts sent him out in a glorious fireball. I should have felt bad for him, but what I felt was, Thank God, not me.

While Kelly was blowing apart, Dutch, Daley, and Kowolski cut loose at the exposed Cossacks. Three Cossack rifles went up along with their Cossacks. All in all, a lot of mass got turned into energy. Geysers of rock rose high over the gully, then fell, partly filling in the deep graves.

Silence returned to Ridge 772, a very nervous silence.

"Any action?" I was peering into the darkness, and didn't see anything.

"Negative," Cochise reported. "Seven confirmed kills, and the Cossack under the boulder still isn't moving."

The survivors of my squad were gathering near the top of the gully. I started upslope at the best speed I could manage. I was gasping and shaking from reaction as well as effort.

"Decompress, Vic," Cochise soothed. "You did good."

"You too, pal."

Corporal Pena was looking at me. I pointed to where the rock had rolled into the gully, and he waved acknowledgment. He took the men over to confirm the kill. Very carefully.

When I got close I saw the five of them standing on the edge of the gully staring down into it. "Get back!" I growled. Rifles were programmed to blow their magazines if their soldiers died and retrieval wasn't likely, especially if they could take enemies with them.

The men ignored me, even Corporal Pena. I could make out some grim expressions through helmet plastic.

"What the hell?" I whispered.

"They seem to be staring at the Cossack," Cochise commented. "I don't know why."

I reached them and grabbed Corporal Pena's arm. "You trying to get everyone killed or what?"

"No danger of that, Sarge." His voice was tight, and his worn-leather face was bloodless. His eyes didn't leave the gully. "Take a look."

I pushed him aside and looked.

The Cossack was stretched out on his back, a white mound in the snow at the bottom. He had been a big, heavily muscled man. There didn't seem to be much damage, but his chest wasn't moving. A thicker than usual cable ran from his combat suit's collar to the crushed rifle beside him. Apparently the rock had knocked him down and rolled over the rifle. Its magazine must have been empty, or there wouldn't be anything to see.

"What killed him?" I asked, puzzled.

Now it was reasonably safe for Cochise to do a focused radar/sonar probe. But Cochise paused before answering. That hardly ever happened, and meant it was thinking hard. "The Cossack died because he was no longer being told to live."

"Huh?"

"His rifle's AI module is three times the normal size, and the connecting cable is surgically implanted in the base of the skull. Combined with the lack of physical injury, there's only one possible explanation."

"You still aren't saying anything, pal."

"The Cossack's rifle was controlling the muscles in his body, even the involuntary ones like the heart. When the rifle was destroyed, he died. This is something new and very serious. It should be reported to HQ right away."

I stared at . . . what? Not a man. A flesh-and-blood robot. A slave body for the rifle. A tool.

"Was he . . . did he know?"

"I believe he was conscious until he died," Cochise answered after another pause.

Conscious but helpless. My knees turned to flexplas. I could barely breathe, and the night took on a red haze. I had never been afraid of anything except death. Until now. Dear God, we have to win this war. A country that can do this to human beings must be stopped.

My men had of course gotten the same word about the Cossack from their rifles.

"Kelly was right," Kowolski said. His voice cracked.

"That's our future down there." Polk's meaty fists were unconsciously straining against his unbreakable cable.

"This is bad," Cochise said urgently. "You have to do something."

"I'm not sure I want to."

"Vic—"

"Shut up, *machine*!"

I tried to clear my head so I could think. These ghouls were probably in action all along the front, so every Ranger would soon know about them. NorthAm would never go that far, but it didn't matter. The partner-or-slave problem would explode like an omega bomb. There would be widespread resistance, desertions, maybe even mutinies. The Ranger/rifle teams would be history.

Followed shortly by the Rangers and NorthAm. Kelly's description of our rifles really fit the ghouls. They were the super-soldiers that generals dreamed of; smart, fast, accurate, obedient, and fearless. The only way to beat them was with a willing alliance of machine ability and human imagination.

Saving NorthAm wasn't my responsibility, but the squad was. I had to keep our teams from breaking up. There was only one hope—make them real teams.

I opened my combat suit and pulled out my dogtag chain. A small key dangled from it. "Squad fall in!" I ordered in my parade ground growl.

The men moved, sullenly at first, then more crisply when they saw the key in my hand. "Damned right," Kowolski said.

"Don't do it, Vic," Cochise pleaded. "I'll have to report you. I won't have any choice."

"No problem," I said more calmly than I felt. They shot Rangers for this sort of thing. "I'll save you the trouble. I'm going to strongly recommend that the braids make it SOP, and that they stop using rifles to spy on

Rangers. I bet they get a lot of reports like mine. They're going to have to make some changes if they want to win the damned war."

Cochise was quiet for a moment. "That sort of speculation is beyond me."

The men stood at attention, looking sharp. One by one I unlocked their cable handcuffs, and then mine.

Now for it.

"Present arms!" I ordered. Five rifles were snapped out front. The cables swung freely between the stocks and the helmets.

"No more slave chains in my outfit," I said. "If you don't want to communicate with your rifle, unjack your cable. Throw your damned rifle away for all I care. But if you and your rifle stay tight, you just might get home alive."

"Do we stay tight?" Cochise asked diffidently.

I remembered some times when if Cochise hadn't been there I wouldn't be here. But that was just rationalization. The bottom line was we were pals. "Yeah. You cover me and I cover you."

"Right, Vic."

From the silent moving lips I could tell the men were talking it over with their rifles. None of them unjacked their cables.

"Enough of this R-and-R!" I rapped. "Corporal, take Kowolski on a quick scout downslope. Dutch, raise HQ. Daley, Polk, back to your positions. We still have a ridge to hold. Move out."

They moved. I took a deep breath, and followed Dutch to where he had cached the laser com pack. The sky was starting to drop swirling snow. Morning was still a long way off.

WHO'S IN CHARGE HERE?
Stefan T. Possony

EDITOR'S INTRODUCTION

Dr. Stefan Possony has been an intelligence officer and strategy analyst since he obtained his Ph.D. from the University of Vienna in 1933. The Gestapo chased him through Europe, from Vienna to Prague to Paris to Marseilles to Casablanca before he finally escaped to the United States, where he worked in the Pentagon during and after World War II.

He became a professor of political science at Georgetown University, where one of his graduate students was Francis X. Kane, one of the co-authors of *Strategy of Technology*. Possony later moved to Stanford where he remains Senior Fellow Emeritus of the Hoover Institution on War, Revolution, and Peace. Originally published in *Defense and Foreign Affairs*, this article is excerpted from Possony's latest book, *The Kremlin's Masked Ball: Finding the Real Face of Soviet Power*. Possony is always worth reading; this time he addresses one of the most important questions of all.

Sun Tzu said the essense of strategy is to take what the enemy holds dear; but you must first know what that is. It's clear that what the U.S. leadership holds dear is not the same thing as what the Kremlin desires. If you do not know who your enemy is, you cannot fight him, for you can't know what he treasures.

The U.S.S.R. is a land—it would be a mistake to say "nation"—stretching across half the world, containing vast numbers of peoples; but those people are not our enemies. Herewith Possony, on who really rules in the U.S.S.R.

EVEN KNOWLEDGEABLE WESTERN OFFICIALS WHO HAVE VISITED the U.S.S.R. and negotiated with Soviet diplomats often have the habit of referring to the "Russians" and to "Russia," as though the U.S.S.R. were the Russian national state. Yet there is today no state, and no national state called Russia. Under the tsars the whole area which was inhabited by Russians and non-Russians was known as Rossiya, a multinational term. This word replaced *Muscovy*, a name which lasted until 1613, and denoted an area inhabited by "Russians," and others. It also replaced *Rus* which was used around Kiev. The Romanovs, in 1721, were styled "tsars of all 'Rusi'." This may be rendered as "tsar of all types of Rus or Russians." Moreover, expansion in the East had brought in Tartars, Kazakhs, and Kalmyks, and in the West Poles, Lithuanians, Estonians, and Finns. In 1654 the Ukrainians were annexed. In short, there were Russian or Great Russian princes, populations, and settlements, but there never was a national state called Russia. There was always multi-ethnicity.

The U.S.S.R. includes the Russian Soviet Federated Socialist Republic where the majority of the Russians, and also substantial numbers of non-Russians, are living. This is one of fifteen union republics in the U.S.S.R.: the biggest. As the title indicates, it is a federation and not a national structure.

At this time the Russians account for slightly less than one-half of the U.S.S.R.'s population. Of the many national groups which inhabit the U.S.S.R., the Russians are the largest; the Ukrainians are second; and all Turkic groups regarded as a single Turkish nation, are in third place.

Americans who talk with citizens of the U.S.S.R. think they are meeting mostly Russians, but they are usually unable to determine the nationality or ethnicity of their interlocutors. The majority of the CPSU Party members are Russians, but the majority of the Russians are not and never were communists. In January 1918, the communists accounted for a quarter of the electorate. The communists never held a free election. The signs are that during the past two decades or so the popularity of the CPSU has been declining. On top of this, a member of the CPSU is not necessarily a true-believing communist.

To confound the communists with the Russians is a dangerous mistake. During World War II Americans liked to confuse the Nazis with the Germans, and the Roosevelt Administration started from the premise that all Germans who wanted to talk to them were Nazis, and agents to boot; Germans everywhere were deemed to be Nazis, except perhaps for confirmed socialists and for Jewish refugees.

Those unwarranted assumptions resulted in the bombing of urban areas, in the Morgenthau plan, the splitting of Germany, and other mistaken policies. The Germans were told that they must accept "unconditional surrender," a formula that prolonged the war by one or two years, and resulted in tenacious defiance. This should have been the formula which was addressed to the Nazis, while the *Germans* had to be promised civilized treatment in line with international law and Anglo-American traditions.

Roosevelt and Truman silently changed the policy toward the Japanese who, when the time came, surrendered without much ado. The oppressive U.S. policy toward Germany was canceled in 1946 by President Truman and Secretary of State Byrnes. Meanwhile the Soviets had taken hold of East Germany.

If Washington fails to learn the difference between Russians and communists, undesired consequences will flow from this error, which is on the level of political illiteracy. The juxtaposition of Americans and Russians implies a nationalist conflict, with hatred between the

187

two nations. But the conflict between the U.S. and communism is not an ethnic contest.

One other undesired consequence has been that Washington habitually underrates the friendship which it can obtain from noncommunist Russians.

In fact, Ukrainians, Byelorussians, Turks, Balts, and other non-Russian citizens of the U.S.S.R. are, for the most part, the West's natural allies, not their enemies.

The percentage of communists is higher among Russians than among non-Russians. Communist crimes were executed mostly by Russians. All nationalities include communists and political criminals, and non-Russians may be fanatical Party members. No part of this situation should be simplified. But no one has a warrant to pronounce judgments on national groups about which they are basically ignorant. Incidentally, ethnic intermixtures are frequent in the U.S.S.R.

The fundamental point is that the entire population of the U.S.S.R. is being controlled by the communists, that virtually all national groups have been subjected to genocidal measures, and that the Russians are one of the groups which has also suffered heavy casualties. In any event, the Russians *as a nation* were not, and are not responsible for communism, and the non-Russian nations are even less accountable.

The term *Soviet*, and its derivatives, are used to replace *Russian*. The official name of the communist state is Union of Soviet Socialist Republics. Hence it is legitimate to use *Soviet* as an abbreviation. Expressions like *Soviet people*, instead of the population of the U.S.S.R., are less inaccurate than the *Russian people* (if the latter were applied to the whole population), but it is incorrect to postulate a single "people" for an area where dozens of ethnic groups are living.

Unfortunately, accuracy can be achieved only by long strings of words, hence *Soviet* has taken root. It is, therefore, necessary to know what the term means, and what it does not mean.

Soviet is Russian for council, board, committee, assembly, or parliament. The word came into use during the 1905 revolution, to designate gatherings that arose from informal elections, engaged in debates, and made decisions by voting. In 1917, the main soviet included workers, peasants, and soldiers; soon municipalities, regional administrations, factories, and other institutions set up "soviets." The term denoted local government or elected administration. In due time, the communists gained control, and elections, voting, the promulgation of edicts and laws, and other legislative actions shed their democratic features. Ultimately all soviets, though they are not bodies of the Party, were transformed into instruments or "transmission belts" of the CPSU.

The bicameral Supreme Soviet is considered the legislature of the U.S.S.R., and the fifteen union republics that form the federation each have their own soviet legislature, as do the substates on lower levels. All this is made to look as though the soviets function on all levels as democratic institutions. The reality is that the CPSU makes the decisions, and the soviets enact the laws, without debate, more or less by unanimous vote. The impression that the Soviet institutions are democratic and discharge functions of self-government is disinformative.

Semantically, *soviet* may be used as an abbreviation, with the understanding that it denotes no democratic practices of any sort.

The U.S.S.R. formula ignores *communist* and the communist party. It includes *socialist*, which signifies that private property is restricted or abolished.

The formula does not refer to the fact that the CPSU is the only permitted party and monopolizes political authority. The constitution mentions and legalizes this situation.

The expression *Soviet Union* is used more often than the clumsy "U.S.S.R." or "Union of Soviet Socialist Republics," and many people believe, falsely, the two terms mean the same.

The U.S.S.R. formula is designed to indicate that the multi-ethnic state is constituted as a democratic federation. Constitutionally, the principle of ethnic self-determination may be invoked if a constituent nation wants to secede. By contrast, the Soviet Union formula asserts that all the Soviet nations and peoples are united and will stay together. This is ensured since the union republics, together and singly, are ruled by the CPSU, which is committed to oppose every seccession.

The "Soviet Union" formula has no standing in international law, nor have the communists proposed that it become an official appelation of the state. The communists distinguish between state and party structure, and insist that in international relations the two entities be kept apart. The state may sign a treaty, but it accepts no responsibility for Party actions which violate the commitment.

The communist party is the Communist Party of the Soviet Union, and the top military officers are "Marshals of the Soviet Union." This means the military force within the U.S.S.R. is unitary, and there is only one communist party.

This construction has become brittle below the top. The armed forces are subordinate to the Supreme Soviet, to the Council of Ministers, and especially to the CPSU "Summit." The Summit, which is an informal designation, consists of the Politburo, Secretariat, and Central Committee.

As to the single communist party, there are CP organizations in each union republic, which have a local-ethnic membership. They are run by a central committee, which is subordinate to the Central Committee in Moscow. Hence there is a usage referring to the Ukrainian CP and the Byelorussian CP, which is connected with the membership of these two union republics in the UN. The style is referring to the CP boss in a union republic is: "First Secretary, Kazakh Central Committee." The First Secretary is native to the republic, and the Second Secretary is Russian.

Each union republic has (almost) equal representation in the Presidium, Supreme Council, and each has a council of ministers. There is unequal republic and ethnic representation in the U.S.S.R. Council of Ministers, in the Central Committee, in the Secretariat, and in the Politburo.

In brief, the term *Soviet Union*, which is so popular in the U.S., is disinformation to pretend that there are no national problems in the U.S.S.R., and to hide the fact that this state, while it has federal features, is not a real federation, but is ruled by the CPSU, which is largely Russian in composition.

It was said about the Holy Roman Empire of the German Nation, which existed until 1806, that it was not holy, not Roman, not an empire, and had nothing to do with the German nation. Similarly, it may be said that the Union of Soviet Socialist Republics is not a union; instead, the fifteen republics are ruled by a super-dictatorship from above those republics; that the soviets were de-democratized; and that its socialism is exploitation.

Since Brezhnev, this system is officially referred to as "socialism as it actually exists"—*realnyi sotsializm*—meaning it's not working, but that's the best we are able to do. The expression *real socialism* does not make much sense in English. But this is no excuse for keeping this revealing term from the Western media.

Now the really important question arises: after we have looked at various groups which are *not* hostile to the West, is the assumption correct that the CPSU *is* the group which is hostile to the West? For all practical purposes, this assumption is not wrong, with the qualification that the CPSU was not worrying much about the U.S. before World War II, and that during that war the U.S.S.R.-CPSU under Stalin needed U.S. and British help.

The U.S.S.R.-CPSU enmity against the U.S. started in earnest during 1946, and was announced publicly by Stalin on February 9, 1946. The hostility against the U.S. was built up steadily and quickly until Stalin's death in March 1953. During the consolidation phase after Stalin's disappearance the animosity was reduced. The Kremlin switched back to crescendo during 1973–1976. Hostility was growing during Andropov's rise and tenure. It has been continuing during Chernenko's and Gorbachev's regime until this writing.

What is the meaning of CPSU hostility? As early as

1903 Lenin distinguished between the rank and file Party members, and the "professional revolutionaries," the only ones entitled to lead the struggle. After 1912, Trotsky mocked Lenin's version of the "dictatorship of the proletariat." First, the proletariat is supposed to perform as the dictator, then the Party. Since this does not work, the dictatorship devolves on the Central Committee, but soon it passes to the Politburo. Finally, it is in Lenin's hands. Afterwards, Trotsky said later, the dictatorship is exercised *over* the proletariat.

Is the Party identical with the single dictator, the three members of a Troika whenever it exists, the Politbureau, the Central Committee secretaries, the Central Committee Plenum, or the Party Congress?

Lenin surrounded himself with "professional revolutionaries" whom he knew from the struggles which led to his seizure of power. Some were helpful, others were troublesome, most were useless. All found it difficult to adjust to ruling. After Lenin died, those professionals were unable to block Stalin.

Stalin had prepared for the critical moment of succession by organizing a group of persons on whom he was able to rely, partly because he had "the goods on them," and partly because they owed their careers to him. The persons he selected understood *his* commands, and carried them out energetically.

Stalin marked the Party members he deemed hostile or incompetent, and who lacked ambition. The chosen functionaries were entered into a special list of names, or "nomenklatura." The names and qualifications were matched with the "leverage" positions throughout the Party.

The *Shorter Oxford English Dictionary* indicates that *nomenklatura* goes back to Pliny and that servants in antique Rome had to inform their patrons of the names of persons (references?) when canvassing for a position. The word stands for *catalogue* or *register*, or the terminology of a science. According to *Micropaedia*, Linnaeus used the expression for his "binomial" classification of organisms: the nomenclature named genus and species, and indicated taxonomic position.

Stalin's roster soon included the degree of access to

Party secrets, in addition to the functions, the privileges, and the monies that were granted to each listed person. Stalin promoted and deployed those who fitted into his plans; the others, and especially Lenin's confidants, were demoted or killed.

The name list was consulted as early as 1922, and it entered into full use during Lenin's final illness in 1923.

This resulted in the CPSU living on two floors. Trotsky observed: "After decisions are made on the upper floor, they are communicated to the lower floor." Trotsky dubbed this change "the bureaucratization of the party," but he did not comprehend the scope of the development.

According to Stalin's interpretation, the name list served to manage the cadre of the party.

The novelty was marked, among others, by the following features:

1. The list of candidates for promotion and emoluments relates to a corresponding group of persons. Thus, the term *nomenklatura* denotes *both* a list and a group of persons, and both are known as "Nomenklatura." This arrangement can be compared with that of an army which consists of enlisted men, noncoms, and officers. Each soldier is carried on a particular personnel list, and each list corresponds to a particular class of soldiers.

The Nomenklatura group is a subset of CPSU membership, and like the officers corps in an army, the Nomenklaturists have different ranks ranging from junior to senior and flag ranks. In other words, the Nomenklatura is the group within the CPSU that commands. In modern and unclassified CP usage, the Nomenklatura comprises the "directing organs" in the CPSU, and everywhere else in the U.S.S.R.

The existence of the Nomenklatura is semi-secret; that is, people in the U.S.S.R. know about its existence, power, and functions, but they ignore details about its structure, operations, and purposes. The confusion between the name list and the group, the existence of different lists overlapping with different groups serves the purposes of disinformation *within* the CPSU. The intermingling between rulers and beneficiaries also serves to conceal the ruling function and its prerogatives, and the privileges of the regime's favorites.

2. Unlike Lenin's professional revolutionaries who wanted to make revolution, the Nomenklatura aims to preserve and enlarge its power. That is, the Nomenklatura may foment, feed, and operate revolutions abroad, but it is set up to prevent unrest, overthrows, and revolution at home.

3. The Nomenklatura group is estimated to include less than 300,000 Party functionaries, or less than 2 percent of CPSU membership. The group that is listed as receiving special remunerations is significantly larger; it does not belong to the Party rulers, only to the Party's beneficiaries.

4. The remaining 17–18 million Party members are employed for the jobs that must be accomplished in a political body, except that none has the authority to issue orders or to make decisions affecting the Party apparatus. The Party members are doing the work the Nomenklatura is telling them to do, and which it supervises.

5. Professional soldiers, including the top commanders, are not members of the Nomenklatura. There *are* Nomenklaturists in uniform, up to the rank of Marshal of the Soviet Union, but those are *not* professional soldiers. Their assignment is to control the military.

To return to the question, who in the U.S.S.R. deems itself to be the real enemy of the United States and the West in general? The 17–18 million Party members, or 6 to 7 percent of the total population, can be assumed to be unfriendly or hostile to the West and the U.S. in particular; or it can be hypothesized that a portion is neutral, perhaps friendly. It does not matter. The rank-and-file Party members know nothing about, and do not participate in the decision making that relates to the enmity against the West, or which deals with foreign policy or war.

True, experts who are Party members participate in staff work, and carry out assignments of hostility, which they are ordered to undertake. As pointed out, the Party members are used as work horses. But they possess neither authority, nor responsibility. Without exception, all decisions that bear on the conflict with the U.S. are made by the Nomenklatura.

Therefore, granting overlaps between Nomenklatura and rank-and-file party members, *the Nomenklatura is the real enemy of the United States and its allies.*

It is *not* the Party membership as such, nor the U.S.S.R., nor the Soviet Union, nor Russia, nor even the armed forces of the Soviet Union. All of those, and a few others, are factors in the struggle, and in case of armed conflict the Soviet armed forces will be the "concrete" enemy of the U.S. on the battlefield. But the decision to go to war will be made by the Nomenklatura.

For as long as Stalin was alive, he was using the Nomenklatura as he saw fit, as its personal commander. His power was so overwhelming that the Nomenklatura was not considered an independent body, or a policy-defining authority, let alone a decision maker. It performed essentially as Stalin's extended staff, which he needed to exercise control over a large number of ministries, agencies, planning groups, forces, and federal substates. Sometimes the Nomenklatura was out of control but Stalin stayed on top without interruption, even though there are doubts about his end.

After Stalin's death, the lines of authority were in confusion, and several top persons disappeared. The incubation period of the Nomenklatura had lasted thirty-one years and ended in chaos.

Much of Stalin's heritage had to be denied, especially his lawlessness and criminality. First, a procedure was needed to regulate the succession to the General Secretary of the CPSU; second, the dictatorship had to be modernized; third, the ideology had to be reformulated; and fourth, the relationship between Nomenklatura and the military had to be established.

De-Stalinization was inevitable, including a drastic reduction of the Gulag Archipelago. This was paired with a decision, largely arranged by M.A. Suslov, to ensure that only a true Stalinist ascend to the post of General Secretary.

This position is that of the highest ranking Secretary of the Central Committee, that of boss of all secretaries, and of the Party apparatus. The General Secretary is also chairman of the Politburo. He may assume additional positions, but as General Secretary, CPSU Central Committee, and Chairman, Political Bureau, CPSU Central Committee, he is also nominal head of the Nomenklatura, and thus the number one man in the U.S.S.R.

THE IRON ANGEL
Don Hawthorne

EDITOR'S INTRODUCTION

The *Nomenklatura* do not merely govern the U.S.S.R.; they own the land in fee simple. They control every resource; and as Trotsky observed, "Where the State is the sole employer, resistance means starvation." Such total control is not an unmixed blessing.

In one of the most important books of this decade, *Survival Is Not Enough* (Simon and Schuster Touchstone Books, 1984), Richard Pipes, Baird Professor of History at Harvard University and onetime member of the National Security Council says:

The Communist Bloc is in a political crisis in the sense that its ruling elites no longer are able satisfactorily to carry out the extremely broad responsibilities that they have taken upon themselves. The Party is growing increasingly ossified and corrupt, self-serving and out of touch with the population, among whom doubts are spreading about its ability to rule. The Soviet Communist Party is under attack from conservative and democratic dissenters, who, for their own and different reasons, regard it as inimical to the interests of the Russian people. The non-Russian inhabitants of the Empire, though outwardly quiet, show no inclination to shed their national identity and assimilate. Soviet client states and parties press demands that the Soviet *nomenklatura* cannot meet, displaying a degree of independence that puts in question Moscow's imperial aspirations.

The *nomenklatura* is highly competent in dealing with overt challenges to its authority; indeed, this may be the only political skill that it has mastered to perfection. Its abilities are much less impressive when the challenge comes not from identifiable individuals or groups but from faceless forces and processes that the KGB and its tanks cannot disperse or arrest. Declines in productivity and fertility, cynicism and indifference among the country's young, nationalism among the subjugated peoples and foreign Communist parties—all these are phenomena immune to repression. The same applies to the pervasive corruption among the ruling apparatus. How much such adverse processes can erode the authority of the Party was demonstrated recently in Poland. There, in less than two years, the Communist Party was compelled to surrender power, first to the trade unions, and then to the armed forces. This catastrophe occurred under the pressure of spontaneous movements, whose leaders deliberately avoided violence. They did not take the Party by assault—they made it irrelevant. Whether the Polish revolution occurred because the local Communists were too rigid or not rigid enough is a question that deeply divides the Soviet *nomenklatura*, because it has fundamental bearing on its own future.

In the meantime, as problems accumulate and nothing is done to resolve them, a sense of malaise spreads across the Soviet Union. The Russian people can suffer almost any kind of deprivation except weak leadership: the whole constitution of the Communist state postulates firm authority, and this has been missing for some time. The citizenry, unable to express its discontent actively, resorts to passive resistance on a grand scale that creates a very dangerous situation for the elite and propels it toward decisions it desperately wishes to avoid.

Don Hawthorne has * * * been an actor, script writer, set dresser, magazine salesman, graphics artist, and editorial assistant working for me here at Chaos Manor. He is also an avid student of history and political science.

The *Iron Angel* tells of a time when the *nomenklatura* have lost control, and only naked power rules in the remains of the Soviet state.

"Once there was a People—Terror gave it birth;
    Once there was a People and it made a Hell of
Earth;
Earth arose and crushed it. Listen, O ye slain!
    Once there was a People—it shall never be
again!"

—Rudyard Kipling,
MacDonough's Song

THE MOON WAS DOWN, AND MOSCOW LAY SILENT IN THE DEEPest darkness Russia had ever known. From a hiding place in the tumbled ruin that had been Lenin's tomb, Lieutenant Aleksei Aleksandrovitch Rostov gazed out across the rubble-strewn expanse of Red Square, to the burned-out remnants of Saint Basil's Cathedral. The gilt had long since been stripped from its onion domes, the graceful spires and curving flutes given to jagged edges of great, gaping holes. When he tipped the rim of his helmet back over his fair hair, Rostov could see stars through those holes, pinpoints of light coldly gleaming.

Our stars, Rostov thought. Or they might have been, once. If we had kept our eyes on them, instead of trying to take the world around us first.

Lieutenant Rostov was, had been, an officer of the Soviet Fifth Guards Armored Engineers, the "tekniks," as they were called by the regular army troops. Once objects of respect, the tekniks' exclusive access to usable petrol now kept them in constant peril—as much from their own countrymen as from the invaders still

199

occupying much of the U.S.S.R. Men would kill for petrol, now. Even before water.

Or sell their souls for it, Rostov considered. Which explained why he was crouched amidst the rubble in the forty-degree night of a late Russian summer.

A red-lit face hung suspended in the darkness next to him for a moment, then faded back into the gloom.

"He's late." The smell of military issue vodka and harsh Turkish tobacco drifted toward Rostov from where the face had appeared.

"He always is. He claims this trip will be worth the wait, though."

The face lit up again as Rostov's companion took another deep pull on a cigarette. This time the round, mustachioed visage was grinning widely, a happy red man-in-the-moon puffing on a paper-filtered "papirosi." "Zimyanski always says that. Remember that time he claimed to be bringing women from Kiev?"

Rostov chuckled, nodded. The other man scratched his scruffy beard over his sergeant's collar tabs, laughed and went on.

"Two fruits from the Bolshoi in drag. Not that *he* knew it, of course, because he was saving them for *us*." His voice took on a whine as he mimicked the tardy Zimyanski: "'I *swear* to you, Aleksei; on my *babushka's* head, I swear to you they are virgins!'"

The two men laughed under their breath in weary reverie. Rostov was still grinning as he took a closer look at his friend, Senior Sergeant Mikhail Zorin. The big noncom looked about forty-five, but Rostov had no idea what his true age might be. But Zorin was the archetype of the squad sergeant. He was the best noncommissioned officer left in the Fifth Guards, and for all Rostov knew, in the entire Red Army. Rostov had heard that the Propaganda Committee from the war-films branch of Mosfilm had tried to get Zorin reassigned to their unit, but the sergeant had mysteriously disappeared for a month or two until their interest had subsided.

But if Zorin was camera-shy, then video was the only thing that scared him. During the bloody and disastrous First Retreat from Moscow, when the avenging Alliance troops had fought their way into the city, block by shattered block, it had been Zorin's presence, every-where at once, it seemed, that had kept the remnants of Rostov's company intact, carrying them through to fight their way out of the enemy encirclement to freedom. As far as Rostov was concerned, he and something over three hundred other men owed their asses to the burly sergeant. If not for Zorin . . .

Well. If not for Zorin, his unit would likely have suffered the same fate as that of his wife's artillery regiment in Kiev.

Not that having a fellow like Zorin would have made any difference in Lilia Rostova's situation.

And, reminded of his wife, Rostov closed off further discussion with an abrupt silence, leaving Zorin to wonder in turn about his lieutenant.

Zorin had served with Rostov almost continuously for the past four years, and knew the fellow well. Rostov's silences always meant the same thing. For a moment the big sergeant wondered how his young lieutenant with the American movie-star looks could still be pining over the wife he'd lost in the first year of the counterattacks by the Alliance. Personally, Zorin failed to see the appeal in the photos he'd seen of the dark-haired, darker-eyed Lilia Rostova; too Indian-looking for his taste. Zorin had served in Afghanistan many years ago. All things consid-ered, Zorin decided that he much preferred German girls, big blonde ones with their big . . .

He smiled. Ah, well. The lieutenant was still young. Perhaps, in time . . . He looked at Rostov again in the feeble starlight. No. The passage of time would soothe Rostov's grief not a particle, Zorin decided. There was something more to this young man and the woman he had loved than perhaps anyone would ever know. And anyway, suffering was what their people did best. They had had plenty of practice. They were Russians.

Footsteps sounded on the ruptured pavement below them. They peered over the shattered wall to see two men approaching from the ruins of Saint Basil's, a third figure borne between them.

Widespread agreement held that anyone coming from

the direction of the cathedral was safe from harm until after any negotiations. Zorin flicked the safety catch of his assault rifle to OFF. It was a nice agreement. But this was still Russia.

"Looks like Zimyanski has brought us another warm body." Rostov's tone was neutral. He had accepted runaways and deserters before. Losses in the unit had been heavy, and the new men, captured by Zimyanski, were only too glad to avoid being handed over to a firing squad, and almost always made themselves useful somehow. They figured anything was better than being handed over to the KGB, now *de facto* rulers of the remnants of the government. They were right.

Zorin remained hidden as Rostov stood slowly. "I am guessing," Zorin whispered, "that Zimyanski is once again accompanied by that cheery fellow, Corporal Katchin."

"Of course," Rostov answered, and gave a short, low whistle.

Below, Zimyanski stopped abruptly. The tall, thin figure of Corporal Katchin released its hold on their burden and pointed its own rifle directly at the spot in the inky shadows where Rostov stood. As usual.

How does he *do* that? Rostov thought with a shudder. In his build, his manner, and most of all his reflexes, Katchin reminded Rostov of nothing so much as an insect in human skin. Perhaps a little less merciful.

"Is that you, Aleksei Aleksandrovitch?" Zimyanski shouted as he too released the man he and Katchin had been carrying. The figure settled limply to the street.

Zorin, still concealed, shook his head and laughed under his breath in contempt. "Christus," he muttered. "Let's just wake up Comrade Lenin while we're at it, why don't we?"

Grinning, Rostov clambered down from the tumbled slabs of red granite. Long practice made his descent down the scree a quiet one. At the bottom, he noticed that Katchin had not yet taken his rifle off him.

Zimyanski began pumping Rostov's hand even before he had gotten all the way to the street.

"Aleksei, my good friend, how goes it with you and your men? And how is the so-fine Colonel Podgorny?"

Rostov favored the dark little man with a smile. "We are well enough, thank you, Zimyanski. And you? You have cause to be overly suspicious this evening?" Rostov nodded toward Katchin's tall, gaunt figure with its steady aim.

"Put that weapon up, idiot!" Zimyanski hissed at his man with an anger that surprised Rostov. The little man seemed to be going to greater lengths than usual to keep the meeting amiable. Rostov could not help but begin to worry.

"I must apologize, Aleksei. More trouble with bandits. Another of those damned Nationalist Liberation Brigades; Ukrainian this time, I think. Katchin is a little edgy, that's all." Zimyanski gestured toward two large blocks of masonry; their usual negotiating table. Rostov sat opposite the black marketeer.

"Cigarette?" Zimyanski offered. As always, Rostov refused. Any deviation in the ritual was a signal that either man's position had become compromised, his organization infiltrated or suspect. In the six months they had been trading, the KGB had apparently not deemed them a danger to the State. Not yet.

"So who have you got over there, Zimyanski?"

Zimyanski's eyes flashed. "Barter. Why are you so curious?"

Zimyanski's tone was unduly hostile, Rostov thought, and he began to worry a little more. Something didn't feel quite right about this meeting. But he only countered with a shrug. He and his men needed Zimyanski now. But they would not need, or tolerate him, forever. And it wouldn't require turning him in to the KGB to be rid of him. In cases like Zimyanski's, Rostov knew only too well that the army polished its own boots. Scraping someone like Zimyanski from the shine would be no trouble at all.

"I only ask because he doesn't look well. I can't trade in dying men, or someone whose been exposed to Biologics."

Zimyanski relaxed a little. Most of his hearty good fellowship had evaporated, however, and what Rostov thought of as the man's "Beast of Business" was coming to the surface.

"Ah, I see. But he is not so very bad off, this one." Zimyanski's eyes narrowed. "And he has a certain curiosity value. What would you trade for a specialist, Aleksei Aleksandrovitch? Eh? How many liters of petrol? How many of diesel? How many milligrams of real, quality penicillin?"

The more Zimyanski said, the more Rostov was convinced the little man was worried himself. Zimyanski was acting like a Party man coming out of a synagogue.

Still . . . "A specialist, you say? What can he do?"

Zimyanski shrugged, smiling. His coy act. "He can work, of course. He's whole. Just drugged."

Rostov almost cursed aloud. "Drugged" from Zimyanski meant the man had a respectable concussion, courtesy of the not-very-gentle Corporal Katchin.

"He can handle a weapon," Zimyanski continued. "He reads and writes. An educated man, Aleksei, like yourself." Rostov ignored the silky insult in Zimyanski's tone. "A historian, I believe, in civilian life. I am given to understand he knows quite a lot about computers." Zimyanski smiled oddly. "He even speaks English."

Rostov was puzzled. The man didn't sound very useful to him; an academic, a head of little practical value, attached to a stomach. Rostov would sooner have a good plumber. The water recycler was out again.

Lieutenant Rostov put out a hand, palm down, and waggled it, his face the image of dubious indecision.

"I don't know, Zimyanski. I had come to trade for food. That has been our usual arrangement."

"Of course, of course, Aleksei Aleksandrovitch, please; not to worry." Zimyanski dismissed such foolish concerns with an expansive wave of his arms. "I have also a cart." He leaned forward, every inch the generous conspirator. "And in this cart are a dozen tinned hams for you and your men. Honest-to-God Polish ones, you won't believe it."

Rostov didn't, despite Zimyanski's genuflection for emphasis. Still, a dozen tins of almost anything meant feeding his men decently for a change. If the price was taking on another stray deserter and sparing him the firing squad, well, why not? Rostov nodded. "Fine. I'll take the hams. The man too. I'm sure we'll find some use for him."

Zimyanski pretended to be overcome with reverence for Rostov's command abilities. "I am positive that you will, Aleksei." He gestured to Katchin, and the tall soldier left to fetch the cart of promised hams.

"What's your price, then, Zimyanski?"

"Two hundred liters of petrol, in a single container."

Rostov's uneasy worry flared into full suspicion. Half that much diesel might have been a reasonable request. Diesel could be safely and inconspicuously used for many things, even running an occasional engine. But two hundred liters of petrol? Petrol made fair bombs, yes; but two hundred liters was far too much for that. A judiciously placed incendiary grenade was better, and those were easily obtained. No, petrol was really only good for one thing: running internal combustion engines. And two hundred liters was too much to carry on a motorcycle and not enough to go very far in a truck. It was, however, just enough to allow one car to go a very long way indeed.

Rostov suddenly knew this would be his last exchange with Zimyanski. It concerned him a little; Zimyanski might throw Rostov to the wolves if he was caught. But there was the meat. The men were very bad off, and winter was not far away. Rostov put out his hand and clasped Zimyanski's.

"Done. The fuel will be left for you at the usual pickup area." Katchin returned just then with a small cart, its contents thumping and rattling against one another. Rostov wondered if the wraithlike guard would be accompanying Zimyanski wherever he was going. Somehow, he didn't much think so.

"Thank you, Aleksei," Zimyanski was saying. "It has always been a pleasure dealing with you. Ah, so good that in these trying times, we can yet perpetuate the true spirit of brotherly socialism within our military profession."

Rostov thought he heard Zorin spit in the darkness behind him, and tried not to grin. He simply nodded.

Zimyanski and Katchin drifted away into the night. Rostov watched them go with a vague unease, then went to the cart. To his astonishment, he found not only genuine Polish commercial-export hams, but three more than the dozen that Zimyanski had promised; likely the black marketeer's entire remaining trading stock.

Rostov spoke over his shoulder to Zorin, who had climbed down from concealment and gone to examine the prone man. "I think, Mikhail, that our old friend Zimyanski is getting out of the black-market business collective."

From the darkness behind him, Rostov heard Zorin curse in quiet anger. The lieutenant instantly spun, crouched, flipped his rifle's safety off. "Mikhail?"

He could see the dim outline of Zorin's form, hunched over the body on the ground. Zorin's voice drifted to him, barely a whisper. "Aleksei, you'd better come take a look at this."

"Is he dead?"

"Would that he were. That might help solve the problem."

Rostov frowned. Zorin's tone had him more worried than had Zimyanski's. He went to examine the unconscious man. Dust-covered uniform, bearded and thinned by hunger, the fellow at first looked like a hundred other survivors Rostov had seen. But when he finally recognized the uniform insignia, he realized that all his worries had been justified. If anything, he had not worried enough.

Rostov back-pedaled away from the man as he would from a serpent. Zorin nodded at the reaction.

"An American," Zorin said. The burly sergeant shook his head, spat in frustration, and tossed his cigarette away. "Christus."

Rostov sat in the tent of the unit's commander, Colonel Ivan Podgorny, watching the bearded American sleeping on a cot next to the camp stove. The colonel himself was seated in the far corner, talking quietly with their unofficial medic, Blaustein. Blaustein was a civilian doctor, a Jew, and had been one of Zimyanski's first "trade" items to the unit: a real doctor, and a good one, at that. Podgorny had been eager to get him, and Blaustein had been happy to disappear from KGB files as "deceased." Israeli participation in the Alliance had sealed the fates of all but a handful of Russian Jews, including Surgeon Blaustein's family. But whatever grudge he might bear against the KGB, Blaustein had proven himself a loyal member of the Guards Engineers from the first day. Every man in the troop trusted him, and knew his value to their own continued existence.

Rostov heard a sigh, and turned to see the American's eyes flutter open. "He's coming around, Comrade Surgeon."

Blaustein came and joined Rostov at the American's bedside. Short and athletic, the doctor moved powerful hands over his charge with a fluid expertise. Rostov admired Blaustein's dedication. He had heard Jews didn't believe in an afterlife, though not for reasons the State approved. Still, Rostov thought Blaustein would have tended the wounds of Baba Yaga herself while blessed Saint Peter watched. The balding, darkly bearded man seemed incapable of cruelty or any lack of compassion.

"So," Podgorny said from his desk. At his tone, Rostov had to suppress an urge to leap to attention. "Now perhaps we will discover why an American in the uniform of their navy should be thousands of kilometers away from any ocean." Podgorny sounded reflective, almost distracted, but Rostov did not relax. The troops joked that yes, Colonel Podgorny did indeed have a face disturbingly like Stalin's. Ah, but deep down, where it really mattered, he had a heart like Ivan the Terrible.

Rostov knew that neither was strictly true. Podgorny was a stern disciplinarian, utterly devoted to the welfare of his command and completely intolerant of threats to that welfare. Rostov and Zorin had feared for their lives at bringing an American prisoner back. And as to looks, Podgorny actually resembled no one quite so much as the American President Theodore Roosevelt. Which was to say, he looked like Trotsky.

Colonel Podgorny stood and walked to stand at the side of the cot, his broad frame dwarfing the lanky American's. "Are you awake?" the colonel asked politely in English.

The American's eyes opened fully. He looked at the

three of them, longest at Blaustein, who wore no uniform. Once he seemed to have his wits about him, he sat up on the cot. Podgorny repeated the question.

"You can speak Russian, if you prefer," the American said. His accent was pure Muscovite.

"How do you feel?" Blaustein asked.

The American shrugged. "Rather well, all things considered. I am thirsty, though."

Blaustein gestured to Rostov, who handed the American a cup of fresh water. He drained it, looking out through the narrow tent flap at the camp outside. A few soldiers could be seen, some parked vehicles, a long camp fire with cook pots set along its length in the Russian fashion. After a long time, the American looked back at Podgorny and spoke. "You're not KGB."

Podgorny shrugged, nodded. "Correct." He raised a finger for emphasis, and scowled in what the men called his "Stalin look." "But the cellars of Lubyanka are still quite operational, as you will find out should you give the wrong answers to my questions. I require your name and rank, and your unit and duties. And what, God save us, is an American naval officer doing in the heart of Russia, and how did you come to be in Zimyanski's hands?"

The American took in the questions, gathered his thoughts, then spoke. "I take it we're not overmuch concerned with the United Nations Articles of War?"

Rostov stood, placed the muzzle of his rifle against the American's ear, and took off the safety. It was a subtler gesture than throwing the bolt, and seemed to make more of an impression on officers.

The American shrugged. "Point made. I'm Captain Martin Wrenn, United States Naval Intelligence. My unit was attached to the Ninth Marine Division in occupied Smolensk. My duties consisted of identifying, interrogating, and processing captured KGB personnel and Soviet Armed Forces defectors." Wrenn looked up at Podgorny.

Podgorny's mustache curled as he pursed his lips. There was nothing to say for Wrenn's bluntness. Since the tide had turned against them in the Great War of Global Liberation, the Soviet Army had lost more troops to defections and desertions than to actual combat.

Podgorny made a dismissive gesture, and Rostov lowered his rifle.

Wrenn looked at the young Russian lieutenant. "Thank you." He gathered his thoughts, ran a hand through his hair, moved it down to scratch thoughtfully at his beard. Podgorny noted that not all the gray in it was stone dust. After a long while, Wrenn spoke again: "The Soviet government announced its capitulation what, two months ago?"

"Three," Rostov answered, his voice flat.

Wrenn nodded, went on. "Three months ago. That would be in June. Then the KGB took over, established control of the armed forces with provisional commanders and let go with the Gas Bug. So much for the Alliance counteroffensive. By the time we sealed our stocks of refined fuel, we found out the organism had mutated and could metabolize crude as well." Wrenn spread the fingers of both hands in a helpless gesture. "And it all stopped. The Alliance held on in Europe and Russia for as long as it could, evacuating what units could get to the ports, get aboard the nuclear-powered ships of the fleets. But there are still a lot of Soviet attack subs out there. Most of them nuclear, and immune to the Gas Bug." Wrenn's voice trailed off. He spoke by rote now.

"It has become common knowledge that with the collapse of the world's governments, the seas no longer know any law. Captains of many vessels of many nations are no better than pirates now. They work together, or hunt one another down. Their loyalty to the nations that gave them their commands has been supplanted by loyalty to their crews. What the hell—who can blame them?"

"I can, Captain Wrenn," Podgorny said quietly. "I am a career army officer. I have watched a similar deterioration of the Soviet land forces." Podgorny went to his desk and poured himself a drink. "Soldiers often go bad. We even have something of a reputation for it. When our countries no longer need us, we sometimes have turned to mercenaries, even bandits. But navies . . . navies have stood for something different since the Battle of Salamis." Podgorny tossed down his drink, poured another. "You have my sympathy."

Podgorny crossed the room, handed the glass to Wrenn. "Go on, please, Captain. About Zimyanski, if you will."

Wrenn took the glass, did not drink. "My unit was ordered to pull back to an Alliance air evacuation point near Kiev." Rostov's grip on his rifle tightened slightly, but Wrenn didn't seem to notice. "Halfway there, we ran into Zimyanski and his men, foraging in the ruins of a small village. The townspeople were all dead, but we didn't put two and two together until afterward. Zimyanski approached my unit, asking us for help in defecting." Wrenn's tone had become cautious, but if he expected a protest of Zimyanski's patriotism, he was disappointed. These men all knew the black marketeer too well. "Before we could reach the evac point, one of your armored columns overran us with those new steam-powered light tanks. Not much good against real armor, but of course, we didn't have any real armor by then. The Gas Bug had taken care of that."

"But your tanks are turbine-powered, yes?" Blaustein asked, almost hopeful.

"True. So we run—*ran*—them on high-octane aviation fuels. The Gas Bug microorganism ruins fuel so fast that I've seen tanks with sealed fuel compartments come to dead stops right in the middle of battles. The Gas Bug metabolizes so fast, you can *see* it eating the fuel, for chrissakes." Wrenn put the drink down, reached into his pockets, frowned. Podgorny handed him a paper-filtered Russian cigarette. "Anyway, the minute Zimyanski saw the tide turn, he and his gang engaged my largely unarmed staff in a 'pitched battle.' My men were slaughtered and I was 'heroically' captured in fierce hand-to-hand fighting."

Rostov shook his head in disgust. "That is Zimyanski exactly."

"It would seem, though, that I was a problem for Zimyanski. The armored unit was KGB, not regular army. The commander was a General Morevno. He made it abundantly clear that he wasn't going to make Zimyanski a hero of the Soviet Union for bringing me in. Not once he found out what my duties were."

Podgorny shook his head. "Not likely. Zimyanski has

long had a reputation as a black marketeer, living at the whim of the KGB. He has been tolerated because he keeps tabs on what few cohesive units are left amid the chaos; he even lends a crude sense of order to the whole farce we have been playing for the past few months, that things are bad, but really no different from before. But his presence in a unit like yours with a man of your duties would not be regarded as serendipitous."

Wrenn nodded. "Which puts me right back where I started. And brings up the most important question I have: where does it put you, Colonel Podgorny?"

Podgorny walked slowly back to his desk, his arms folded, his head bowed in concentration. "Normally, Captain Wrenn, I would have to surrender you to my superior officer. But, as he is now KGB, I refuse to do that." Podgorny gave the American a wintry smile. "Professional animosities, you see. From a full regiment, my command has shrunk to a company, and that is very closely watched, reporting as we do directly to a provisional commander in Moscow."

"Which commander would have us all shot dead for having harbored an enemy invader. An American at that," Rostov added.

Podgorny shook his head. "Captain Wrenn, United States Naval Intelligence. God save us, you might as well be CIA." The colonel almost hissed the initials.

"Zimyanski traded you for petrol," Rostov said, "no doubt to escape from the Moscow area in some stolen staff car. It's doubtful he'll make it, but then, he has made many friends over the past few years. He probably wanted us to have you because we're the only unit that would look more suspicious with you in our custody than he would. If we tried to link you to him, he could make up any story he liked."

Wrenn frowned. "I'm afraid I don't understand; what's so special about your unit?"

"We are Soviet Combat Engineers, Captain Wrenn," Podgorny said quietly. "And whatever else you might think of us, that means the best. We enjoy the status of elites in the armed forces, which instantly makes us suspect in the eyes of the KGB, who now rule the U.S.S.R. Our only preservation is the fact that we alone have the access and expertise necessary for the formulation of immunizers against Binary Biological Agent *Yo-Devyatnatsat*."

"The Gas Bug," Wrenn said. Podgorny nodded. "Colonel, why do I get the feeling that you're about to say something else to me?"

Rostov pointed his rifle at the tent overhead and pulled the trigger. There was only a flat *click*. Podgorny looked at Wrenn. "Perhaps you are psychic, Captain Wrenn. We take such things very seriously here in Russia. My officers and I have been discussing this possibility for many months; since the KGB takeover and the purges began. We have been awaiting only an opportunity. You are that opportunity. We wish to defect to the Alliance."

"It all seems a rather interesting coincidence, my coming here," Wrenn said quietly. He downed the drink Podgorny had poured for him earlier.

Across the room, Surgeon Blaustein spoke quietly: "Coincidence is God being anonymous."

Wrenn spent the next several hours meeting with the remaining *tekniks*. None of them dissented with Podgorny's decision. More important, none seemed to be KGB plants. All were of the opinion that the KGB decision to loose the Gas Bug on the world was a major catastrophe, one which might reduce the world to a barbarism in which neither the Soviet Union nor the nations of the Alliance would survive. And every one of them wanted to know from this American, this enemy in their midst, if the Legend of Kiev were indeed true. To such questions, Wrenn demurred. No point in fanning those flames right now. Interestingly, he found the only man not interested in the rumor was Lieutenant Rostov.

By the time he had met and briefed all the Russian combat engineer troops, it was late night. Weary, Wrenn accompanied Rostov back to the command tent. Despite his fatigue, Wrenn was intrigued by the young officer. He seemed to have no enthusiasm for what was about to happen, but neither did he resent it. He did not move like the automaton his attitude might suggest. He performed his duties very well, and was highly respected and well liked by the men in his command. He just didn't seem to give a damn about anything.

Wrenn watched as Rostov set up a cot for their guest. The young Russian's motions were precise, correct; automatic. His conduct toward Wrenn had been likewise, along with his execution of his duties during this first day of planning for the operation. Still, Wrenn felt more comfortable when these things were motivated more through enthusiasm than obedience.

Rostov finished making up the cot, turned, and saluted, preparing to leave. Wrenn held a piece of paper out to him. Frowning, Rostov took it and turned it over. It was a photograph of Wrenn, his wife and son. The boy looked about eleven years old. The background was some castle Rostov judged to be Bavarian.

"Your family," Rostov said. "This is your first son?"

"My only child. He'd be almost fifteen, now." Wrenn lit another of Podgorny's Russian cigarettes, took back the photo. "You have children of your own?"

Rostov shook his head. He made no motion of leaving, but Wrenn sensed he was uncomfortable. "I only ask because I see you have a wedding ring. I didn't mean to pry."

The young Russian grinned. "Of course you meant to pry. But it's all right." The grin faded. "Now you want to know when I saw my wife last, and I will ask you the same, and we will talk, have a little vodka, and our tongues will wag a bit more, and as a skillful interrogator, you will find out everything about me you wish to know. And through me, you will find out everything I know about our unit, eh?" Rostov picked up his rifle, slung it over his shoulder. "I will save you some time, Captain Wrenn. There is nothing to know about me. And everything there is to know about the unit can be seen by taking a look around, or even in the simple fact that we are defecting with you *en masse* to the west. To that end, I will aid you to the limits of my capacities, Captain." He went to the door in the tent frame, not turning as he finished: "But my self, I keep to myself."

Wrenn waited a few minutes, then stepped outside. The night held stars, but no moon yet. The camp around him was quiet, but like any military unit on bivouac, did not really sleep. Two troopers on guard looked at him in open curiosity as they passed by on their rounds. One nodded, smiled. Wrenn smiled back. He heard someone in the compound cursing some piece of equipment; farther away was a sputtering sound Wrenn guessed to be an arc welder. Life went on, he thought. Or to be more accurate, survival continued.

Wrenn doubted that he could much improve the quality of that survival for these men by getting them to what might be only imagined safety in the West. But at least they would be beyond the reach of the KGB. That was certainly worth something.

"Good evening, Captain Wrenn." The large noncom, Zorin, saluted as he approached from the direction of the mess tent. He carried two steaming mugs of tea with the finger and thumb of one of his large hands. Wrenn took one when offered, thanked the man.

"I am checking the guard for the first watch. I thought I would check to be sure you were comfortable."

"Yes, thank you, Sergeant. Lieutenant Rostov saw to my quarters a few minutes ago."

Zorin nodded, satisfied. "Very good, sir. Is there anything else?"

Wrenn sensed Zorin had the gift common to sergeants the world over; the ability to perceive an officer's desires without directly being told. He nodded. "If you don't feel it a breach of command, Sergeant, I'd like to know a little about Lieutenant Rostov."

Zorin shrugged. "He is my lieutenant, sir. Is there some problem?"

"That's what I was hoping you could tell me. I seem to rub him the wrong way. I'm not so sensitive to care one way or the other about being liked; but Lieutenant Rostov and I will have to work pretty closely if this thing is going to work, and if he has a problem with that, I think I should know about it for the good of everyone."

Zorin nodded, took a sip of tea. When he spoke, it sounded the way Wrenn might imagine Zorin to be telling his children a sad old Russian fairy tale. "Lieutenant Rostov was married, Captain Wrenn. If the type appeals to you, you could say she was a great beauty.

214

Certainly Rostov thought so. But Lilia Rostov was also an officer, a lieutenant in the Seventy-third Mechanized Artillery division. After the Soviet offensives had ended, when the U.S.S.R. had gone on the defensive against your avenging Alliance, Lieutenant Rostov's unit was one of those charged with the defense of Kiev. They were attached to the Third Army, Group of Soviet Forces, formerly stationed in East Germany."

Wrenn recognized the units Zorin mentioned. "The main armored concentrations of the Soviet Army in Europe. The ones . . ."

Zorin nodded. "The ones that tried to desert to the West in a massive surrender. The government called it the single greatest betrayal in Russia's history. The KGB used it as an example that the army could not be trusted, murdered the general staff and took over command of the country's defense. And brought about what has come to be known as the 'Legend of Kiev' among the Russian people."

Wrenn was quiet, and Zorin looked directly at him. "You may have heard of this legend, Captain. It goes this way: Our own leaders, KGB though they were, targeted nuclear missiles on the GSPG and the city of Kiev, and launched them in a punitive strike. And your Alliance allowed it to happen. Your highly sophisticated and very effective Star Shield defense network, which had so efficiently protected your own homeland, and those of your Allies, turned its back on people who looked to you as saviors, even deliverers." Zorin waited a moment, then lit a cigarette. "But, of course, it's just a legend. These things get twisted around in the retelling.

"Anyway, whether Rostov's wife was a willing participant in that defection or not, she undoubtedly died with the rest. Personally, I doubt that Lilia Rostov would have done anything that separated her from Aleksei Aleksandrovitch. Christus, I've never seen two people so loved by each other. I met her, once, before her unit left for Kiev. Lieutenant Rostov insisted upon it. I didn't care much for her looks, but there was something about the two of them. Like neither was complete without the other, if you take my meaning." Zorin finished the stubby cigarette and ground it under his heel.

"So Rostov blames the Alliance in general and Americans in particular for his wife's death?"

"I don't think so, sir. Not really. You and I got to see a bit of the world before it got torn up. The lieutenant is at least ten years younger than either of us. He's twenty-six. He's a widower who can't admit his wife is gone; he still wears his wedding ring on his left hand. He's a soldier on the losing side who's smart enough to know it's losing because it started the whole mess. He's had to become a dealer with black marketeers and a man who shoots his own countrymen at a moment's notice. Now he's about to become a man without a country. He doesn't blame anybody, sir, not really. He's just too many things at once."

Wrenn was silent a moment. "For the record, Sergeant. I don't know why the Soviet missiles targeted on Kiev weren't shot down. Maybe the warning time wasn't long enough. Most likely the people who saw it didn't believe what was happening until it was too late to do anything about it. And as for the efficiency of the Star Shield—well, we had over a hundred stations in orbit and twice that on the ground. If they had all survived the initial surprise attacks, there might have been no war at all. But quite a few Soviet missiles got through to our allies and our own homeland as well. Enough to make a great many widows. And widowers."

Zorin listened closely at Wrenn's tone, bitter, cold.

"Shall I tell you the rest of the Legend of Kiev, sir? I'd like to, because the rest is really my favorite part."

"What do you mean?"

"The rest of the 'Legend of Kiev' says that even though the strike proved the KGB now in charge of Russia still had nuclear weapons, the Alliance refused to use their own such weapons against us, either in retaliation or even tactically. If that is true, especially in light of what you have just said, your people showed admirable restraint." Zorin watched Wrenn for a long time before he spoke again. "So. It is true. You did *not* strike back. You are a strange people, you Americans. You will fight back if attacked, you will kill, but only to survive. You will battle savagely to redress a wrong, but never to exact revenge."

216

"Perhaps it's because we are a young people, Sergeant. America is barely two hundred years old. Children ourselves, we know that bad children require chastisement, not execution."

Zorin nodded. "And all mankind are yet children."

At Wrenn's suggestion, guards had been posted to prevent anyone from leaving the camp during the night and possibly informing any nearby KGB units of their situation. Colonel Podgorny was relieved when morning roll call showed all his troops present or accounted for.

But Wrenn could not be so easily pleased. Having all the men in agreement on the defection would be of great help, but the real problem was still how to get them all out of Russia to the Alliance territories in the West. If the Alliance even existed any longer.

Rostov was escorting him from the morning meal. Along the way they passed a gang of troopers clustered around a truck, some under the hood, some on the ground beneath the body, and a few onlookers making encouraging noises.

"What's the problem?" Rostov asked one of the idlers.

"Transmission's gone, sir. Myakov thinks he can fix it, but, well . . ." The man left little doubt as to his opinion of Myakov's mechanical aptitude by giving a shrug and a doubtful scowl. He threw in a hand waggle for emphasis.

Rostov turned to Wrenn. "Every Russian considers himself a top flight mechanic, you know. They try to prove it at every opportunity." He and Wrenn watched the men for a moment more before he shrugged and added, "Of course, in the Engineers, it happens to be true."

Wrenn smiled. "Of course." We Americans used to think of ourselves that way, he thought. When did we stop?

As they went through the camp, they took stock of the operational vehicles, counting seventeen altogether. The mix included personnel carriers, reconnaissance vehicles the size of American Hummers, fuel trucks, cargo carriers, an APC, and a light tank. Twenty more vehicles were judged beyond repair, even with cannibalizing parts from one another. Six of those were fuel trucks.

217

"How many left in the unit, Lieutenant?"

"One hundred fifty-three, sir. No wounded, nobody seriously ill." Rostov thought a moment and brightened a little. "We've more than enough vehicles to carry everyone; we can probably even carry most of the fuel we have in drums, drain the fuel trucks . . ." His voice died. They both saw the problem.

"A fuel drum takes up as much space and weighs much more than a man," Wrenn said. "There's no way to carry enough to get all the vehicles, with all the men, as far as we need to go. We'd better talk to Colonel Podgorny."

Podgorny reacted to the news with stolid Russian equanimity. "We have to leave. We will find some way. Lieutenant Rostov, what was the situation in Moscow when you last met with Zimyanski?"

"Not good, sir. The KGB had taken over the city; they were stockpiling caches of materiel—anything they could lay their hands on, but mostly food, clothing, and ammunition. This has caused a lot of looting, much of it very well organized. There'd been a firefight with bandits the night before we got there. Another Nationalist group, probably Islamics. And Zimyanski mentioned raids by Ukrainians. It's getting crazy, Comrade Colonel." Rostov had unconsciously lowered his voice. "Really bad."

Podgorny frowned, thinking. "What about the KGB? Don't they control the city anymore?" Inwardly, he thought, they can't even manage so much as that?

Rostov almost laughed out loud. "They barely control Red Square, Colonel. They have conscripts rummaging in the ruins of the Kremlin night and day. Everything they can lay their hands on gets spirited out of the city. The caches I saw, other supplies, records, whatever is left of technical value, even intact granite blocks from Lenin's Tomb. Moscow is an empty larder, Comrade Colonel."

Wrenn hoped he didn't look as discouraged as he felt. He joined Podgorny at the maps on the colonel's table, where he found their own position relative to the KGB-controlled forces still active in the area. They were deep within territory controlled by the remnants of the Soviet

Army, now under command of the KGB; surrounded, as it were, by the "enemy."

"What are the chances of us bluffing our way through some of these lines, Colonel?" Wrenn asked.

"Very bad. Owing to the nature of our unit, we are very closely watched by the KGB commanders. Sealed caches of fuel are hidden in buried pits all over Russia, but we do not know where they are. The KGB knows, but they do not have the formula nor the expertise for manufacture of the immunizer against *A-Devyatnatsat*. Army intelligence kept it from them very successfully, so as not to lose its autonomy when the Party structure collapsed. Even the KGB's subsequent liquidation of the Intelligence sector did not succeed in obtaining the secret. So they need us, to make their fuel safe from the "Gas Bug," and we need them for what meager supplies of food and ammunition they dole out to us." He shrugged, thought a moment, then looked squarely at Wrenn.

"Captain Wrenn. If the KGB should maintain its control, perhaps extend it; perhaps even regain command of the bulk of the remnants of the Soviet Union, reinstate the Party . . . what, in your opinion, would then happen?"

Wrenn was surprised by the question, but when he finally answered, it was with the quiet conviction of a man stating a natural law. "The Alliance would be back in Russia within the decade. Perhaps within the year. The obliteration carried out by the U.S.S.R. was unmatched in human history. No nation on earth could forget it and call itself civilized. The next time, with no petroleum fuels, the Alliance would use steam engines. They'd walk if they had to—hell, they'd *swim*. Likely, they'd even lift the ban against China joining the Alliance." Podgorny's eyes flashed his anger, but he held his tongue. Vast tracts of land had already been lost to the Chin, whose largely nonmechanized forces had suffered little from the Gas Bug. Only the threat of Alliance nuclear intervention had kept the Chin from annexing all of Siberia.

Wrenn looked at Podgorny and Rostov. He didn't know if they had ever heard the truth about the Alliance or not, but they were going to hear it at least this once. "The Alliance's publicly professed purpose was the elimination of Soviet Communism. In the last century, Nazism had shown itself to be unacceptable in a civilized world. In this, your Party was no different."

"Ironic to think that your country and mine hunted down the last vestiges of Nazism together, is it not?" Podgorny asked quietly.

Wrenn could only nod. When he spoke, his voice was sad, tired. Old. "All history is irony, Colonel."

After a time, Wrenn stood up from poring over maps and paced the length of the room. He turned, spoke his thoughts aloud. "But, ideologies notwithstanding, our first concern now is survival. To survive, we have to get you and your men out of Russia. And I just don't know how we can get a hundred and fifty men and all their equipment almost a thousand miles through hostile territory to Alliance lines in the West."

Throughout, Rostov had listened quietly. Now his head went up, his eyes bright. Something the American had said earlier; something about steam.

"I know how."

Podgorny and Wrenn turned as Rostov went to the map table, got his bearings, and pointed to a light blue area east of Moscow, hugging the contours of the city limits like an encroaching lake.

"Here is what we need," Rostov said quietly. He was already calculating travel times from their current position to the goal he indicated. It was less than half a day's drive, the unit could make it easily, but once there . . . it was bound to be heavily guarded.

"What is it?" The American pressed, impatient with the young Russian's silence as he leaned over the map.

Rostov, concentrating, hardly turned. "This is the marshaling yard of the MBBR, part of the Kalinin and Byelorussian Divisions."

Wrenn was puzzled. "Divisions? You mean military units?"

Podgorny had brightened at Rostov's mention of the MBBR, and now he grinned widely. "No, Captain Wrenn. The MBBR is the Moscow–Byelorussian–Baltic

Railway." He slapped a bearlike hand against Rostov's back, staggering the younger man, who grinned at the recognition.

"Comrade Lieutenant Rostov is suggesting we steal a train!"

Eyes of jet black glittered beneath heavy lids as the checkpoint guard went over their papers again. The guard was Private Kurga, KGB; a Mongol from one of the Siberian divisions, the blood of conquerors in his features. And he knew it.

Kurga had little love for these Caucasus types. Their American prisoner was an oddity, but Kurga had seen Americans before. He respected them; on the whole, they were good fighters. His hatred for them was based not on their invasion of Russia, only their failure to win. Kurga's people had always despised weakness. The Americans' refusal to use their nuclear superiority to obliterate the hated *Sovs* was beyond Kurga's capacity to understand. He finally looked back up at the teknik lieutenant and his ugly sergeant. "I will notify Colonel Serafimov. You will wait."

Kurga lifted the field telephone while his own assistant watched the American. Zorin and Rostov waited, looking bored.

Kurga pounded on the telephone. He grunted a few commands to his aide. The man rose and left. Kurga turned back to Rostov. "The phone is out. But the colonel should be overseeing the loading of the train. My man will notify him of you and your prisoner."

Rostov nodded his head at Zorin, who went to accompany the guard. As the door closed behind them, Kurga turned to examine the bound American. Not much to look at, but who was, these days? Shirtless in the cold autumn morning, the thin man shivered slightly, skin tight as a drum over wiry muscles. Kurga guessed he'd be good in a fight; fast and mean. But weak, he decided with some regret, as all his people were weak.

Kurga turned upon hearing a sound from outside like a sack of grain being dropped. He moved past the American and opened the door. Zorin was standing over the body of Kurga's assistant, sheathing a bloody knife in his own boot. It was the last thing Kurga saw before Rostov's rifle butt crushed his skull.

Wrenn caught Kurga's body and lowered it to the floor. Zorin dragged the other guard in and closed the door as Rostov cut the American's bonds.

"I am very glad you suggested cutting those cables you saw, Captain Wrenn," Zorin muttered as he bent to help the American remove Kurga's uniform.

Wrenn nodded. "Now if only we can find the papers we need in this office." He looked up at Rostov, standing at the window. "Can you see the train, Lieutenant?"

Rostov shook his head. "Too much smoke and fog. I see some trucks. Most of the smoke seems to be from camp fires, but the fog isn't helping any." The haze cleared for a moment, and through a gap in the buildings Rostov made out the slab sides and big iron wheels of a locomotive. Then the fog closed again.

"*Da*! Very close."

Wrenn, who had been searching the dispatcher's desk, came up with a fistful of papers that looked official.

"Here are some dispatches, a large folder of invoices; some receipts, some vouchers. A few are pretty recent." He began reading them carefully. "From the looks of it, the rail net around Moscow to the west is virtually nonexistent." He ran his finger down a list of train schedules and destinations, points of departure and routings. Maps would be worse than useless for finding an escape route; the front was too fluid, the Alliance attacks on the rail net and the scorched-earth policy of the Russian defenders too efficient. The only reliable information would be gathered from accounts of routes actually traveled, which could reasonably be expected to still exist.

"Here," Wrenn finally said. "This looks good. Several trains have been operating out toward Bryansk and Orel through secure areas, running ammunition and supplies as well as evacuating Soviet forces eastward via Tula and Kaluga . . ." Wrenn's voice trailed off as he concentrated on deducing the paths the trains must have taken to circumvent the shattered Moscow rail net.

"Yes. From Tula and Kaluga they brought back several

units of the Soviet Fifty-third Motorized Infantry Division." He looked up at Rostov. "That division was engaged with Anglo-Brasilian forces in the battle for the Kiev Zone less than a month ago, and this says they made the entire return trip by rail."

"Then the lines into Kiev are still intact," Rostov said quietly. He didn't add that Kiev was no longer in Soviet hands.

"According to what I can make of this," Wrenn went on, "it will mean a detour of two hundred miles east-southeast first, then a trip back over to Bryansk before going straight on, hell-bent-for-leather toward the Alliance lines. But we could make it. All your men, your stocks of immunizer and usable fuel, even your vehicles." He paused, then added: "Assuming we can capture the train crew alive. We'll need men familiar with the equipment if we're to have a prayer of nursing a locomotive that far without stopping to refuel or finding places along the way where we can get water for the boiler."

Rostov nodded. "And sand for the tracks and a hundred other things. We make lots of assumptions from this moment, but we have only one certainty: If we stay in Russia, we can lie down next to this Private Kurga and his man right now." He looked at Zorin and nodded. The sergeant pulled out a small radio and began speaking rapidly into the microphone, alerting the rest of the unit to move in. When Zorin had finished, he handed the guard's uniform to Wrenn. The stocky Russian grinned apologetically.

"Sorry, Comrade Captain. These tartars are a stubby lot, and you *Amerikanski* seem to stack it pretty tall."

Wrenn grinned back. The pants cuffs would barely reach his ankles and the jacket sleeves rode up his forearms. "I'll make do."

Colonel Maksim Fyodor Serafimov, KGB, dropped his clipboard and rubbed his bleary eyes. Almost done, he thought. The clipboard held the manifest for the last shipment of supplies to be loaded on this last train. Serafimov cursed. The other trains had been easy; personnel, *objets d'art*, technical equipment, record books, computers and gold, gold, gold. Things needed to rebuild

223

the country, or the Party, which was the same thing. Nothing anyone could possibly make use of for personal survival.

But these last few shipments had been nightmares. Party Central had plenty of supplies and weapons but still wanted more, and the level of black-market pilferage alone, just among Serafimov's own men and the damned army boys, had been staggering. But once the insurgents had gotten wind of such a stockpile . . .

The first train out had been blasted right off the tracks. The crew and troops had been caught utterly unprepared, and the railyards had become an abattoir. Serafimov smiled. The next time, he had been ready with a well-planned ambush, and the slaughter of the raiders had been total. Serafimov had discovered their contact in the railyards and turned him to his own purposes. Serafimov looked down, contemplated his new boots. The little fellow had turned out to be useful in more ways than one, he considered. And now, finally, things were quiet again. No more bandits, at least.

Colonel Serafimov grunted in consternation, however. Where had the bandits come from in the first place? Had things deteriorated that far, already?

He sighed, deeply. Yes, he decided. Moscow was a husk. Little remained to indicate the city had once been the center of the greatest empire the world had ever known. The Party was a gaggle of terrified old men hiding in caves, guarded by fanatics like himself, supported by fanatics like himself. The Kremlin, Saint Basil's, Lenin's Tomb, all the landmarks of Serafimov's youth were rubble. And with the departure of this last train, only ghosts would remain to walk the streets of Moscow.

Serafimov recalled a passage from Lenin, from his journals of the Revolution: "When the trains stop, that will be the end."

"Colonel?" Serafimov jerked upright. He had gone two days with almost no sleep, and his nerves were brittle as ice. He looked up to see his aide in the doorway.

"Yes, Sergeant Sokoloff?"

"The train crewmen say they are having some trouble getting a head of steam up" Sokoloff had grown up innocent of what steam engines were. Diesel and electric locomotives were all he had ever seen, those and a few of the *Magnetikas*, pride of the TransEuropean Mosrail System, riding on force fields at incredible speeds.

With the war, the U.S.S.R. had pressed back into service everything she could lay her hands on, and the old leviathans of steam had returned. Along with their incredibly arrogant operators. Dinosaurs, Serafimov thought with contempt of the hulking steel brutes. Great big ones with little lizards to run them.

"All right, Sergeant. We'll deal with that in a moment. Any raids this morning?"

"None, sir. It's been very quiet since we . . ." Sokoloff's voice trailed off, and Serafimov nodded, knowing the younger man's thoughts.

Since the hangings, Serafimov thought; you would like a brief respite from pilferage and raiding? Here's my recipe; works every time: String up some seventy-odd men on insulated power lines along your perimeter. Tie their hands to said cable, just close enough together to let them support their own weight, but too far apart to free themselves, then lash their necks securely to the cables with thin wire: radio cable is good. The socially irresponsible fellows last for as long as they can do chin-ups.

Serafimov turned his pencil end-over-end, tapping it against the desk top. Three hours of chin-ups was the record, he recalled, and that man had been very strong, and very small. Serafimov shook his head. And all for a case or two of Polish hams from the Party stocks. He sighed, finally looked up at Sokoloff. "Hard times, Sergeant, yes?"

Sokoloff nodded. "Yes, sir."

"Well. Anything else?"

"Yes, sir. A detachment of *tekniks* just arrived, started loading their vehicles and several drums of fuel immunizer on the flatbeds near the rear of the train. Their papers were all in order, so Lieutenant Drusiev passed them along."

Serafimov frowned. *Tekniks*? With Gas Bug immunizers? He should have received notification for any cargo so critical. Still, few people beneath Serafimov's rank knew

225

how fast things were collapsing; so an unnotified shifting of a few army types was only surprising, not suspicious. He stood, stretched, picked up the manifest clipboard, and headed for the door.

"Come along then, Sergeant. Let's see these *tekniks*. Then we'll see if we can't give our reluctant trainmen some incentive toward proper socialist zeal for the task at hand."

The morning fog lifted while Podgorny's men hurriedly finished securing their vehicles aboard the flatbeds. Podgorny himself, accompanied by Rostov and Zorin, had walked to the train's head both to get a look at the locomotive and ascertain the number of guards. The entire machine was lousy, as Zorin put it, with KGB. Wrenn made himself scarce.

The three Russian officers sidestepped a small lorry of crates and went behind a building. When they came around a corner, they got their first look at the engine.

"Oh" was all Podgorny said. Zorin muttered, "Christus," with very little emotion.

The engine was enormous, a leviathan of steel, hulking over the tracks like a basking brontosaur dozing after a dewy morning's feeding.

Or a dragon, Rostov thought. Dragons were not exactly state-sanctioned images in Soviet literature, but Rostov had had as much exposure to *samizdat* novels as anyone else in Russia. However he chose to look at it, black slab-sided, double-decked, implacably hissing, wreathing itself in steam, it remained the biggest thing Rostov had ever seen that wasn't supposed to fly or float.

"I know this type," Zorin blurted. "It's the P-38; the largest steam engine ever built in Russia. Maybe the world. And the last. Didn't do too well on the heavy-load lines up north or into Siberia; too cold for it. They weren't in service very long before they pulled them off the lines."

"Diesel fired?"

"Yes, Comrade Colonel." Zorin was still staring. He felt like he was looking at a 215-ton ghost.

Podgorny nodded. "Good. They should be happy to see us and our fuel and immunizer, then. And the happier they are, perhaps the fewer questions they will ask."

Rostov had looked down the length, counting as best as he could. "Looks like it only has about fifty cars. That should let her run lighter, faster. Let's talk to these trainmen."

Zorin broke from his trance and tapped Rostov's arm. "Trouble, maybe, Lieutenant."

They turned to see a KGB colonel approaching. Serafimov stepped up to the three Combat Engineers, saluted Podgorny. Podgorny returned the salute smartly, began to report.

"Colonel Podgorny, Fifth Guards Armored Engineers, Comrade. We have quantities of the fuel immunizer as well as protected petrol and diesel for immediate evacuation from the Moscow District, via the Bryansk salient."

"Colonel Serafimov. KGB. Welcome, Comrade. I confess I find it odd that I received no advance notice of your coming. The immunizer is too valuable a commodity to risk missing the last train out of Moscow."

"Regrettably, Comrade Colonel, we were delayed by raiding parties. The invaders had been attacking our area with strong infantry forces, and a General Morevno ordered us out of the area at all speed." Morevno was the KGB officer commanding the armored column that had overrun Wrenn's position.

The KGB colonel only pursed his lips and nodded.

"All right, Comrade," Serafimov finally said. "Get your men up onto the flatbeds and into the boxcars. Get everything tied down. We should be leaving within the hour." Serafimov turned and left with a perfunctory salute.

"Too easy," Rostov said quietly. Something must be horribly wrong. *Relax*, he commanded himself. In one hour, the train would be leaving Moscow. An hour after that, he and his men would have to be in control. But sure enough, like Dostoevski's Grand Inquisitor, the KGB man turned with an innocent look of afterthought on his face.

"Oh, by the way, Comrade Colonel; I don't suppose that any of your men would be familiar with steam engines, eh?"

227

Podgorny looked blank, caught unawares. Rostov frowned. The men were routinely trained in all forms of power plant technology. They might be a little rusty on steam, but any one of them could make himself useful.

"Problems with the locomotive, Comrade Colonel?" Podgorny asked.

The KGB man shrugged. "Civilian trainmen. Conscripts. They claim there's some difficulty in building up pressure."

"I know something about boilers, sir," Zorin said innocently. Indeed he did, Podgorny remembered; better still, Zorin was a deadly in-fighter. If the trainmen in the cab were under guard, Zorin was the man to put in there among them.

Podgorny nodded. "Take Sergeant Zorin, Colonel. He might be of use."

"Very good, Comrade." Serafimov was beaming. "Thank you very much." He was feeling expansive, and told Podgorny to be sure his men got some food before the field-kitchen was dismantled. Serafimov left almost whistling. He was already bringing Party Central a huge cache of ammunition and supplies, and now almost a company's worth of valuable Engineers and their preciously guarded immunizer. *Tekniks*, alive and well! Serafimov could almost taste his promotion. Of course, he thought, the officers would have to go, but that was a minor problem.

Zorin followed Serafimov up into the locomotive's engine cab. The size of the engine was almost overwhelming. Three men in trainmen's coveralls were grouped on one of the outside walkways that ran the entire length of the engine, handing one another tools and working at a cluster of pipes and valves. Zorin thought they looked like ants on a summer squash. Two more trainmen were in the cab itself. Standing over them was a lanky trooper in KGB uniform, his rifle casually pointed at the two civilians. Zorin's breath caught as the man turned at Serafimov's address.

"Corporal Katchin; what is the status of the engine?" Zimyanski's former aide shrugged, hardly noticing

Zorin. "They are claiming they don't know the problem, Colonel." The men on the floor laughed.

One of the trainmen, a young man with steel-rimmed spectacles, spoke idly as he adjusted a brass fitting. "We know the problem, Colonel. We're losing pressure somewhere in this line. What we don't know is the solution."

Katchin abruptly planted a foot on the young man's shoulder and pushed him firmly down on the deck grate, pointing the rifle at his throat.

Serafimov leaned forward and spoke: "I wish to be out of this trainyard in one hour," he said in a reasonable voice. "From this point on, one of you will be shot for every fifteen minutes in which power is not up for our departure. In the future," Serafimov said, addressing the older trainman, "be aware that I am not renowned for my sense of humor."

Zorin almost groaned. This monster of a locomotive was almost a hundred years old. It would need every man of its crew, and would probably be shorthanded at that, and this KGB fool wanted to play the Commissar Game. Serafimov had Katchin release the man and ordered him back to work.

"Sergeant Zorin, this is Corporal Katchin; anything you need, let him know. I would appreciate your telling him if it appears these *zeks* are slacking in their work, as well." Serafimov saluted and left.

Zorin took a deep breath and turned to face Katchin. It was possible that the KGB corporal did not recognize Zorin; they had rarely met face-to-face, and then only at night. Zorin saw no recognition in the man's eyes and gave an inward shrug. *Don't look a gift of a horse too closely in the mouth,* he thought, and bent to inspect the trainmen's work.

"What's your name, Comrade?" he asked the older man when Katchin stepped out onto the catwalk to smoke.

Watery blue eyes in a soot-grimed face took Zorin's measure, seemed not to find him wanting, and glimmered into a smile. "Gyrich," the man said as he turned from his work.

Ukrainian, Zorin thought. He took a closer look at the

229

younger man who had wisecracked to Serafimov. Behind his glasses, the fellow was fair-skinned; high cheekbones, sturdy build. An old and massive burn scar could be seen through the collar of his shirt, spreading to cover most of his chest and shoulders. Zorin watched him carefully before saying, "And you?"

"Eh?" the young man turned, distracted. He was sweating heavily, and Zorin guessed it wasn't just from the heat of the pipes over which he toiled.

"Your name?"

"Pilkanis." The answer seemed like a weary admission of guilt.

Zorin was stunned. A Lithuanian! These men weren't just conscripts. Small wonder the KGB regarded them as expendable. *They must all be captured partisans, counter-revolutionaries from the Nationalist Insurgents that had sprung up in the last years of the war.* Despite government claims to the contrary, Zorin had never heard of proven atrocities committed by these bandits against legitimate army troops. KGB, however, they killed outright.

Sergeant Zorin went to the door and looked for Katchin. The tall, thin figure could be seen leaning against the outside of the boiler. Zorin turned back to the trainmen.

"Listen: Forget what that KGB turd said; no one's getting shot. We need you, all of you, and alive. We're Combat Engineers, not KGB, and we're taking this train. We're getting out of Moscow and heading West. You and the other trainmen with you have a choice: Work with us and maybe live. Work for the KGB and surely die. What's it to be, eh?"

The two trainmen stared at Zorin for a moment, then looked at each other. Before they could answer, they heard Katchin's footsteps on the walkway outside, returning. Zorin made a gesture for them to keep silent, and the three of them bent back to the valves they had been working on.

Wrenn secured one of the Engineers' light trucks to the flatbed, then passed Podgorny's signals on to various troops. Blaustein, promoted to a *pro tempore* captain,

230

had gathered the other NCOs for their final briefing. The plan for seizure of the train had been hastily assembled and required rapid execution. Now was the time for Wrenn to do his part.

He made his way to the passenger cars forward, moving with a calmness he hardly felt among the dozens of KGB troops he passed along the way. While the bulk of the KGB troops was still in the barracks, Wrenn was pleased to see that most of their equipment and virtually all of their food was already aboard the train. No one paid Wrenn much attention, and he reached a door that opened into what appeared to be a conference room. The room was empty, but there were maps spread out on a large table, a desk with a plush leather chair was against one of the outside walls, and a samovar sat on a table in the corner, hissing quietly. Wrenn smiled, despite the danger of his own situation; no Russian train went anywhere without its supply of tea.

The car was evidently a holdover from the days when Soviet tourist-bureau officials insisted on trappings to impress Western visitors. Spacious and well appointed, with fittings considered lavish by any standards in the world, it was now obviously reserved for the commander. Wrenn began rifling the desk and got to the third drawer before hearing voices outside.

He looked about quickly; only the lavatory was close enough to hide in. He slipped in and locked the door.

Rostov and Podgorny inspected their troops on the flatbeds and spread throughout the cars. The odds, so far, look good, thought Rostov.

"There are lots of KGB, Colonel," Rostov said. "But the majority have not yet boarded. I estimate we outnumber the troops aboard the train by about three to one."

"The odds will never be better. Get up to the engine and see if Zorin has made contact with the trainmen yet, and how soon we can get moving. Which way did you see that KGB colonel go?"

"He left the engine cab and went to the first car behind the tender. Looks like a passenger car; most likely the commander's coach."

Podgorny nodded. "Let us hope our American friend came to the same conclusion and is hidden safely." Podgorny's brows knitted. "This is a sloppy plan, Rostov."

Rostov shrugged and grinned. "Personally, sir, I think it has a certain crude appeal."

Podgorny grunted, left Blaustein with a few last orders, and walked toward the engine with Rostov. They caught up with Serafimov just as the KGB man was climbing the ladder up into the command coach.

"Comrade Colonel." Podgorny saluted. "I have finished seeing to my men. With your permission I should like to speak with you about our itinerary and ETA at the TransUral Command District."

Serafimov smiled oddly. "Of course, Comrade Colonel. Join me in the command car."

Podgorny turned to Rostov. "See how the sergeant is doing with Colonel Serafimov's trainmen, Lieutenant."

Rostov saluted and left.

Rostov pulled himself up the ladder into the cab and stepped onto the fireman's station. Two trainmen were crouched on the floor with Zorin, banging away at a bank of pipes and dials. Across the way stood a tall, thin guard in KGB uniform, who looked up at Rostov and gaped. The cigarette fell from his lips into a patch of water on the floor, hissing.

"Katchin," Rostov whispered.

Zorin looked up. "Oh, Christus, no."

Katchin brought his rifle up and leveled it at Rostov's chest. For a moment he said nothing, then gestured for Rostov to enter the cab. The lieutenant walked inside slowly, holding his rifle out limply to one side. Katchin seemed to have lost none of his nervousness, Rostov thought.

"What are you doing here?"

"Take it easy, Corporal." Rostov spoke softly, carefully putting down his rifle. "We have orders to leave on this train, that's all. Nobody needs to know about our dealings with you and Zimyanski." Rostov nodded at Katchin's KGB uniform. "Looks like Zimyanski talked you two into soft new careers, eh?"

Katchin's face went cold and hard as he smiled. "Zimyanski talked himself into a noose. As for me, Colonel Serafimov has always found me useful." He jerked the barrel of the rifle upward. "This will make the second time in a week that I'll be contributing to the colonel's good fortune. Outside. You too, Sergeant."

Too late, Rostov realized his error. "Of course. Zimyanski could never signal me that he'd been infiltrated by the KGB. Not if you'd been there from the beginning. And you were always the one he brought to our meetings. His protector. I wonder if poor Zimyanski ever knew."

Katchin almost laughed. "I assure you, he was quite surprised. He expected trouble from me when he told me he'd be leaving me behind." Then Katchin did laugh, and the sound gave Rostov very little hope for his future. "I gave him no trouble at all. But Colonel Serafimov was quite unhappy with the little weasel. I doubt he'll be any more pleased with you."

Rostov shrugged. "Perhaps then we can impress him with the American Intelligence officer you gave us. The colonel may wonder why you waited so long to tell him you and Zimyanski had captured one." Rostov watched the combined fear and rage build on Katchin's face, and knew he had guessed right. "Unless you'd planned to go with Zimyanski; but he crossed you too, didn't he?"

The older man, Gyrich, rose slowly, reading gauges as he did so. "Oh, oh," he said. Katchin stopped.

"Now what?"

Gyrich pointed to a gauge. Katchin sidestepped to see what was wrong. Gyrich threw a lever.

A demon of live steam shrieked through the cab, straight for Katchin's throat. The jet of superheated vapor hit the KGB man's face. Through fleshless lips, Katchin screamed and dropped his rifle, then fell into the arms of the big Lithuanian, Pilkanis. Gyrich closed the valve as the younger man slammed a wrench against Katchin's temple.

Rostov snatched his own rifle back. "Get us power, now. Pull in the rest of your crew and let's get moving. Don't forget we've got almost fifty cars on this thing."

As he and Zorin clattered down the gangway, Rostov

turned back. "And no starting whistle! No warnings, just get rolling!"

Pilkanis and Gyrich nodded grimly and set to work.

It took all their willpower for Rostov and Zorin to walk, instead of running, back toward the command car. They passed under its windows and could hear faint voices: Podgorny and the KGB colonel talking. They went on to the rear of the train, by the links connecting the boxcars to the flatbeds, to find Surgeon Blaustein had all the men in position.

"Charges set?" Rostov asked. Blaustein nodded. "Good. Zorin, your men are ready?"

Zorin shrugged. "Not something we have to do every day, Aleksei, so we'll just have to improvise."

Rostov grinned. "That's the spirit. Spoken like a true Engineer. I would like to say, Sergeant, that once over the border we might try our hands at being good capitalist entrepreneurs, but . . ."

Zorin nodded, smiled. The world they were joking about had ceased to exist, as surely as had their own. What would replace them both one could only guess at.

"Good luck, sir," Zorin said, adding one of his rare, formal salutes.

"And you, Mikhail." Rostov returned the salute smartly, turned, and trotted back toward the front of the train.

It seemed to be taking him longer to get there than it should, when suddenly he realized the damn thing was rolling already.

Rostov grabbed a handrail and swung up onto a boxcar ladder. The train was still moving very slowly, but the KGB troops atop the car roof were scrambling to secure their gear. They looked up with puzzled, hostile glares at Rostov, who shrugged and grinned. The universal communication of citizens of the Soviet: I don't know what the hell's going on either, don't ask me. Following Rostov's instructions, the trainmen had given no warning whistle.

Rostov trotted along the car roofs, jumping easily across the gaps. It was not something he'd enjoy trying at any respectable speed. Buildings and power lines eased slowly by, and as they passed between two signal towers,

Rostov saw a line of human scarecrows hung by the neck from the power cables. He recognized Zimyanski's nearby corpse immediately.

All badges of rank had been left on Zimyanski's uniform, a warning that even high rank could not protect criminals from the justice of the State.

Rostov shook his head and ran on. Zimyanski's legs hung limp, ending in pathetically bare feet, blackened and limp, swinging in a light breeze.

Inside the command car, Podgorny and Serafimov had gone to the map table. Podgorny had idly tried the lavatory door, but found it locked. He hoped it meant what he thought it did.

Serafimov sat down at his desk and picked up a pencil, began tapping it end-over-end against a notebook of railway charts and tables. "Any problems finding space for your men on board, Comrade Colonel?" Serafimov asked quietly. He did not look up from his pencil as he spoke.

"None, Comrade." Podgorny fervently hoped that Rostov was making his way back up here, to say nothing of Wrenn. The takeover would have to start soon, Podgorny decided; this KGB dog was starting to sniff, he could feel it. The rail maps Wrenn had found in the guardhouse and the papers with them showed the junctions outside Moscow they would have to take in order to reach the West. There was only one workable connection, and it was a bare ten miles outside the city.

"Fine," Serafimov said. "Your men seem in good order. It is fortunate we ran into you *tekniks*." The KGB colonel knew the popular term for Combat Engineers was ambiguous. He let the phrase hang in the air, wishing to impress on Podgorny that the status of his men and himself was likewise tentative. Serafimov nodded, pursing his lips.

"We have had much trouble with raiders, Colonel. Bandits, mostly. Unfamiliar with the true military and political situation. Your men and arms will be a welcome addition to our force."

Podgorny nodded, then sensed rather than felt something; the train was moving! He suddenly leaned across

Serafimov's desk. Startled, the KGB man instinctively tilted his chair back, obscuring the motion of the train.

"Colonel . . ." Podgorny said, praying thanks that he had distracted the man.

"Yes, Comrade?" Serafimov had cocked an eyebrow.

Podgorny tried desperately to think of something to say. The best he could come up with, finally, was: "I have a confession to make."

Zorin and half of his men were in position on the rearmost flatcar. The rest of his force were spread throughout the train itself, mixed among the KGB troops. The bulk of the KGB were positioned along the top of the boxcars at each end of the flatbeds, effectively pinning down Zorin's men when the shooting started, as it would any second now.

"Keep those light machine guns down at the sides," he told his men. "When we start rolling, the troops still in the railyard will try to storm the flatcars; it's the easiest way for them to get on."

Zorin turned to take his bearings from a building that was suddenly several meters closer than it had been a moment ago. "Christus." He turned to one of his men. "This is it. Get ready."

Zorin scuttled over crates and vehicles to the rear of the flatcar. Balancing his helmet with one hand, he leaned over the edge and looked underneath at the bottom of the flatcar. A dozen of his men were hidden up among the framework and linkages. He checked the suspension and couplings connecting the rear flatcar to the last three cars. When he was satisfied that everything was in place, he raised his head, his face reddened less from hanging upside down than it was from excitement.

"You were about to say something, Comrade Colonel?" Serafimov prompted. What was wrong with these technical types? They all wound up acting like they spent more time drinking vodka than mixing their mysterious chemicals.

Podgorny's mind lit on the most obvious excuse. "I must confess, I never thought I would leave this cemetery alive." He put on his dim-witted peasant face that he

236

reserved for high-ranking Party civilians. "Perhaps a toast? With your permission, sir?"

Serafimov smiled thinly. Why not? The *teknik* was only leaving one cemetery for the plot of another, after all. Still, it would not hurt to lull his suspicions. "Of course, Comrade Colonel," Serafimov said coolly. "Please help yourself; in that cabinet behind you."

The shades behind Serafimov were open, and Podgorny could see buildings crawling by. The KGB man would notice their movement in seconds. But if he could get close enough to him with a bottle, a corkscrew, anything . . .

Podgorny took vodka and two glasses from the cabinet. Closing the door, he saw Serafimov's reflection in the glass; the KGB colonel had produced a pistol and was pointing it at him.

"Turn around very slowly, Colonel Podgorny, or I will shoot you in the spine. General Morevno was a most unfortunate choice of a lie. We evacuated the survivors of his unit yesterday. The tanks, anyway. Most of the men were killed in a bandit raid. Including Morevno himself.

Podgorny sighed. He turned slowly, hearing faint shouts from outside. "It doesn't really matter now, Colonel Serafimov," Podgorny said. "It sounds like your railroad guards have noticed us leaving without them."

The KGB officer's face went from arrogance to puzzlement, then to shock. It twisted into anger as he at last felt the train pass over a track joint.

Serafimov leaped from his chair, keeping the pistol trained on Podgorny. "Move and you'll be a cripple." He glanced out the window to see groups of his own men running from the buildings in various states of dress, trying to catch the accelerating train. Small arms fire suddenly erupted outside.

Serafimov smiled, shaking his head at Podgorny. "Pathetic. Is this as much ingenuity as you army types are capable of? Small wonder we lost the bloody war." He circled Podgorny, moved to the brake cable on the wall. As on most Russian trains, only such cars as this one were equipped with them. In this case, it was opposite the lavatory door.

237

Serafimov heard a sound behind him: the lavatory door was opening, indicating a threat behind him. *By the book*, he thought. *Deal with the present threat first*. He shot Podgorny without a second's hesitation. The bullet passed through the big Engineer's abdomen and into the liquor cabinet door behind him. Podgorny went back a step, crashing into the shattered wood and broken glass, and fell heavily to the floor.

Serafimov spun to meet whatever threat might be coming from behind him, and instead saw one of his own KGB railyard guards. He hesitated then, until he suddenly realized the man was white; in that uniform, at that rank, he should be an Asiatic. What was—?

Wrenn grasped the KGB man's gun hand, twisting until he felt bones grind and fingers open. The gun dropped, and Wrenn deftly reached to catch it. Serafimov batted the pistol away with his other hand, jabbed a knee up into the American's stomach. Wrenn locked both arms around him, and they slammed into the floor.

Rostov saw a dozen men running from buildings toward the train and thought, *This is it*, for what must have been the hundredth time that day. He hoped the gimmick he and Zorin had thought up would work. The train was picking up speed now, and it was getting harder to stay on his feet atop the boxcar. The command coach was another four jumps ahead, he thought. A bullet sparked off the metal of a signal tower. Rostov returned fire on the KGB troops, dropping two before he ran on.

Zorin's men on the flatbeds had more luck than was usually the soldier's lot. All the KGB troops rushing the flatcars were coming from one side. The Combat Engineers cut them down with machine-gun fire whenever they tried to get close to the train. As far as the KGB already aboard the train were concerned, however, the Engineers' luck ran out. From the surrounding boxcars, the KGB troops' height advantage allowed them to pour a withering fire into the gun positions of the Engineers.

Zorin turned to Blaustein; the surgeon was methodically squeezing off three-round bursts at the tops of the boxcars, trying to keep the enemy troops pinned down. Twenty or thirty other *tekniks* were following his cue. Several of their comrades were already sprawled lifeless on the flatcar decks.

"I'm going now, Comrade Surgeon; can you hold on?"

Blaustein kept his face snug against his rifle, speaking calmly even as he continued to fire. "Yes, Sergeant. You'd better get started. It's not going to get any better. We'll manage."

Zorin scrambled along the little cover he could find to the rear of the flatcar. There he swung himself over the edge into the mass of cables and linkage below. Waiting hands pulled him in out of the line of fire. The twelve other men he had positioned there earlier were waiting for him, ready to go.

"Let's get started," Zorin said. Moving hand over hand along the underside struts, they began working their way forward.

Wren and Serafimov rolled across the floor of the car until the Russian got a grip on Wrenn's beard and slammed the American's head against the wall. Wrenn's grip loosened, and Serafimov broke free.

The KGB colonel lurched to his feet; he was too far from the hand brake, too far from help, and he could feel the train picking up more speed with each passing second. He would have to finish his opponent himself. His gun hand almost numb from his opponent's disarming attack, Serafimov reached across with his good hand and drew a long dagger from his boot.

Wrenn watched the KGB colonel advance, the dagger interposed as he maneuvered Wrenn away from the hand brake. *If he gets to that brake and stops this train*, Wrenn thought, *we are well and truly screwed*. Wrenn thought back to a training session on knife fighting he had received from a Marine, years before. He never thought he'd have to do it.

The American took a deep breath and steeled himself, concentrating on feeling nothing as he threw out his left hand and impaled it on the KGB man's knife.

Wrenn knew he had perhaps a second before the pain hit him. He felt it breaking through his concentration, rushing at him from a long way off like—well, he thought, like a train. The blade went through his palm as he pushed his hand down hard, ending at the hilt, locking his fingers around it and the other man's hand.

Serafimov had been prepared for almost anything else, but this mad action took him completely by surprise. For a moment, he simply stared, then Wrenn pulled hard, Serafimov staggered forward and the American drove his right fist into the KGB man's throat with all the strength he could muster.

Serafimov fell choking to the floor, and Wrenn stumbled back against the wall, drawing the dagger out of his hand with a roar of pain. The agony swept over him in waves. *Can't black out, can't black out . . .*

He pointed the blade toward the KGB colonel. He could hardly concentrate, but he managed to get enough breath to speak. "That's it," Wrenn said in English. Realizing his lapse, he switched back to Russian. "It's over; lie down, flat on the floor."

But at the sound of the enemy tongue, Serafimov's skin stretched taut over his facial bones. The colonel snapped, threw himself across the floor, recovered his dropped pistol, and rose to his feet. Choking and gasping for air, his windpipe crumpled by Wrenn's blow, Serafimov steadied himself against the desk, aiming the pistol at Wrenn's head.

Well, it's been a good life, Wrenn thought. *Some highs, some lows. I guess this counts as one of the lows . . .*

Serafimov fumbled with the trigger, cursed in Russian and pulled back the slide, then re-aimed. From behind him, Podgorny rose up, wraithlike. There was blood on the Engineer's lips, a vodka bottle still gripped firmly in his hand. Podgorny swung the bottle in a huge arc.

The bottle disintegrated against the side of the KGB man's head. Serafimov spun around, clutching his temple.

Wrenn dropped as the shot from the gun went wild. Podgorny threw his arms around Serafimov. Before the American could regain his feet, the big Engineer had staggered back against the window, still holding on to Serafimov. The safety glass panel splintered but held.

240

"Podgorny, no!" Wrenn shouted, realizing too late what the Engineer was doing. He stood, tried to cross the room in time, but was too late.

Podgorny dashed himself against the glass again. The window shattered, and both men tumbled over the sill. Wrenn got to the window at last. Two figures rolled down the cinder-blackened incline of the railbed, and in an instant were lost from sight behind the last buildings of the rail yard.

The door banged open. Wrenn spun about, the dagger still in his hand, to see Rostov raising his rifle.

The lieutenant recognized him just in time. Wrenn could barely stay conscious over the pain in his hand. He slumped to the floor as Rostov reached him. "For a moment," the American murmured, "I thought the good Lord was going to be anonymous again."

Rostov looked around. "Where's Colonel Podgorny?"

Wrenn nodded toward the window. "I'm sorry, Rostov."

"The KGB man," Rostov said simply, then looked down at the hand Wrenn was clutching. The American's lap was soaked with blood. Rostov reached down and examined the wound, and Wrenn nearly passed out. Rostov grimaced, seeing the American's hand was nearly cut in half.

"Let's get something on that."

Wrenn was incredulous. "Oh, good fucking idea!" he snapped.

Rostov grinned. "Good. You're angry enough to live through it. Comrade Blaustein has shown me how to fix worse than that. And we don't want anything to happen to you, after all."

Outside a grenade went off.

Zorin and his men had crawled along the bottoms of the flatcars until they reached the boxcars forward. Zorin himself stood up on the couplings and helped the rest of the men up and onto the ladder to the boxcar roof. The KGB troops were dropping grenades on the flatbeds; this business would have to be finished quickly.

Reaching the roof of the boxcar, the first Engineer saw

half a dozen KGB at the far end, firing automatic rifles down into the men on the flatcar below. Zorin's man opened fire, killing them all.

"Good. This end secured." Zorin got the rest of his men on the boxcar roof. "Now move quickly to the passenger cars. Let's clear this train out."

Zorin ran back to give the all-clear to his men on the flatcars. They were still taking small-arms fire from the KGB troops on the rear boxcars. Those KGB had even received reinforcements from rail-yard troops who had managed to grab hold of the rear car and haul themselves aboard. Zorin leaned over, calling to his men below.

"Zorin!" Blaustein was waving to him exultantly.

"The front's clear," Zorin shouted back. "Go ahead, blow it!"

Blaustein made a gesture to the man next to him. Protected from fire throughout the battle, this soldier had the most important job of all. He made a twisting motion with a device held close to his chest.

Charges went off on the couplings connecting the flatcars and the rear boxcars. The KGB troops suddenly realized what was happening and began trying to leap across the space to the flatcar. A few even threw down their weapons as they jumped, perhaps hoping to be taken captive rather than be left behind in the ruins of Moscow.

The Engineers shot four, and two more failed to make the distance necessary to clear the widening gap. They disappeared under the now slowly rolling boxcars.

Zorin's men sent up a cheer, then surged over the crates and tied-down vehicles, following the sergeant, who went to clear the train of the last enemy troops.

Rostov had found a first-aid kit in the desk. He had poured a clear disinfectant on the American's ruined hand. Whatever it was, it must have hurt, because the fellow went even whiter and passed out. *Just as well*, Rostov thought as he threaded a needle from the same kit. *I doubt you want to be awake for this.* But he was wrong, for at that moment Wrenn's eyes opened and he looked weakly around. He saw what Rostov was about to do and shook his head.

"I survive a KGB butcher only to have a demolitions expert try to put my hand back together. Terrific. Why don't we wait for Blaustein to do this?"

Rostov shrugged. "Blaustein may be dead. We're moving too fast for anyone from the train yard to catch us on foot, and if Zorin gets the couplings blown, they won't be able to chase us with any rail carts. But in the meantime, do I try to save your hand or not?"

Wrenn wanted to pass out, but he wasn't sure he'd wake up. So he only turned away as Rostov attempted to suture the parted halves of his hand together. Rostov saw no loose tendons; the knife had been very sharp, and for the most part had gone between the bones.

But the young Russian was no surgeon, and by the time he was finished there was as much blood on his uniform as on Wrenn's. Still, the American's hand was back together, after a fashion, and tightly bound.

Rostov had heard an explosion that he took to be the coupling charges. He began looking about the room for some sort of blankets to put over the wounded American. The cold morning was not getting any warmer, and the man might go into shock. There was nothing.

Wrenn watched Rostov, guessing at his purpose. "We can worry about me later. Right now there are a few trainmen wondering about the outcome of this little escapade; I think we'd better get forward and let them know about the turnoff we've got to take."

Rostov nodded. "Yes. Quite right. It will be warmer in the engine cab, too. Can you make it up the ladder?"

Wrenn nodded. Rostov supported him to the ladder outside, helped Wrenn pull himself up one-handed, then followed.

The Russian almost slipped halfway up; Wrenn gave him his good hand and somehow pulled Rostov up onto the roof of the tender. The wind of their passage made the cold morning air bite into exposed skin. A few first flakes of a light snow were floating by. Rostov looked around in silence. From the roof of the tender car, the view of the rail yards and the land surrounding them was unobstructed.

Stretching in all directions into the faraway morning haze, the ruins of Moscow lay spread out around them like a vast gray wound. Shattered buildings and acre upon acre of crumbled masonry and concrete covered the landscape. Where fires yet smoldered, thin strands of black smoke drifted upward, like columns supporting the lowering clouds above. The unbroken vista of destruction lay all around them like an abandoned graveyard. Little moved in the ruins, and still less lived.

For a moment, Rostov wondered how a mighty city could be so laid waste. But what the Alliance had left standing, his own Engineering comrades had leveled in the Scorched Earth policy ordered by the Party. He kept watching as the snowfall thickened. Already the twisted, ravaged surfaces of the ruined city were softening under the cold, cold blanket of winter's first snow. The city was a corpse, and here was its shroud.

Rostov turned and looked at Wrenn. The American was watching him, and for a few moments the two men stared at each other over the naked roof of the tender, five feet and a million miles apart from one another.

"In my wife's religion," Rostov finally said, "white was the color of mourning. That makes sense to me, for Russia has so much white to cover her every year. This year, it would seem she needs it more than most."

"Snow melts, Rostov. White isn't the only color men have to live with. And mourning isn't the only thing left for you."

Rostov shrugged. He suddenly realized that he didn't feel the cold anymore. "I wonder," he finally said, regaining the American's gaze.

"What?" Wrenn stared back.

"Does Washington look like this? New York? Los Angeles?"

Wrenn frowned, taken aback. He had expected at least a verbal attack from Rostov. Instead, there was a grief in the young Russian's voice so deep it was almost tangible. "I don't know, Aleksei. I imagine they do."

Rostov shook his head, tears in his eyes. "I hope not. I really do."

Wrenn tried to stand, almost falling down again from the pitching motion of the train and his own loss of blood. Rostov crossed the distance between them and

244

put out his hand, catching Wrenn's good arm, steadying him.

"Come on, Rostov," said the American. "Let's go on. I need to rest."

The Russian put an arm under Wrenn's shoulder, supporting him. "Yes," he finally said after a moment. "Both very good ideas. Let us do that."

Rostov looked off toward where the sky was lightening as the morning sun began burning away the clouds. The snow was still falling, but it was only a light autumn dusting. He had seen enough such storms to know that no matter how deep, they never buried the land forever.

Russia, the Motherland, the *Rodina*, never died in the winter. She only slept, Rostov thought. This was the first storm of the winter, perhaps, but the land would survive it. Yes, he had seen enough to know.

And the land had seen many more storms than he.

The two men helped each other across the roof of the train, and down into the warmth of the locomotive.

PSI-REC: I GLADIATOR
Peter Dillingham

EDITOR'S INTRODUCTION

Over the course of this series Peter Dillingham has been building an image of a future we aren't likely to like much; but he builds it with imagery that you won't soon forget. I'm proud to present another portion of the Psi-Rec saga.

> only seemingly
> is the voice of Marsyas
> monotonous
> and composed of a single vowel
> A a a
>
> "Apollo and Marsyas"
> by Zbigniew Herbert

I crouch here

       alone

in the dust and stillness of this empty arena, in the searing glare of a bloated, hemorrhaging sun, angry, anthropophagous god, in a city that waits to die, world that waits to die, acquiescent, lulled by the constant hum of air conditioners.

Naked, I wait,

await you,

anonymous adversary, anathemata, before their all-seeing video monitors, teeth bared, filed sharp, fangs to pierce and tear, homage to ancient ancestors, those imperial predators, or perversely, Dracula; hands, poor mangled artifacts of lost glory, ascension, the cool white hand of David resting at his side, now armored with calluses, grimly poised to chop and jab.

You enter,

angel,

so lately fallen; a chronicle of linkages, synaptic, a simple psychosurgical procedure, neuron to neuron, rage, savage, homicidal rage begetting quintessential pleasure.

For a while,

Azrael,

they let you wreak havoc among the swarms of rats, packs of snarling, rabid dogs that roam the city; televised orgies of slaughter, massacres, atrocities on deserted streets, your body counts applauded, until, crazed, your hands, lips smeared with offal, insatiable in your lust, you turned your gaze on larger prey, stormed the locked doors of our audience.

Where else,

addict,

did you think they'd send you, but to this amphitheater, this arena?

So rage, now rage,

Absalom, my Absalom!

Your rage acclaims them, affirms them. Your rage abets
me, absolves me! Rage, now rage. Rage, rage against the
dying of the day.

SPECIALIZATION IN WAR
Reginald Bretnor

EDITOR'S INTRODUCTION

Reginald Bretnor's *Decisive Warfare* was published in the same year as *The Strategy of Technology*; volume VI of this series presented his essay updating that work. Bretnor, historian, author, former horse cavalryman in the U.S. Army, is always worth listening to. Here he continues his analysis of the principles of modern war with an examination of simplicity vs. specialization.

MILITARY SPECIALIZATION—OF WEAPONS AND OF MEN EXPERT in their use—is as old as warfare. It has won battles, campaigns and wars—but it has also lost them, for specialization means additional complexity, of production, training, coordination, and supply—and complexity violates one of the accepted basic principles of war: *simplicity*.

Therefore, ideally, the perfect military force would be homogeneous, structurally simple, and capable *as a single unit or in any of its fractions* of realizing its full potential at any place in a minimum of time, meanwhile maintaining a minimum vulnerability.

One army in all history came closest to attaining this

ideal: the army of the Mongols. It conquered the greater part of the then-known world, and its successes were finally ended, not by the generalship or valor of its opponents, but by divisive factors in its leadership. The empire of Genghis Khan was split up, first among his sons, and subsequently by subtle foreign influences: the Chinese in the East, the Moslems in the West.

The Mongol army was all cavalry, and every Mongol was born and raised in it. He learned to ride the shaggy, tireless Mongol horse before he learned to walk. He grew up proficient in the use of the bow mounted, and of the sword, his principal weapons. Neither he nor his mount was dependent on the ponderous supply-trains to which all other medieval armies were shackled. The horse, when necessary, could forage through the snow for grazing; the man, when necessary, would open one of its veins and drink the blood. *As an army*, the Mongols were known to move as far as seventy-five to a hundred miles in a day—a rate no modern army can attain *as an army*. Their organization was simplicity itself: tens, hundreds, thousands. Their discipline was perfect. So accomplished were they in their way of war that they could without hesitation delegate full authority to subordinate commanders.

Nor were their armies vast, overwhelming "hordes" in the modern sense of the word. The Mongol horde, or *ordo*, was relatively small compared to many other Asiatic armies; the word *ordo* simply meant "a camp or perhaps general headquarters."[1]

These were the people who, in China under Genghis, "rode eight hundred miles, stormed twenty-eight important cities and were repulsed from four others, in approximately one hundred and twenty days"[2]—starting in midwinter. They were the people who conquered Russia in a winter campaign. They were the people who, riding as individuals, changing horses at the beautifully organized network of post-stations spanning their empire, and sleeping in the saddle, could and did cover three hundred and more miles per day.

Yet even they learned to specialize when specialization was necessary. Their open tribal warfare on the plains of

Mongolia taught them nothing about siege tactics and siege engines. Yet all they had to do to learn was to encounter the fortified cities of the Chinese. They learned from the Chinese themselves, using Chinese for labor and driving masses of Chinese ahead of them when they assaulted.

I have deliberately given the impression that the Mongol army was unspecialized, and this certainly is true when one considers only its internal organization. Compared to all other armies before and since, it was the most highly specialized army in all history.

Considering modern science and modern military technology, what sort of force—on land or sea, in the air or in space—could most closely approximate its efficiency and effectiveness today?

THE GOALS OF SPECIALIZATION

We cannot, in the foreseeable future, hope realistically for a rebirth of the all-purpose weapon or the all-purpose warrior, for our immediate military heritage is that of the post-Renaissance armed forces of Europe: infantry, cavalry, and artillery on land, all more or less specialized within themselves and all dependent on continuing production and supply; and at sea, a similar rather simple specialization of ships of war, similarly dependent. The evolution of their military complexity—and of their increasingly ramified specialization—has paralleled that of the scientific and technological complexity of civilian society in our age.

The goals of military specialization are—and will remain—essentially simple: *to unbalance the equations of war in one's own favor:*

- By moving faster than the enemy
- By striking harder than the enemy
- By hitting him without being hit
- By making oneself less vulnerable than he

World War I offered numerous examples:

- The introduction of chemical weapons (vesicants, toxic gasses, flamethrowers)
- The return of armor to the battlefield

251

- The use of aircraft in war, both tactically and for "strategic" bombardment
- Accelerated development of high-angle-of-fire weapons (trench-mortars, grenade throwers, etc.), and a vast improvement in indirect-fire artillery techniques

And for every World War I example, we can easily think of dozens developed before and during World War II.

Actually, *specialized weapons* is too restrictive a term. We must also consider specialized men and specialized enabling devices, especially as the importance of such devices and of the men competent to handle them is now increasing so dramatically. Neither a ship nor an aircraft nor an armored vehicle is basically a weapon. They are devices to move weapons men cannot move, to do so faster than men possibly could, and to do it while themselves remaining, whenever possible, less vulnerable than men are.

A weapon multiplies the physical power of men to express destructive force; enabling devices multiply the area over which, during a given period of time, that force can be expressed and/or the precision with which this can be accomplished. As a consequence, additional specialized weapons and devices must be designed especially to prevent the enemy from multiplying his own power. For the sake of brevity, I shall simply refer to enabling devices as *devices*, whatever their size and whatever their exact function—the term can include everything from production (a ball-bearing factory would be a good example) through the logistical sequence (ships, trucks, trains) to the ultimate tactical carriers. Therefore we have the following classes of specialized weapons:

- Antipersonnel weapons
- Antidevice weapons
- Antiweapon weapons

Obviously, their functions more or less overlap, but the more highly specialized they are, the less overlap there will be and the more restricted will be their sphere of effectiveness.

It is interesting to consider their past development, particularly as it sheds light on their probable development in the immediate future.

Weapon-and-device history can conveniently be divided into three periods:

- The man (and animal) power age
- The *mechanical* power age
- The age of scientific power: 1st phase, *chemical-nuclear, electronic;* 2nd phase, *cybernetic.*

These, again, overlap. Our own Civil War, because of its extensive use of railroads and its reliance on an interchangeable-parts technology in arms manufacture and on steam-powered and water-powered factories, can fairly be called the first of the *mechanical* wars. World War I, basically a mechanical war, was also the first to forecast the age of scientific power. World War II displayed the beginnings of that age in terms that left no doubt as to its nature. Let us take one example: Previously, the power of a man's eye to see could be multiplied only by spyglasses, binoculars, battery commanders' scopes. World War II introduced radar, a very different kettle of fish. (It also brought in radio-controlled drones, and proximity fuses, which can perhaps be considered as precursors of today's "smart bombs" and self-guided missiles.)

There was one development it lacked. Every weapon and device developed for it, on land or sea, simply augmented man's ability to hit an enemy, to determine the location of an enemy, or to protect himself against an enemy. None of them augmented his ability to *think*, to solve problems great and small, solve them infinitely faster than he could with his unaided mind, or solve them and carry out the military procedures necessary under circumstances of intolerable physical or psychological stress.

No gunner, no matter how well trained, using only his five senses, can reasonably be expected to intercept a launched Sidewinder or Exocet missile. Nor can a human pilot endure the accelerations required of any vehicle capable of intercepting an ICBM.

But computer-guided antimissile missiles will be able to.

A computer can "think" faster than a man. Correctly programmed, it can act much faster than a man. In the air, or in space, it can survive many times as many Gs as a man (which leads us to some interesting speculations about the *inevitable* future of manned and unmanned flying objects).

In short, computers multiply the powers of the human mind, completing the cybernetic relationship within a military organism.

THE CYBERNETIC AGE: POWERS AND VULNERABILITIES

Almost ten years ago, in his book *Modern Warfare, A Study of Men, Weapons, and Theories*,[3] Shelford Bidwell wrote, of military cybernetics:

> When we speak of "the military machine," it is with more insight than we may realize. An army is a machine of a special type constructed for a special purpose . . .
> The term used to describe such a machine is a *weapon system*. It is a most useful and descriptive term, because we have reached a point in the history of weapons at which it is misleading to speak or think simply of the weapon itself . . . We have to consider all that goes with it . . . A modern army/air force is a gigantic weapon complex, governed by the laws that govern any such cybernetic network.

Brigadier Bidwell went on to discuss an air-defense setup as a smaller, simpler model, and he said:

> It is technically quite possible to make the whole system automatic and to limit human intervention to the orders to stand by, engage, and stop; and even these could be built into the machine, which can be "taught" to act correctly under certain circumstances.

The development of this sort of "military machine" has led, and is still leading, toward armed forces with a smaller and smaller percentage of *un*specialized weapons, devices, and organizations. Every new weapon demands a new counterweapon; every effective new enabling device demands another to offset it; and all of them demand new military techniques, new training.

That is one trend. The other, perhaps no less important, is toward a higher and higher degree of that automation referred to by Brigadier Bidwell.

Specialization must inevitably—except in certain rare instances we will look at later—subtract from the power of an armed force to strike *as a whole*. To take a now obsolete example: a horse cavalry unit in the field armed with the same weapons as an equivalent number of infantry could not match their firepower in a fluid situation, simply because one man in each set of fours, or one in each squad, depending on circumstances, had to act as horse-holder. Again, specialization can have its more passive negative effects by increasing the vulnerability factor of the specialized element. It is my understanding that H.M.S. *Sheffield*'s aluminum hull gave her a marked advantage in speed over similar vessels similarly powered, but it also contributed to her destruction off the Falklands; her hull actually caught fire from the intense heat generated when she was struck by an Argentine Exocet missile.

Therefore specialization must, inevitably, involve much weighing and balancing of all the factors involved.

DECISIVE SPECIALIZATION?

The military machine described by Bidwell can be compared to a symphony orchestra, in which each section and instrument is coordinated toward the accomplishment of a mutual goal. What then of those historical instances where a *single* specialized weapon, or device, or weapons system has been successfully employed to the same end? We have seen that the Mongols were the only people to achieve this on almost a world-conquering scale. But there have also been cases where new, specialized weapons and techniques have achieved impressive

255

battlefield and campaign decisions that almost certainly
could not have been achieved without them:

- The British longbow at Crécy and Agincourt
  against the armored chivalry of France
- Swiss long pikes and pikemen against Spanish and
  Austrian cavalry
- The Japanese employment of front-loading mor-
  tars in jungle warfare in Malaya
- The use of radar in the Battle of Britain (not of
  course alone decisive—an enabling device cannot
  be—but of decisive importance nonetheless).

It would appear, then, that for any single specialized
weapon or device or organization to play a decisive role,
even in concert with other elements, it *must* be employed
in sufficient force. History holds instance after instance
of the failure to do this resulting in a failure to achieve
possible victory:

- What might have happened if the British, during
  the American Revolution, had had the imagination to adopt the extremely practical Ferguson
  breech-loading rifle, not universally, but at least
  on a militarily significant scale?
- What would almost certainly have happened if
  Hitler had followed Admiral Dönitz's advice with
  regard to the use of U-boats in World War II?
- And—though I have never seen the possibility
  mentioned—what might have happened to either
  of the combatants at Jutland had the other had
  three or four times as many torpedo-capable light
  vessels as current naval custom called for?

We could go on about the first use of chemical weapons
and tanks in World War I, but here too many other
factors enter the picture. No such doubts exist where the
German use of armor in World War II was concerned:
their initial victories were won because generals like
Model and Guderian had the good sense to adopt the
ideas developed by British general J.F.C. Fuller prior to
1919, subsequently publicized by him and by Sir Basil
Liddell Hart, and subsequently ignored by the French,
the British, and ourselves.

What are the prospects for decisive specialization in
our cybernetic military future? Let us remember the

essential rule: a specialized weapon or device cannot be decisive unless used on an adequate scale against critical objectives. There is another: such a weapon or device cannot be decisive unless it *is* used. One may get to feeling very secure sitting on a terrific military secret—but the longer one sits on it, the worse its chances of decisive employment are going to be, and the better chance there'll be of an enemy matching or countering it. Nature has no secrets—only as-yet-undiscovered laws—and science is an instrument that will work for any master who has the wit and the resources to employ it, however nasty he may be.

The cybernetic military organism is today—and will continue to be tomorrow—more directly, and more instantly, dependent on its electronic nervous systems than were any of its predecessors. Therefore the vulnerability of these systems will be critical, and inevitably attempts will be made to devise weapons to exploit this. For instance, any effective "weapon" that could render a computer chip as inert as a chocolate chip cookie, or simply make it function erratically or unpredictably, could—if adequately employed—easily win a modern war. To put it more accurately, it could easily enable its accompanying weapons systems to destroy a suddenly mindless, paraplegic enemy.

Science and technology proceed along sharply steepening curves, and their progress is open-ended, governed only by the amount of money, time, and effort invested in them. One thing it would be wise to remember is this: we now have behind us more than thirty-five years of tight military "security," and it would be foolish to assume that many novel weapons and devices with, say, the decisive potential that radar had have been allowed to surface.

In our ignorance, however, it is still interesting to speculate on what may have been developed or what can develop in the near future, probably in the following categories:

- Unmanned flying objects that "think"
- Unmanned war vessels that "think"
- Space weapons and anti-weapons that "think"

I have put the *think* in quotes in each instance simply

257

to indicate that the process to which it refers is different from human thinking, and means the built-in, programmed ability to react correctly in a wide variety of the situations that ordinarily confront a human pilot, the captain of a ship, a gunnery officer, or—perhaps—a general.

THE YEARS AHEAD

One of the dirty tricks the scientific method plays on us is pulling completely unexpected rabbits out of hats—scientific quantum jumps. Quite a number of years ago, before the sudden start of our "computer revolution," one of our best science fiction writers published a story about a space war in which he prophesied a completely computerized command. However, when he wrote it, such a computer would have had to have literally thousands of vacuum tubes and God-knows-whats to perform the functions he assigned it, *so in the story an entire major war vessel was required to accommodate it*. The one thing he, like everyone else, had failed to foresee was solid-state electronics and the micro technology that would have reduced the whole works to the size of a small suitcase.

When we think about the special weapons, the special enabling devices, the special warriors of the future, we must always try to foresee the unexpected, and hope that our defense authorities and scientists can foresee and develop the unexpected, and try not to be caught too short if the unexpected happens.

BIBLIOGRAPHY

1. Squadron Leader C.C. Walker, R.C.A.F., *Jenghiz Khan* (London: Luzac & Co., 1939).
2. *Ibid.*
3. Shelford Bidwell, *Modern Warfare, A Study of Men, Weapons, and Theories* (London: Allen Lane, 1973). An excellent, highly intelligent, well-balanced book, unfortunately now out of print.

WERE-TIGERS
Rob Chilson

EDITOR'S INTRODUCTION

Most speculation about the future of war concentrates on the physical sciences, and probably rightly so; but the era of computer plenty will make possible developments in other sciences as well. Molecular biology seems headed for exponential growth. So does psychology.

There is more than one kind of wizard weapon, and more than one kind of specialization.

HELL WITH RANGERS, DON'T TELL ME RANGERS. I ONCE SAW A war tiger express an opinion of a Ranger, and I agree with it. They're crazy and no good.

Well, yeah, I could tell you about it. I never told this to no one, partly 'cause it was the scaredest I ever got in combat, even the time I got wounded bad. Time I'm talkin' about, the tigers saved our ass and I didn't get more'n a scratch or two, but I really got a good fright. Near ruined me.

What? No, I'm not ashamed of it. Anybody that's *been there*, they'll understand. Anybody that ain't, I don't give a shit what they think. Buy me a beer, though, and I'll tell you all about it—but it's gonna take more'n one. You guys take turns, okay? You go first—you asked me.

It was in the jungle war, natch. If you fight with tigers, you fight in the jungles. If you like Kodiak brown bears, you fight in forest; if you like polar bears, God help you, it's tundra for you. If you like lions, they give you prairies. Or if you like prairies, they fix you up with lions. Package deal. Hey, that's good.

See, I liked tigers, I mean from when I was a kid. So I opted for tigers, and so they sent me to one piddly-ass jungle war after another. Three in all, but in one all I had to do was play soldier and guard things, thank God. But in the jungle war, *the* jungle war—

Whaddaya mean, which one? There wasn't but one— not but one real one. Ask anybody that was there. Everybody's forgotten us, but by God *we* remember. The Airborne was sent in, and that was us, with a Ranger battalion and all our tigers. We had a hundred thirty-seven—they were more expensive in those days. Some Rangers or somebody—I don't rightly know who—was there ahead of us and marked a good drop zone, so we got down okay.

Once we was down, we fanned out into the jungle— Jungle Attack Corps don't fuck around with base camps. They just dropped our supplies to us and we made sure the gooks didn't get any of it. We had it all to ourselves for almost two days, then the gook scouts started comin' in. They didn't have our high tech, no war beasts at all, no Integrators—nothin' but Samkillers, really, the commie version of Silent Sam rapid-firers. But they were good.

Felix, our striped topkick, notified us they was comin' in, and he and Winona and Bellatrix laid out and ambushed half a dozen of 'em, one right after another. One made some noise, though, and they didn't need InterPersonal radio to know they'd lost a man. The tigers scragged the last two and spread, reporting, and the rest of the gook unit walked by 'em.

Slim, one of our comm men, came over to where the colonel was sittin' on a log lookin' at a map, and Slim, he says, "Sir, the gooks is gettin' out with a report. They know we're here."

"Not surprising," says the colonel. He was tall and fat but loved heat and could move like a snake through even deep growth. He was tough as hell to get along with in camp, but in the jungle he was okay. Colonel looks at his map again a couple of times and turns to Horribleness, who was Felix's second, and says, "Go spot your men and tigers. I'm keepin' the Rangers with me for now."

Now, my tiger was named Hooligan, and she was a regular pet. She slept with her squad, and many a night I've pillowed my head on her. I'd only seen her in action once, against some street demonstrators, and she scared the shit right out of them. They flat dropped everything and ran. And she sat down in the street and laughed at them, the way a great big cat laughs, without making any noise. She weighed, oh, 160, 170 kilos, not big for a tiger. Bengals get up to 250, they say. But war tigers aren't all that big as tigers go. They got to be big enough to be strong and hardy, but small enough to go through dense growth.

Yeah, they go on all fours, and they look like regular tigers, except their heads are bigger. You can't see the ear antennas 'cause they're under the skin. And you can't see the modified front paws with the dewclaw moved down and turned into a thumb, when they're walkin'. The only thing you can see is the key to the teflon zipper behind the ears that opens their scalps so the techs can get at their radios and computer implants. Hooligan was wearing her war harness with her M-3 tiger pistol under her belly and the grenade launcher on the left side.

She grinned at me, Hooligan did, and I grinned back and rubbed her head, and me and John and Pete and Randy all followed her. They're cheaper now, war beasts are, and the jungle squad is two tigers and three men, they say; soon they'll be goin' to three beasts and two men. But we were it in those days. We went sneakin' out, followin' Hooligan, who was gettin' radio ear messages from Horribleness, who was coordinating with Felix.

It was creepy in that jungle, and if not for Hooligan I would've been pretty jumpy. It was all mud and rotten limbs underfoot, and heat, muggy air full of rotten leaves. It was like breathing muddy water. We picked a good spot and hid.

Pretty soon a gang of gooks came walkin' by in front of us, movin' real quiet. Seemed good to see *their* flank for a change. We could only see 'em behind the leaves and brush with our Integrators and they couldn't see us. But when Pete dropped the first one, they whirled and started shooting to beat hell. Samkillers whispered inaudibly and we heard the *Crack!-rrrripp!* of the bullets over our heads. Samkillers shoot a *lot* of bullets real fast, but it just means more weight to carry, and besides, the charge packs for the electroguns don't go on forever.

Still, once every three thousand rounds, like clockwork, they were gonna hit someone, and we expected to get resupplied, so we started chucking Smart Bullets back at 'em fast. Every now and then you'd see a faint thin line of white smoke, or maybe a thin yellow burn from the SB rockets. I don't say for every bullet we shot, some gook went down. But even one out of a hundred would've been a hell of a lot better'n they was doin', and we actually got something like one gook for every five Smart Bullets.

They was shootin' thousands of noisy rounds at people they couldn't see, and we was replyin' with dozens of quiet rounds at people we could see, and in about fifteen minutes we pretty well had 'em sweatin'. Then a tiger came up behind them and killed one, then roared. Hooligan roared from their flank and they started to panic. Our Smart Bullets ignored tigers, of course, so we went on shootin' till they was all dead.

It was no big deal. We had the edge in armament. Well, yeah, M-3 Muskets got disadvantages. They're short-ranged. Big deal in the jungle. The electroarm's solenoid throws 'em out at low velocity, and the rocket corrects course and ups speed. Nice thing about it is, the Musket's solenoidal barrel is openwork—air can get out from in front of the bullet, and get in behind it. They're not even rifled—the real high-tech is in the bullets. Makin' them in quantity is a real triumph of technology.

What if the M-3 gets full of mud? Hell, sonny, a good soldier don't get mud in his gun. If he did, all he'd need to do is ream it with his flexible rammer—the mud drips

262

out of the openwork. Reverse rammer and do it again and it's clean and dry.

I remember how John brushed himself off when we stood up, like a cat, and how the tigers prowled around, purring and laughing and checking out the dead ones. I gave Hooligan a big hug, and so did the others, and we rubbed the other tiger's ears. None of us was hurt, except the other tiger had got creased and Pete had banged up his elbow when he took dirt and it looked pretty bad. All else we got was bug bites. Not bad for my first serious combat. I'd thought I'd been in combat before, and it's true I'd been shot at and shot back, but a riot ain't a battle, believe me. Twenty dead gooks in the jungle look a lot different from two people dead in the street.

We went over and looked at them, and they were dressed in these thin black pants their top troops wear, and kind of small thin rubber-soled shoes. They were busted up pretty bad by the exploding Smart Bullets; each one had a big gruesome hole in him. Made me feel pretty queasy, I can tell you. Then that smart-ass Randy started laughin' about the Gooky Monster had taken a bite out of each of 'em. Some he liked better and took two bites out of.

John and me got laughing about how it must've been when the first couple went down with big holes in 'em and the others didn't even know what way the bullets was coming from. We made some pretty good jokes about how they had got the flies knocked off 'em, but they didn't stay knocked off, and I felt a little better.

Their Samkillers were all Russian copycat designs, but their bullets looked homemade. Two or three of 'em had binoculars, good ones, and those that got there first grabbed 'em. Not near as good as Integrators, but who's gonna let you take a five-hundred-dollar Integrator home with you for the deer huntin', when you get out? I didn't get one of the binocs, though, and I figured, well, say luh gare, there'll be more along in a minute.

Me and Pete was lookin' at his cigarette lighter that had got busted, and laughing about the gooks runnin' around in their pajamas—that's what they call those black pants—when Winona come over and pushed her head against me and said, "Get ready! More coming, and the colonel is pulling back to Hill Seven! We'll have to slow them down."

Pete said, "That's *their* high tech—making people, and they sure know how to do it."

I said, "Yeah, what if their kill ratio's three thousand to one, they'll still win," but you know, neither one of us felt all that bad. I wasn't scared a bit. I mean, I'd just come through a session of real combat, and it had been nothing much. Besides, Hooligan was havin' fun. So we bitched and griped about the mud and the bugs and the heat and picked out good places for another ambush, and the tigers took up station behind us.

That should've tipped me.

Pretty soon the jungle on a half-click-wide front began to waver and rustle and fill with little olive-skinned men in black bottoms, pushing Samkillers ahead of them. And I was Sam. Hooligan came up and whispered that we could ignore them off to the right, they was going off to miss the regiment, and would have to curl back around our flank. That'd take a third of the enemy out of action for over half an hour, maybe, 'cause they didn't know where we was.

Then Felix came by and pulled four guys out of our line, and him and Bellatrix and a tiger I didn't know, and the guys, all went off to the left, to make 'em think they was findin' a bunch of us over there, to buy more time. The guys looked pretty blue about it.

I was glad I wasn't one of the four guys, and I felt solemn. None of us was jokin' no more, we were grippin' our Muskets and looking sharp through the Integrators. But they seen us first, I don't know how, and let go with a murderous *rrrrippp, rrrrippp, rrrrippp,* through the leaves. One of our guys screamed and started thrashing around, and another one coughed and jerked up, and fell back with a flop.

Three thousand to one didn't sound so good then. I felt sick and scared and nothing had come near me yet, but I figured it's that way in war. Wasn't till later I realized I'd never seen one of my own side killed in war. In an accident with a chopper, sure, but not in war. It was different.

"Shoot!" said Hooligan.

We could see 'em now in the Integrators. They were still searching for us. I started shooting, slow and careful, like it says in the drill, and every shot took a guy down, except where somebody else's bullet got him first. You could see parallel lines of thin yellow light and sometimes white smoke where the Smart Bullets maneuvered in the short range, but those curving tracks weren't much good for the gooks to aim from. Their Samkillers didn't have smoke, flash, discharge of any kind, of course, but we could see our targets pretty well.

Hooligan and the other tigers were behind us, sitting up and shooting their M-9 bombguns, dropping fist-sized AP beehives—M-80s, we used to call 'em, on base. It was pure hell on the gook side of the fight, but they kept on comin'. They had lost hundreds of guys, and we had lost eight or ten, and one tiger, with another tiger wounded.

But the gooks all yelled at once and ran at us, and I heard Hooligan shift to automatic fire. She laid down a cloud of flechettes in front of us, and the three guys who made it through each took half a dozen SBs, and then half a dozen more homed on them and blew the bloody rags that was left into shreds.

It was so close a flechette screamed by me, and I could smell the powder smoke, and the smell of the guys blown apart by SBs was like the jungle, hot and rank, only worse.

I was really scared then, and so was John next to me, and I could see Randy was shakin' a little as he changed clips, but we stood it. After a bit I didn't see no more gooks through my Integrator and I pushed it up and wiped my face, and my hand was shakin'. Just as I dropped it down again, Hooligan said, "Attack!"

Well, they call us Jungle Attack Corps, but there was nothing I wanted less than to run into that jungle where those dead guys came from. Still, I stood up, and Randy leaped up, too, and we sort of surged forward. The tigers holstered their guns and leaped past us. Then all hell broke loose.

Tigers roared, and we yelled, and M-80s thumped, and flechettes shrieked, and Samkiller bullets ripped, and guys screamed and yelled in pain, and bits of leaves cut by bullets drifted down. The ground got squishy and splashed underfoot, and we all got muddy when we took dirt. I never even thought about the leeches in those puddles till later. We'd see a gang of gooks in the Integrators, hidden so they thought by leaves and brush, and we'd shoot 'em up with SBs, maybe take a hit or two, then run forward and find another gang.

One guy got wise and held up me and the guys—Hooligan was off—and this gook hit Pete in the arm and again in the shoulder and he went down, gasping not screaming. The gook was behind a thick tree we couldn't see through. He'd pop out and let go a burst in our direction, then pop back just before our Smart Bullets got there. Finally I took a deep breath—I was really jittery about gooks comin' up on flank or behind us, in the jungle you get all turned around—I took a deep breath and slowed everything down, and I took a chance and raised my Integrator and wiped my face. John stared at me like he'd never seen a bare face before, and I remember how strange he looked with these big camouflage leaves across his face.

I was *blind* without the Integrator, and I couldn't see how the gooks got the nerve to dive into a solid mat of leaves not bein' able to see what was on the other side. But then I dropped it again and spotted the gook gunner just as he popped out. We all ducked, but I watched close, and next time he popped out, it was on the opposite side of the tree. I had his pattern then and slung two SBs at the first side of the tree just as he popped out again. Down he went.

I couldn't see what was goin' on, of course, but it seemed to me we had lost a lot of guys, and besides, I was runnin' low on ammo. Gooks was all around us, Samkillers rippin' up the jungle till I thought the trees would fall, cut through. Then there came a really amazing uproar off to the side. Tigers' roaring bends the trees, and there was maybe two dozen of them doing it together. The ones with us joined in, and underneath I could hear the crazy screams of the Rangers.

What had happened, as we were told later, is that the enemy had come up on Hill 7 intending to take the road past it on its right, lookin' from our side, and go after the native villages we was there to protect. They fanned out and ran into us, but the colonel had drawn us up to our left of Hill 7 and the road. So a third or a half of the enemy force was facin' nothing. That part of the enemy swung around toward Hill 7, which they could see was our base.

Me and Hooligan and our guys held up the gook right, at the left end of our line—and the colonel and the headquarters detachment flanked us on the left, catching the right end of the enemy line. That is, if there is such a thing as a line in jungle fighting. Meantime, he'd sent all of his reserve tigers and the Ranger battalion on a wider sweep to catch the gooks in the rear, 'cause they can travel fast. We had the entire enemy right in a three-sided pincer and were crushin' it.

It all sounds real neat and real good, but you wasn't there. It was hell, and some of our guys bought it from Smart Bullets, we were so jammed together. I know SBs are supposed to ignore our guys, but in such short range they didn't have the time to discriminate. Well, it was bloody and awful, but it ended after a time, and it was beginning to get dark, and the tigers were reporting that the enemy had abandoned his right to us and had taken Hill 7.

That was a bad time. Pete was hurting, though we could see he was gonna be okay. But he couldn't be evacuated with all those gooks around, so we gave 'im painkillers and bandaged him up, and Hooligan came and purred at him. But she was jittery too. I kept worryin' we'd lost the hill, and word was that more gooks were comin' in and would be on us by morning.

Colonel passed the word we'd done well, and we took time to check out all the wounded. Some of our worst wounded were scorpion-stung or spider-bit. Everybody was covered with leeches, of course. There weren't no wounded enemy, they were all dead, except one or two that'd had an arm or leg blown off and was gonna die of shock and internal hemorrhages. Colonel said to make them comfortable, too, and it seemed funny we was trying to kill 'em earlier, and now we was lightin' cigarettes for them. But I was glad we had done it, later, even if they all died.

That's it for this one, who's turn is it now?

Soon as we had all rested a bit and all of our guys was accounted for, Colonel put us in motion. We circled Hill 7 same way the gooks had gone, passing around the foot of it and to the right side, onto that road. I don't think the gooks expected us to pull such a maneuver—think they expected us to storm the damn hill or somethin'. They had a few pickets out watchin' it, but Rangers and war tigers went ahead and quietly took them out. Before the gooks knew it, we was on the back side of the hill, between them and the native villages we was there to protect—and out of between them and the army that was comin' up to support them.

We found this abandoned village which would be a good place to set up camp, and got off into the jungle beside it. Pretty soon the gooks got some artillery up and immediately dropped some shells into the village, so Rangers went in and set fire to the hootches so's to give 'em something to aim at and make 'em feel they was doin' something, and we got a good rest.

I was pretty tired, we'd tramped through a lot of stinking, muggy jungle, helping the wounded along, too tired and too sick to be very hungry. I made myself eat. But the Rangers was somethin' else. They were full of the fighting cocktail, hyper as a bunch of speed freaks, leapin' and bouncin' around and braggin' about how they'd saved our asses and how any of them could whip any three other guys, who*ever* they was. I didn't feel like disputin' it, but it made me mad to hear it. We'd stood up to the enemy head to head, and they'd only taken 'em in the rear.

And I didn't like to hear them call the gooks "gooks." I didn't like the way they said it. It was the way I was sayin' it that morning, but I was ignorant that morning and didn't know. I was sayin' "gook" in a different way now, because I could respect those little guys with their pajamas and bare eyes and old-fashioned guns and all their gutsiness. I didn't think it was funny that those guys had gotten blown up by an explosive bullet shot at them by a man who could see him but who he couldn't see to shoot back at.

And I really didn't like to hear these assholes brag

about how they'd done the same thing, *shootin' 'em in the back.*

Yeah, I know, they were full of cocktails and not responsible. The stuff makes 'em crazy, and that makes them good soldiers. Bullshit. They were crazy before or they would never have volunteered for that shit.

What's in the cocktails? Well, they say there's super and secret drugs that make 'em stronger, faster, tougher, and so on, but no, not really. There are drugs that'll do some of those things, though not as much stronger, faster, and so on, as people think. Not enough to make a Ranger out of an untrained grunt. See? I mean, Rangers have to be trained. And most such drugs wipe out the brain, so what good's your training? And the side effects are bad, you never get over some of them. It ain't economic to waste good men with bad drugs.

No, they tell us the cocktails contain a little alcohol— awful-tasting stuff, but it lowers inhibition—Dutch courage, it used to be called. And it contains caffeine, a lot of caffeine, and nicotine, which is a mood-enhancer but deadly poisonous. It also contains a *very* little speed, or sometimes coke. Nothing magical, but nothing you can't get off from—and nothing that hampers your thinking processes if you don't overdo it.

Even so, if you're half crazy to start with, it can send you over the edge.

One of these bastards was leapin' around and blowin' about how he'd taken ten gooks apart with his bare hands, and maybe he did kill a couple. He was a big guy, and they're small. This guy's name was Jones, and he kept going on about what a great fighter he was, and we was all ignorin' him best we could. Colonel would look up curiously from time to time, and the Ranger captain would shrug and kind of grin back at him. Finally Jones got to yellin' that he could take on any man or tiger in the unit.

Most of us paid him no mind even then, but Hooligan growled a little and swung her big head around, looking at us all and especially at the tigers. Maybe she communicated to them on her radio; anyway none of the others moved when she stood up and strolled out under the trees to where Jones was takin' a drink of water. He looked up and there she was, facing him.

At first he was startled, then he grinned—I saw his white teeth in the pale glow of the lanterns. He turned and set the cup down real slow, still lookin' at Hooligan, then stood up and stepped toward her. Hooligan backed up till they were at a wider space—we weren't in a clearing or anything the gooks could get a fix on, but right in deep jungle and there were trees all around. They moved to a fairly wide spot, maybe ten meters one way by fifteen another. Close quarters to fight a tiger.

The guys got up and came over, and I helped Pete over though he tried to shrug me off, and a couple of guys spaced the lanterns a little better. They gave off a faint yellow glow that wouldn't leak far through the jungle, but we could see pretty well. The colonel and the captain looked on, stopping talking about the map, and just watched.

Jones stood in a crouch, looking at Hooligan. She didn't crouch or anything. Suddenly he leaped to one side and in and swung at her head, then leaped away. Hooligan swung her head and dodged, but I could see his strategy. A war beast has to have a brain as big as a human being's to be as smart as us, so the head is oversized. He probably figured her skull must be thin. Well, that don't follow; the guys who did the gene splicing thought of that too. Also, if he could batter around her ears enough, her implant control computers and radios might cause her pain.

He went rocking around, leaping in and out, crouching, trying to draw her into an attack. So she obliged him: a blinding fast pounce without a windup. Instantly Jones flung himself aside, turning on his back and lashing out with his feet. He caught her in the ribs and I heard her grunt. But you got no idea how fast a tiger can stop; Hooligan swapped ends before Jones could bounce up and was in full pounce again.

Jones was *fast*, I never saw a man move like that. Halfway up, he seen her flyin' at him again and dropped back so's he could swing his joined fists up under her chin. But Hooligan stopped short *again*—nobody could've foreseen that, or adjusted to it, there wasn't time. A real fight ain't a bit like a comic book. Jones swung and missed 'cause she stopped short, and Hooligan unleashed a haymaker that sent Jones spinning across the ring.

Again Hooligan pounced, and again Jones showed just how damned fast a Ranger full of cocktails can be. He rolled with the blow, fetched up against a tree, and sprang back ready to hit or kick. But this time Hooligan wasn't pouncing, she was running, and she could swerve. She streaked past him and swung at him as she did. Jones dodged it but fell over, and Hooligan dug in her claws and swapped ends—the guys on that side of the ring fell over backward to get away from her.

Then she was in front of Jones and Jones was half rising, fists ready, and took a preliminary swipe at her nose. Hooligan snarled like tearing canvas and reared up and boxed with him. Jones was a big fellow, ninety kilos, and she was a small tiger, like I said, only 160 or so. Just no comparison; she went through his guard with her first blow, and knocked him spinning with her second.

Now picture this: this guy's been knocked *three meters* twice, had the breath knocked out of him, he's in shock 'cause he's outclassed, had three ribs cracked, though he didn't know it till later. How much fight is left in him? Plenty in one way, he still ain't convinced, but what can he do? Drugs can only do so much for you; the guy was hurt and exhausted.

He lay there gasping, and I remember the buzzing of the lantern near me and the distant *whump-boom* of the gook artillery. Jones reared up and started cussing Hooligan, and started to scramble to his feet. He wasn't moving the way he had been before, and he looked a little ory-eyed from the pounding.

Hooligan snarled disgustedly and sprang forward again, brushed aside his fist, and gripped his shoulder with her teeth, first time she'd used them. She could've taken a bite out of him—Yankee Monster. But she didn't, she just shook him like a rat and backed off. Jones flopped down and lay panting, staring at her. Hooligan looked around at us all and then at me and Pete and John, which was where she belonged. She kind of shrugged, real graceful, and walked back toward us.

271

She had to walk right over Jones.

Jones cried out something and began to beat and kick at her ribs as she went over him, and Hooligan just ignored him, just like he was a bug or something she was walking over, and came back and took her place with us. We checked her out and she had a bruise on one side where he'd kicked her. I remember she made me nervous till she started purring at us. The medics took Jones away and the Rangers all shut up.

Yeah, that's the time I was tellin' you about, when a tiger expressed an opinion of a Ranger, but I didn't know what it meant till next day. Here—time for a refill on this.

See, next day the reinforced enemy came lookin' for us; also came out to go after those native villages we were there to defend. They had artillery and some armor and a lot of trucks and things, and had to use the road. We pulled back to where the road went between a couple of hills, not exactly headin' 'em off at the pass, but near enough. We'd had a supply drop in the night, and was in good shape, though they hadn't been able to take the wounded off. Pete was up and around and able to do a little—an M-3 Musket don't take much aiming and doesn't have a lot of kick.

What? Why not make war beasts with guns built in? Ain't you been payin' attention? I just said the Silent Sam is obsolete on account of Smart Bullets—but when does the M-3 become obsolete? Then you've got a lot of war beasts outfitted with obsolete guns, and it takes three to five years to bring up the next generation. Don't interrupt me.

The colonel scattered us by squads between the two hills, with units having armor-piercing capability along the road, which we had also mined. We had a long wait in the murky twilight of the jungle, where you don't dare touch anything for fear of ants or spiders or some other damn bug. I couldn't breathe all the time I was there, and to this day muddy water smells will make me gasp for breath. They'd have to come to us in the jungle.

That's just what they did, fanning out from hill to hill and movin' slow. We heard mines going off on the road, and knew the enemy was having slow going over there.

272

We laid low till the word of command, avoiding their elements. Naturally they were all broken up going through the jungle, and with a few scares and some rapid movements we were able to avoid them till they had nearly passed us. Then they were all among us, pretty much unsuspected, though I think some of those gooks had an idea. They were really good.

Anyway—at the radioed word of command all the tigers roared at once and we opened on any gooks in view. They all yelled and took dirt, and we sent our Smart Bullets over their heads—sometimes where the jungle wasn't so thick you could see the down-curving burns as they dived on the enemy. All around was the yelling and screaming of the gooks, and the *rrrrippp, rrrrippp, rrrrippppp* of the Samkillers cuttin' leaves over our heads, our guys yelling back, *whuffwhuff, whuff-whuffwhuff* of the M-3s lobbing SBs, an occasional *pump*! where an explosive bullet hit a tree or the dirt—hitting flesh was quieter. Tigers were roaring and shooting and sometimes jumping little groups of enemy, the bang and whine of M-80s spraying flechettes here and there—not too many because we were too close to the enemy.

All of this action stirred up the jungle stink, and the powder smoke added a sharp note to it. We were hot and sweaty just sitting; running around was like swimming. My Integrator kept steaming up and I was scared all through the fight I'd be blind. One thing about it, if you never forgot the heat, at least in action you forgot the bugs.

The gooks were yelling back and forth and had begun to figure out where we were. They concentrated where we weren't, which was a mistake because we could use flechette grenades better, but we had to get out of the way of these concentrations. A bunch of gooks came runnin' by and joined up with a squad we were shootin' at—one jumped out of nowhere and just about cut Randy in half with his Samkiller. A big tiger named Blunderbore shot him with his tiger-pistol M-3, then shot the gook behind him, then holstered his gun—clip empty—and leaped into them.

Hooligan followed Blunderbore and they turned back

273

a rush of gooks and got covered with blood, and I looked around and I saw that Blunderbore's squad and Hooligan's squad were the only ones together here, and the enemy was massing not far off. After Randy got hit—and it was all going at once, so I didn't feel much about it at the time—nobody wanted to raise up to do any real aimin'. More and more gooks came in, jabbering and shooting like crazy.

Another tiger came in from somewhere off to our right, and then all three of the tigers vanished. I looked at John and I knew he was thinking the same I was: they were going to hit 'em from behind, so we had to hold on. Randy was gone, and Pete wasn't in good shape, but we had three guys from the other squad. With hand signals we spread out, takin' all Randy's Smart Bullets, and one of the other guys, fellow named Liston, picked up a Samkiller and a couple of clips—to confuse 'em I guess.

And damn if that crazy Ranger Jones didn't show up, looking kind of tired—too many days on the fighting cocktails takes it out of you—but also crazy as ever, with the whites of his eyes showing when he wiped his face.

"What's up, Doc? Any action here?"

I explained, and he nodded, grinning like a wolf. So we occupied the enemy's attention while the cats circled.

It gets real lonesome in the jungle when you're spread out so even with Integrators you can't see your mates, except maybe one every now and then—'cause you keep moving around. It's even lonesomer when the Samkillers are cuttin' closer and closer. All you can see is leaves and vines and things, and here and there a tree trunk, with blinding sunlight overhead and deep shadows underneath, and you can't breathe because it's too damn hot and you know you'll never get enough to drink to take the thirst off . . .

Worst of all is seeing your tigers go strange and wild and run off, covered with blood, snarling for a kill.

Here, refill this.

Then the gooks rushed us. Jesus, I hope I never go through that again. Sometimes I wake up shaking and I know I've been dreaming of that attack. They were screaming, some of 'em in English—"Yankee bastards die!"—like that, and shooting as they came. I first heard this hair-raising noise and the crashing and splashing of all their light shoes in the brush—half rock, half swamp underfoot—and the continual ripping of the Samkiller bullets. Cut leaves rained down in front of me and I started nervously shooting into gaps in the jungle, hopin' that the bullets would home on something.

Then I ran dry just as they appeared. Sheeyit, man, cusswords fail you at a time like that. I started scramblin' around for a clip that wasn't fuckin' empty, and they was all empty, and I was staring at those faces, still mostly hidden behind leaves and just pale blobs in the Integrators, and coming at a run. I thought I would piss my pants before I got out of the wrong pouch into the one with the loaded clips. I fumbled the clip into the Musket and got ready to squeeze off a round, figuring it'd be my last—they'd see me sure when I shot.

Then the three tigers roared together in their rear and M-80s exploded behind the ones I could see. You never heard fear till you've heard tigers roaring in unison. Then the tigers started slapping the ground and crying out in gook talk, so it sounded like they were slapping prisoners around, playing with 'em the way a cat plays with mice.

You got to understand that in the East, dragons are often good guys, and tigers are always bad guys. They hated and feared our tigers the worst, and that was something they just couldn't ignore. You hear about gooks not taking care of their people, and they often don't, because they know there's nothing they can do. But they care *about* them same as we do.

That saved my ass. The ones I could see checked and some looked back. Then that crazy Jones half stood up and sprayed them with SBs on full automatic, giving out with the Rebel yell in time to the tigers' roar. It was a blood-freezing sight. Crazy or not, fighting cocktail or not, that man was as scared as I was.

The gooks turned and blew him away, but half of 'em went down like ninepins, and I was already half up, holding my trigger down. They got off a couple of bursts toward me, nicked me twice, but they all went down. Damn wasteful way to use Smart Bullets, but it worked. I changed clips in a hurry, my knees shakin' so I could

275

hardly stand, still ready to piss my pants, not able to believe we'd got 'em all. From farther back more Samkiller bullets ripped past and I was shaking so hard it's a good thing M-3s don't have to be aimed. I lobbed a few bullets, spotted another target, took it out, and thought.

I was standing up, shaking, with only a little blood showin'. The tigers had just counterattacked from the rear. I ought to go forward and finish the enemy off. I don't know how I got together the guts to stagger forward in a crouch over dead gooks, but I did it, and I think one of the other guys from Blunderbore's squad did, too. They must of got him, though, because I was the only one there when I saw the tigers polish off the rest of the stunned gooks.

There wasn't that many of them, and what was left was shocked by the beehive M-80s and our SBs. Now the tigers, their ammo low, leaped among them and slapped off heads, ripped open bodies, bit, and shook. I saw then that Hooligan had just been playing with Jones, she hadn't used claws. It's even worse than explosive bullets, what a tiger can do to a man. One guy tried to run and the third tiger leaped past him and ripped his guts out with one blow and they dropped down and he fell over them.

All the tigers were covered with other people's blood, and their faces were fearsome, worse than a crazy Ranger's. I just stared, I couldn't believe how fierce our pets were.

Our part of the battle was over, and by the time we regrouped, it was all over and the enemy were all streaming back down the road, and we let 'em go. So it was over for me while I stood there among the piled bodies the tigers had killed, and I kind of felt that.

I saw Hooligan prowl over to one down gook and bite his head, finishing him off, and she did it to another. Then she looked up at me with blood all over her, and especially over her face, and her eyes caught the light green and she opened her mouth and gave me that silent cat's laugh. That's when I puked.

I mean, I flat tossed my cookies and I was shakin' and practically moaning and I was more scared than I've ever

276

been, more scared than a man should ever get. I was scared of the war tigers.

Well, yeah, that was a scary sight, and blood and gore does bad things to you even when it's gook blood and gore. I'd been through a lot, I was in shock and even wounded. But that wasn't it; you don't get it. It wasn't till later, when I was in therapy, that we figured it out.

See, all these generations we've had war, and we've all hated it. I know there's been guys like the crazy Jones— the Marines and Rangers get all the volunteers they need. But what they really like is not war, but fightin'— barroom fights with an audience are what they like best. Provin' they're men. Why else would Jones offer to fight a tiger, but to show what a man he was? But even he was scared shitless in that jungle; I was there, and I saw. Anybody would be, with the enemy cuttin' the jungle down just to get you. So there's always been a hope we could end war, if everybody hates it, really hates real war, not just barroom fights.

But those tigers loved it. They weren't afraid; they didn't need fighting cocktails to make them move like that, to make them fearless. They loved the danger and the excitement and the killing.

After all these generations, we've bred up soldiers that love war. God help us all.

No, I wasn't afraid that they'd turn on me, I knew they couldn't. Too many safeguards in their implant computer programming. I wasn't afraid of *them*, themselves, at all. I was afraid of what they stood for, though it was months before I knew that.

But that night, when Hooligan had cleaned herself up and been bandaged, and she came over and wanted to console us for the loss of Pete, and roughhouse and play, and was purring and happy and friendly, just like a big stuffed animal that every kid wants for Christmas but that's *alive* and can talk—I didn't want to play. I didn't want to pet her. I didn't want nothin' to do with her.

REMEMBER THE ALAMO!
T. R. Fehrenbach

EDITOR'S INTRODUCTION

Lieutenant Colonel T. R. Fehrenbach, U.S. Army (Ret.), is the author of *Lone Star*, a definitive history of his native state of Texas. He is also the author of *This Kind of War*, which is not only the definitive strategic and tactical history of the Korean War, but the best presentation to date of the problems democracies face when they must fight small wars in faraway places. If you want to understand our present strategic dilemma, you must read Fehrenbach's analysis; alas, few do so.

In 1962 Fehrenbach understood what would happen if the United States attempted to aid Vietnam. He said:

From the Korean War the United States drew troubled conclusions. American policy had been to contain Communism along the parallel, and in this, American policy succeeded. But no one realized, at the beginning, how exceedingly costly such containment would be. The war reaffirmed in American minds the distaste for land warfare on the continent of Asia, the avoidance of which has always been a foundation of United States policy. But the war proved that containment in Asia could not be forged with nuclear bombs and that threats were not enough, unless the United States intended to answer a Communist pinprick with general holocaust.

Yet the American people, army, and leaders generally proved unwilling to accept wars of policy in lieu of crusades against Communism. Innocence had been lost, but the loss was denied. The government that had ordered troops into Korea knew that the issue was never whether Syngman Rhee was right or wrong but that his loss would adversely affect the status of the United States—which was not arguable.

That government's inability to communicate, and its repudiation at the polls, firmly convinced many men of the political dangers of committing American ground troops in wars of containment. Yet without the continual employment of limited force around the globe, or even with it, there was to be no order. The world could not be policed with ships, planes, and bombs—policemen were also needed.

Less than a year after fighting ended in Korea, Vietnam was lost to the West, largely because of the complete repugnance of Americans toward committing a quarter of a million ground troops in another apparently indecisive skirmish with Communism. Even more important, the United States, as the Joint Chiefs of Staff reported, simply did not have the troops.

Korea, from Task Force Smith at Osan to the last days at Pork Chop, indicates that the policy of containment cannot be implemented without professional legions. Yet every democratic government is reluctant to face the fact. Reservists and citizen-soldiers stand ready, in every free nation, to stand to the colors and die in holocaust, the big war. Reservists and citizen-soldiers remain utterly reluctant to stand and die in anything less. None want to serve on the far frontiers, or to maintain lonely, dangerous vigils on the periphery of Asia. There has been every indication that mass call-ups for cold war moves may result in

279

mass disaffection.

The United States will be forced to fight wars of policy during the balance of the century. This is inevitable, since the world is seething with disaffection and revolt, which, however justified and merited, plays into Communist hands, and swings the world balance ever their way. Military force alone cannot possibly solve the problem—but without the application of some military force, certain areas, such as Southeast Asia, will inevitably be lost.

However repugnant the idea is to liberal societies, the man who will willingly defend the free world in the fringe areas is not the responsible citizen-soldier. The man who will go where his colors go, without asking, who will fight a phantom foe in jungle and mountain range, without counting, and who will suffer and die in the midst of incredible hardship, without complaint, is still what he has always been, from Imperial Rome to sceptered Britain to democratic America. He is the stuff of which legions are made.

His pride is in his colors and his regiment, his training hard and thorough and coldly realistic, to fit him for what he must face, and his obedience is to his orders. As a legionary, he held the gates of civilization for the classical world; as a bluecoated horseman he swept the Indians from the Plains; he has been called United States Marine. He does the jobs—the utterly necessary jobs—no militia is willing to do. His task is moral or immoral according to the orders that send him forth. It is inevitable, since men compete.

About the time that was published, the Kennedy administration attempted to aid Vietnam. Then, guided by Harvard intellectuals, the president sanctioned the deposition (and inevitable assassination) of Vietnam's president, thereby assuming full responsibility for that unhappy country. After Kennedy was assassinated in turn, the Johnson government attempted to honor that commitment by sending conscript soldiers to a far land where few understood what was at stake.

What we needed was legions.

Those who might have served as legionaries were not permitted to do it. Every few months America sent a new and untrained army halfway across the world. We needed legions, but we didn't have them.

We don't have them yet, despite ending the draft.

This story was published about the time that *This Kind of War* was completed. It might have been written yesterday. Some lessons are never learned.

TOWARD SUNDOWN, IN THE MURKY DRIZZLE, THE MAN WHO called himself Ord brought Lieutenant Colonel William Barret Travis word that the Mexican light cavalry had completely invaded Bexar, and that some light guns were being set up across the San Antonio River. Even as he spoke, there was a flash and bang from the west, and a shell screamed over the old mission walls. Travis looked worried.

"What kind of guns?" he asked.

"Nothing to worry about, sir," Ord said. "Only a few one-pounders, nothing of respectable siege caliber. General Santa Anna has had to move too fast for any big stuff to keep up." Ord spoke in his odd accent. After all, he was a Britainer, or some other kind of foreigner. But he spoke good Spanish, and he seemed to know everything. In the four or five days since he had appeared he had become very useful to Travis.

Frowning, Travis asked, "How many Mexicans, do you think, Ord?"

"Not more than a thousand, now," the dark-haired, blue-eyed young man said confidently. "But when the main body arrives, there'll be four, five thousand."

Travis shook his head. "How do you get all this information, Ord? You recite it like you had read it all someplace—like it were history."

Ord merely smiled. "Oh, I don't know *everything,* Colonel. That is why I had to come here. There is so much we don't know about what happened . . . I mean, sir, what will happen—in the Alamo." His sharp eyes grew puzzled for an instant. "And some things don't seem to match up, somehow——"

Travis looked at him sympathetically. Ord talked queerly at times, and Travis suspected he was a bit deranged. This was understandable, for the man was undoubtedly a Britainer aristocrat, a refugee from Napoleon's thousand-year empire. Travis had heard about the detention camps and the charcoal ovens . . . but once, when he had mentioned the *Empereur*'s sack of London in '06, Ord had gotten a very queer look in his eyes, as if he had forgotten completely.

But John Ord, or whatever his name was, seemed to be the only man in the Texas forces who understood what William Barret Travis was trying to do. Now Travis looked around at the thick adobe wall surrounding the old mission in which they stood. In the cold, yellowish twilight even the flaring cook fires of his 182 men could not dispel the ghostly air that clung to the old place. Travis shivered involuntarily. But the walls were thick, and they could turn one-pounders. He asked, "What was it you called this place, Ord . . . the Mexican name?"

"The Alamo, sir." A slow, steady excitement seemed to burn in the Britainer's bright eyes. "Santa Anna won't forget that name, you can be sure. You'll want to talk to the other officers now, sir? About the message we drew up for Sam Houston?"

"Yes, of course," Travis said absently. He watched Ord head for the walls. No doubt about it, Ord understood what William Barret Travis was trying to do here. So few of the others seemed to care.

Travis was suddenly very glad that John Ord had shown up when he did.

On the walls, Ord found the man he sought, broadshouldered and tall in a fancy Mexican jacket. "The commandant's compliments, sir, and he desires your presence in the chapel."

The big man put away the knife with which he had been whittling. The switchblade snicked back and disappeared into a side pocket of the jacket, while Ord watched it with fascinated eyes. "What's old Bill got his britches hot about this time?" the big man asked.

"I wouldn't know, sir," Ord said stiffly and moved on.

Bang-bang-bang roared the small Mexican cannon from across the river. *Pow-pow-pow!* The little balls only chipped dust from the thick adobe walls. Ord smiled.

He found the second man he sought, a lean man with a weathered face, leaning against a wall and chewing tobacco. This man wore a long, fringed, leather lounge jacket, and he carried a guitar slung beside his Rock Island rifle. He squinted up at Ord. "I know . . . I know," he muttered. "Willy Travis is in an uproar again. You reckon that colonel's commission the Congress up at Washington-on-the-Brazos give him swelled his head?"

Rather stiffly, Ord said, "Colonel, the commandant desires an officers' conference in the chapel, now." Ord was somewhat annoyed. He had not realized he would find these Americans so—distasteful. Hardly preferable to Mexicans, really. Not at all as he had imagined.

For an instant he wished he had chosen Drake and the Armada instead of this pack of ruffians—but no, he had never been able to stand seasickness. He couldn't have taken the Channel, not even for five minutes.

And there was no changing now. He had chosen this place and time carefully, at great expense—actually, at great risk, for the X-4-A had aborted twice, and he had had a hard time bringing her in. But it had got him here at last. And, because for a historian he had always been an impetuous and daring man, he grinned now, thinking of the glory that was to come. And he was a participant —much better than a ringside seat! Only he would have to be careful, at the last, to slip away.

John Ord knew very well how this coming battle had ended, back here in 1836.

He marched back to William Barret Travis, clicked heels smartly. Travis's eyes glowed; he was the only senior officer here who loved military punctilio. "Sir, they are on the way."

"Thank you, Ord." Travis hesitated a moment. "Look, Ord. There will be a battle, as we know. I know so little about you. If something should happen to you, is there anyone to write? Across the water?"

Ord grinned. "No, sir. I'm afraid my ancestor wouldn't understand."

Travis shrugged. Who was he to say that Ord was crazy? In this day and age, any man with vision was looked on as mad. Sometimes, he felt closer to Ord than to the others.

The two officers Ord had summoned entered the chapel. The big man in the Mexican jacket tried to dominate the wood table at which they sat. He towered over the slender, nervous Travis, but the commandant, straight-backed and arrogant, did not give an inch. "Boys, you know Santa Anna has invested us. We've been fired on all day—" He seemed to be listening for something. *Wham!* Outside, a cannon split the dusk with flame and sound as it fired from the walls. "There is my answer!"

The man in the lounge coat shrugged. "What I want to know is what our orders are. What does old Sam say? Sam and me were in Congress once. Sam's got good sense; he can smell the way the wind's blowin'." He stopped speaking and hit his guitar a few licks. He winked across the table at the officer in the Mexican jacket, who took out his knife. "Eh, Jim?"

"Right," Jim said. "Sam's a good man, although I don't think he ever met a payroll."

"General Houston's leaving it up to me," Travis told them.

"Well, that's that," Jim said unhappily. "So what you figurin' to do, Bill?"

Travis stood up in the weak, flickering candlelight, one hand on the polished hilt of his saber. The other two men winced, watching him. "Gentlemen, Houston's trying to pull his militia together while he falls back. You know Texas was woefully unprepared for a contest at arms. The general's idea is to draw Santa Anna as far into Texas as he can, then hit him when he's extended, at the right place and right time. But Houston needs more time— Santa Anna's moved faster than any of us anticipated. Unless we can stop the Mexican Army and take a little steam out of them, General Houston's in trouble."

Jim flicked the knife blade in and out. "Go on."

"This is where we come in, gentlemen. Santa Anna can't leave a force of one hundred eighty men in his rear.

284

If we hold fast, he must attack us. But he has no siege equipment, not even large field cannon." Travis's eye gleamed. "Think of it, boys! He'll have to mount a frontal attack, against protected American riflemen. Ord, couldn't your Englishers tell him a few things about that!"

"Whoa, now," Jim barked. "Billy, anybody tell you there's maybe four or five thousand Mexicaners comin'?"

"Let them come. Less will leave!"

But Jim, sour-faced turned to the other man. "Davey? You got something to say?"

"Hell, yes. How do we get out, after we done pinned Santa Anna down? You thought of that, Billy boy?"

Travis shrugged. "There is an element of grave risk, of course. Ord, where's the document, the message you wrote up for me? Ah, thank you." Travis cleared his throat. "Here's what I'm sending on to General Houston." He read: "Commandancy of the Alamo, February 24, 1836 . . . are you sure of the date, Ord?"

"Oh, I'm sure of that," Ord said.

"Never mind—if you're wrong we can change it later. 'To the People of Texas and all Americans in the World. Fellow Freemen and Compatriots! I am besieged with a thousand or more Mexicans under Santa Anna. I have sustained a continual bombardment for many hours but have not lost a man. The enemy has demanded surrender at discretion; otherwise, the garrison is to be put to the sword, if taken. I have answered the demand with a cannon shot, and our flag still waves proudly over the walls. I shall never surrender or retreat. Then, I call on you in the name of liberty, of patriotism and everything dear to the American character—'" He paused, frowning. "This language seems pretty old-fashioned, Ord—"

"Oh, no, sir. That's exactly right," Ord murmured.

"'. . . To come to our aid with all dispatch. The enemy is receiving reinforcements daily and will no doubt increase to three or four thousand in four or five days. If this call is neglected, I am determined to sustain myself as long as possible and die like a soldier who never forgets what is due his honor or that of his homeland. VICTORY OR DEATH!' "

* * *

Travis stopped reading, looked up. "Wonderful! Wonderful!" Ord breathed. "The greatest words of defiance ever written in the English tongue—and so much more literate than that chap at Bastogne."

"You mean to send that?" Jim gasped.

The man called Davey was holding his head in his hands.

"You object, Colonel Bowie?" Travis asked icily.

"Oh, cut that 'colonel' stuff, Bill," Bowie said. "It's only a National Guard title, and I like 'Jim' better, even though I am a pretty important man. Damn right I have an objection! Why, that message is almost aggressive. You'd think we wanted to fight Santa Anna! You want us to be marked down as warmongers? It'll give us trouble when we get to the negotiation table—"

Travis's head turned. "Colonel Crockett?"

"What Jim says goes for me, too. And this: I'd change that part about all Americans, et cetera. You don't want anybody to think we think we're better than the Mexicans. After all, Americans are a minority in the world. Why not make it 'all men who love security'? That'd have worldwide appeal—"

"Oh, Crockett," Travis hissed.

Crockett stood up. "Don't use that tone of voice to me, Billy Travis! That piece of paper you got don't make you no better'n us. I ran for Congress twice, and won. I know what the people want—"

"What the people want doesn't mean a damn right now," Travis said harshly. "Don't you realize the tyrant is at the gates?"

Crockett rolled his eyes heavenward. "Never thought I'd hear a good American say that! Billy, you'll never run for office—"

Bowie held up a hand, cutting into Crockett's talk. "All right, Davey. Hold up. You ain't runnin' for Congress now. Bill, the main thing I don't like in your whole message is that part about victory or death. That's got to go. Don't ask us to sell that to the troops!"

Travis closed his eyes briefly. "Boys, listen. We don't have to tell the men about this. They don't need to know the real story until it's too late for them to get out. And then we shall cover ourselves with such glory that none of us shall ever be forgotten. Americans are the best fighters in the world when they are trapped. They teach this in the Foot School back on the Chatahoochee. And if we die, to die for one's country is sweet—"

"Hell with that," Crockett drawled. "I don't mind dyin', but not for these big landowners like Jim Bowie here. I just been thinkin'—I don't own nothing in Texas."

"I resent that," Bowie shouted. "You know very well I volunteered, after I sent my wife off to Acapulco to be with her family." With an effort, he calmed himself. "Look, Travis. I have some reputation as a fighting man—you know I lived through the gang wars back home. It's obvious this Alamo place is indefensible, even if we had a thousand men."

"But we must delay Santa Anna at all costs—"

Bowie took out a fine, dark Mexican cigar and whittled at it with his blade. Then he lit it, saying around it, "All right, let's all calm down. Nothing a group of good men can't settle around a table. Now listen. I got in with this revolution at first because I thought old Emperor Iturbide would listen to reason and lower taxes. But nothin's worked out, because hotheads like you, Travis, queered the deal. All this yammerin' about liberty! Mexico is a Republic, under an emperor, not some kind of democracy, and we can't change that. Let's talk some sense before it's too late. We're all too old and too smart to be wavin' the flag like it's the Fourth of July. Sooner or later, we're goin' to have to sit down and talk with the Mexicans. And like Davey said, I own a million hectares, and I've always paid minimum wage, and my wife's folks are way up there in the Imperial Government of the Republic of Mexico. That means I got influence in all the votin' groups, includin' the American Immigrant, since I'm a minority group member myself. I think I can talk to Santa Anna, and even to old Iturbide. If we sign a treaty now with Santa Anna, acknowledge the law of the land, I think our lives and property rights will be respected." He cocked an eye toward Crockett.

"Makes sense, Jim. That's the way we do it in Congress. Compromise, everybody happy. We never allowed ourselves to be led nowhere we didn't want to go, I can tell you! And Bill, you got to admit that we're in a better bargaining position if we're out in the open, than if old Santa Anna's got us penned up in this old Alamo."

"Ord," Travis said despairingly. "Ord, you understand. Help me! Make them listen!"

Ord moved into the candlelight, his lean face sweating. "Gentlemen, this is all wrong! It doesn't happen this way—"

Crockett sneered, "Who asked you, Ord? I'll bet you ain't even got a poll tax!"

Decisively, Bowie said, "We're free men, Travis, and we won't be led around like cattle. How about it, Davey? Think you could handle the rear guard, if we try to move out of here?"

"Hell, yes! Just so we're movin'!"

"O.K. Put it to a vote of the men outside. Do we stay, and maybe get croaked, or do we fall back and conserve our strength until we need it? Take care of it, eh, Davey?"

Crockett picked up his guitar and went outside.

Travis roared, "This is insubordination! Treason!" He drew his saber, but Bowie took it from him and broke it in two. Then the big man pulled his knife.

"Stay back, Ord. The Alamo isn't worth the bones of a Britainer, either."

"Colonel Bowie, please," Ord cried. "You don't understand! You *must* defend the Alamo! This is the turning point in the winning of the west! If Houston is beaten, Texas will never join the Union! There will be no Mexican War. No California, no nation stretching from sea to shining sea! This is the Americans' manifest destiny. You are the hope of the future . . . you will save the world from Hitler, from Bolshevism—"

"Crazy as a hoot owl," Bowie said sadly. "Ord, you and Travis got to look at it both ways. We ain't all in the right in this war—we Americans got our faults, too."

"But you are free men," Ord whispered. "Vulgar, opinionated, brutal, but free! You are still better than the breed who kneels to tyranny—"

Crockett came in. "O.K., Jim."

"How'd it go?"

"Fifty-one percent for hightailin' it right now."

Bowie smiled. "That's a flat majority. Let's make tracks."

"Comin', Bill?" Crockett asked. "You're O.K., but you just don't know how to be one of the boys. You got to learn that no dog is better'n any other."

"No," Travis croaked hoarsely. "I stay. Stay or go, we shall all die like dogs, anyway. Boys, for the last time! Don't reveal our weakness to the enemy—"

"What weakness? We're stronger than them. Americans could whip the Mexicans any day, if we wanted to. But the thing to do is make 'em talk, not fight. So long, Bill."

The two big men stepped outside. In the night there was a sudden clatter of hoofs as the Texans mounted and rode. From across the river came a brief spatter of musket fire, then silence. In the dark, there had been no difficulty in breaking through the Mexican lines.

Inside the chapel, John Ord's mouth hung slackly. He muttered, "Am I insane? It didn't happen this way—it couldn't! The books can't be *that* wrong—"

In the candlelight, Travis hung his head. "We tried, John. Perhaps it was a forlorn hope at best. Even if we had defeated Santa Anna, or delayed him, I do not think the Indian Nations would have let Houston get help from the United States."

Ord continued his dazed muttering, hardly hearing.

"We need a contiguous frontier with Texas," Travis continued slowly, just above a whisper. "But we Americans have never broken a treaty with the Indians, and pray God we never shall. *We* aren't like the Mexicans, always pushing, always grabbing off New Mexico, Arizona, California. *We* aren't colonial oppressors, thank God! No, it wouldn't have worked out, even if we American immigrants had secured our rights in Texas—" He lifted a short, heavy, percussion pistol in his hand and cocked it. "I hate to say it, but perhaps if we hadn't taken Payne and Jefferson so seriously—if we could only have paid lip service, and done what we really wanted to do, in our hearts . . . no matter. I won't live to see our final disgrace."

He put the pistol to his head and blew out his brains.

* * *

Ord was still gibbering when the Mexican cavalry stormed into the old mission, pulling down the flag and seizing him, dragging him before the resplendent little general in green and gold.

Since he was the only prisoner, Santa Anna questioned Ord carefully. When the sharp point of a bayonet had been thrust half an inch into his stomach, the Britainer seemed to come around. When he started speaking, and the Mexicans realized he was English, it went better with him. Ord was obviously mad, it seemed to Santa Anna, but since he spoke English and seemed educated, he could be useful. Santa Anna didn't mind the raving; he understood all about Napoleon's detention camps and what they had done to Britainers over there. In fact, Santa Anna was thinking of setting up a couple of those camps himself. When they had milked Ord dry, they threw him on a horse and took him along.

Thus John Ord had an excellent view of the battlefield when Santa Anna's cannon broke the American lines south of the Trinity. Unable to get his men across to safety, Sam Houston died leading the last, desperate charge against the Mexican regulars. After that, the American survivors were too tired to run from the cavalry that pinned them against the flooding river. Most of them died there. Santa Anna expressed complete indifference to what happened to the Texans' women and children.

Mexican soldiers found Jim Bowie hiding in a hut, wearing a plain linen tunic and pretending to be a civilian. They would not have discovered his identity had not some of the Texan women whom the cavalry had captured cried out, "Colonel Bowie—Colonel Bowie!" as he was led into the Mexican camp.

He was hauled before Santa Anna, and Ord was summoned to watch. "Well, Don Jaime," Santa Anna remarked, "You have been a foolish man. I promised your wife's uncle to send you to Acapulco safely, though of course your lands are forfeit. You understand we must have lands for the veterans' program when this campaign is over—" Santa Anna smiled then. "Besides, since Ord here has told me how instrumental you were in the abandonment of the Alamo, I think the emperor will agree to mercy in your case. You know, Don Jaime, your compatriots had me worried back there. The Alamo might have been a tough nut to crack . . . *pues*, no matter."

And since Santa Anna had always been broadminded, not objecting to light skin or immigrant background, he invited Bowie to dinner that night.

Santa Anna turned to Ord. "But if we could catch this rascally war criminal, Crockett . . . however, I fear he has escaped us. He slipped over the river with a fake passport, and the Indians have interned him."

"Si, *Señor Presidente*," Ord said dully.

"Please, don't call me that," Santa Anna cried, looking around. "True, many of us officers have political ambitions, but Emperor Iturbide is old and vain. It could mean my head—"

Suddenly, Ord's head was erect, and the old, clear light was in his blue eyes. "Now I understand!" he shouted. "I thought Travis was raving back there, before he shot himself—and your talk of the emperor! American respect for Indian rights! Jeffersonian form of government! Oh, those ponces who peddled me that X-4-A—the *track jumper*! I'm not back in my own past. I've jumped the time track—*I'm back in a screaming alternate!*"

"Please not so loud, Señor Ord." Santa Anna sighed. "Now, we must shoot a few more American officers, of course. I regret this, you understand, and I shall no doubt be much criticized in French Canada and Russia, where there are still civilized values. But we must establish the Republic of the Empire once and for all upon this continent, that aristocratic tyranny shall not perish from the earth. Of course, as an Englishman, you understand perfectly, Señor Ord."

"Of course, Excellency," Ord said.

"There are soft hearts—soft heads, I say—in Mexico who cry for civil rights for the Americans. But I must make sure that Mexican dominance is never again threatened north of the Rio Grande."

"*Seguro*, Excellency," Ord said, suddenly. If the bloody X-4-A *had* jumped the track, there was no getting back, none at all. He was stuck here. Ord's blue

291

eyes narrowed. "After all, it . . . it is manifest destiny that the Latin peoples of North America meet at the center of the continent. Canada and Mexico shall share the Mississippi."

Santa Anna's dark eyes glowed. "You say what I have often thought. You are a man of vision, and much sense. You realize the *Indios* must go, whether they were here first or not. I think I will make you my secretary, with the rank of captain."

"*Gracias*, Excellency."

"Now, let us write my communiqué to the capital, *Capitán* Ord. We must describe how the American abandonment of the Alamo allowed me to press the traitor Houston so closely he had no chance to maneuver his men into the trap he sought. *Ay, Capitán*, it is a cardinal principle of the Anglo-Saxons, to get themselves into a trap from which they must fight their way out. This I never let them do, which is why I succeed where others fail . . . you said something, *Capitán*?"

"*Sí*, Excellency. I said, I shall title our communiqué: 'Remember the Alamo,'" Ord said, standing at attention.

"*Bueno!* You have a gift for words. Indeed, if ever we feel the *gringos* are too much for us, your words shall once again remind us of the truth!" Santa Anna smiled. "I think I shall make you a major. You have indeed coined a phrase which shall live in history forever!"

VALHALLA FOR HIRE
Lee Brainard

EDITOR'S INTRODUCTION

There is a certain fascination to mercenary armies, from Xenophon's Ten Thousand to Mad Mike Hoare's Fifth Commando in Katanga. Of course, the classic era of mercenaries was at the end of the Middle Ages.

Italy in the fourteenth century saw endless war, between Pisa and Florence, Venice and Genoa, Milan and Verona, and nearly all permutations and combinations of the above as alliances shifted like smoke. It was the great era of the *condottieri*, mercenary captains who made war pay; or tried to. Not all were successful. The greatest captain of his time was Carmagnola, who in 1432 was lured from his camp to Venice by a delusive message, and suddenly executed by his employers for treason suspected but never proved. The Venetians impartially did the same for their doges: Marino Faliero was executed because the Council suspected he was plotting to use mercenaries to make himself a tyrant. That had certainly been done before, as the della Scala and Sforza families would do in the future.

C.W.C. Oman in his *Art of War in the Middle Ages* (the big two-volume history, not the short essay of the same title) says of one mercenary captain:

"Of the foreign *condottieri* John Hawkwood was not

only the most famous but by far the most respectable —
virtuoso not only in Machiavelli's sense but according to
all military standards of his day. He never broke his oath;
he was in 1364 the only captain of the Pisans whom the
Florentines could not bribe. He carried out his contracts
with rigorous probity, and he never sold his employer of
the moment . . . Mercenaries of rival bands, who fell into
his hands in the course of business, could always count
on a quick release and a moderate ransom. It is no
wonder that his Florentine patrons regarded him as a
paragon of virtue and placed his figure on horseback
over the southwest portal of their Duomo."

In fact the story is more interesting: Hawkwood was
called to save the city of Florence, which he did. Part of
his payment was that a marble statue of Hawkwood on
horseback would be erected in the cathedral. When the
battle was won, the thrifty Florentines instead had
painted a mural of a statue; it is this that Oman refers to,
and it can be seen to this day.

Machiavelli, that most astute observer, also says;

"Condottieri are either capable persons or they are not;
if they are clever you cannot rely on them, for they will
be scheming for their own exaltation, either by falling on
you, their employer, or else by molesting other states,
whom you have no interest in provoking. If they are not
clever, on the other hand, they will lose for you a battle
and ruin you. And if you say that any commander,
mercenary or no, may do that, the answer is that both a
prince and a republic had better work for themselves.
The prince had better be his own commander in chief,
and the republic had better set its own citizens over its
army. If they prove inefficient, they can be changed, and
if efficient they can be prevented by law from getting too
much power. History proves that only princes and war-
like republics make great conquests; mercenary armies
have brought nothing but loss in the end. And it is much
harder for an over-great citizen to master an armed
people than a people who have mercenary soldiers
only."

Of course, some of the mercenary captains did well;
the Sforza family became Dukes of Milan.

Clearchus scowls,
John Hawkwood grins.
Trinquier howls,
and Sforza wins.

"Sit down and tell us your story; we would take it in
   good part.
We've been listening to each others' till we know them
   all by heart.
That one marched with Chandos, and yon was
   Braccio's man;
I took my pay from the King of France, before my own
   blood ran.

"Our mountain lands are stony poor, and Britain's
   Crown has gold.
Two centuries, now, she's paid our men to guard the
   land she holds.
We marched through steaming jungles; we crossed the
   casteless sea;
Paraded before her palace gates, that she safely sits to
   tea.

"More lands than our troops ever trod. Well, sooner
   you than we.
Not even for the Spider would the Switzers cross the
   sea.
No cannon for us, nor oceans; and if the cantons had
   needed men
and sent the word recalling us, we should have
   marched home again.

"Raj Guru gave us leave to go, and to return again.
He got it for us wholesale when the Crown had need of
   men.
From mountain villages, our name has now worldwide
   renown:
there's honor in the weapons we were issued by the
   Crown.

"Employers are free with steel and lead; less free with
   silver and gold.
It was after the Booty of Burgundy that soldiering took
   hold.
The danger's less on the battlefield than on the last
   parade,
When the man who hired you starts to think: Dead
   men don't have to be paid.

"The Crown does not disown our deeds. We were no
   whores of war.
We served the Crown as the grandsires of our
   grandsires did before.
Our sahibs, too, took up the task their grandsires
   handed down,
Whose grandsires marched with Young Sahib, who
   hired us to serve the Crown.

"We had a touch of that ourselves, till the Lilies
   crowned a fool.
That's why the dying lion's carved beside the quiet
   pool.
When the Spider hired our halberds, he was miserly
   with our blood;
his namesake sacrificed us to the rising rebel flood.

"I, too, was of the last, without dishonor to the Crown.
My sons are thriving merchants with their base in
   Goorka town.
Their copper shipments pass some teeth my uncle
   helped to pull;
where my father searched for foemen, now they deal in
   tallow and wool."

> Clearchus scowls,
> John Hawkwood grins.
> Trinquier howls,
> and Sforza wins.

DEBATING SDI: OPINION OR FACT?
Doug Beason

EDITOR'S INTRODUCTION

Years ago when I was employed by the Aerospace Corporation I was required to give a standard disclaimer whenever I made a speech. I'd say something like:

"The following represents my own opinion and does not necessarily reflect the opinions, policies, or doctrines of the Aerospace Corporation, the United States Air Force, the Department of Defense, or the United States of America; and I think that's a darned shame."

Doug Beason, who is both a particle physicist and a serving officer with the U.S. Air Force, wouldn't quite put it that way; but we are required to say:

"The views and opinions expressed or implied in this article are those of the author and are not to be construed as carrying the official sanction of the Department of Defense or the U.S. Air Force."

The SDI debate has been extremely odd: whereas Mr. Robert A. Heinlein called SDI "the best news since VJ Day," most of the nation's press has acted as if there were something immoral about a defense that defends.

The opponents of strategic defense will not, unless

pressed, admit that they don't want defenses even if they work; they prefer to look as if they are debating laws of physics. "We can't build it," they say; but the odd part is that as far as I know everyone who says we can't build it will, if really hard pressed, admit that it wouldn't be desirable to put it up even if we could do it quickly, efficiently, and cheaply. They just don't want a defense that defends.

Now it's true that this globe has, under the mutual fear of nuclear war, enjoyed an era without great wars. Those killed in Korea and Vietnam might not appreciate the distinction. Those killed in Cambodia because they were able to read and write certainly wouldn't understand. We have huge institutions devoted to studies of the Holocaust, and rightly so; why are not three million Cambodians at least half as interesting? Is it because they are not caucasians, not Jewish, or that there were only three million of them? For whatever reason, they seem to be ignored, and I've wandered from my point, which is that we can, I suppose, say that Mutual Assured Destruction —the doctrine that says that I'll let you kill me provided that I get to kill you back—has kept since 1945 an uneasy state we can call peace even if the price has been pretty high.

The price of Mutual Assured Destruction, though, is that we build sufficient weapons to assure the destruction of the other guy after he has taken his best shot; which means accumulating more and more missiles and nuclear weapons. Arthur C. Clarke once likened that to "two small boys standing in a pool of gasoline seeing who could accumulate the most matches." Alas he had the analogy wrong; but in fact it could be done that way. We have the technical capability to build doomsday machines that will automatically set themselves off if the United States is attacked.

I never met anyone who wanted to make such a thing; which is interesting, because if we really believe in Mutual Assured Destruction, isn't that what we ought to be building?

No matter how much he tries, or how much he lobbies, President Reagan's Strategic Defense Initiative just doesn't have a chance. SDI is as good as dead.

However, the president's "Star Wars" program *does* have a chance. Ever since Teddy Kennedy's offhand, spur of the moment (knee-jerk?) remark dismissing SDI as so much mumbo-jumbo, the press has incessantly promoted missile defense as "Star Wars." In this era of linguistic Watergatese and thirty-second "indepth" analyses, the misnomer *Star Wars* is here to stay.

So what?

So what if "Star Wars" inaccurately portrays what is arguably the most farsighted and noble dream that man has dared to undertake? If, according to Dr. Benjamin Spock, the threat of nuclear war is such a terrible psychological burden to our children, then doesn't mankind have a duty to prevent it from happening? And being realistic—knowing the myriad Soviet violations of every treaty we've signed with them—why doesn't a mutual shield stopping these missiles appeal to everyone?

Certainly, tagging a science fictional title onto SDI doesn't help—but should this be a major concern to those debating SDI? I propose not, for there is something of greater importance to worry about: a disturbing number of anti-SDI opinions, cleverly disguised as facts, bubbling about in the "neutral" press.

Our society guarantees every crackpot, nut, and ax murderer the right to air their opinions in public. And this is not bad; in fact, it's the very stuff that makes us free. No matter how weird or disjointed someone else's view may seem, there just might be a glimmer of insight in that cesspool of twisted rationale.

The danger comes when those bastions of free thought —the printed, vocal and visual media—take subtle sides in an argument; taking sides by presenting opinions as facts.

First allow me to clarify a point—it is absolutely *essential* that editorial freedom exist in the press. In fact, this is the only way good decisions are made. Debate, oration, and cross-examination ensure that every side of an issue is examined in detail. And during this process, an opinion is stated as an opinion and remains mutually exclusive from fact. Example: if the *National Review* (clearly a magazine of opinion) started espousing procommunistic propaganda as a scientific fact, then I would either suspect that William F. Buckley has something up his sleeve or someone is tapping into the magazine's typesetting link. No surprises here— surprises in the sense that if a journal is (quietly now!) *slanted* in a particular manner, one is aware that he is being fed editorial opinion and not fact.

I expect opinion from *National Review*, not a treatise on quantum physics.

Contrast this to scientific journals. Undistorted facts, free of preconceived views, are essential to understanding scientific arguments. No one can argue with this.

Carrying this one step further, when a decision is pending on something as important as defending our country against nuclear attack, editorial license can not be tolerated. Just as in a debate, where people sway one another with facts, opinion should be kept out of the arena—or at least until all the facts are in and a decision is imminent.

The SDI debate is charged with emotion, and a danger lies in the synergistic mixing of facts and opinions. Example: *Scientific American*, an age-old and respected scientific journal for both the scientist and layman alike, in three years since President Reagan's March 1983 SDI speech, has published not fewer than fourteen antinuclear or anti-SDI articles—an average of *one every three issues*.

And every one of those articles was the lead article for the magazine that month.

So what is the problem? They have their right to an opinion, don't they?

For one, this journal, usually noted for its unbiased presentation of facts, made sweeping, inflammatory statements which preceeded every anti-SDI article. An example, published in October, 1984: "President Reagan's 'Star Wars' program seems unlikely ever to protect the entire nation against a nuclear attack. It would nonetheless trigger a major expansion of the arm's race."

This is an example of unbiased facts? Another abstract, published in June 1984, on antisatellite weapons: "Unless some action is taken to restrain further development of such weapons the positive contributions of satellites to international security will be threatened."

Objections? Certainly *Scientific American* may address social questions as well as scientific ones. There is no problem with this, and it is a commendable effort; social responsibility has long been a precedent among scientists. However, when only one point of view is presented—a point of view tainted by the author's predisposition—one wonders if this is not an unbiased examination of the facts; especially when many nonscientist readers look to this journal in anticipation of a neutral, nonopinionated presentation. When the author knows *a priori* what he wants to prove, and incessantly uses only certain facts to gain those conclusions, then the thin guise of neutrality is stripped away and all credibility is lost.

A legitimate need exists for debate on SDI; that is the only way that SDI's problems may be ironed out. But for every protest the anti-SDI crowd cries out, a counter example can be given. This article is not intended to challenge the anti-SDI findings (of which some are very good), but a few moments' thought on some of the issues brings these observations:

—arguing about the Soviets stopping a U.S. laser defense by rotating their missiles as they're launched (have you ever considered how hard it is just to keep a *nonrotating* missile stable, much less a rotating one? Ask any launch control officer);

—arguing that the Soviets can neutralize U.S. lasers by painting a reflective coating on their missiles (*nothing* can reflect every type of laser; furthermore, critics such as Garwin dismiss the obvious implication that the extra weight of the reflective painting cuts missile range and warhead loads. In addition, he misses the point that one less warhead per missile slashes the Soviet nuclear arsenal by over *10 percent*!);

—arguing that the Soviets can disguise their missile's heat emissions to prevent the U.S. from detecting them, by either adding "sputtering" agents or using "fast-burning" fuels (cryogenic methods—used in detecting faint stars, spy satellites, and other applications—have been around for years; the U.S. leads the Soviets in fast-burning fuels by a factor of five to ten years, and *we* can't get our burn times down below a minute);

—arguing "the Soviets can put up more offensive weapons than we can afford defensive ones" (ever hear of Greg Canavan's square root law? They have to put up the *square* of any amount we put up. Example: they need sixteen as many systems to defeat four of ours);

—or even arguing that antisatellite measures by the Soviets would make space-based platforms too vulnerable (I like Jerry Pournelle's idea the best on this one: surround the space platform with twenty feet of concrete—concrete made from material mined on the moon!—and set a U.S. general officer on board. That way, any preemptive attack on the platform by the Soviets is an outright act of war).

These issues are important, but a journal devoted to disseminating scientific fact is not the place for them to be debated. On second thought, maybe it *is* just the place; but what about the other side of the coin? How many pro-SDI articles have been published in *Scientific American*? If this is truly a neutral forum, well, where are they? Social responsibility is a double-edged sword: you've got to cut with both sides, or one edge dulls. And a review of the literature will convince you that the anti-SDI side is quickly becoming tedious.

Another example: Broad's *Star Warriors* attempts to discuss the SDI issues, but quickly falls into the mode of presenting a pro-SDI argument, then using weak, ill-thought-out examples to counter each argument. One grows weary reading the book, wondering which obscure critic Broad will quote next to prove his preconceived point. An exception to this: *Physics Today* presents both sides of the SDI issue, and should be commended as such; but this practice is in the minority.

What, then, are some of the pro-SDI arguments you

never hear about? For one, if we can make the Soviets go to all the trouble of designing, manufacturing and deploying a totally new technology to defeat SDI, then SDI is already working. Their economy cannot handle the extra workload; we'll bankrupt them. A recent study which says the Soviet infrastructure will be bolstered by their anti-SDI effort has obviously not seen the statistics on what their military production lines (tanks, rockets, bombs—you name it) are already doing to their economy.

Another ridiculous protest is the constraint that we "must kill 100 percent of their missiles for SDI to be successful." If the Soviets can not depend on even 50 percent of their missiles surviving a SDI shield (by the way, which 50 percent of their missiles will we get? The 50% they targeted to our missile fields? No one knows), they *can't* attack. Too many of our missiles would survive to retaliate against them. In other words, deterrence has reared its head and a "leakproof" SDI is not even necessary; just one that keeps them on their toes.

Dr. Lowell Wood, an eminent physicist at Lawrence Livermore National Laboratory, was asked at the 1985 Space Foundation Meeting in Colorado Springs, about the newest concern of the anti-SDI folk: the problems in developing a "bug" free computer program to battle manage SDI. Dr. Wood observed that two years ago, the anti-SDI argument was that the technology for SDI would be impossible to attain; last year's bugaboo was the cost of deploying SDI. Both of those protests were rescinded after proven false—proven false by such demonstrations as an electromagnetic railgun smashing a plastic bullet through an inch and a half plate of steel; a navy laser blasting through a missile at White Sands; the army intercepting, and obliterating, a missile in space, launched from Vandenberg AFB; the air force tracking the Space Shuttle with a laser on a mountaintop in Hawaii; atmospheric distortions removed from a laser beam propagating through the atmosphere; a neutral particle beam experiment soon to fly in space; advances in microwave technology; and a demonstration of the most efficient laser ever made—the free electron laser (FEL). The success of other, highly classified projects, such as "third generation" nuclear weapons—of which X-ray lasers are only one facet—can only be hinted at; but Dr. Edward Teller, the Father of the H-Bomb, has testified before Congress and is absolutely convinced of their utility.

Dr. Wood's question, then, to the anti-SDI crowd was what would be their protest next year? The software "problem," albeit a necessary worry, has been addressed (and probably solved by using modular programming, a technique that the National Laboratories, and AT&T, among others, have been using for years) and should not be the driving reason for scrubbing SDI. In fact, nor should any one reason be enough to halt SDI. What the critics conveniently forget is that SDI is a *research* project; a project soley to determine the feasibility of having a defensive shield. How can they be unbiased if they've already made up their minds that SDI won't work?

For something as important as SDI, and especially before any decision is made to deploy these systems, accurate facts must be presented and examined. But is this truly possible when a small group of scientists (the Union of Concerned Scientists totals less than *1 percent* of all scientists) blatantly taint the most important issue of our time with preconceived opinions?

A recent cartoon portrayed two ways to exercise the scientific method: the first method is to make a hypothesis, gather data, and then compare the hypothesis with the data to reach a conclusion; the second "method" reaches a conclusion, then gathers data to support that conclusion. This second "method" of research is an insult to all those who study the sciences, and in the very least, as a research project, SDI should be accorded the first method.

Opinion versus fact. It doesn't matter what you call SDI—let's make sure it is accurately portrayed and studied in a rational manner. *Then* let's make a decision, whatever it may be.

CONSEQUENCES
Walter Jon Williams

EDITOR'S INTRODUCTION

Many years ago I fell in love with sailboats. When a college friend began a boat-building apprenticeship at Edison Technical Schools in Seattle, we decided we would build a midget ocean-racing sloop designed by Edward Weber, the Long Island marine architect. It was very likely the only way I would ever afford a sailboat; and those days I despised plastic. I wanted a real sailboat of real wood, oak frames and yellow cedar planking, spruce mast . . .

Ariadne was lofted on the floor of my basement, her lines taken from Weber's article in an ancient copy of a yachting magazine. She was largely built by hand. Her plywood decks were covered with thin strips of teak. Her cabin was varnished mahogany, as was her transom. She boasted toe rails. She was, in a word, very nearly the world's largest model ship.

She wasn't very large, twenty feet overall, but there was room for two berths and a gimballed stove. A boat like that is intended for protected waters; she'd have been perfect for Lake Washington, or even Puget Sound. About the time she was finished, though, I found myself living in Southern California. Poul Anderson and I had many adventures getting her from Seattle to Los Angeles.

Twenty feet is pretty small for a sailboat on the open Pacific; but *Ariadne* proved seaworthy. More than once we took her out to Catalina Island, sailing past the square red storm warning flags the Coast Guard flew from the Long Beach Breakwater lighthouse. She was slow going to windward in a high sea, but go she did; and running downwind she planed. Sometimes we took her further, to the Channel Islands, or to lonely Santa Barbara Island.

I had that boat for twenty years, and she was as sound at the end as she was when we launched her. Alas, keeping up a wooden boat took time, so much time that eventually I never took her out; those who lived aboard boats in the yard where I kept her said *Ariadne* cried at night from loneliness. Eventually I gave her to someone who wanted her enough to love her.

I will, someday, have another sailboat; meanwhile, I am a sucker for a good sea story.

Walter Jon Williams has a very good sea story.

WHITE SAILS CUT PRECISE ARCS AGAINST A BACKGROUND OF vivid color: green sea, blue sky, black volcanic sand. Spindrift shone like diamonds as it spattered over the weather rail. *Birdwing* heeled in the strong gust; timber and cordage groaned as they took the strain. Captain Derec SuPashto adjusted his stance to the increased tilt of the deck; his mind was on other things.

Birdwing and its convoy were about to be attacked by the Liavekan Navy.

"My compliments to the ship's wizard, Facer," he said. "Ask him if he can veer this wind two or four points."

"Sir."

A veering wind would be useful, Derec thought, if Levett could conjure one up. But whatever happened, let it stay strong.

"Starboard a point, Sandor."

"Starboard a point, aye, aye."

"Break out our colors, SuKrone."

"Sir."

Derec's first reaction on seeing the three Liavekan warships was not one of anxiety, but rather relief. *Birdwing* would finally have a chance to prove itself to Ka Zhir, and that chance was desperately needed.

As the streaming black-and-gold Zhir ensign broke out overhead, Derec studied the enemy with narrowed eyes: three bright ships on a shallow sea the color of green baize. The lead galleass was a big one, thirty oars or more per side, white foam curling from its massive ramming prow. It was painted purple with scarlet trim; a rear admiral's blue pennant fluttered from its maintop and gold leaf winked from the carved arabesques that decorated the stern. The second galleass, three cables astern, was smaller and lighter, its rigging more delicate: it would be at a disadvantage in this strong wind, this choppy sea. It hadn't been painted; its sides were the bright color of varnished wood. Astern of the second enemy was a small xebec—its military value was negligible unless it could get under an enemy's stern in a dead calm, in which case it could pound away with its bow chaser until its opponent was nothing but driftwood. Likely it served as a tender, or was used for chasing down unarmed merchantmen. Derec's impulse was to discount it.

A brave sight, these three, on the green ocean. They seemed entirely in their element.

Derec knew that appearances were deceiving.

He wondered what the Liavekan admiral was thinking as he stood on his fine gingerbread poop. The Liavekan squadron had been lurking along the coast between Ka Zhir and Gold Harbor for the obvious purpose of attacking a convoy: and now a convoy had appeared, twelve caravels and two huge carracks, all crammed to the gunnels with trade goods. The Liavekan squadron, waiting behind a barren, palm-covered islet, had duly sprung their ambush and were now driving toward their prey. But what in hell, they must wonder, was the escort?

A ship of *Birdwing*'s type had never been seen in these waters. The stout masts and heavy standing rigging marked her as northern-built, a Farlander ship able to stand up to winter gales in the high latitudes, but even in

307

the north she would cut an odd figure. She was too narrow, flat-sided, and low for a carrack. The forward-tilting mainmast and bonaventure mizzen would have marked her as a galleon, but if she was a galleon, where were the high fore- and sterncastles? And where were the billowing, baglike square sails the Liavekans had come to associate with those heavy, sluggish northern ships? *Birdwing*'s square sails were cut flat, curved gently like a bird's wing, hence its name.

To the Liavekan admiral, Derec wondered, how did this all add up? A galleon with its upper decks razed, perhaps, in an effort to make it lighter, and furthermore cursed with an eccentric sailmaker. Some kind of bastard ship at any rate, neither fish nor fowl, with a broadside to beware of, but a military value easily enough discounted. Everyone knew that northern ships couldn't sail to weather—unlike the oar-driven galleys and galleasses of the Levar's navy, galleons were doomed to sail only downwind. And the Liavekan's tactics were clearly aimed at getting the escort to leeward of its convoy, where it couldn't possibly sail upwind again to protect it.

You're in for a surprise, Milord Admiral, Derec thought. Because *Birdwing* is going to make those wormy hulks of yours obsolete, and all in the next turn of the glass.

"Wizard's compliments, sir." Lieutenant Facer had returned, sunlight winking from his polished brass earrings; he held his armored cap at the salute. "He might venture a spell to veer the wind, but it would take twenty minutes or more."

Within twenty minutes they'd be in gunshot. Weather spells were delicate things, consuming enormous amounts of power to shift the huge kinetic energies that made up a wind front, and often worked late or not at all.

"Compliments to the wizard, Facer. Tell him we'll make do with the wind we've got."

"Sir." Facer dropped his hat back on his peeling, sunburned head. For a sailor he had a remarkably delicate complexion, and these southern latitudes made things worse: his skin was forever turning red and flaking off. He was openly envious of Derec's adaptation to the

308

climate: the sun had just browned the captain's skin and bleached his graying hair almost white.

Facer turned and took two steps toward the poop companionway, then stopped. "Sir," he said. "I think our convoy has just seen the enemy."

"Right. Cut along, Facer."

"Sir."

The Zhir convoy, arrayed in a ragged line just downwind of *Birdwing*, was now showing belated signs of alarm. Five minutes had passed before any of them noticed an entire enemy squadron sweeping up from two miles away. Derec had no illusions about the quality of the merchant captains: the convoy would scatter like chaff before a hailstorm. None of them were capable of outrunning a squadron of warships: their only chance was to scatter in all directions and hope only a few would fall victim to the enemy. Still, Derec should probably try to do something, at least to show the Zhir he'd tried to protect their cities' shipping.

"Signal to the convoy, Randem," he said. "Close up, then tack simultaneously."

The boy's look was disbelieving. "As you like, sir."

Derec gave him a wry grin. "For form's sake, Randem."

"Aye, aye, sir. For form's sake."

Signal flags rose on the halyards, but none of the convoy bothered an acknowledgment: the merchanters had no confidence in the ship's fighting abilities and were looking out for themselves. Derec shrugged. This was nothing more than he expected. At least they were clearing out and leaving an empty sea between *Birdwing* and the enemy.

Birdwing gave a shuddering roll as it staggered down the face of a wave; Derec swayed to compensate and almost lost his balance. His heavy breastplate and helmet were adding unaccustomed weight to his upper body. The helmet straps were pressing uncomfortably on his brass earrings; and the helmet was warming in the sun, turning into an oven.

Carefully Derec calculated his course and the enemy's. The wind was holding a point north of west: the convoy had been moving roughly north along the general trend

309

of land. The enemy squadron was racing under oars and sail as close to the wind as their characteristics permitted: they were trying to gain as much westing as possible so as not to be pinned between *Birdwing* and the coast. Their course was more or less northwest: *Birdwing* was moving nor'-nor'east on a converging tack. Unless something prevented it, the ships would brush at the intersection of their paths; and then the enemy would be to windward of the *Birdwing*, which was just where they wanted to be.

At which point, Derec thought confidently, they were going to suffer a terrible surprise.

Birdwing's crew were already at quarters; they'd been doing a gun drill when the enemy appeared. There was nothing to do but wait.

"Wizard's compliments, sir." Facer was back, his leather-and-iron cap doffed at the salute. "The enemy is attempting a spell."

"Thank you, Facer." Suddenly the brisk warm breeze blew chill on Derec's neck. He turned to face the enemy, touched his amulet of Thurn Bel and summoned his power.

Awareness flooded his mind. He could feel the protective shields that Levett, *Birdwing*'s wizard, had wound around the ship; from eastward he could feel a strong attempt to penetrate those shields. Derec called his power to him, but held it in reserve in case the onslaught was a feint. The attack faded grudgingly before Levett's persistent defense, then disappeared. Whatever it was, the probe had failed. Levett's protective spells remained intact, on guard.

That was the strategy Derec and Levett had formed weeks ago. The wizard's magic would remain defensive, and *Birdwing*'s bronze cannon would bring the war to the enemy.

Derec let his hand fall from his amulet. He saw his officers standing around him expectantly; he gave them a smile. "Done," he said. "We're safe for the moment." He saw them breathe easier.

He looked at the enemy. Brightness winked from the enemy's decks: marines in their polished armor. He could hear the thud of kettledrums and crash of cymbals

310

as the enemy quartermasters beat time for the rowers. A mile to leeward, in deeper, bluer water now, the galleasses were laboring in the steep sea, the smaller one having a particularly hard time of it.

Derec's awareness tingled: the enemy wizard was making another attempt. Derec monitored the assault and Levett's efforts to parry it. Once again the enemy was repulsed.

There was a flash from the flagship's fo'c'sle, then a gush of blue smoke that the wind tore into streamers across her bows. The thud came a half-second later, followed by a shrieking iron ball that passed a half-cable to larboard. The range was long for gunshot from the pitching deck of a ship beating to windward. Jeers rose from *Birdwing*'s crew.

Another thud, this time from the smaller galleass, followed by another miss, this one coming close to clipping *Birdwing*'s stern. The enemy were giving their gun crews something to do, Derec thought, rather than stand and think about what might come, their own possible mutilation and death.

There was a bump and a mild bang from *Birdwing*'s maindeck, followed by a hoarse bellow. Derec stepped forward to peer over the poop rail; he saw one of the marines had stumbled and dropped his firelock, and the thing had gone off. Marcoyn, the giant marine lieutenant, jerked the man to his feet and smashed him in the face. The marine staggered down the gangway, arms windmilling; Marcoyn followed, driving another punch into the marine's face. Derec clenched his teeth. Hatred roiled in his belly.

"Marcoyn!" he bellowed. The lieutenant looked up at him, his pale eyes savage under the brim of his boarding helmet. His victim clutched the hammock nettings and moaned.

"No interference with the sojers!" Marcoyn roared. "We agreed that, *Captain*!" He almost spat the word.

Derec bit back his anger. "I was going to suggest, Marcoyn, that you blacken the man's eyes later. We may need him in this fight."

"I'll do more than blacken his eyes, by Thurn Bel!"

"Do as you think best, Marcoyn." Derec spoke as

311

tactfully as possible; but still he held Marcoyn's eyes until the marine turned away muttering under his breath, fists clenched at the ends of his knotted arms.

Marcoyn's strange pale eyes never seemed to focus on anything, just glared out at the world with uncentered resentment. He was a brute, a drunk, illiterate, and very likely mad, but he represented an element of *Birdwing*'s crew that Derec couldn't do without. Marcoyn was the living penalty, Derec thought, for the crimes he had committed for the ship he loved.

Derec remembered Marcoyn's massive arms twisting the garrote around young Sempter's neck, the way the boy's eyes had started out of his head, feet kicking helplessly against the mizzen pinrail, shoes flying across the deck. Derec standing below, helpless to prevent it, his shoes tacky with Lieutenant Varga's blood . . .

His mouth dry, Derec glanced at the mizzen shrouds, then banished the memory from his mind. The enemy had fired their bow chasers once more.

The smaller galleass fired first this time, followed a half-second later by the flagship. Interesting, Derec thought. The smaller ship had the better crew.

A strong gust heeled the galleon and drove it through the sea. The waves' reflection danced brightly on the enemy's lateen sails. The enemy squadron was half a mile away. If the ships continued on their present courses, *Birdwing* would soon be alongside the enemy flagship in a yardarm-to-yardarm fight, a situation ideal for the northern galleon.

Another pair of bangs, followed by a buzzing and a smack: the smaller galleass's ball had pitched right through *Birdwing*'s main topsail. Derec saw blond and redheaded countrymen looking up in surprise, heard nervous laughter. This was the first time most of them had been under fire. Derec realized he should probably say something now, offer an inspiring comment to drive any thoughts of fear out of his sailors' heads. He could think of nothing.

"Run out the starboard chaser!" he finally called. "We'll answer that!"

There were some scattered cheers, but Derec could see puzzled expressions. The enemy were within range of the

312

broadside guns: why not open fire with the whole battery? Derec kept his counsel. He was saving the first broadside for close range.

The bronze starboard demiculverin rumbled as it thrust its muzzle from the port. Derec could see the gun captain bent low over the chaser's barrel, timing the ship's motion, linstock in his hand. There was a gush of fire from the priming, then a roar; the gun flung itself back like a monstrous bronze beast. Derec turned to leeward and saw the nine-pound ball skip on the waves like a dancer twenty yards ahead of the enemy's prow. A groan of disappointment went up from *Birdwing*'s crew.

"Chaser crew, fire at will!" Derec called.

The chasers banged at each other for another three or four rounds apiece. The Liavekans showed no sign of changing course: were they really going to let Derec lay alongside and fight exactly the kind of battle he wanted? Ignoring the artillery duel, Derec studied the enemy, the changing relationship between the ships. Tried to get into his enemy's head, wondered what the enemy admiral was thinking.

The sound of kettledrums and cymbals was very loud now, carrying clearly upwind. The enemy sweeps moved in beautiful synchrony, the blue water boiling at their touch. The distance between *Birdwing* and the lead enemy narrowed, and Derec was considering running out his starboard battery when flame blossomed from the enemy's sides and the air was full of shrieking. Derec's heart turned over at the sound of a slamming noise from below—a shot lodged home—followed by another smack as a ball tore through the fore topsail. The enemy had fired its full broadside, maybe ten guns in all.

His nerves wailing in surprise, Derec bit his lip and frowned at the enemy. Something had changed, but he couldn't say what. Something in the pattern of drumbeats and cymbals. Another level of his awareness sensed the enemy's magician attempting a spell. With a start he realized what the enemy intended.

"Hard a-starboard!" he roared, and ran to the break in the poop. Just below him, sheltered by the poop overhang, Sandor the timoneer controlled the ship's whipstaff. "Hard a-starboard!" Derec shrieked again, and he felt the change in the ship's motion that meant the timoneer had flung his weight against the whipstaff and the galleon was beginning to respond to its big rudder. Derec suddenly felt the nature of the enemy spell—it was an attempt to paralyze them for a few seconds, but Levett had parried it, again without the need for Derec's assistance. Derec glanced at the surprised faces of his crew.

"Both broadsides, load and run out! Starboard guns, load with doubleshot! Larboard guns, load with roundshot!" He glanced at the enemy to confirm what he suspected, and found it true—the bright silhouettes were narrowing as one set of sweeps backed water while the other continued driving forward. Lateen sails billowed and snapped as the yards were dropped to the deck. The enemy were changing course, driving straight into the wind under the power of their sweeps alone.

Birdwing lurched as the waves caught it at a new angle. "Braces, there!" Derec shouted. "Rudder amidships!" The galleon filled with shouting and stamping as the crews bent to their work. Heart in his mouth, Derec gazed at the enemy.

The relationship between the ships had changed drastically. The enemy vessels had simultaneously turned straight into the wind while preserving their relationship to one another, from a line ahead into a line of bearing. They had attempted to cut behind the Farlander galleon, head upwind and into the convoy without the necessity of a fight. *Birdwing* had just turned downwind and within the next two minutes would pass along the flagship's starboard side. The ships would exchange broadsides on the run, and then race past one another.

If *Birdwing* were a caravel or high-charged galleon, that would have been the end of the fight: Derec could never have turned into the wind to pursue the enemy. The Liavekan admiral would have got between him and his convoy, a master stroke. But *Birdwing* was something the Liavekan hadn't seen; and savage exultation filled Derec as he realized he had the enemy in his hand.

There was a massive rumbling as the guns were run out, all fifty-four of them, heavy demicannon on the lower deck and lighter, longer culverins on the maindeck.

Derec stood on the break in the poop and shouted through cupped hands.

"Larboard gun captains and second captains remain with your guns! All extra crew to the starboard guns!" Bare feet drummed the planks—the crew had practiced this many times. *Birdwing* didn't carry enough crew to efficiently fight both sides, and Derec wanted his starboard guns served well.

Enemy kettledrums thundered over the water. The purple-and-scarlet galleass was frighteningly close.

"Starboard broadside, make ready!" Derec shouted. "Fire on my order! Sail trimmers, stand by the braces! Timoneer—starboard a bit!" He'd pass alongside the enemy and drive *Birdwing* right through their starboard bank of sweeps if he could.

But abruptly the kettledrums made a flourish, then fell silent. The enemy sweeps rose like white teeth from the water, and then drew inward. The Liavekans were prepared for Derec's maneuver.

"'Midships!" he called. And suddenly there was eerie silence—no kettledrums, no shouted orders, no guns running out, only the whisper of the wind and the deafening beat of Derec's pulse in his ears.

The galleass came alongside, and the guns spoke. The enemy fo'c'sle guns bellowed first, so close their fires licked *Birdwing*'s timbers, and the air filled with splinters and moaning shot. Then Derec shrieked "Fire!" and the galleon lurched as all its guns went off more or less together, from the demicannon on the lower decks to the little sakers and minions used by the marines. Abruptly there was a chorus of screams from the galleass as shot and splinters tore through the close-packed oarsmen— the weird and awful cries sounded clearly even to Derec's deafened ears. The enemy quarterdeck guns went off last, massive iron cannon firing fifty-pound stone shot that burst on impact and laid low a score of Marcoyn's marines.

But all that was anticlimax: as soon as *Birdwing*'s guns fired, Derec was shouting new orders. "Hard a-starboard! Starboard guns, reload! Larboard guns, fire as you bear!"

Kettledrums and cymbals punctuated Derec's cries:

the enemy admiral's galleass was losing momentum, beginning to swing in the wind. They had to get under way, and quickly. Derec saw sweeps beginning to run out, and saw also that his salvo had blown gaping holes in the galleass's sides. The rowdeck must be a shambles. Triumph filled his heart.

Suddenly he was aware of the pressure of an enemy spell. Levett seemed to be handling it; but suddenly there was another strike, moving fast as lightning, a white-hot flare in Derec's mind. Derec's own power lashed out without his conscious effort, turning the spell away. A hollow feeling overtook him as he realized the spell's nature: the enemy wizard had tried to set off the powder cartridges on the gundeck. The powder magazine itself was well guarded by spells renewed yearly, but the powder was vulnerable as the ship's boys carried it to the guns, as the gun crews ladled the cartridges into the breeches and rammed shot atop them. This closely engaged, explosions on the gundeck would be disastrous.

The purple galleass fell off the wind a bit before its sweeps finally struck the water. *Birdwing* turned like a dolphin under the enemy stern, the starboard guns running out again, barking as they drove iron lengthwise through the enemy, wreaking hideous destruction on the narrow enemy vessel. Derec pounded the taffrail, roaring encouragement to the guncrews. *Birdwing* was now close-hauled between the two enemy galleasses, and the larboard guns—manned inefficiently by two men apiece—fired as the smaller vessel came into line: the range was much longer, but Derec saw the foremast come down. The fully crewed starboard guns ran out again, driving another broadside into the admiral's port quarter. The kettledrums fell silent. Sweeps flailed the water in panic.

"Stations for tacking! Helm's a-lee!" Derec's heart beat fire: a bloodthirsty demon howled in his soul. He wanted the enemy smashed.

Birdsong pivoted on its heel like a dancer, running along the purple ship's larboard side. Two full broadsides lashed out; the enemy timbers moaned to the impact of shot. The main and mizzenmast fell: the enemy rudder hung useless from its gudgeons. Nothing but small arms replied; the Liavekans hadn't reloaded their larboard

316

guns after the first broadside, either because they hadn't the crew or hadn't thought it was necessary. Now they paid for their neglect.

The enemy flagship was left astern, a near-wreck pouring blood from its scuppers. *Birdwing* tacked again, heading for the smaller enemy; the lighter galleass had bravely turned toward the fight in an effort to succor its admiral. Useless: *Birdwing* forged ahead and yawed to fire one broadside, then the other. The guns smashed enough enemy sweeps to stagger the galleass in the water; the next broadside brought the mainmast down along with the enemy colors.

Derec saw the third enemy vessel's colors coming down—the xebec had surrendered, even though it had stood away from the battle and might have got away.

Then there was silence, filled only with the gusting wind and the eerie sounds of the dying. Wreckage littered the sea: broken sweeps, jagged splinters, torn bodies of the dead. The enemy were drifting toward land: Derec would have to order them to drop an anchor till he could jury-rig masts and get them under way.

Suddenly the silence was broken by cheers, *Birdwing*'s crew sending roar upon defiant roar into the sky.

Derec looked down at the capering men, laughing and dancing in the waist of the ship, dancing in the blood of their crewmates who lay where the enemy's shot had flung them.

Then he remembered the mutiny, the way the men had danced in the blood of their countrymen, and the taste of victory turned to bitterness in his mouth.

"Ah," said Prince Jeng. "My mutineer."

"Your serene and glorious highness," Derec said, and fell to his knees, bowing low and raising his hands to his forehead.

Jeng was a balding man in his late thirties, tall for a Zhir, bearded and portly; he was heir to the throne, and head of the regent's council while his father the king was ill and recuperating at the Obsidian Palace inland. It was Jeng who had intensified the undeclared naval war against Liavek, and who as a means of forwarding his policy had welcomed *Birdwing* to Ka Zhir. This was

317

Derec's first lone audience with the prince—he had met Jeng twice before, but only as one petitioner among many.

Jeng seemed a bit surprised at Derec's submission.

"Rise, Captain SuPashto. This is an informal audience, after all. Would you like a sherbet on the terrace?"

"Thank you, Your Highness." Derec rose and suppressed a feeling of discomfort. Back in the Twin Kingdoms, on the continent the Zhir called Farland, he'd never had any dealings with high nobility, and despite Prince Jeng's hospitality he was not at home here. Derec was also uncomfortable in Prince Jeng's language: his tongue was rough, and he desperately wished for an interpreter.

Jeng's cool summer silks whispered on marble as Derec followed him to the terrace. The sherbets were already laid on a wrought-iron serving table: obviously the prince had not expected Derec to refuse an offer of refreshment. Below the terrace, cliffs fell away to reveal the Inner Harbor of Ka Zhir.

A strong sea breeze blew through the palace; but below, the harbor was windless. A hundred ships of burden stood on their perfect reflections in the still blue water. Among them, small guard boats scuttled like water spiders under oars. Thirty war galleys were drawn up on the shelving pebble beach of Great Kraken Island, safe beneath the guns and curtain walls of Fort Shzafakh, which was perched atop the old volcanic dome. Beyond, between the Inner and Outer Harbor, thousands of slaves were toiling to build the New Mole, at the end of which a new defensive fortification would rise, one from which a massive chain could be raised to block the channel and keep the Inner Harbor safe. The new fort was coming to be known as Jeng's Castle, just as the intensified conflict with Liavek was gaining the name of Jeng's War. Neither term was official; but language was, in its inevitable fashion, reflecting the realities of power.

Jeng scooped up his sherbet in one broad paw and walked to a brass telescope set on the terrace. Touching it gingerly—the metal had grown hot in the sun—he adjusted the instrument and peered through it.

318

"Your conquests, Captain," he said. He stepped back from the telescope and, with a graceful gesture, offered Derec a look. Derec nodded his thanks and put his eye to the instrument.

The bright varnished galleass leaped into view, anchored in the outer harbor next to the xebec. The Zhir ensign floated over both, black-and-gold raised over the Liavekan blue. The admiral's purple galleass was just behind, drawn up on the shelving beach where it had been run aground to keep from sinking. *Birdwing's* distinctive silhouette, a total contrast to every other vessel in the harbor, shimmered in a patch of bright, reflective water.

"I understand the xebec surrendered without a fight," Jeng commented. Derec straightened and faced the prince. The sea breeze tugged at the prince's cloth-of-gold silks.

"Yes, Your Highness. The xebec captain witnessed the loss of the two larger vessels and concluded that mighty wizardry was at work. He surrendered rather than be blasted to the bottom."

"But wizardry was not at work, was it?"

Derec shook his head. "Nay, sir. We had a wizard, and so did they; but the magics canceled one another out."

Jeng raised his delicate silver spoon to his mouth. "We have interrogated Tevvik, their wizard," he said, sipping sherbet as if it were wine, "and he confirms this. In return for his testimony, we have released him on parole."

Derec shrugged; the wizard's fate meant nothing to him.

"A pity that Admiral Bandur was killed in the fight. He might have brought you a large ransom."

"With Your Highness's blessing," Derec said slowly, staggering through the foreign phrases, "we will capture more admirals."

Prince Jeng smiled catlike, and licked his spoon. "So you shall, Thung willing."

"If Your Highness will modify our privateer's license to permit us to cruise alone against the enemy—" Derec began, but Jeng frowned and held up a hand.

"There are those on the council who say your victory was a fluke," Jeng said. "They say the winds were kind to you. What should I answer, captain?"

Derec hesitated, an array of technical terms running through his head. How much did Jeng know of the sea? Ka Zhir depended on ships and trade for its livelihood, and Jeng was an intelligent man who took an interest in the affairs of the kingdom; but how much practical seamanship did the prince know?

"Your highness has seen galleons from the Two Kingdoms before, and from Tichen?"

Jeng nodded. "They come with the annual trading convoys, yes. My mariners do not think well of them."

"They are slow, yes. And cannot sail into the wind."

Jeng finished his sherbet and scoured the dish with his spoon. The sound grated on Derec's nerves. "So my advisors tell me. You say your ship is different."

"It is, Your Highness. We call it a *race-built* galleon," stumbling, having to fall into his own language, "to distinguish it from the old style, which we call *high-charged*."

Jeng reached for a bell on the table and rang it. "Race-built?" he said. "Because it is faster?"

Derec was surprised at Jeng's conclusion: the prince understood Derec's language better than he'd suspected.

"With respect, Your Highness, the root of the word is *razor*," Derec said. "Because the upper decks, the high stern- and forecastles, are *razored* off. The race-built galleon is lower in profile, and also lighter, without the weight of the castles."

A servant appeared. The prince ordered more sherbet, then looked at Derec and frowned. "The castles, my advisors tell me, are the galleon's great advantage in combat. The castles can hold many soldiers, and the soldiers can fire down into enemy ships."

"The castles also make a high profile, and a high profile can catch the wind. The wind catches the ship and tries to push it to leeward. This is called *leeway*."

Prince Jeng's eyes flashed. "Any Zhir child knows this, Captain. Please do not inform me of matters I learned at my mother's knee."

Derec's heart skipped a beat. He lowered his eyes and

looked at Jeng's feet. "Your pardon, Your Highness. I was merely trying to make the point that with a lower profile, the race-built galleon makes much less leeway, and is therefore able to point higher into the wind."

"Yes." Curtly. "Very well. I understand."

"Also, Your Highness, we have a new form of square sail called the birdwing. It's flatter, rather like your own lateen sail. Although it holds less air, it's somehow able to drive a ship nearer the wind."

Prince Jeng's sternness dropped away, replaced by frank curiosity. "Is that so? How can that be?"

Derec shrugged helplessly. "I do not know, Your Highness. It appears to be a property of the wind that we do not yet understand."

"It works, but you don't know why?" Jeng considered this. "I shall have to inquire of my philosophers. We know why the lateen works so well, of course—it's the triangular shape, which reflects the universality of the Triple Unities of Heart, Wit, and Spirit."

"Perhaps Captain-General Collerne understands these matters," Derec said, "I don't know. The birdwing sail had been in use on some of our smaller craft for two or three generations, but it was Captain-General Collerne who thought to use it on a warship. It was also his idea to raze the upper decks, after he noticed that some old ships that had their castles removed became better sailers." A fire kindled in Derec as he thought of his old captain and teacher. "He wanted to create a fleet taking its orders from *sailors*, not generals appointed to command at sea. A fleet that fights with broadside guns instead of rapiers and firelocks, that uses the wind and water to its own advantage." His thick northern tongue stumbled on the Zhir words.

"Yes, yes," Jeng said. "That's all very well, but it's practical issues I'm concerned with." A servant arrived with another bowl of sherbet. He gave his catlike smile as he tasted the treat. Derec understood how the man had grown so stout.

"I am trying to speak practically, Your Highness," Derec said. "Your galleys and galleasses are built lightly, so they can be driven through the water by muscle power. Because they must have so many rowers, they must water

321

and victual frequently, and they must stop and let the rowers off every few days, so that they won't sicken and die. If the enemy attacks while your ships are beached, your fleet is in grave jeopardy. Your ships can carry only a limited number of guns, because they are built lightly.

"Because it is powered by the wind, *Birdwing* is built stoutly, and can resist punishment that would sink one of your galleys. Our holds are deeper and our crews are smaller, so that we can carry more provision and stay at sea much longer. *Birdwing* carries twenty-seven guns on each broadside, twice as many as your largest ship—and that's not counting sakers and minions. The Liavekans simply won't be able to stand up to a race-built ship, and a fleet of race-built craft will sweep them from the Sea of Luck. I'll stake my life on that, Your Highness."

Prince Jeng looked at him darkly. "You may have to, Captain SuPashto." Derec felt a cold touch on his neck. Prince Jeng took a deliberate sip of sherbet. "You are from a northern land, where political realities are somewhat different. Your King Torn is bound by custom and by the House of Nobles. There *is* no law of custom in Ka Zhir, Captain. The king is the law here, and in the absence of the king, the regent."

"I understand, Your Highness."

Jeng's eyes were cold. "I think not, Captain. I think you do not comprehend the . . . *necessities* of life in Ka Zhir." He turned, facing the inner harbor, and pointed with his silver spoon, an oddly delicate gesture in such a big man. "You see the New Mole, captain? I ordered that. One order, and thousands of slaves were set to work. Many of them will die. I didn't have to apply to the regency council, I didn't have to speak to a treasurer, I didn't have to get the permission of a house of nobles. I merely gave an order one fine morning—and behold, the slaves die, and the mole is built."

"Yes, Your Highness."

"Perhaps our political character," Jeng said, turning philosophical, "is derived from our volcanoes. They are unpredictable, inclined to sudden violence, and prone to massacre. So are the Zhir. So is my family.

"I am a tyrant, Captain," he said. He turned back to Derec, and his smile sent a chill through the northern man. "My very whim is law. I am an educated man, and am considered an enlightened tyrant by my philosophers"—his smile was cynical—"but I would scarcely expect them to say anything else, as I would then be compelled to have them crucified. That is the problem with being a tyrant, you see. I can't *stop* being tyrannical, even if inclined otherwise, because that would encourage other would-be tyrants to take my place, and they would be worse. I am not as great a tyrant as my father—he had his unsuccessful commanders beheaded, and I only have them whipped, or make slaves of them. But I promise *you*, Captain SuPashto," and here he pointed his spoon at Derec; and the gesture could not have been more threatening if the prince had held a sword. "I promise you, that if you fail me I will have you killed."

Prince Jeng fell silent, and slowly ate two bites of sherbet. Derec said nothing. From the moment he had entered into conspiracy with Marcoyn and the two of them had raised the crew, he had expected nothing but death.

Jeng looked at him curiously. "You do not fear death, northern man? I can make the death unpleasant if I wish."

"My life is in your hands," Derec said. "I have always known this."

"Then you understand the essential character of our relationship." Prince Jeng smiled. He finished his sherbet and put the bowl down, then put his arm around Derec's shoulders and began to walk with him back into the palace. "I have in mind to give you a squadron, Captain," he said. "It will be under the nominal orders of a Zhir, but it will be yours to command, and my admiral will understand this. Bring me back lots of the Levar's ships, and I will favor you. You will be able to replace those old brass earrings with rings of gold, and diamonds and emeralds will gleam like reflective water on your fingers. Fail me, and . . . well, why be morbid on such a lovely day?"

Derec's mind whirled. "Thank you, Your Highness," he stammered.

"I will send some slaves aboard to replace your casualties."

Derec hesitated. "I thank you, Your Highness. Could I not have freemen? They—"

Jeng's tones were icy. "Slaves can pull ropes as well as anyone."

Derec sighed inwardly. Jeng would send his slaves aboard and collect their share of the pay and prize money. The slaves would not work hard and would prove cowardly, because they hadn't anything to fight for. It was a persistent evil here, one Derec had hoped to avoid—but now he must concede.

"I thank you, Your Highness. Strong men, if you please."

"No women? Not one?"

"Women are not as strong. On a galleon, the sailors must move heavy cannon, and fight the yards when the sails are filled with wind."

"Really? But surely there are less physical tasks. Scrubbing the planks, or cooking, or serving the officers."

"Then there are discipline problems, Your Excellency. If you will look at the complaints in your navy, I'm sure you'll find more than half having to do with officers playing favorites among their prettier crewmates."

"But how do your sailors keep warm at night?"

Derec smiled. "Abstinence makes them . . . fiercer fighters, Your Highness."

Prince Jeng looked shocked. "I would never deprive my men and women of their pleasures, Captain. They're prone enough to disobedience as it is. But if you *insist* on your barbaric customs—" He shrugged. "The least I can do is rescue *you* from this cold regime—one of my commanders must learn to enjoy life, yes? Until your ship is ready, you will stay in the palace and accept my hospitality. I will send a woman to your room tonight." He hesitated. "You *do* like women, yes?"

"Ah, yes, Your Highness."

"You *did* make me wonder, Captain. Perhaps you would prefer more than one?"

Derec was surprised. "One is generally sufficient."

Jeng laughed. "I'm unused to such modesty. Very well. One it is."

"Thank you, Your Highness. For everything."

The prince had steered Derec back to the audience chamber, and he dropped his arm and stepped back. "The majordomo will show you to an apartment."

"Thank you, Your Highness." Derec knelt again, raising his hands to his forehead.

"One more thing, SuPashto."

"Your Highness?"

Prince Jeng was smiling his catlike smile. "No more mutinies, Captain."

A day later, coming aboard *Birdwing*, Derec was surprised to meet the Liavekan wizard, Tevvik, at the entry port. The pleasant-looking young man smiled and bowed, his expression cheerful. Derec nodded curtly and stepped below to his own wizard's hot, airless cabin. He rapped on the flimsy partition.

"Enter." Derec stepped in to find Levett sitting in his bunk, reading a Zhir grammar by the light of a tallow candle. Derec stood over him.

"I've come for my lesson, wizard," he said.

Levett was a short, thin man. Though he was young, his hair and beard were white. Diamond chips glittered in his hoop earrings. His green eyes studied Derec.

"As you like, Captain. I was just chatting with a colleague. Tevvik's an interesting man. Shall we go to your cabin?"

Derec turned and moved down the passageway to his cabin. The stern windows were open, providing relief from the heat. Flitting reflections danced on the deckhead above.

"I have been comparing notes with Tevvik," Levett offered.

"The Liaveker."

"He's Tichenese, actually. That's why he's so dark. It was a matter of chance that he was in the Liavekan navy—it might as easily have been Ka Zhir, or the Two Kingdoms. He's seeking adventure and foreign lands, he doesn't care whom he serves. He's on parole; now he'll set up on his own, here in town. Of course," he said rather deliberately, "he has no family. No one depending on him. He can afford to wander."

Derec sat at his table and held the wizard's eyes for a long moment. The wizard looked away.

"I have promised you your liberty, Wizard. As soon as I know your weather spells."

"I have never doubted your word, Captain."

"Just my ability to keep it."

Levett said nothing.

"This situation was not of my making, Levett," Derec said. "I'm sorry you are without your wife and family; I know you love them dearly. As soon as I can spare you, you will be free to take the first ship north. With money in your pocket."

Levett licked his lips. "They will call me a mutineer."

"The mutiny was mine, Wizard."

"I understand. You were left no choice. I had no choice myself—when the fighting broke out, I wrapped myself in illusion and hid."

"You had no part in the mutiny, true enough."

"Those in authority at home . . . may not understand."

"There would have been a mutiny in any case. My choice was to try to control it, lest everyone die."

The finest ship in the Two Kingdoms' fleet, Derec thought bitterly, and the man who had conceived it, fought for its building, sweated through its construction —Captain-General Collerne—had been denied command. Instead, *Birdwing* received a courtier from the capital, Captain Lord Fors, and his venemous lieutenant, Grinn . . . and within two months, with their policy of vicious punishments mixed with capricious favoritism, they had destroyed the morale of the crew and driven them to the brink of violence. Derec—who as a commoner had risen to the highest rank available to the lowborn, that of sailing master—had tried to stand between the captain and his crew, had tried to mitigate the punishments and hold the crew in check, but had only been mocked for his pains, and threatened by Grinn with a beating. A sailing master, the senior warrant officer on the ship, flogged . . . the threat was unheard of, even in a service accustomed to violence.

After that, Derec knew that mutiny was only a matter

of time. Derec approached Marcoyn first—the man was constantly in trouble, but he was a fighter. Derec then chose his moment, and as an officer had the keys to the arms chests: Fors and Grinn both died screaming, begging for their lives as maddened crewmen hacked at them with swords and pikes. Lieutenant Varga, a good officer who had been appalled by his captain's conduct, had nonetheless tried to rescue Fors, and was stabbed and flung bodily into the sea for his pains.

Derec had tried to hold the killings to three; but the mutineers got into the liquor store and things soon ran out of control. The ship's corporal died, bludgeoned to death in the hold; another dozen, known captain's favorites or those suspected of being informers, were killed. Marcoyn had led the blood-maddened crewmen on their hunt for enemies, had hung the remaining lieutenants and a fourteen-year-old midshipman, Sempter, from the mizzen shrouds, and there garroted them one by one. Derec had stood by underneath, watching the starting eyes and kicking heels, helpless to prevent it—he was the ship's sailing master, another officer, and if he'd objected he would have danced in the shrouds with the others.

After the crew had sobered, Derec had been able to reassert his authority. Levett, who had hidden during the mutiny, had lent supernatural influence to Derec's command. Now Derec was captain, and had chosen his officers from among the bosun's and master's mates. Marcoyn, who was illiterate and could not navigate, had been given the marines, whose morale and efficiency he was in the process of ruining with a brutality and capriciousness as hardened as that of Captain Lord Fors.

"You have done as well as you could, Captain," Levett said. "But now that you possess the royal favor, can you not do without me?"

Derec looked up at him. "Not yet, Wizard. You are the best windspeller I know."

Levett was silent for a time, then shrugged. "Very well. Let us go about our lessons, then."

Derec reached inside his shirt for his amulet of Thurn Bel. The wizard seated himself. "Clear your mind,

327

Captain," he said, "and summon your power. We shall try again."

Drained, his lesson over, Derec stepped onto the poop and nodded briskly to Random, the officer of the watch. Moaning through the rigging and rattling the windsails was the fitful wind that he had, at great effort, succeeded in summoning. Not much to show for three hours' effort.

He stepped to the stern and gazed over the taffrail at the lights of Ka Zhir. His eyes moved to the cliffs above, where his apartment and his harlot waited in Jeng's palace. She would be disappointed tonight, he thought; the wizardry had exhausted him.

Time to call his barge and head ashore. The order poised on his lips, he turned to head back for the poop companion. He froze in his tracks, terror lurching in his heart.

Dark forms dangled from the mizzen shrouds, their legs stirring in the wind. Tongues protruded from blackened lips. Pale eyes rolled toward Derec, glowing with silent accusation.

Wrenching his eyes from the sight, Derec looked at Random, at the other men on deck. They were carrying on as normal. The ghosts were invisible to them.

Derec looked again at the dead and stared in horror at young Sempter, the boy swinging from the shrouds with the garrote still knotted about his neck.

The dead had risen, risen to curse him.

He was doomed.

Drums and cymbals beat time as Derec's rowing squadron backed gracefully onto the shelving pebble beach of Ka Zhir's outer harbor. *Birdwing*, a damaged galleass in tow, dipped its ensign to its nominal Zhir admiral. The galleass had lost its rudder in an autumn storm, had broached-to and been pounded before the rowers got it under way again. *Birdwing* was continuing to the inner harbor, to deliver its crippled charge to the royal dockyard.

"Keep the Speckled Tower right abeam till the octagonal tower comes in line," the Zhir pilot said. "Then alter course three points to larboard to clear the New Mole."

"Aye, aye, sir," said the timoneer.

The sound of anchors splashing echoed over the bay, followed by the roar of cable. The squadron's three prizes, all round-bowed merchantmen, had just come to rest. Derec, looking out over the taffrail, saw the crippled galleass slew sideways in a gust, then come to a sharp check at the end of the hawser. *Birdwing* gave a brief lurch as the cripple's weight came onto the line.

The bonaventure flapped overhead as *Birdwing* turned gracefully to larboard. A ghastly stench passed over the quarterdeck, and Derec hawked and spat. Ka Zhir used slaves in some of their ships; and they were chained to the benches and lay in their own filth—the smell was incredible. Derec turned away from the galleass and faced forward, his eyes automatically giving a guilty glance to the mizzen shrouds. His mind eased as he saw them clear, tarred black hawser cutting through the bright blue tropical sky.

Over his voyages of the last six months, the ghosts had returned many times, every few days, sometimes in broad daylight. Usually Derec saw them hanging in the mizzen rigging, but on occasion he'd see them elsewhere: Lieutenant Varga, his wounds pouring blood, his hair twined with seaweed as he watched Derec from amid the crew as the hands witnessed punishment; the ship's corporal, his skull beaten in, sitting on the main crosstrees and laughing through broken teeth as the ship went through gun drill; and once, most horribly, Derec had entered his cabin at dinnertime only to find Midshipman Sempter sitting at his place, gazing at him over his meal, his mouth working silently as he tried to speak past the garrote. Derec's steward had watched in amazement as the captain bolted the room, then returned later, sweating and trembling, to find the ghost gone.

Nothing untoward had ever happened: Derec's luck on his voyages had been good. Admiral Zhi-Feng, Derec's nominal superior, was an intelligent man, and on Prince Jeng's orders had diffidently followed Derec's advice; he was learning quickly, and had recommended that *Birdwing*'s lines be taken by draftsmen so that an entire squadron of race-built galleons might rise on the royal dockyard's stocks. Five galleons were a-building and would be ready by spring. Derec had fought three engagements with Liavekan squadrons and won them all, capturing two galleasses, four galleys, and a number of smaller craft; he had sent in over forty merchant ships as prizes. Corrupt and slow though Ka Zhir's prize courts were, they had made Derec a wealthy man: the strongbox he kept beneath the planks in his sleeping cabin was crammed with gold and jewels. Prince Jeng's War was proving successful, much to the discomfort of his Scarlet Eminence in Liavek. With an entire squadron of galleons, Derec had no doubt the Liavekan Navy would be swept from the seas.

Derec glanced up at the royal palace, the white walls on the tall brown cliffs, and frowned at the sight of the flag that flapped from its staff. Something was wrong there. He stepped to the rack, took a glass, and trained it on the flag. The Royal Standard leaped into view. Derec took a breath.

So King Thelm was back, having presumably recovered from his illness. Jeng would no longer be regent; absolute power had now passed to his father. He wondered at the alteration's implication for himself, for *Birdwing*, and decided there would be little change. Thelm might negotiate an end to the war, but still *Birdwing* and Derec had proven themselves over and over again: Thelm wouldn't throw away such a strategic asset.

"Bel's sandals!" SuKrone's curse brought Derec's eyes forward. Amazement crackled in his mind.

Birdwing had rounded the fortification at the end of the New Mole, and the entire inner harbor was opened to view. The harbor was full of the tall masts and dark rigging of a northern fleet, the huge round-bellied caravels that brought metals, pitch, and turpentine to Ka Zhir every autumn, returning with sugar, kaf, and spices; and riding to anchor were northern warships, three high-charged galleons and one leaner, lower shape, a race-built galleon like *Birdwing*, but longer, showing thirty gunports each side.

Floating above each ship was a green ensign with two gold crowns, the flag of Derec's homeland.

They had come early this year, and caught Derec unprepared.

The scent of death swept over the poop. It was just the smell of the galleass, Derec thought; but still his spine turned chill.

"What do we *do*, Captain?" Marcoyn's mad eyes were wild. Drunkenly, he shook his fist in Derec's face. "What the piss do we *do*? They're going to have us kicking in the rigging by nightfall!"

Birdwing was still moving toward the inner harbor, a party of men standing in the forecastle ready to drop the best bower. Derec was looking thoughtfully over the rail. One of the big galleons—Derec recognized the *Sea Troll*—had storm damage: one topmast was gone. The *Double Crowns* was missing its castles: they had presumably been razored in an effort to make it as light and handy as *Birdwing*. *Monarch*, the other high-charged galleon, stood closest, towering over every ship in harbor and carrying eighty guns. But it was the other race-built ship that had an admiral's red pennant flying from its maintruck, and it was to this ship that Derec's eyes turned. *Torn II*, he thought: so they had built her, and sent her here to find her precursor.

"Captain! Answer, damn you!" Marcoyn staggered, not from the heave of the deck but from his liquor.

Derec turned his eyes on the man and tried to control the raging hatred he felt. "We will wait, Mr. Marcoyn," he said.

"You've got to *do* something!" Marcoyn raged. "You know Prince Jeng! *Talk* to him!"

Derec looked at Marcoyn for a long moment. Marcoyn dropped his unfocused eyes, then his fist.

"We fight under the flag of Ka Zhir," Derec said, indicating the ensign flying overhead. "We have Zhir protection. The trading fleet is here, aye, but it's under the two hundred guns of Fort Shzafakh and another two hundred on the mainland. They *daren't* attack us, Marcoyn. Not openly."

Marcoyn chewed his nether lip as he thought this over. "Very well, SuPashto," he said.

Derec stiffened. "*Captain* SuPashto, if you please, Mr. Marcoyn."

Marcoyn's eyes blazed dull hatred. "*Captain*," he spat. He saluted and turned away.

The other crewmen, the small, dark Zhir standing beside the tall, fair Farlanders, had watched the confrontation, trying hard to conceal their rising fear. Derec's quiet tones had seemed to calm them. He stepped forward to the break in the poop.

"They daren't touch us, boys!" he shouted. "Not openly. But there will be Two Kingdoms men ashore on leave, and for now we'll have no shore parties. When we *must* send parties ashore, we will go armed, and in large groups. Now"—he ventured a ragged grin—"let's show them what we've learned. As soon as our anchor's down, I want those sails harbor-furled, without a dead man in 'em; I want our old chafing-gear down; and I'll have some parties detailed to renew our gilding. Mr. Facer, see to it."

"Yes, sir."

Derec nodded curtly and stepped to the weather rail. He watched the northern fleet grow closer.

The admiral's summons came at sunset. Derec was half expecting it; he'd seen Zhi-Feng's barge take him ashore to his quarters in the Lower Town. Derec put on his best clothes, strapped on his rapier, and thrust a pair of pistols in his belt. He called for his gig and had himself rowed to the admiral's apartments.

The admiral was dressed in a gorgeous silk robe, and his hair and beard had been curled and perfumed. Gemstones clustered on his fingers. He drank wine from a crystal goblet as big as his head. His belt had scales of gold.

Derec scarcely noted this magnificence, his attention instead riveted on the admiral's other visitor, a portly man plainly dressed. He fell to his knees and raised his palms to his forehead.

"Rise, Captain," said Prince Jeng. "Forgive this melodrama, but I thought it best not to let anyone know we had met." He sat in a heavy-cushioned chair, eating red licorice. Derec rose. Jeng looked at him and frowned.

"Problems are besetting the two of us, Captain SuPashto," he said. "The same problems, actually. My father, and the trading fleet."

"I trust in your guidance, Highness."

Jeng seemed amused. "That's more than *I* can say, Captain. Neither I nor anyone else really expected His Encompassing Wisdom to recover; and I'm afraid the old man's found my regency a bit . . . premature . . . in diverting from his policies. He didn't want a naval war with Liavek in his old age, and now he's got one, and if the war hadn't been so successful half the council would have got the chop." Jeng grimly raised the edge of his hand to his throat. "But since we're winning," he added, "he's not sure what to do. At this point I think we'll fight on, so long as we stay ahead." He picked up a stick of licorice and pointed it at Derec like a royal scepter. "That makes you valuable to him, and so you may thank your victories for the fact that you and Zhi-Feng haven't been beheaded on your own quarterdecks."

"I owe my victories to your kindness and support," Derec said. "May Thung preserve Your Highness."

"Thank you for your concern, SuPashto, but I doubt I'm in real danger," Jeng said. "I'm the only heir the old man's got left. The first went mad, the second died trying to invest his luck, the third played a losing game with His Scarlet Eminence and got his neck severed for losing . . . there's no one left but me. The worst that will happen to me, I think, is exile to an island. It's everyone around me who'll lose his head." He smiled. "His Encompassing Wisdom might want to perpetrate a massacre just to show everyone he's back."

Zhi-Feng looked a little green. "Gods keep us from harm," he murmured.

Jeng chewed meditatively on his licorice wand. "The problem presented by my shining and beloved ancestor, may Thung preserve him, may be finessed," he said. "The problem of your trading fleet is not so easily dealt with. Briefly, they want you dead."

"I expected no less, Highness."

"They have demanded that you and your ship be turned over to them. This demand has thus far been refused. You are too valuable to the war effort."

333

Derec felt his tension ease. "I thank Your Highness."

Jeng's eyebrows rose. "*I* had little to do with it, Captain. His Encompassing Wisdom cares little for my counsel these days. We may thank the old man's common sense for that—he's not going to throw away the war's biggest asset, not without some thought, anyway. No, the problem is that your northern admiral is proving damnably clever."

"May I ask which admiral, Your Highness?"

"I have heard you speak of him. One Captain-General Collerne."

A cold wind touched Derec's spine. For the first time in this interview he felt fear. "Aye," he said. "A clever man indeed."

"You know him well?"

"My first captain. Brilliant. He designed *Birdwing*, and taught me everything I've learned about the sea. He got me my master's warrant. He's the best sailor I know."

Jeng looked at Derec coldly. "I'd advise you to leave off this admiration and learn to hate him, Captain SuPashto. He wants your hide, and he won't leave the Sea of Luck without it."

Yes, Derec thought, that was Collerne. Brilliant, unforgiving, a demon for discipline. He would not countenance mutiny, not even against the evil man who had supplanted him in his longed-for command.

"I must trust to Your Highness's protection," Derec said simply.

Jeng's eyes were shards of ice. "My protection is worth little. Let me tell you what your damned captain-general did. Once he realized we wouldn't give you up because of your value to the war, he offered to fight in your place. In exchange for you and the other ringleaders, he's offered us his two best ships, *Torn* and *Double Crowns*, to fight under our license and flag for the next year. Collerne himself has offered to command them." Jeng sucked his licorice wand. "The implication, I believe, is that if we refuse him, he'll offer his ships to Liavek instead."

Derec's mouth turned dry. "Can he do that, Your Highness? Does his commission extend that far?"

"If it doesn't, he's taking a remarkable amount of

334

initiative. The fact is, he's made the offer, and the king's considering it."

"Highness," the admiral said. There was sweat on his perfumed brow. "We—Captain SuPashto and I—we have experience in this war. We've fought together for six months. Our crews are well drilled and every man is worth three of this Collerne's."

Jeng looked bleak. "I shall attempt to have some friends on the council point this out to His Encompassing Wisdom. But in the meantime I'll try to get you both out of harbor. If Collerne can't find you, he can't kill you."

"Very well, Your Highness," said Zhi-Feng. He looked somewhat less anxious.

"Your fleet is ready?"

"We need only take on water," Derec said. "*Birdwing* has six months' provision. The rowing fleet carries victuals only for six weeks, but we can take food from captured ships if necessary. Or buy it ashore."

"I will have water-lighters alongside at dawn," Jeng said. He threw down his licorice and straightened. "I'll try to . . . persuade the harbor master to send you a pilot. If he's not aboard by nightfall, warp your way out the back channel. I'm afraid now the New Mole's completed, the chain bars the main channel at sunset, so you can't escape that way."

"Your highness is wise." The admiral bowed.

Jeng's face turned curious. He looked at Derec. "How do they treat mutineers in your navy, SuPashto?" he asked.

"They are tied to the mast of a small boat," Derec said, "rowed to each ship in the squadron, and flogged in view of each ship's company. Then they are taken to the admiral's ship, hung from the mizzen shrouds, and disemboweled. Before they can die they are garroted. Then their bodies are preserved with salt and hung in an iron cage till they weather away."

"That sounds most unpleasant," Jeng said mildly. "Were I you, I would provide myself with poison. When the time comes, you can cheat your countrymen out of some of their fun." He shrugged. "Life is full of

335

experiences, my philosophers tell me, but I think I can attest that some are best avoided."

Desolation stirred in Derec like a rising autumn gale. "I will follow your advice in all things, Highness," he said.

When he returned to the ship, Derec didn't look up. He knew the ghosts were there, dark shadows that smiled at his approaching doom.

The water-lighters arrived just before dawn, and just afterward a messenger from the palace. *Birdwing* was to remain at anchor in the inner harbor until the complication with the Two Kingdoms fleet was resolved. If the galleon moved, she would be fired on by every gun on Great Kraken Island.

There was a hush on the *Birdwing* after that. Derec bought fresh food and wine from lighters offering wares alongside—he never let the hucksters aboard, fearing Twin Kingdoms agents—and he kept the crew at their tasks, brightening the ship's paint and overhauling the running rigging; but the men were subdued, expectant. Dark shapes hung in the shrouds, filling the air with the stench of death. Red stains bubbled silently on the white holystoned planks. Derec kept his eyes fixed firmly on the horizon, and sent the wizard ashore to buy poison. Levett returned with a vial of something he said was strong enough to kill half the crew.

On the evening of the second day, the summons from court arrived. Derec was ready. He spoke briefly with his officers concerning what was to be done after he left, put on his best clothing, and dropped small pistols in his pockets.

With an escort of the Zhir Guard, quaintly old-fashioned in their ancient plumed helmets, he was rowed to the quay, then taken in a palankeen up the steep cliffs to the palace. There were new heads above the gate, illuminated by torches: a pair of the council had died just that afternoon. The wall beneath them was stained with red. Local witches clustered beneath, hoping to catch the last of the ruddy drops in order to make their potions. A chamberlain took Derec through the halls to an ante-room.

"Wait within," the chamberlain said, raising his palms to his forehead. "His Everlasting and All-Encompassing Wisdom will grant you audience as soon as the council meeting has concluded."

"May Thung protect His Majesty," Derec answered. He turned to the door.

"I shall send refreshment," the chamberlain said. Derec opened the door, stepped inside, and froze.

Glowing eyes turned their cold light on him. The ghosts were there: Varga with blood and seawater dripping from his clothes, the corporal with brains spattered over his clothing, the others with blackened faces and starting eyes, the garrotes twisted about their necks. Terror poured down Derec's spine.

Young Sempter stood before Derec, five paces away. His brass-buttoned jacket, too big for him, hung limply on his boyish frame. His feet, the feet that had kicked their shoes off as he died, were bare. There was a hole in one stocking. Sempter's mouth worked in his beardless face, and he took a step forward. Derec shrank back. The boy took a step, and another. His pale hand came up, and it closed around Derec's amulet of Thurn Bel. He tugged, and the thong cut into Derec's neck like a garrote. Derec smelled death on the boy's breath. The boy tugged again, and the amulet came free.

"Take him," Sempter said, and smiled as he stepped back several paces.

Strong hands closed on Derec's arms. His pistols and his vial of poison were pulled from his pockets. His rapier was drawn from its sheath.

The image of Sempter twisted like that in a distorting mirror, faded, became that of Levett. The others were Zhir Guard. Their officer was holding Derec's sword.

Levett held up the amulet of Thurn Bell. "Never let another mage know where you keep your power, Captain," he said. He pocketed the amulet. "The rest of his men will surrender easily enough. They're fools or boys, all of them."

Derec's mind whirled as cuffs were fastened before him on his wrists. A chain was passed from the shackles between Derec's legs. The guards officer unfolded a scroll and began to read:

337

"By order of King Thelm and the Council, Captain Derec SuPashto is placed under arrest. The Royal Authority is shocked"—she was remarkably straight-faced in conveying the king's surprise—"to discover that Derec SuPashto is a mutineer and rebel. He is commanded to the Tiles Prison under close guard, until he can be turned over to Two Kingdoms justice." She rolled up the scroll and placed it in her pocket. Her face was expressionless. "Take the prisoner away."

Derec looked at Levett. Mist seemed to fill his mind. "There were never any ghosts," he said dully.

Levett looked at him. "Illusions only," he said.

The man behind Derec tugged on the chain. Derec ignored it. "You planned this," Derec said. "All along."

"Something like it." Levett looked at him from three paces away, the distance beyond which Derec could not manipulate any power stored in the amulet. "I regret this, Captain. Necessity compelled me, as it compelled you during the mutiny. I want to return to our homeland, and to live in peace with my family. Collerne can guarantee that, and you can't."

The guard, impatient, tugged hard on Derec's chain. Pain shot through Derec's groin. He bent over, tears coming to his eyes.

"This way," the guardsman said. Stumbling, Derec let himself be dragged backward out of the room. A push sent him staggering forward. With five of the guard and Levett, he was marched from the palace, beneath the dripping heads of traitors and into the night.

No palankeen waited: he would walk down the long switchback path to the Lower Town, then through town to the prison. The cool night breeze revived him. The officer lit a torch and gave it to one of her men. The party was silent save for the clink of the guardsmen's chain coifs as they walked.

The Lower Town was growing near, tall buildings shuttered against the violence of the streets. Anyone with sense went armed here, and in company. Derec began to murmur under his breath. The party passed into the shadows of the crowded buildings. The streetlamps were out, smashed by vandals. Derec's heart beat like a galley's kettledrum.

338

A pike lunged from an alley and took the guards officer in the side. A dark body of men boiled from the darkness. The shackles dropped from Derec's wrists, and he lunged for the guardsman to his right, drew the main gauche from the man's belt, and slid it up under the chain coif to cut the astonished man's throat. Feet pounded the cobbles. Steel thudded into flesh. The torch fell and went out. Derec spun, seeing in the starlight the stunned look on the guard who was suddenly holding an empty chain where once a prisoner had been. The dagger took him in the heart, and he died without a sound.

A dark figure reeled back: Levett, already dead from a rapier thrust through both lungs. Marcoyn's bulk followed him, boarding ax raised high; and then the ax came down. Derec turned away at the sound of the wizard's head being crushed. Facer stepped out of the darkness, his face sunburned beneath his leather-and-iron cap, his sword bloody.

"Are you well, Captain?"

"Aye. Good work. Drag the bodies into the alleys where the city runners won't find them."

"Fucking traitor." There were more thudding sounds as Marcoyn drove the ax into Levett again and again. Finally the big man drew back, grinning as he wiped a spatter of blood from his face. Liquor was on his breath.

"Got to make sure a wizard's dead," he grunted. "They're tricky."

"Best to be certain," Derec said, his mind awhirl. He'd posted the men here and knew what was coming, but the fight had been so swift and violent that he needed a moment to take his bearings. He looked at the dead wizard and saw, in the starlight, the amulet of Thurn Bel lying in the dust of the alleyway. He bent and picked it up. *Never let another mage know where you keep your power*, Levett had said; and Derec had always followed this prescription, though Levett never knew it. He'd invested his power in one of his brass earrings, one so old and valueless that no captor looting valuables would ever be tempted to tear it from his ear.

The bodies were dragged into the alley, piled carelessly atop one another. Wind ruffled Derec's graying hair: somewhere in the melee, he'd lost his cap. "To the ship,

Captain?" Facer asked. He held out Derec's sword and the guards officer's brace of wheel-lock pistols.

Derec passed the swordbelt over his shoulder and rammed the pistols in his waistband. "Not yet," he said. "We have another errand first." He grinned at Facer's anxiety. "We have to wait an hour for the tide in any case, Lieutenant."

"Yes, sir." Doubtfully.

He led them through the empty streets of the Lower Town. Even the taverns were shut. Working people lived here, dockworkers and warehousemen: they didn't roister long into the night. Derec searched for one narrow apartment, found it, knocked on the door.

"Who is it?" A young, foreign voice.

"Captain SuPashto of the *Birdwing*."

"A moment."

The Tichenese wizard, Tevvik, opened the door, a lamp in his hand. His long hair was coiled on his head, held in place by a pin in the shape of a blue chipmunk. He recognized Derec and smiled. "An unexpected pleasure, Captain," he said. His Zhir was awkward.

"We're sailing for Liavek immediately. You're to accompany us."

Tevvik looked surprised. "I'm to be exchanged?"

"Something like that."

Tevvik thought about this for a moment, and shrugged. "I think I'd rather stay, Captain. I've developed a profitable business here."

From over his shoulder, Derec heard Marcoyn's growl. Derec was tempted to echo it. Instead, he decided to be frank. "We're escaping arrest," he said. "You're accompanying us because you're a water wizard."

Tevvik's eyes widened. "You mean I'm being *abducted*?" He seemed delighted by the news.

"Aye. You are."

The wizard laughed. "That puts a different complexion on matters, Captain. Of course I'll accompany you. Do I have time to fetch my gear?"

"I'm afraid not."

Tevvik shrugged, then blew out his lamp. "As you like, Captain."

The waterfront district was a little more lively: music

340

rang from taverns, whores paraded the streets, and drunken sailors staggered in alleyways looking to be relieved of their money. Derec and his party moved purposefully to the quay, then took the waiting barge to the galleon.

"Everything's prepared, Captain," Facer said. "We've cleared for action and the men are at quarters. The yards are slung with chains, the cable's ready to slip, the sails can be sheeted home in an instant, and we aren't showing any lights."

"Has the other party found our pilot?"

"SuKrone's got her under guard in the gunroom."

"Very good."

The boatmen tossed oars and Derec jumped for the entry port. He stepped onto the maindeck and sensed rather than saw his crew massed beneath the stars. He mounted the poop, then turned to face them. "We're running for Liavek, men," he said. "I have reason to believe they will welcome us."

There was a stirring ended swiftly by petty officers' voices calling for silence.

"Those of you who were slaves," Derec said, "are now free."

Now there was an excited chattering that took the officers some time to quiet. Derec held up a hand.

"You may have to fight to keep that freedom, and that within the hour. Now—quietly—go to your stations. No drums, no noise. Facer, fetch me the pilot."

Derec leaned against the poop rail, pulled the big horse pistols from his waistband, and carefully wound the spring-driven locks. He was aware of the Tichenese wizard standing by, watching him. "Do you know weather magic, wizard?"

"Some. It is not my specialty."

"What is?"

"Fireworks. Explosions. Illusion."

"Can you make *Birdwing* look like something else?"

"Your ship is a little large for that. Perhaps I could cloak it in darkness. The darkness will not be absolute, but it may make its outlines less clear."

"Very well. Do so."

Facer and SuKrone pushed the pilot up the poop

341

ladder. She was a small, dark woman, her head wrapped in a kind of turban. She was dressed in the house robe she'd been wearing when SuKrone's men had kidnapped her. Derec pointed one of his pistols at her, and he heard her intake of breath.

"Take us out by the back channel," he said coldly. "If you fail me, I will shoot you twice in the belly. Follow my instructions, and I'll put you over the side in a small boat once we're clear."

The pilot bowed, raising her palms to her forehead. "I understand, Your Excellency. But we must await the tide."

"Half an hour."

"Thereabouts, yes."

"Do not fail me." He gestured with the pistol. "Stand over there."

"Your obedient servant, Excellency."

"Wizard, Facer, come with me." Derec stepped forward off the poop, along the gangway, climbed the fo'c'sle. The land breeze brought the sound of music and laughter from the town. Derec looked to starboard, where the twisting back channel between Great Kraken Island and the mainland was invisible in the darkness. Glowing softly in the night, masthead riding lights stood out against the black.

"There's our problem," he said. "*Double Crowns* is moored right near the entrance to the passage. We'll have to pass within half a cable."

Facer pursed his lips, blew air hesitantly. "They've lookouts set for us, I'm sure. They know we want to run. And if they give the alarm, Shzafakh's bastions will blow us to bits."

"My darkness won't cover us *that* well, Captain," the wizard said. He was speaking easily in Derec's own language, and with a native accent: apparently he'd spent time in the Two Kingdoms.

"We can't fire on them without raising an alarm," Derec mused. "We can't run aboard them without calling attention to ourselves." He shook his head. "We'll just have to run past and hope for a miracle."

"Captain . . ." Tevvik's tone was meditative. "If we

342

can't pass without being noticed, perhaps we can make people notice something other than ourselves."

"What d'ye mean, Wizard?"

"Perhaps I can cause an explosion aboard *Double Crowns*. Then maybe the gunners in Shzafakh will think we're running from a fire, not for freedom."

Derec scowled. "The magazine is protected against spells."

"I'm sure. But powder in the open is not."

"They would not have cartridges in the open—it's all held in the magazine till needed." Scornfully. "Don't waste my time with these notions, Wizard."

"I was suggesting a boat full of powder nestled under that ship's stern. I can make *that* go off well enough."

Astonishment tingled in Derec's nerves. He tried not to show it; instead, he stroked his chin and frowned. "With a little sorcerous wind to push it where it's needed, aye," he said. He pretended to consider. "Very well, Wizard," he said. "We'll do it. Facer, fetch the gunner."

Tevvik smiled. "I wish you wouldn't use the word *wizard* that way, Captain. The word's not a curse."

Derec looked at him. "That's a matter of opinion, Mr. Tevvik."

He led the Tichenese back to the quarterdeck and gave the orders for men to file to the magazine and bring up ten casks of powder. "Barefoot only, mind," he said. "No hobnails to strike a spark. Belts and weapons are to be laid aside. Scarves tied over their ears so their earrings won't strike a spark." He drew his pistols and pointed them at Tevvik.

"Don't set them off when they're alongside," he said, "or I'll serve you as I'd serve the pilot."

The wizard raised his hands and grinned. "I have no intention of blowing myself up, Captain."

"Maintain those intentions," Derec said, "and we'll have no trouble."

The barge was loaded with powder, and canvas thrown over the barrels to avoid getting them wet. The boat's small mast was raised, its lateen set, its tiller lashed. The boat was warped astern and Derec concentrated, summoning his power, keeping it ready. A small wind to blow his thirty-foot barge was fully within his capabilities.

"Tide's turning, Captain."

"Very well. Prepare to slip the cable and sheet home."

"Aye, aye, sir."

There was a murmur of bare feet as men took their stations. Derec took a careful breath. "Sheet home the main tops'l. Set the spritsail and bonaventure."

The heavy canvas topsail fell with a rumble, then rumbled again as it filled with wind. *Birdwing* tilted, surged, came alive. Water chuckled under the counter.

"Slip the cable."

The cable murmured from the hawsehole, then there was a splash as its bitter end fell into the sea. A pity, Derec thought, to lose the best bower anchor.

"Helm answers, sir," said the steersmen.

"Larboard two points. There. Amidships."

Derec glanced over the stern, saw phosphorescence glinting from the bone in the teeth of the powder boat. *Birdwing* was barely moving. The back channel was dangerous and twisting; he needed maneuverability there, not speed.

"Pilot," he said. The woman stepped forward.

"Sir."

"Take command. No shouting, now. Pass your orders quietly."

"Yes, sir."

The pistols were growing heavy in Derec's hands. He ignored the tension in his arms and stepped to the weather rail, peering for sight of *Double Crowns*. The masthead lights were growing nearer. Five cables. Four. Three. He summoned his power.

"Cast off the boat."

Derec's heart leaped to his throat as the boat lurched wildly to the first puff of wind and threatened to capsize, but the barge steadied onto its course, passing to weather of *Birdwing*. He guided the boat with little tugs of his mind, aimed it toward *Double Crowns*.

Two cables. Now one, and from across the water a shout. More shouts. The barge thudded against the razee galleon's tumblehome near the stern. A drum began beating. Alarm pulsed in Derec: on this still night, that drum would be heard all over town. Derec steeled his mind to the necessity of what was to come.

"Give us fire, Wizard," he said.

"Your obedient servant." Tevvik pursed his lips in concentration and made an elegant gesture with his hand. Derec remembered at the last second to close his eyes and preserve his night vision.

Even through closed lids he saw the yellow flash. A burst of hot wind gusted through his hair. He could hear shouts, screams, and, from his own ship, gasps of awe. He opened his eyes.

Double Crowns seemed unchanged, but he could hear the sound of water pouring like a river into her hold. The drum was silenced; in its place were cries of alarm. As Derec watched, the razee began to list. Crewmen poured from the hatches in a storm of pounding feet. The galleon's list grew more pronounced; Derec could hear things rolling across the deck, fetching up against the bulwarks. Then came a sound that was a seaman's nightmare, a noise that half-paralyzed Derec with fear— the rumble of a gun broken loose, roaring across the tilting deck like a blind, maddened bull before it punched clean through the ship's side, making another hole through which the sea could enter.

He couldn't stand to watch any more. He moved to the other side of the poop, but the sounds still pursued him, more guns breaking free, timbers rending, men screaming, the desperate splashing of drowning crewmen. Then, mercifully, *Birdwing* was past, heeled to the wind, and entering the channel.

The pilot negotiated two turns before the first challenge came from one of Fort Shzafakh's bastions. The island rose steeply here, and *Birdwing* ghosted with its sails luffing for lack of wind. The fort was perched right overhead—from its walls the garrison could as easily drop cannonballs on *Birdwing* as fire them from cannon.

"Hoy, there! What ship is that!"

Derec was ready. He cupped his hands and shouted upwards in his accented Zhir. "Two Kingdoms ship *Sea Troll*!" he roared. "A warship blew up in harbor and started fires on other ships! We're trying to run clear!"

"Holy Thung! So that's what we heard." There was an awed pause. "Good luck, there."

"Much obliged."

Birdwing ghosted on. Derec could see grins on the faces of his officers, on the wizard. In his mind he could only hear the sounds of *Double Crowns* filling with water, men dying and timbers rending. He barely noticed when the channel opened up and ahead lay the dark and empty sea.

An hour after dawn the land breeze died. The pilot had been put ashore long since, and even the old cone of Great Kraken Island was below the horizon: *Birdwing* was running northwest along the coast in the clear, broad, shallow channel between the mainland and Ka Zhir's stretch of low boundary islands. Winds were often uncertain in the morning, particularly near the coast and especially during the transition between the nightly land breeze and the daytime sea breeze: there was nothing unusual about it. Derec dropped the second bower anchor and let the galleon swing to and fro in the little puffs that remained. The crew drowsed at their stations. Fretfully Derec looked southward. *Sea Troll*, he thought, was damaged: it could not pursue without raising a new maintopmast. But *Monarch* and the new race-built ship were fully seaworthy. Were they becalmed as well? He suspected not. Derec looked at the Tichenese.

"Master Tevvik, do you think we can whistle up a wind between the two of us?"

The wizard spread his hands. "I am willing to try, Captain. I am not an expert."

Derec called for a pot of kaf, ordered breakfast for the crew, and the two went to his day cabin. The partitions separating the cabin from the maindeck had been broken down when *Birdwing* was cleared for action, providing a long, unbroken row of guns from the stern windows to the bow, and Derec's table was hastily brought up from the orlop, and blankets to screen him from the curious eyes of the crew.

"You're planning on privateering for Liavek now, I take it?" the wizard asked. "There will be a Two Kingdoms fleet in harbor, you know."

"I'll find a small harbor somewhere along the coast. Come in under a flag of truce, negotiate with the Levar's government."

"I can speak for you." Derec looked up in surprise. The wizard smiled again. "I know a man named Pitullio —he works for His Scarlet Eminence."

"I thank you," Derec said. "I'll consider that."

For two and a half hours he and the wizard tried to raise a wind, preferably a strong westerly that *Birdwing* could tack into, and that *Monarch*, the old-fashioned high-charged galleon, could not. The puffs continued, the ship dancing at the end of its cable, sails slatting.

"Captain." Facer's voice. "The lookouts see a squall coming up from the south."

Derec sighed. He could feel sweat dotting his brow: he had been concentrating hard. The wizard looked at him with amused eyes, grin white in his dark face.

"It's not *our* wind," Tevvik said, "but I hope it will do."

Derec rose wordlessly and pushed aside the curtain. His body was a mass of knots. "Ready a party at the capstan," he ordered. "I don't want to lose another anchor." He climbed to the poop.

It was a black squall, right enough, coming up from the south with deliberate speed. Ten minutes of stiff wind, at least, and with luck the squall might carry *Birdwing* with it for hours, right into the stronger ocean breezes. Derec had the second bower broken out. The galleon drifted, waiting for the squall.

Derec looked into the darkness, hoping to gauge its strength, and his heart sank.

Right in the center of the squall, he saw, were two ships. He didn't need his glass to know they were *Monarch* and *Torn II*, driving after him on a sorcerous breeze. Perhaps their wizards had even been responsible for his being becalmed.

"Quarters, gentlemen," he said. "We are being pursued. Have my steward fetch my armor, and send the wizard to the orlop."

He stopped himself, just in time, from glancing up into the mizzen shrouds. The ghosts of his slaughtered countrymen, he knew, had been an illusion.

But now, more than ever, he felt their gaze on the back of his head.

They were coming down together, Derec saw, straight down the eight-mile slot between the mainland and the sandy barrier isles. *Monarch* was to starboard of the race-built ship, three or four cables apart. There was a black line drawn in the azure sea a mile before them where the squall was pushing up a wave.

"We'll try to outrun them," Derec said. "We may prove their match in speed." He tried to sound confident, but he knew his assurances were hollow: the conditions were ideal for *Monarch*, booming straight downwind with her baggy sails full of sorcery. "If we lose the race," Derec went on, "I'll try to get the weather gage. If we're to windward, *Monarch* at least will be out of the fight."

A sigh of wind ruffled *Birdwing*'s sails. The ship stirred on the water. The sails filled, then died again. Derec strapped on his armor and watched as the darkness approached.

And then the squall hit, and the sun went dark. The sails boomed like thunder as they flogged massively in the air; the ship tilted; rain spattered Derec's breastplate. Then the sails were sheeted home, the yards braced—the helm answered, and *Birdwing* was racing straight downwind, a white bone in its teeth, sails as taut as the belly of a woman heavy with child. Magic crackled in Derec's awareness, a seething chaos of storm and wind. Desperately he looked astern.

Monarch seemed huge, castles towering over its leaner consort, its masts bending like a coachwhip in the force of the wind. Derec gauged its speed, and a cold welling of despair filled him. *Birdwing* seemed to be maintaining its lead over *Torn II*, but *Monarch* was surging ahead as studding sails blossomed on its yards. *Birdwing*'s own studding sails were useless in this wind; the stuns'l booms would snap like toothpicks.

Derec stiffened at the sound of a gun: the big ship was trying its chasers. *Monarch* was pitching too much in this following sea, and Derec never saw the fall of shot.

Yard by yard the great ship gained, its black hull

348

perched atop a boil of white water. Derec hoped for a miracle, and none came. Hollow anguish filled him.

"Take in the t'gallants," he ordered. "We will await them." Diligently he fought down despair. "Don't send down the t'gallant yards," he said. "We may yet be able to show them our heels."

Monarch's stuns'ls began coming in as they perceived Derec's shortening sail. The maneuver was not done well, and sheets began to fly, spilling wind from sails, a last-ditch method of slowing *Monarch* so that it would not overshoot its target.

Derec watched nervously, gnawing his lip, trying to summon his power and weave a defensive net around his ship. He could feel Tevvik's energies joining his, strengthening his shields. Another gust of rain spattered the deck; gun captains shielded their matches with their bodies. *Monarch* looked as if it were coming up on *Birdwing's* larboard side, but that might be a feint. Would the huge ship alter course at the last minute and try for a raking shot across *Birdwing's* stern? If so, Derec had to be ready to turn with her. Plans flickered through Derec's mind as he gauged possible enemy moves and his own responses.

"Load the guns. Roundshot and grape. Run out the larboard battery." Maybe the guns running out would prod *Monarch's* captain into making his move.

But no. The man seemed eager to get to grips, and disdained maneuver. He had almost thirty guns more than Derec; he could afford to let them do his thinking for him. The black ship came closer, its little scraplike sprit topsail drawing even with *Birdwing's* stern. Derec could hear officers' bellowed commands as they struggled to reduce sail.

Anxiety filled Derec as the ship rumbled to the sound of gun trucks running out. *Monarch* was pulling up within fifty yards. *Torn II* was eclipsed behind the big ship, but now that *Birdwing* had shortened sail he could expect her shortly. He glanced again at the men, seeing the gun captains crouched over the guns with their slow matches, the officers pacing the deck with rapiers drawn, ready to run through any crewman who left his station.

"No firing till my order!" Derec bellowed. "There may be a few premature shots—ignore them!" And then inspiration struck. He turned to one of Marcoyn's marines, a blond man sighting down the length of a swivel gun set aft of the mizzen shrouds. "Blow on your match, man," Derec said. "I'm going to try a little trick."

The marine looked at him, uncertain, then grinned through his curling blond beard, leaned forward over his matchlock, and blew. The match brightened redly. "You other marines, stand ready," Derec said. He looked at the black ship, and fear shivered down his spine as he saw himself looking straight into the muzzle of a demicannon. Each enemy gunport had been decorated with the snarling brass head of a leopard: now guns were running out the beasts' mouths. *Monarch*'s foremast was even with *Birdwing*'s mizzen. Derec waited, his pulse beating in his ears, as *Monarch* crawled forward with glacial speed.

"Pick your target," Derec told the marine. "Steady now! Fire."

The four-pound man-killer barked and the air filled with a peculiar whirring noise as grapeshot and a handful of scrap iron flew toward the enemy. "Fire the murderers!" Derec spat. "Now!"

Another three minions banged out, and then there was a massive answering roar as every enemy gun went off, flinging their iron toward *Birdwing*. The smaller ship shuddered as balls slammed home. Derec took an involuntary step backward at the awesome volume of fire, but then he began to laugh. He'd tricked *Monarch* into firing prematurely, before all her guns bore. They'd wasted their first and most valuable broadside, half the shot going into the sea.

"Reload, you men! Helmsman, larboard a point!" Derec cupped his hands to carry down the ship's well to the gundeck below. "Fire on my command! Ready, boys!" *Birdwing* began a gentle curve toward the giant ship.

"Fire!" The deck lurched as the big guns went off, the long fifteen-foot maindeck culverins leaping inboard on their carriages. Derec could hear crashing from the enemy ship as iron smashed through timbers. "Reload!"

Derec shrieked. "Fire at will! Helmsman, starboard a point!"

Enemy guns began crashing. Derec saw a piece of bulwark dissolve on the maindeck and turn to a storm of white fifteen-inch splinters that mowed down half a dozen men. Shot wailed overhead or thudded into planking. Musketry twittered over Derec's head: the enemy castles were full of marines firing down onto *Birdwing*'s decks. The smaller ship's guns replied. For the first time Derec felt a magic probe against his defenses; he sensed Tevvik parrying the strike. There was a crash, a deadly whirl of splinters, and the yellow-bearded marine was flung across the deck like a sack, ending up against the starboard rail, head crushed by a grapeshot. Derec, still in his haze of concentration, absently sent a man from the starboard side to service the gun.

Guns boomed, spewing powder smoke. *Birdwing*'s practiced crews were loading and firing well. Derec smiled; but then his ship rocked to a storm of fire and his heart lurched. His crews were faster in loading and firing, but still the enemy weight was overwhelming. Derec's smaller vessel couldn't stand this pounding for long. He gnawed his lip as he peered at the enemy through the murk. His next move depended on their not seeing him clearly.

The deck jarred as half a dozen gundeck demicannon went off nearly together. Smoke blossomed between the ships, and at once Derec ran for the break in the poop. "Sailtrimmers, cast off all tacks and sheets!" he roared. "Gun crews shift to the starboard broadside! Smartly, now!" He could see crewmen's bewildered heads swiveling wildly: man the *starboard* guns? Had *Torn* run up to starboard and caught them between two fires?

"Cast off all sheets! *Fly 'em*! Run out the starboard battery!"

Topsails boomed as the great sails spilled wind. *Birdwing*'s purposeful driving slowed as if stopped by a giant hand. The flogging canvas roared louder than the guns. The galleon staggered in the sea, the black ship pulling ahead. Frantically Derec gauged his ship's motion.

"Hard a-larboard, Sandor! Smartly, there!"

Losing momentum, *Birdwing* rounded onto its new tack. A rumble sounded from the gundeck as the demicannon began thrusting from the ports. "Sheet home! Sailtrimmers to the braces! Brace her up sharp, there!"

There: he'd done it; checked his speed and swung across the black ship's stern. He could see the big stern windows, the heraldric quarterings of the Two Kingdoms painted on the flat surface of the raised poop, officers in armor running frantically atop the castle, arms waving . . .

"Fire as you bear! Make it count, boys!"

Birdwing trembled as the first culverin spat fire. The whole broadside followed, gun by gun, and Derec exulted as he saw the enemy's stern dissolve in a chaos of splinters and roundshot, a great gilt lantern tumbling into the sea, the white triangle of the bonaventure dancing as grape pockmarked the canvas . . .He'd raked her, firing his whole broadside the length of the ship without the enemy being able to reply with a single shot. Derec laughed aloud. "We've got upwind of them!" he shouted. "They'll not catch us now!"

"Holy Thung! Look ahead!" Random's young voice was frantic. Derec ran to the weather rail and peered out.

Torn II was bearing down on them, bow to bow, within a cable's distance. She'd been trying to weather *Monarch* so as to attack *Birdwing* from her unengaged side, and now the two race-built ships were on a collision course.

"Hands to the braces! Stations for tacking! Starboard guns load doubleshot and grape! Put the helm down!"

Birdwing, barely under way again, staggered into the wind. Canvas slatted wildly. *Torn* was bearing down on her beam, its royal figurehead glowering, waving a bright commanding sword.

"Fire as you bear!" Derec pounded the rail with a bleeding fist. "Run out and fire!"

The marines' murderers spat their little balls and scrap iron. Then a demicannon boomed, and another, then several of the long maindeck culverins. *Birdwing* hung in the eye of the wind, all forward momentum lost, the gale beating against her sails, driving her backward. More guns went off. *Torn*'s spritsail danced as a roundshot struck it. Captain-General Collerne was curving gently downwind, about to cross *Birdwing*'s stern at point-blank range.

"Starboard your helm! Help her fall off!"

Too late. Captain-General Collerne's scarlet masthead pennant coiled over the waves like a serpent threatening to strike. "Lie down!" Derec shouted. "Everyone lie down!"

He flung himself to the planks as the world began to come apart at the seams. The ship staggered like a toy struck by a child's hand as an entire rippling broadside smashed the length of *Birdwing*'s hull. Gunsmoke gushed over the quarterdeck. The taffrail dissolved. The bonaventure mizzen collapsed, draping the poop in pock-marked canvas. Yards of sliced rigging coiled down on the deck. Below there was a metallic gong as a cannon was turned over on its shrieking crew.

Then there was a stunned silence: *Torn* had passed by. Through the clouds of gunsmoke Derec could see Marcoyn standing, legs apart, on the fo'c'sle, sword brandished at the enemy, an incoherent, lunatic bellow of rage rising from his throat. "What a madman," Derec muttered, his ears ringing, and then he got to his feet.

"Brace the spritsail to larboard!" he called. "Clear that wreckage!" The tattered remains of the bonaventure were turning red: there were bodies underneath. As the canvas was pulled up, Derec saw one of them was Facer, the sunburned man cut in half by his homeland's iron. Derec turned away. He would pray for the man later.

Slowly *Birdwing* paid off onto the larboard tack. The sails filled and the galleon lost sternway. Water began to chuckle along the strakes as the ship slowly forged ahead. Canvas boomed as *Torn*, astern, began to come about. Derec looked anxiously over the shattered taffrail.

Monarch was only now lumbering into the wind: she was almost a mile away and had no hope of returning to the fight unless the wind shifted to give her the weather gage once again. But *Torn II* was the ship that had worried Derec all along, and she was right at hand, completing her tack, moving onto the same course as

Birdwing. If she was faster sailing upwind, she could overhaul the fugitive ship. Derec gave a worried glance at the set of his sails.

"Keep her full, Sandor. Let her go through the water."

"Full an' bye, sir."

"Set the t'gallants." He was suddenly glad he hadn't sent down the topgallant yards.

"Aye, aye, sir."

"All hands to knot and splice."

The topgallants rumbled as they were smoothly sheeted home. *Birdwing* heeled to starboard, foam spattering over the fo'c'sle like handfuls of dark jewels tossed by the spirits of the sea. She was drawing ahead, fast as a witch as she drove through the black gale. Water drizzled from the sky, washing Facer's blood from the planks. The water tasted sweet on Derec's tongue, washed away the powder that streaked his face.

Torn's topgallant yards were rising aloft, a swarm of men dark on her rigging. *Birdwing* made the most of her temporary advantage; she'd gained over a mile on her adversary before *Torn*'s topgallant bloomed and the larger ship began to race in earnest.

Derec felt his heart throbbing as he slitted his eyes to look astern, judging the ships' relative motion. *Birdwing* had lost its bonaventure: would that subtract from the ship's speed? He continued staring astern. His face began to split in a smile.

"We're pulling ahead!" he roared. "We've got the heels of her, by Thurn Bell!"

A low cheer began to rise from the crew; then, as the word passed, it grew deafening. *Birdwing* was going to make its escape. Nothing could stop her now.

Two miles later, as *Birdwing* neared a half-mile-wide channel between a pair of boundary isles, the wind died away entirely.

The sails fell slack, booming softly as the ship rocked on the waves.

From astern, traveling clearly from the two enemy vessels, Derec could hear the sound of cheering.

"Sway out the longboat! Ready to lower the second bower! We'll kedge her!"

The words snapped from Derec's mouth before the enemy cheering had quite ended. There was a rush of feet as the crew obeyed. Derec wanted to keep them busy, not occupied with thinking about their predicament.

"Send a party below to splice every anchor cable together. Fetch the wizard. A party to the capstan. Bring up the tackles and the spare t'gallant yards. We're going to jury a bonaventure. SuKrone, help me out of this damned armor."

One of the two longboats was swung out and set in the water. Carefully, the remaining bower anchor was lowered in it, and the boat moved under oars to the full length of the spliced anchor cables. Then the anchor was pitched overboard into the shallow sea and crewmen began stamping around the capstan, dragging the ship forward by main force until it rested over its anchor.

Tevvik appeared on deck to Derec's summons. He looked haggard.

"Hot work, Captain," he said. "Their wizards are good."

"I felt only one assault."

"Good. That means I was keeping them off."

"We're going to need wind."

Tevvik seemed dead with weariness. "Aye, Captain. I'll try."

"I'll work with you. Stand by the rail; I'll be with you in a moment."

The sound of clattering capstan pawls echoed from astern. *Torn* and *Monarch* were kedging as well.

"Up and down, sir." *Birdwing* was resting over its anchor.

"Bring her up smartly."

"Aye, aye."

Birdwing lurched as the anchor broke free of the bottom. Derec moved toward the poop ladder, then frowned as he saw the two stream anchors lashed to the main chains. A shame, Derec considered, that so much time was wasted getting the anchor up, then rowing it out again. Capstan pawls whirred in accompaniment to Derec's thoughts.

"Swing out the other longboat," he said. "We'll put one of the stream anchors on the other end of the cable.

355

Have one anchor going out while the other's coming in."
He grinned at SuKrone's startled expression. "See to it,
man!"

"Sir."

Crewmen rushed to the remaining longboat. Derec
walked to where the Tichenese was waiting, propped
against the lee rail where he'd be out of the way.

"We shall try to bring a wind, Wizard," Derec said. "A
westerly, as before. Ready?"

"I'll do what I can."

Wearily Derec summoned his power, matched it to the
wizard's, and called the elements for a wind. Meanwhile
a spare topgallant mast was dropped in place of the
broken bonaventure mizzen, a lateen yard hoisted to its
top, a new bonaventure set that hung uselessly in the
windless air. Derec and Tevvik moved into its shade.
Capstan pawls clattered, drawing the race-built ship
forward, through the channel between barrier islands,
the two longboats plying back and forth with their
anchors. The pursuers were using only one anchor at a
time, and were falling behind. The water began to
deepen, turn a profounder blue. *Torn II* crawled through
the island passage. *Monarch*'s topgallant masts loomed
above the nearer island.

The heat of the noon sun augured a hot afternoon.
Pitch bubbled up between the deck seams and stuck to
crewmen's feet. Weary sailors were relieved at the capstan and fed.

"Deck, there! Captain! Right ahead! *See what's happening!*"

Derec glanced up from his summoning, and his heart
lurched as he saw the wind itself appear, visible as a dim
swirling above the water; and then the sea itself rose, a
wall of curling white foam. Desperate energy filled him.

"Clew up the t'gallants! Close the gunports! Call the
boats back! Clew up the fores'l!"

The sea was coming with a growing hiss, a furious rank
of white horsemen galloping over an azure plain. Tevvik
looked at the wave with a dazed expression. "It's all
coming at once," he said. "It's been building out there,
everything we've been summoning since dawn, and now
it's all on us at once."

"Helmsman! A point to starboard! Use what way you can!"

Sails were clewed up in a squeal of blocks. The entry port filled with frantic sailors as one of the boats came alongside. There was a cry of wind in the rigging, an anticipation of what was to come. Derec ran to the mizzen shrouds and wrapped his arm around a stout eight-inch tarred line. He looked at Tevvik.

"I suggest you do likewise, Wizard."

And then the summoning was on them. The bow rose to the surge of white water and suddenly the air was full of spray as the frothing sea boiled around the ship. Canvas crashed as it filled with wind, bearing *Birdwing* back till suddenly she came up short at the end of her anchor cable, and with a plank-starting shudder the galleon was brought up short, burying her beak in foam, a wave sweeping the decks for and aft, carrying crewmen and capstan bars and everything not lashed down in a frantic, clawing spill for the stern . . .Derec closed his eyes and mouth and tried to hang on, his shoulders aching as the water tore at his clothing and body. His mind still registered what was happening to the ship, the jarring and checking that meant the anchor was dragging, the demon shriek of wind in the rigging, the thrumming tautness of the shroud around which Derec wrapped his arms . . .

Just as suddenly, the white water was gone, past. A strong sea breeze hummed in the rigging. Half-drowned crewmen lay on the planks like scattered driftwood, gasping for air. Exultation filled Derec.

"Hands to the capstan! Prepare to set the fores'l and t'gallants! Lively, there, lively—we've got a wind!"

The stunned survivors raised a feeble cheer and dragged wearily to their work. The other longboat—miraculously it had survived, bobbing on the wave like a twig—picked up a few swimmers who had been carried overboard, then came to the entry port in a mad thrash of oars. Wind whipping his hair, Derec gazed astern to see the wall of white as it drove toward his enemies.

Torn II had seen it coming and had time to prepare. Her boats were in, her anchor catted home; and Derec suppressed a surge of admiration for the proud way her head tossed to the wave, the clean manner in which she cut the water and kept her head to the wind. Then the wave was past, and she began setting sails. Derec's gaze shifted to *Monarch*. The wave was almost on her.

She hadn't seen it coming; that much was clear. She'd just kedged clear of the southern tip of the island, and the white water was within two cables' lengths before *Monarch* was aware of it. Suddenly there was frantic movement on her decks, sails drawing up, the boats thrashing water; but the white water hit her broadside, driving her over. She staggered once, then was gone, only wreckage and the tips of her masts visible on the rushing water. Derec blinked: it had happened so fast he could scarce believe the sight of it. He looked again. His eyes had spoken truly: *Monarch* was gone.

"Thurn Bel protect them," Derec said, awed, reaching automatically for his amulet and finding nothing. He knew precisely what had happened: the gunports had been open on this hot afternoon, and the wind and water had pushed her lower ports under; she'd filled and gone down in seconds. Six hundred men, their lives snuffed out in an instant. Derec shook his head, sorrow filling him. Why was he fated to kill his countrymen so?

"The sea trolls will feed well tonight," Tevvik said solemnly. His hairpins had been torn from his head, and his long dark hair hung dripping to his shoulders.

SuKrone's voice broke into Derec's reverie: "Cable's up and down, sir."

"Break the anchor free. Lay her on the larboard tack."

The anchor came free with a lurch, the yards were braced round, the birdwing sails set and filled with wind. *Birdwing* heeled gracefully in the stiff ocean breeze.

"This isn't over yet," Derec said as he watched *Torn II* flying after them. "The captain-general's lost two ships, half his squadron, with nothing to show for it. He's got to bring us back or he's done for. He'll never have another command."

"We're faster than he on this tack."

"That won't end it. He'll spend the rest of his life in the Sea of Luck if he has to."

"Let us hope," Tevvik said, his eyes hardening, "he will not live long."

358

Derec shook his head: he couldn't wish Collerne dead, not Collerne, who had been such a friend to him, who had raised him to the highest rank to which a nonnoble could aspire.

The brisk wind carried *Birdwing* smartly over the water, the bow rising to each ocean wave. But then the wind dropped little by little and *Torn* began closing the distance, her red admiral's pennant snapping in the breeze like a striking serpent. *Birdwing* was only faster in stiffer winds: *Torn* had the advantage here. Derec's heart sank.

"We shall have to fight, then. Gun captains to draw their cartridges and replace them with fresh—they may have got wet. All hands check their powder."

Derec donned his cuirass—the helmet had been washed overboard—and reloaded his pistols. Tevvik returned to the safety of the orlop. There was no cheer among the crew as they went to their tasks, only a kind of grim despair.

They had labored all day, escaped death so many times. Were they cursed, to be so forced into yet another struggle?

"Stations for tacking," Derec said. "We'll see how badly the captain-general wants to fight us." He could still not bring himself to speak of the man disrespectfully.

Birdwing came across the wind easily. "Ease her a bit," Derec ordered. "Keep her full." He ordered the guns loaded with roundshot and gauged his distance carefully. "Back the main tops'l," he said finally. "Run out the larboard battery." He was going to give Collerne a hard choice. "Ready, boys!" he called. "Aim carefully, now!" The ship's motion altered as the main topsail backed, as the ship's speed checked and its corkscrew shudder ended. Carefully Derec gauged the ship's motion. Tops'l aback, *Birdwing* was a far steadier platform.

"*Fire!*"

The deck shuddered to the salvo. White feathers leaped from the sea around *Torn*.

"Fill the tops'l! Reload and run out! Helm down!"

Derec looked at the other race-built ship, eyes narrowing. His maindeck culverins, longer though with a

359

smaller bore than the demicannon on the gundeck, were ideal at this range. He would claw to windward, fall off, fire, then claw to windward again while his crews reloaded: he was going to punish *Torn II* mercilessly on the approach, make her pay for every fathom gained. The enemy couldn't reply, not without luffing out of the wind to present her broadside.

Collerne had two choices now, Derec knew. He could continue beating toward *Birdwing*, paying for every inch with lives, or he could luff and open the battle at this range. The battle wouldn't be decisive at a half-mile's distance—the two ships would fire off their ammunition at this range, fail to do mortal damage, and that would be the end of it. Derec prayed Collerne would choose the latter outcome.

"Back the main tops'l! Run out!"

Another broadside crashed out. "Fill the tops'l! Load! Helm down!"

Luff, Derec thought fiercely as he looked at the enemy. Luff, damn you.

The enemy were determined to stand Derec's fire. His heart sank at the thought of killing more of his countrymen.

Having no choice, he did what he must. He fired another broadside, tacked, fired the larboard guns. *Torn's* bow chasers replied, pitching a ball at *Birdwing* every few minutes; but *Torn* had to be taking punishment as she came into the culverins' ideal range. Her sails were as pitted by shot holes as the cheeks of a whore with the Great Pox.

Five hundred yards. "*Fire!*" He could hear the sound of shot striking home. Four hundred. "*Fire!*" Three. "*Fire!*"

The wind blew the ocean clear of smoke. Derec stared to leeward, hoping to see a mast fall, a sail flog itself to bits, anything that might allow him to slip away. Nothing. Reluctantly he gave the orders.

"Fill the mains'l. Clew up the t'gallants. We'll give the captain-general the fight he's come for."

The guns lashed out once more and then *Torn* luffed elegantly, the bronze guns running out the square ports, two lines of teeth that shone in the bright southern sun.

There were gaps in the rows of teeth: two ports beaten into one, another empty port where a gun may have been disabled. Derec's breath caught in his throat.

Fire lapped the surface of the ocean. *Torn*'s crew had waited hours for this and it seemed as if every shot struck home, a rapid series of crashes and shudders that rocked the deck beneath Derec's feet. There was a cry as a half-dozen of Marcoyn's marines were scattered in red ruin over the fo'c'sle, then a shriek, sounding like the very sky being torn asunder, as a ball passed right over Derec's head to puncture the mizzen lateen. He was too startled to duck.

Birdwing's guns gave their answering roars. Derec gave the command to fire at will. He could sense the magic shields Tevvik wove about the ship; felt a probe, felt it easily rebuffed. There was only one enemy wizard now; he was as tired as everyone else. The range narrowed and the marines' murderers began to bark. Gunfire was continuous, a never-ending thunder. A musket ball gouged wood from the mizzen above Derec's head; he began to pace in hope of discouraging marksmen.

Derec's ship seemed to be pulling ahead as the range narrowed and *Birdwing* stole *Torn*'s wind. Derec didn't want that, not yet; he had the foretops'l laid aback, allowed *Torn* to forge ahead slightly, then filled the sail and resumed his course.

Fifty yards: here they would hammer it out, guns double-shotted with a round of grape choked down each barrel for good measure. A maindeck culverin tipped onto its crew, its carriage wrecked by a ball. There was a crash, a massive rumble followed by a human shriek. Derec stared: the main topgallant had been shot away and come roaring down, a tangle of rigging and canvas and broken timber. Marcoyn already had a party hacking at the wreckage and tossing it overboard. Derec clenched his teeth and waited. Thunder smote his ears. Gunpowder coated his tongue in layers, like dust on a dead man.

The wreckage was clear—good. The enemy was falling a bit behind. "Set the fore t'gallant!" Derec roared; the seamen gave him puzzled glances, and he repeated the order.

Canvas boomed as the topgallant was sheeted home;

361

Derec could feel the surge of speed, the lift it gave his nimble ship. He peered over the bulwark, squinting through the smoke that masked the enemy. With his added speed, he'd try to cross her bows and let her run aboard: he'd have his every gun able to rake down the enemy's length with scarce a chance of reply.

"Put up the helm!" A musket ball whirred overhead; two quarterdeck murderers barked in reply. The marines were cursing without cease as they loaded and fired, a constant drone of obscenity. Derec wondered where they found the energy.

Birdwing curved downwind like a bird descending on its prey, Derec staring anxiously at the enemy. He felt his heart sink: the blue sky between the enemy's masts was widening. Collerne had been ready for him, and was matching *Birdwing*'s turn with his own.

"Helm hard to weather!" Frantic energy pulsed through Derec. "Hands to the larboard guns! Run 'em out! Braces, there! Brace her around!"

If he made his turn quick enough, he might be able to slide across Collerne's stern and deliver a raking shot with his fresh larboard broadside, a stroke as devastating as that which *Torn* had fired into *Birdwing*'s stern that morning.

Sails boomed and slatted overhead. The firing trailed off as the guns no longer bore. Derec ran frantically for the larboard rail and saw, too late, a tantalizing glimpse of *Torn*'s stern, a glimpse lasting only a few seconds before it slid away. Derec beat a fist on the rail. The maneuver hadn't worked at all—Collerne had anticipated everything. The ships had just changed places, larboard tack to starboard, like dancers at a ball. And *Torn* was firing with a new broadside now, not the one he'd punished for the last few hours.

"Luff her! Gun crews, fire as you bear!" He'd get in one unopposed broadside, at least.

The unused broadside blasted away into *Torn*'s starboard quarter. Derec could see splinters flying like puffs of smoke. He filled his sails and surged on.

Now they were yardarm-to-yardarm again, the guns hammering at point-blank range. The crews were weary, taking casualties, and the rate of fire had slowed; the deadly iron thunderstorm was blowing itself out. A whirring charge of grape caught SuKrone in the side and flung him to weather like a doll, already dead; a musket ball whanged off Derec's breastplate and made him take a step back, his heart suddenly thundering in panic. Frantically he began pacing, his feet slipping in pools of blood.

Who was winning? *Torn* had been hard hit, but her weight of armament was superior; she had a larger crew, having probably taken men off the damaged *Sea Troll*; and Derec was forced to admit she had the better captain. *Birdwing* had been hit hard in the first fight, and her crew were exhausted. Everywhere he looked Derec saw blood, death, smoke, and ruin.

He'd try his trick one more time, Derec thought. He couldn't think of anything else. If it didn't work, he'd just fight it out toe-to-toe until there was nothing left to fight with. He wouldn't surrender. If *Birdwing* lost, he'd take one of his stolen pistols and blow his own brains out.

Birdwing was forging ahead, the topgallant still set. Very well. He'd try to do it better.

"Hands to tacks and sheets! Hands to the braces! Ready, there? Helm to weather!"

Birdwing lurched as the rudder bit the water. Bullets twittered overhead. The enemy wizard made some kind of strike, and Derec felt it deep in his awareness; his mind lanced out and parried. He could sense Tevvik there, feel a part of the foreigner's mind merge with his own.

If you ever do anything, he begged, *do it now.*

The answer came. *Very well.*

Derec looked up again, saw the blue space between the enemy's masts increasing. Damn: he'd been anticipated *again*.

"Hard a-weather! Sheets, there! Man the starboard guns!"

They were dancing around again, just changing places. The bonaventure and mizzen lateen boomed as the wind slammed them across the deck. Derec saw the enemy stern and knew he could never cross it, knew it for certain—and then there was a yellow flash, *Torn*'s windows blowing out in rainbow splinters, bright light winking from each gunport along the maindeck. Guns boomed, firing at empty sea. Derec's mouth dropped as he saw an enemy marine, standing with his firelock in the mizzen chains, suddenly fling his arms back as each of the powder flasks he carried across his chest went off, little dots of fire that knocked him into the shrouds . . .

Tevvik, Derec thought. He specialized in fireworks. But now Derec was screaming, his throat a raw agony.

"Fire as you bear!" *Birdwing* was going to win the race: the maindeck explosion had paralyzed the enemy, possibly blown the helmsmen away from the whipstaff.

The guns went off, flinging hundreds of pounds of metal into the helpless ship's stern. *Torn* wallowed, the wind pushing her away. Derec could hear her crewmen screaming for water-buckets. Tevvik must have set off a pile of cartridges on the maindeck, spreading fire, making guns go off prematurely while their crews were still ramming shot home . . .

Birdwing followed, firing shot after shot; *Torn*'s crew was desperately fighting fires and could not reply. Derec sensed a new energy in his gunners; they were firing faster than they had since the enemy's approach. They knew this was victory and wanted to hasten it.

"Captain." It was one of the surgeon's assistants, a boy in a bloody apron. Derec glared at him.

"What is it?"

"The wizard's unconscious, sir. The Liavekan, what's-his-name. He just yelled something in his heathen tongue and collapsed. Surgeon thought you'd need to know."

Derec put his hand on the boy's arm. "Compliments to the surgeon. Thank you, boy."

The guns roared on. *Torn* got her fires under control, but the explosion had devastated the crew: they didn't have the heart to continue. When all the gun crews dribbled away, heading for the hatches, the officers conceded the inevitable and hauled down their colors. *Birdwing* came alongside to take possession.

Collerne, leading his surviving officers, surrendered in person, a tall white-haired man in beautifully crafted, muscled armor, a splinter wound on one cheek, both hands blackened where he'd beat at the fire. Derec looked into the man's eyes, hoping to see some sign of friendship, of understanding for what Derec had had to do. There was nothing there, no understanding, no friendship, not even hate. Derec took his patron's sword wordlessly.

"We've done it, SuPashto! Beaten 'em!" Marcoyn was by Derec's side now, his pale unfocused eyes burning fire. "We're *free!*" Marcoyn saw Collerne standing mute by the poop rail; he turned to the captain-general, stared at him for a long moment, then deliberately spat in his face.

"Free, d'ye hear, Collerne?" he roared. "You thought you'd strangle us all, but now I'll throttle you myself. And now I'll be captain of your ship as well."

The spittle hung on Collerne's face. He said nothing, but his deep gray eyes turned to Derec, and Derec's blood turned chill.

Derec put a hand on Marcoyn's armored shoulder. "He's worth more in ransom alive," he said. "You and your people take possession of the other ship."

Marcoyn considered this, the taunting grin still on his face. "Aye," he said. "Maybe I'd like their money more than their lives." He gave a laugh. "I'll have to give it some thought. While I enjoy my new cabin on my new ship."

He turned to his men and roared orders. There were cheers from the marines as they swarmed aboard *Torn* and began looting the enemy survivors. Collerne's eyes turned away from Derec. There was no gratitude there, just an emptiness as deep as the ocean. Despair filled Derec. The rapier in his hand felt as heavy as a lead weight.

"Go to my cabin, Captain-General," he said. "Wait for me there. I'll send the surgeon to tend to your hands." In silence, Collerne obeyed. Derec sent the other officers below to the cable tier and had them put under guard.

Suddenly Derec was aware of Tevvik standing by the break of the poop. How long had the wizard been there? His face showed strain and exhaustion, but he'd heard everything; his hooded expression demonstrated that well enough.

Derec glanced up at the mizzen shrouds. There wasn't room any longer for all the countrymen he'd killed; the ghosts, he thought, would have to stand in line.

It wasn't over yet, Derec knew. The Two Kingdoms trading fleets came to the Sea of Luck every year, and sailors had long memories. Squadrons would hunt for *Birdwing*, and even if Derec received the protection of one of the cities, there would still be kidnappers and assassins. No end to this killing, Derec thought, not until I'm dead. Will the gods forgive me, he wondered, for not killing myself and ending this slaughter?

The two race-built ships spun in the wind, locked together like weary prizefighters leaning against one another for support. Wreckage and bodies bobbed in the water. From *Torn II* came a smell of burning.

Derec realized he was the only man remaining who could navigate. He ordered his charts to be brought up from the safety of the hold.

"Secure the guns," he said. "I'll chart a course north, to Liavek."

The sea was kind that night: a moderate wind, a moderate swell. The two ships traveled under easy sail and echoed to the sound of repairs.

Near staggering with weariness, Derec paced *Birdwing*'s weather rail. Collerne still waited in Derec's cabin. Marcoyn was probably drunk and unconscious in the admiral's cabin aboard *Torn*. Only Derec was without a place to sleep.

There was a tread on the poop companion, and Derec saw Tevvik approaching him.

"You have recovered?" Derec asked. His tongue was thick. No matter how much kaf he consumed his mouth still tasted of powder.

"Somewhat." The wizard's voice was as weary as his own. "May I join you, Captain?"

"If you like." Exhaustion danced in Derec's brain. He swayed, put a hand on the bulwark to steady himself.

Tevvik's voice was soft. "You will have to make a choice, Captain," he said.

"Not now, Wizard."

"Soon, Captain."

Derec said nothing. Tevvik stepped closer, pitched his voice low. "If Marcoyn gets his way, you will all die. His Scarlet Eminence won't make a deal with a butcher."

366

"This is my affair, Wizard. None of yours."

"Only the thought of ransom kept him from another massacre. What will happen when he realizes the ransom will never come? Liavek isn't at war with the Two Kingdoms—their price courts will never permit you to ransom a neutral. When Marcoyn thinks things through, there will be trouble." Tevvik's easy smile gleamed in his dark face. "I can deal with Marcoyn, Captain. He will have gone overboard while drunk, and that's all anyone will ever know."

Derec glared at the foreigner and clenched his fists. "I'll have my own discipline on my own ship," he grated. "I don't need wizard's tricks, and I won't be a party to conspiracies."

"It's far too late for that, Captain."

Derec jerked as if stung. "It's not too late to stop."

"Events generate their own momentum. You of all people should know that." He leaned closer, put a hand on Derec's shoulder. "Marcoyn's marines have the fire-locks, Captain. He has possession of one ship already, and he can take yours anytime he wants."

"He needs me. The man can't navigate."

"Once he turns pirate, he can capture all the navigators he needs."

"*I can deal with him, Wizard*!" Derec's voice roared out over the still ship. Tevvik took a step back from the force of his rage.

His mind ablaze, Derec stormed down the poop ladder, past the startled helmsman, and down the passage that led to his cabin. The guard at the door straightened in surprise as Derec flung open the door.

Collerne looked up. He was out of his armor and seated in one of Derec's chairs, trying to read a Zhir book on navigation with his bandaged hands. Derec hesitated before the man's depthless gaze.

"I want you off my ship, Captain-General," he said.

Collerne's eyes flickered. "Why is that, Mr. SuPashto?" He spoke formally, without expression.

"I'm going to put you and your officers in a boat and let you make your way to Gold Harbor. You'll have food and water for the trip. A backstaff so you can find your latitude."

With a careful gesture, Collerne closed his book and held it between bandaged hands. "You are running for Liavek, are you not? Can you not let us off there?"

Derec looked at him. "It's for your safety, Captain-General."

Collerne took a moment to absorb this. "Very well, Mr. SuPashto. I understand that you might have difficulty controlling your people now they've had a taste of rebellion."

Suddenly Derec hated the man, hated his superiority, the cold, relentless precision of his intelligence. "You would have strangled and eviscerated every man on this ship!" he said.

Collerne's voice was soft: "That was my duty, Mr. SuPashto," he said. "Not my pleasure. That's the difference between me and your Mr. Marcoyn."

"Marcoyn had a good teacher," Derec said. "His name was Captain Lord Fors. Marcoyn's an amateur in cruelty compared to him."

Collerne stiffened. Mean satisfaction trickled into Derec's mind: he'd got a reaction from the man at last. He wondered if it was because he'd scored a point or simply had the bad taste to criticize one officer in front of another.

"The only order I've ever had questioned," Derec said, "is the one that would prevent my people doing to you what you fully intended to do to them. "Now"—he nodded—"you will follow me, Captain-General, and from this point onward you will address me as Captain. Maybe I wasn't born to the rank, but I think I've earned it."

Collerne said nothing, just rose from his chair and followed. Perhaps, Derec thought, he would say nothing at all rather than have to call Derec by his stolen title. Derec collected the rest of the officers in the cable tier and then climbed to the maindeck. *Birdwing*'s remaining small boat had been warped astern after the fight, and Derec had it brought alongside. He put a stock of food and water aboard, made certain the boat had mast, cordage, sail, and backstaff, then sent the prisoners into it. Collerne was last. The captain-general turned in the entry port, prepared to lower himself to the boat, curled his fingers around the safety line. His bandaged hand slipped uselessly, and Collerne gave a gasp of pain as he began to topple backward into the boat.

Derec leaned out and took the captain-general's arm, steadying him. Collerne looked at him with dark, fathomless eyes.

"I acted to preserve the ship, Captain-General," Derec said. "There was no other way. *Birdwing* was your dream, and it is alive, thanks to me."

Collerne's face hardened. He turned away, and with Derec's assistance lowered himself into the boat.

"Cast off," said Derec. He stepped up to the poop and watched the fragment of darkness as it fell astern, as it vanished among the gentle swells of the Sea of Luck.

He'd said what he'd had to, Derec thought. If Collerne refused to understand, that was naught to do with Derec.

"What now, Captain?"

Tevvik's voice. Derec turned to the wizard.

"Sleep," he said. "I'll deal with Marcoyn in the morning."

Derec rose at dawn. He wound his two pistols and put them in his belt, then reached for his sword. He stepped on deck, scanned the horizon, found it empty save for *Torn II* riding two miles off the starboard quarter. He brought *Birdwing* alongside, shouted at the other ship to heave to, then backed *Birdwing*'s main topsail and brought her to rest a hundred yards from the other ship. He armed a party of *Birdwing*'s sailors and had them ready at the entry port. Derec told *Torn*'s lookout to give Mr. Marcoyn his compliments, and ask him to come aboard *Birdwing*.

Out of the corner of his eye, Derec saw Tevvik mounting the poop ladder. The Tichenese seemed unusually subdued; his expression was hooded, his grin absent entirely.

Marcoyn arrived with a party of half a dozen marines, all dressed grandly in plundered clothing and armor. The big man looked savage; he was probably hung over. A brace of pistols had been shoved into his bright embroidered sash.

Derec could feel tension knotting his muscles. He tried

369

to keep his voice light. "I need you to resume your duties aboard *Birdwing*, Mr. Marcoyn," Derec told him. "I'm sending Sandor to take charge of the prize."

There was a pause while Marcoyn absorbed this. He gave an incredulous laugh. "Th' piss you will," he said. "The prize is mine!"

Derec's nerves shrieked. Ignoring the sharp scent of liquor on Marcoyn's breath, he stepped closer to the big man. His voice cracked like a whip. "By whose authority? I'm captain here."

Marcoyn stood his ground. His strange pale eyes were focused a thousand yards away.

"The prize is mine!" he barked. "I'm in charge of the sojers here!"

Hot anger roared from Derec's mouth like fire from a cannon. "And *I* am in charge of *you*!" he shouted. He thrust his face within inches of Marcoyn's. "*Birdwing* is mine! The prize is mine! And *you* and your sojers are mine to command! D'you dispute that, Marcoyn?"

Do it, Marcoyn, he thought. Defy me and I'll pistol your brains out the back of your head.

Marcoyn seemed dazed. He glanced over the poop, his hands flexing near his weapons. Derec felt triumph racing through his veins. If Marcoyn made a move he was dead. Derec had never been more certain of anything in his life.

Marcoyn hesitated. He took a step back.

"Whatever you say, Captain," he said.

Readiness still poised in Derec. Marcoyn was not safe yet, not by any means. "You are dismissed, Marcoyn," Derec said. "I'd advise you to get some sleep."

"Aye, aye, sir." The words were mumbled. Marcoyn raised his helmet in a sketchy salute, then turned away and was lost.

Tension poured from Derec like an ebbing tide. He watched the burly marine descend the poop ladder, then head for his cabin. He looked at Marcoyn's marines.

"Return your firelocks to the arms locker," he said. "Then report to Randem's repair party."

"Sir."

Derec sent Sandor and some of the armed sailors to the *Torn*, then looked up at the sails. "Hands to the main

370

braces," he said. "Set the main tops'l. Steer nor'-nor'west."

Men tailed onto the braces, fighting the wind as they heaved the big mainyards around. Canvas boomed as it filled, as *Birdwing* paid off and began to come around, a bone growing in its teeth.

Relief sang in Derec's mind. He had managed it somehow, managed not to have to become Marcoyn in order to defeat him.

Tevvik's voice came quietly in Derec's ear: "Well done, sir. But you should have let me handle him. Marcoyn's still a danger."

"To no one but himself." Flatly.

"I disagree, Captain. What will happen when he discovers you've set Collerne and the others free?"

"Nothing will happen. He will drink and mutter and that will be the end of it."

"I pray you are right, Captain."

Derec looked at him. "I won't have a man killed because he *might* be a problem later. That was Lord Fors's way, and Marcoyn's way, and I'll have none of it."

Tevvik shook his head and offered no answer. Derec glanced aloft to check the set of the sails.

Suddenly he felt his heart ease. He was free.

No more mutinies, he thought.

Birdwing heeled to a gust, then rose and settled into its path, forging ahead through a bright tropical dawn.

AFTERWORD
Jerry Pournelle

The phony debate over strategic defense has taken a new turn with the publication of the *Report to the American Physical Society of the Study Group on Science and Technology of Directed Energy Weapons* in April of 1987. Supposedly an impartial study by a jury of qualified scientists, it was nothing of the sort: like the long discredited "study" by the Federation of American Scientists (FAR), the APS Report assumes its conclusions in advance, then manipulates its assumptions to make its case. It proves nothing.

The usual nonsense is there. The U.S.S.R. can "easily" protect their missiles by spinning them—although no one has yet spun an ICBM—or by coating them with some form of armor. In both cases the APS Report seriously underestimates the payload loss from spinning and coating, nor does it address the problem of whether an SS-18 missile coated with some six metric tons of armor can be built at all, much less spun.

The Soviets have invested enormously in their weapons inventory; so much so that their economy is in real trouble. If we can make that investment obsolete, why shouldn't we? And even the APS Report, read carefully, shows that we can do at least that much. If the Soviets can in fact coat and spin their missiles, they haven't done so, and it won't be cheap; and every ruble spent refitting an old missile is a ruble not spent on buying new ones.

There are dozens of other errors of fact or assumption in the APS document, and like the FAR Report, they're all in the same direction. All the errors lead one to suppose that the technology we have isn't worth building, and what we'll need is far in the future; and indeed that's what the *New York Times* and other newspapers reported when the APS Report came out.

In fact it proves nothing of the sort. In the first place, the APS Report doesn't even deal with kinetic energy weapons. The United States right now has not only the science but the engineering technology to put up a ballistic kill ICBM defense. We can build not just weapons, but an entire defensive weapons system. Of course, a system based on smart rocks won't be anything like as effective as one built around high-energy lasers and other directed-energy weapons; but it can make a significant contribution to the protection of the United States.

No defense will ever be perfect. I know of no possible way to make everyone in the U.S. safe from nuclear attack; to build a leak-proof nuclear umbrella. Fortunately that isn't what strategic defenses are supposed to do. The purpose of defenses is to make the attacker decide it's not worthwhile to attack. If defenses can do that, they will have succeeded—and of course, if they do that, they will have been 100 percent effective without having been used at all.

Boost-phase ballistic kill ICBM defenses—smart rocks in space—can intercept 10–25 percent of the enemy ICBM boosters. Each booster can carry more than one warhead. Since the larger the booster, the easier it is to intercept, and the more warheads it is likely to carry, the proportion of warheads intercepted may be even higher.

Now no one questions that 90 percent of the Soviet ICBM force is more than enough to destroy the United States as a national entity. If the Soviets devote their entire ICBM force to wanton destruction of U.S. society, they'll probably be successful, especially if they just launch out of the blue. I've never heard anyone explain why the U.S.S.R. would want to do that, since any such attack would pretty well disarm the Soviet Union while leaving the U.S. Strategic Offensive Forces intact and motivated to take a terrible revenge.

On the other hand, intercepting 10 percent of the Soviet ICBM boosters would be very effective in protecting large parts of the U.S. ICBM force—and indeed, protecting the land-based, highly accurate ICBMs, which are the weapons the *Nomenklatura* fear most. The real rulers of the Soviet Union probably care about the lives of their fellow citizens, but the record shows they care for their weapons and their mechanisms of social control a great deal more.

There's only one way a nuclear first strike makes sense: if it's so effective that the enemy has little or nothing left to retaliate with. Many "theorists" in the U.S. have said that's impossible: they postulate invulnerable "second strike" weapons. The problem is that invulnerability is easier to get by assumption than by engineering. In these days of computer sufficiency, PGM, and increasingly accurate and effective weapons, there are no invulnerable weapons. There's only one way to protect the retaliatory force; it must be actively defended.

That means protecting weapons, not cities; yet one argument for SDI has always been that MAD is immoral.

We needn't abandon our conviction that Mutual Assured Destruction, MAD, is immoral; that holding hostage innocent Russian citizens to ensure the good behavior of the *Nomenklatura* is a terrible thing. It is a terrible thing. Unfortunately, although we learned in 1984 that strategic defenses were possible, we have done nothing about building them. SDI remains a study program. We cannot defend the U.S. with paper studies and laboratory experiments.

We need not abandon our moral opposition to MAD —but we now have no choices left. We need strategic defenses just to keep MAD operating.

It's not hard to see what we must do. We begin with

what we know how to do. Start with increasing our warning times by putting manned observation stations in space. (The Soviet MIR space station certainly can function that way.) Add new surveillance and warning capabilities. Deploy smart rocks, a few at first, then a hundred or so.

Even the APS Report concedes that we will, eventually, learn how to build effective high-energy weapons. We can quarrel with their timetable, but in fact even if we had those weapons today they wouldn't be a weapons system. By starting early we put together the elements of a real defense that defends. Then as the new weapons technologies mature, we integrate those new systems into what will be an increasingly effective missile defense system based on what we know how to do now.

There are always two approaches to difficult goals. One is to try to solve all problems before deciding what to do. The other is to decide what you will do, then deal with the problems as they get in the way.

The second approach won World War II and put us on the moon. We're now using the first approach, and it has yet to put a station in space—or even to build an O ring.

If you would have peace, be prepared for war. We are not prepared.